Devil's Mistress

Heather Graham

Devil's
Mistress

(1)

WHEELER
PUBLISHING, INC.
ROCKLAND, MA

★ AN AMERICAN COMPANY ★

Published in Large Print by arrangement with The Bantam Dell Publishing Group, a division of Random House, Inc., in the United States and Canada.

Wheeler Large Print Book Series.

Set in 16 pt Plantin.

Library of Congress Cataloging-in-Publication Data

Graham, Heather.
   Devil's mistress / Heather Graham.
      p. (large print) cm.(Wheeler large print book series)
   ISBN 1-58724-011-4 (hardcover)
   1. Ship captains—Fiction. 2. Mistresses—Fiction. 3. Witches—Fiction.
4. Scotland—Fiction. 5. Large type books. I. Title. II. Series

   [PS3557.R198 D48   2001]
   813'.54—dc21   2001017877
                                                                CIP

For my sisters near and far,
Victoria Graham Davant
and Jenifer Anne Graham

Preface

In the late afternoon the fog began to roll in, curling across the water like a misted silver blanket. It slowly moved to the wharf, and danced and shivered over grass and road, shimmering with its ethereal magic. It rose high above the bluffs and cliffs of the old Burial Point, and spiraled downward again, swirling with a haunting intrigue around the ancient markers and the bases of the few skeletal trees. When I first arrived, the day had been overcast and from the sea, a breeze—the same breeze that now carried the fog—seemed to have cast a spell over the Charter Street Cemetery.

In this place the wind seems to whisper plaintively of dramas gone by, of lives played out, in joy and in travesty—and in tragedy. As is the play of nature, some stones are better preserved than others; some stand straight, others are worn smooth. Some even appear to arise from the gnarled roots which have grown about them. Some stones can be read, and others are unreadable.

1

In that cemetery in Salem the past came to life for me. Closing my eyes, I could feel the breeze, touch the ancient stones—almost seeing the people who had been buried here approximately four hundred years ago. Among them is the grave of John Hathorne, one of the original magistrates and most ardent examiners of one of our country's greatest tragedies and controversies.

While kneeling at his marker—old and worn and bolted together—I first had the strange feeling that I was no longer alone. Of course I wasn't "alone"; Dennis was wandering about somewhere. But suddenly I had a feeling that crept along my neck, chilling my spine—I sensed someone near me. It was frightening in this place covered by fog where the naked trees let down their branches like bony fingers reaching out.

I jumped up and saw a young woman about twenty years old. She seemed to have been cast straight from the fog, coming from nowhere, and I must have started severely, for she smiled apologetically. She was one of the most striking individuals I'd ever seen, with brilliant blue eyes and feathered hair as dark and sleek as India ink. She pointed toward the grave and said, "A witchcraft student, eh?" and I laughed a little self-consciously, for I had been caught touching the old gravestone with my eyes closed.

"Sort of—but really just a dreamer," I told her.

She smiled again and pointed past the ceme-

2

tery to the street. "Once the Burying Point's base was swept by the seawater of the tidal river. They filled in and made Derby Street, oh, somewhere in the eighteen hundreds. The oldest stone still standing here goes back to '73—1673, that is. Bradstreet's here, and more of the members of the court."

"The court?" I asked her curiously. As I talked to her the street seemed to slip away in mist. I could almost hear the tidal wash again, and the gray day seemed to turn into a shrouded, swirling twilight.

"The witchcraft court," she told me solemnly, but her eyes were a blue that twinkled even with darkness. She looked off into the distance then. "What tales the earth could tell! But then it wasn't so very bad here, you know. They burned and hanged 'witches' by the thousands in Europe; we killed but a few dozen." She looked at me again. "But then tragedy is a personal thing, isn't it? One thing that hasn't changed in all this time is human nature. They were dreamers too. They knew happiness, and they knew sorrow, and some survived and some did not." Then she winked as she rose, beckoning me over to the base of a tree.

There was a grave marker on the ground, but one I wouldn't have taken much interest in, since it was twined with metal, badly broken, and not at all legible. "A dreamer, eh?" she asked me. Her fingers, delicate and fine, moved over the stone, and I saw the date, 1756. "The year she died," she told me. "Having outwitted them all! You see, they say that none of the 'victims' are buried here—this ground was for the affluent. But she wanted to come here."

Well, of course I had to ask her "Who?" And then, "How do you know all this?" in the same breath.

She laughed and waved to the row of houses beyond the street. "I'm from here and there's all sorts of local gossip and legend. But I've always been especially fond of this story. Just the type of thing for a dreamer..."

She then sketched out a picture for me of seventeenth-century Europe and the Colonies, and of some special, individual people. For as she had told me, life cannot always be seen in numbers and dates, we must know the people of the times—for human nature never does change. No matter how far we come along, we will love and laugh and suffer—and love and laugh again.

I listened to her story with eager fascination. I fingered the stone again, and I could almost see the people she described—their gowns and old-fashioned trousers, caps, and hats; horses on unpaved roads; vast ships with tall white sails—I thought I heard their whispers, and their tears, and their laughter.

I don't know when she ended her story, but when I turned around again, my husband Dennis was there, and the girl was gone. I frowned and asked Dennis if he had seen her; he shook his head and smiled a little ruefully. "I didn't see anyone at all."

Well, I wasn't about to argue with him, but I was confused about the disappearance of my visitor. When Dennis suggested we find a place for dinner, I agreed that it was time to go.

In the days that followed, we went on to see Salem, Massachusetts, and the town now called Danvers which was once Salem "Village," where the witch-hunts really began. I was never really sure if there was a girl in the cemetery or not that day. But then, Salem had long ago proven to be a place of illusion—and delusion.

So if you will, come along with me. Bear in mind that witch hunters were different men from different times who had not long left the dark ages behind. A medieval world was shifting and changing and the feudal system had reached its dying stages. Many men believed in the power of witchcraft, in charms, in curses, and in evil eyes.

Keep in mind also that reality—like fantasy—is often a state of the mind.

1
Enter the Devil

> *"Thou shall not suffer a witch to live."*
>
> King James version of the Bible

Chapter 1
Glasgow, Scotland: August, 1688

The sky was ominously gray. People lined the common and the streets, their faces resembling that silent, brooding sky. Oh, there were those with bloodlust in their eyes, but most of the spectators awaiting the execution were as somber as the air with its hovering expectancy, as grave as the death pall around them.

"She comes! She comes! Blessed saints preserve us!" The cry went out as the procession came forward led by fat old Father Timothy, his jowls heavy, his rheumy eyes bleary with tears, for he was a kind old man, only carrying out his duty. Behind him walked Matthews, a tall handsome man, with broad shoulders, wearing his tall hat and cape with an arrogant air. His intense eyes were as dark as his hair and filled with determination and the wrath of God. His face was young, his eyes as old as death. Following him was the cowled executioner, the man who would light the flame.

And then...came the witch.

The woman in the rickety cart that was made more unsteady by the mud and pockmarked road and was surrounded by the official witchfinder's lackeys, was not ranting or raving. She did not stare at the spectators with fire and brimstone in her eyes. She threatened no repercussions upon those who so self-righteously abused her. Instead, her beautiful blue eyes were filled with sadness and pity for those about her. Her eyes were about all that was left of her once great beauty!

Torture was illegal in these times. But a murmur went through the crowd, for it was obvious that she had, indeed, suffered serious abuse while the court sought her confession. Her gown was stained with blood, her complexion more pale than a summer's cloud, and she could barely stand.

"God bless you and keep you, lady!" a voice called out.

The witchfinder stopped in his tracks, his eyes raking over the crowd. His silence created a tension as still as the day, as terrifying as the portent of lightning.

Nothing else was said. He began to walk again.

The cart drew up before the stake. The kindling set below the stake was raw, damp, and thick. The region executioners' duty was abhorrent to them; therefore they had done everything in their power to assure that dense smoke would rise quickly, asphyxiating the poor lady before the flames touched her flesh.

A sob suddenly broke the stillness but was quickly hushed. To sympathize with one condemned for witchcraft was a quick path to inquisition by the witchfinder. And once the witchfinder had pointed his finger, there was little chance of remaining alive...

Pegeen MacCardle, her midnight hair caught by the wind, tried to stand. "Help me, good sir," she told her executioner with quiet dignity. The man's body spoke of his fear. Beyond the ashen gray of her features Pegeen offered him a beautiful smile. "If they would burn me, good sir, they must first attach me to the stake."

The witchfinder nodded to the executioner. Pegeen was carried and tied to the stake. She offered no resistance as she was bound. Her crimes and sentence were read to the assembled crowd; then she was given her last chance to speak.

"Pray for me, friends," she said, her voice gentle yet ringing clearly through the somber air and rising tension. "Pray that I meet my Maker quickly, and that I may abide with Him, as I will pray for you that He may guard all of you from the demons that walk the land under the order of a pathetically misguided king. I do, even here, pray for our sovereign James, that he may see the error of his ways, and find his own welcome in the home of our merciful God."

"Enough!" roared the witchfinder. Merciful God, he wondered, could he not get this over with! He was not a man immune to temptation, and he had fallen prey to her great beauty himself. He had fallen into wicked ways, for she had bewitched him. He would have saved her—oh, God, he would have

11

saved her—had it not been for her pride, and surely for her lust for the devil. He had been so bewitched he had almost forgotten his commitment in life, his determination to fight the devil. He had begged to take her into his own bed, to take her away, and she had denied him. When he looked at her, he saw his own failure, the weakness of his own flesh. *Die!* he cried out silently. *Die with your carnal lust for the devil in your heart, and leave me in peace.*

The witchfinder nodded his head gravely toward the executioner.

The masked man was trembling. Pegeen closed her eyes tightly for a minute. "Before God!" she said, weeping quietly. "Light the flame! Let it end!"

The fire was lit.

"Burn, witch! Burn!" The cries rang in a chanting crescendo.

The flames rose in an outer ring, soaring to touch the sky, but not brushing Pegeen. In between the angry flashes of blood-red, bright orange, and brilliant yellow, her face could be seen, her eyes staring upward, a blue as beautiful as the sky. Then her face was blotted out by a wall of flame.

She emitted one high-pitched, shattering scream that rent the air as cleanly as the stroke of a knife. Its echoes held the spectators in a haunting silence.

She was dead before the flames touched the hem of her skirt, asphyxiated by the pummels of dense smoke that turned the gray air almost black.

She was spared the hungry consumption of her flesh by the fire, but the spectators were not. The terrible scent, acrid, permeating, embraced them, held them in a grip of mortal terror. It stung the eyes, it filled the lungs, it hideously pervaded their senses and their souls. Many were held in the dark grip of their conscience, ready to cry out now against the horrible death. But it was too late.

The crowd remained silent. Pegeen, the witch, the lady, the healer, was gone. To move, to speak now, could do nothing for her. She was in God's hands while they were still alive. Matthews and his men watched for any reaction with sharp eyes.

But suddenly, from the rear of the crowded throng, a scream rang out, again and again, shattering, haunting echoes of the first, wave after wave of agony, of despair, of abject horror. The screams were, in fact, so similar to that first one emitted by the witch, that even Matthews was seized for a moment by chills that tore through his spine. It was as if the witch were still alive, mocking him.

He shook off his trembling and started walking through the crowd, searching out the perpetrator who had momentarily terrified him. It was difficult even for his determined stalking frame to pass through the people who hovered there in confusion, looking about. The smoke was very thick; people hacked and wheezed; ladies brought little sachets of fragrance to their noses in futile attempts to escape the stink of death.

Finally, the witchfinder saw the girl.

Again the chills of trembling terror temporarily debilitated him. He was stunned; caught motionless by fear. For as her screams had mocked had haunted him, so did her appearance.

Her hair was black, as black as a moonless night, so very dark and glossy that it might have been indigo. It was loose, and it waved in curls over her shoulders, down the length of her back.

Her skin was as pure as snow, as smooth as marble. Her coloring was ashen at the moment, but beneath her pallor lurked a complexion of ivory and rose. Her tense, white lips were full and shapely. Matthews could imagine, as he stood in his paralyzed state, that when she laughed her mouth would be like a rose, red and soft, and would taste like wine, sweet and potent.

She was the witch! Oh, sweetest Jesus! He had burned the witch, but she had come back. The devil had taken her from the flames, given her succor, and brought her back to haunt him, tempt him, beguile him, rob him of his senses and his manhood.

The townspeople knew who she was. This was no ghost to haunt them, but merely Brianna, Pegeen's niece. She had lived in the forest with her aunt, growing wild and beautiful beneath Pegeen's gentle tutelage.

Those who had opposed the execution, and those who had held doubts, no longer wavered. They had watched one die in the flames.

Enough. They saw Brianna now—in the wake of that terror—for what she was: young, with all the loveliness and freshness of youth. She was one of them and they were proud of her exceptional beauty. Perhaps they hadn't the nerve to risk their own lives, but if they could, they would help her.

Matthews kept staring at her, trembling inwardly.

She looked like Pegeen MacCardle but she was much younger. She was a girl still, but a maiden as tempting as ripe fruit, in the full bloom of youthful grace. In a plain dress of simple gray homespun she was the most beautiful creature he had ever seen walk the earth.

Something stirred within Matthews's state of spellbound fear. That something was desire, as riddling and gripping as the fear.

The look she gave him was of the most contemptuous disgust and horror he had ever witnessed. He was, he knew, from the clear message in her crystal-blue eyes, more heinous to her than the lowest of rats or snakes.

Fear suddenly passed. Desire remained. And fury. She was definitely the spawn of the devil. Only the devil could make a woman so provocative that she could reduce a man to a trembling, mindless creature lost to carnal thoughts and to dreams of her tempting ripeness...

How dare she stare at him with fire burning brightly in her blue eyes, full of accusation and loathing! Only the devil could lift her chin so, could give the look of haughty aristocracy to the delicate features of this mere peasant girl.

15

This witch! The devil's own!

He lifted a bony finger and pointed it toward her. "Seize her!" he cried out. "In the name of James II, Lord of all England, Scotland, and Wales, I accuse thee..."

Brianna MacCardle heard the words faintly— they came to her from the depths of a thick gray fog. Death had stunned her; horror held her tightly in a vise. Pegeen was dead. Oh, God, she was really dead. They had dragged her to the stake, tied her there, and set fire to her. The air stank with the scent of her charred flesh; it was too horrible to believe or fully comprehend.

Now this man, Matthews—the witchfinder— was staring at her.

His dark, probing eyes were on her. In them she could see a reflection of fire—the fire of the stake. He was calling her "witch."...

And she turned to run.

Chapter 2

Huddled in an alleyway, Brianna remembered that she had been strenuously warned by those neighbors who had loved Pegeen not to come anywhere near the execution. But since the day when the men had burst into her aunt's cottage and dragged Pegeen out into the midday sun, Brianna had been living a nightmare of confusion and horror.

She had been in the woods when the men had come. From the shadows of the huge and sheltering oaks that surrounded the little cottage, she had seen her aunt taken away.

The shouts in the streets seemed to be coming closer. Brianna tore down another alley, leaning back against the rear wall of a bakery. She was somewhat shielded from view by a series of grain crates, and she took the opportunity to breathe in great gulps of air. Closing her eyes, she couldn't help but think back.

She had been stunned when they took Pegeen, shocked into immobility. When the truth of what was happening seeped through to her dazed mind, she had torn out after them, scattering the herbs and roots she had been collecting along the way.

The men on horseback—with her aunt their prisoner—were halfway down the road before she had panted her way to the front of the cottage. Needles of pain shot through her healthy young legs, and through her laboring lungs. She had paused only a second, then started to run again, her bare feet pounding down the dirt lane with a speed almost equaling that of the horses.

But Mistress Willow, their nearest neighbor in the forest, had managed to stop her, hurling her rounded form upon that of the slip of a girl.

"Brianna! You mustn't go after her!" Mistress Willow pleaded, tears in her eyes, as she looked into the accusing eyes of the girl. "There's naught you can do now, girl."

17

"They've taken her...Pegeen... They've taken Pegeen. The witchfinder has taken Pegeen..."

Mistress Willow cradled the girl against her. "Pegeen is in God's hands now, girl. And you can't help her—but you can get yourself arrested too! We can do naught but wait, child, and pray that the Lord intervenes."

But the Lord did not intervene.

Until the very last moment Brianna had prayed that he would. Pegeen MacCardle had been the kindest, most gentle person alive. She loved the forest, she loved the creatures. And she loved Brianna. She had spent her life caring for the ill and wounded—her neighbors, and any creature, great and small. Her determination to heal had brought her to the stake. The wife of a farmer who had been cured of croup by Pegeen's potion of herbs had accused her of "bewitching" her husband because the husband had revered Pegeen as a saint in thanks for his life.

Brianna opened her eyes. Had she come far enough? No. The voices had been distant but now she could hear them more clearly. She pushed away from the wall of the bakery and ran blindly eastward, through the alleyways between huddled houses, smiths, and barns. Once again she found seclusion beneath an overhang, and paused, breathing deeply, feeling the pain ravage her again.

Pegeen! It was impossible that she was gone—so brutally, so cruelly. Orphaned at eleven when her parents had both succumbed to a plague, Brianna had at first been sent to live with her mother's family, the Powells, in England. They had been kind people, but strict Puritans, and after life with her handsome and fun-loving father, it had been quite a change. They were also extremely poor, and knowing that she had been a burden to them had hurt Brianna terribly.

Robert, her second cousin and ten years her senior, had tried very hard to convince her—but to no avail—that she was added help, not a burden. He was a religious, serious young man, but his dark eyes had always been warm and tender and he had spoken to her in the gentlest of tones. Then Pegeen had come, and immediately she had loved Brianna. Both the Powells and Brianna knew that she would be loved and cherished if she returned to Scotland with Pegeen.

During the eight wonderful years Brianna had grown up in the small woods home of her aunt, she had come to know that Pegeen MacCardle was very simply, very basically, one of the finest human beings alive. In an era when blood was shed over the slightest discrepancy in belief, Pegeen was truly good. Her religion was the forest; her God was one of goodness.

Oh, yes—the Lord should have intervened!

But he hadn't, and Pegeen MacCardle had died.

When Brianna had realized that no miracle was going to occur, she had lost all sense of reason in the face of horrible reality. And so she had come to face Matthews, official witchfinder.

Her heart caught suddenly and skipped a beat. She could hear him again—Matthews!

"Find her! Find the witch!"

He was close, oh, very close! And it seemed that the alleyways were full of whispers, full of the sound of running feet. She turned a corner and collided with a wizened old man. She almost screamed but he touched a finger to his weathered lips.

"Run, girl, run!"

She had to run. But there seemed to be nowhere to go; no safe place. Run—because if she did not, she, too, would become charred flesh and ash in the wind...

Desperation and deep-rooted instincts for survival spurred Brianna's young limbs into fluid action. She couldn't cry for her aunt; she couldn't even afford the time to feel her pain. It didn't matter. She was numb. Her feelings and emotions were deadened by horror.

She raced north through the city; behind her she could hear the shouts of the king's men as they lashed out against the pressing throng that detained them. They couldn't move against the sea of humanity.

Brianna began a zigzag course, one that started to take her westward as well as north. A new sound, rasping, heaving, reached her ears.

It was the sound of her gasping breaths; it mingled with the rush of the blood that filled her ears like the sound of waves, and with the terrible thudding and pounding of her heart.

The woods, she thought. She had to get out of the city and into the woods. She could find shelter in the dense forests; there were caves and crannies and cliffs and she could disappear as easily as a doe—until she could find a way back to the Powells! Oh, yes! They would help her now. Robert, or his father, would know what to do, how to hide her...

She couldn't seem to outrun the smell of burning flesh, or the sound of the chase behind her.

She ran down another alley rank with the stench of emptied chamberpots and decaying garbage. A cat, skeleton-thin, screeched in her path, arching his back. She tried to run around it, but the panicked creature bolted with her. She tripped over it, and sprawled into the mud and dust and garbage. Spitting dirt out of her mouth, she scrambled to her feet.

"This way," cried a soldier of the crown.

"Down the alley!" shouted another.

"Suffer not a witch to live!" returned the first voice.

Brianna lost all conscious thought and logic as she heard the voices of the soldiers. Like a cornered rat, she had no reason. She would have kicked and clawed and bit at stone to escape her pursuers.

As she rounded the corner, she left behind her the alley of the slums. A scent of salt and tangy sea breezes finally began to clear that of the acrid smoke.

She came upon a row of dockside houses. Not elegant mansions, but townhouses that belonged to sea captains and merchants.

Across from the townhouses were the docks and ships, everything from tiny fishing boats to the massive merchant ships and the men-of-war that sailed across the Atlantic to the Colonies.

And beyond that there was nothing, except the sea, as gray and tempestuous as the sky.

Brianna paused for a moment, drawing in great gulps of air as she pivoted about on her toes, desperately seeking a hideout. Her zigzag course had taken her into a trap of her own making.

As she spun about, the gray of the sky was brilliantly lit by a jagged streak of lightning. A peal of thunder followed so quickly, it sounded as if the heavens had split. And as if the sky had truly been torn asunder, rain began to fall in torrents.

Brianna stared desperately about herself once more, blinking against the rain. At the far end of the townhouses she could make out a sign. It creaked and swayed beneath the wind and rain, but she could make out the words. HAWK'S TAVERN. Knowing only that she could not stand awaiting capture in the pouring rain, she raced for the three rickety steps that led to the tavern's door.

It was gray inside, almost as gray as it was outside. The air was heavy too; but heavy with odors that were pleasant to the senses. The delicious scent of fresh bread was in the air; the appetizing scent of braised and seasoned meat.

Brianna stood against the door for a second, wide blue eyes scanning the tavern. There were rough wood tables about the room, a fireplace against the far wall that offered a mellow, comforting heat. A number of the tables were filled with male customers—crusty old sea salts, from the looks of them. But, Brianna noticed, her heart giving a little leap of relief, there was another woman in the room. She was dressed in a rather startling low-cut gown of red, and she sat with one of the sailors. There were also females waiting upon the tables, two of them, both engaged at present in slamming down tankards of ale and hunks of mutton before boisterous customers.

Brianna prayed desperately that she had enough coins in her shoe to purchase a tankard of ale. If she could slip quietly into one of the shadowy corners of the gray room, she could bide a little time.

Her decision made, she moved quickly, keeping close to the wall to reach the secluded corner table. It was concealed by a broad structural beam as well as by the darkness. Nervously Brianna sidled around the beam in hopes of quickly sliding into a chair and avoiding notice by any of the tavern's other patrons. All she wanted to do was disappear into the woodwork.

Instead, she found herself drawing in a sharp gasp, and then swallowing quickly so that she wouldn't cry out.

The chair she had sought behind the beam was not empty, and she did not sit down upon cold wood. Through the wool of her dress and the linen of her chemise she could feel heat, and something as hard and firm and strong as wood; but unlike the wood, the form she came in contact with was alive and vital. She tried to rise again with her gasp, but found she could not—because a pair of arms as strong as steel were tightly around her. She twisted quickly to stare into a pair of arresting green eyes.

A high-arched black brow rose with amusement within the contours of a strongly chiseled and handsome face. Full, mobile lips curved into a dry smile. "I've been waiting for you. Welcome to the tavern."

"What?" She gasped out.

He was frowning then, assessing her with annoyance. "Damn, but you're a mess! I wasn't expecting the latest fashions from Paris—but clean would have been appreciated."

"I beg your pardon!" Brianna snapped, and then paused with the cold realization that the man had been expecting a whore—and that he was assuming she was the woman he had hired. She could think of nothing at first except escaping his iron hold and the strange tremors that swept through her as he held her.

"No—" she started to protest, but suddenly there was another man striding through the dimly lit tavern toward them. "Get on out of here, girl!" the man, a husky, ill-kempt fellow in an apron, told her grimly. "We do not cater to womenfolk here!"

The man had his hand upon her arm. Brianna was reminded that the streets crawled with the King's men, searching her out.

"Leave her be, Liam," the green-eyed stranger with the iron arms said quietly. "I've been expecting a—companion."

He had spoken so softly, and yet his words carried such force that the harried Liam immediately paused and grinned a smile that was minus a front tooth.

"As ye wish, Captain, as ye wish."

"Oh, Liam, will you see that the lady is brought some wine rather than ale, and some of the lamb stew and that bread you've just baked." He spoke in English rather than in Gaelic with a slight accent that she could not place. That wasn't strange, because English was quite common in Glasgow. But the accent...

"Right away, m'lord, right away." Liam hurried off, wiping his broad hands upon his apron.

Reason began to cut through the haze of fear and numbness that had engulfed Brianna. She glanced quickly from the handsome and stalwart jade-eyed man to the woman in red she had seen upon entering the tavern.

Indignation rose within her as she quickly assessed the woman in red. Her gown was not only shamefully brilliant, but it was cut low over heaving breasts. The woman's cheeks were also heavily powdered and rouged. And

25

this man had grouped her along with the slut in red!

Anger swept over her and she clawed at the little vises of steel that were his fingers locked around her.

"Let me up!" she demanded.

"Let you up?" A single dark brow rose high again with amusement, then lowered as his eyes narrowed with a flash of cynicism. "As you wish."

He stood and she found herself unceremoniously upon the floor, staring up at him. She was too stunned to speak for a moment, made so acutely aware of his height and the breadth of his shoulders. He must stand, she thought with a bit of awe, well over six feet. Fawn breeches clung tightly to well-muscled thighs, and his expertly tailored navy-blue greatcoat accentuated his powerful chest and a torso that tapered handsomely at the waist and lean hips. His calves, of which she was given a bird's-eye view from her ignominious position, were encased in high black boots, and were as long and sinewed as his sturdy thighs.

Brianna suddenly realized that she was giving the stranger a commendable assessment while half seated, half sprawled, at his feet. She rose swiftly, barely aware that the top of her head was well below his chin when she planted her hands firmly upon her hips, arched back her throat, and snapped, "You bastard!"

He shrugged, thick dark lashes half hovering over his radiant eyes with disinterest. "I am not in the mood for games," he told her, the lashes rising again.

That sea-jade stare could sizzle dangerously, Brianna noted, but she was too incensed to heed any danger signals. Her treatment at the hands of this apparent "lord" was simply unacceptable. She lifted her hand and slapped him fully across the face.

She gasped as his hand shot out to catch her wrist, constricting it painfully in his grip. Belatedly she realized that his eyes were indeed as dangerous as the square set of his determinedly formed jaw.

And belatedly she remembered why she had run into the tavern. He might be quite dangerous, but Matthews was the enemy, and this man might just well offer her escape. At the very least she could play for time.

"Madam," he grated harshly, his use of the word a mockery. "I have told you, I am in no mood for games. You appeared hungry and I was willing to feed you. But if our arrangement is not to your liking, please feel free to leave. The tavern door swings both ways."

Brianna quickly lowered her eyes. She couldn't leave that tavern; she didn't dare. The streets could still be swarming with the King's madmen shouting, "Witch!"

Resolution, like the icy waters of a winter stream, flowed through her. Cold. So very cold. So very different from the burning flames of death. She couldn't save her aunt, she could only try now to save herself.

God help her! Having seen the flames of death, she would indeed sell her soul to any devil to escape that fate. He wanted a whore—

she'd have to act the part. She shivered suddenly. Could she do it? Could she? She had to!

"Forgive me," she mumbled sweetly, not raising the shield of her lashes. She slid silently into the chair opposite the stranger and kept her gaze fixed upon the rough planking of the table until she had gathered herself together. Then she raised her lashes and gazed at him with wide eyes and an apologetic smile. "I really am so very sorry! The weather is awful, I had difficulty traveling. I tripped, you see, and was splattered with mud. I'm afraid I'm quite nervous." He kept staring at her and she allowed her lashes to flutter and fall again, praying he would believe her.

She felt his gaze upon her, boring into her. One of his boot-clad legs was stretched out alongside the table; his arm rested upon it and he lightly drummed his fingers against it.

"What is your name?" he asked her.

She glanced up at him—offering him another radiant smile. "Brianna," she said softly. How long, she wondered, could she stay here with him? Was she convincing him that she was what he wanted? Tension gripped her stomach painfully as she grew more and more uneasy with the role she allotted herself. Was he a loyal supporter of King James? Would he eagerly throw her to the man who searched for her?

No! She couldn't allow herself to think that way. She had to play him out, flirt with him, tease him, until...

Until what? she wondered with desperation. Until the king's men cleared the streets, and she could make good an escape out of Glasgow to the forest.

"You're very kind," she said, irritated by her stiff tone. You'll have to do better than that! she reproved herself. And she smiled again, with all the allure she could muster. "I am famished, and the meal will be most appreciated."

"So will soap and water," he muttered, watching her curiously. She returned his scrutiny and discovered that she could act boldly.

She felt very remote watching him as if she were someone else. The past days had begun the change and the past minutes had completed it. Her carefree life had been swept away—and with it her youth, and all her dreams.

She lowered her head, and a bitter smile came fleetingly to her lips. Oh, how life had changed! Just days ago she had been so assured and confident. Her dreams of the future had included a valiant knight falling in love with her, promising eternal devotion. She had been Brianna of the Forest to the local boys— untouchable. She had laughed with them and accepted their adoration, like a snow queen with her courtiers. Ah, she was so chaste, so determined that none should ever touch her until her forever love, the misted knight who would one day claim her!

That had been last week. This was now. The untouchable little "snow queen" was sitting at a table with a man who assumed she was a whore. And the man was no boy, no stripling lad. He appeared as rugged as the highland hills, as vital as the sea that crashed a tempest against the coast.

She grated her teeth together hard. This was also reality and she would do anything for his protection. She would do anything not to burn. Oh, God! She had almost ruined it! She'd almost thought herself that other Brianna—that princess of the forest—and ruined it all with her silly dreams!

Yes! She would do anything to escape the flames. She would beg, borrow, steal—or even bed with this hard, imposing stranger—to escape. If it did come to that, she would withdraw into herself. And if she could just do that, she would remain untouched.

He was watching her—too acutely, too curiously. She smiled quickly, thinking that a whore would be stroking his ego. "It's quite a pleasure to see a man of your strength," she crooned softly.

"Is it?" he asked. She kept smiling, even though she longed to slap him and tell him he was incredibly insolent. What would the real whore respond? Brianna wondered. Worse still, what if the real whore put in an appearance while they were sitting there?

"Yes, it is," she replied quickly. "It's such a pleasure that I'm very anxious to be alone with you."

He leaned across the table. She was made very aware of his scent, clean and male and tangy like the sea.

One of the serving girls came to the table with a steaming bowl of stew, a crude pewter wine-cup, and a new tankard of ale for the captain, or lord, or whatever he might be. She was a pretty wench, busty and well rounded, and she had a saucy smile for the captain and a faint glance of skepticism for Brianna.

Brushing closely against the captain, she asked coyly, "Will ye be needin' anything, m'lord?"

He smiled in return to her, "I think not, Bessie, thank you."

Bessie pouted her lips slightly. "If ye decide that ye do"—her glance suggested that with Brianna as his "companion," it was most likely that he would discover himself in need—"ye just let me know, m'lord."

"He won't, Bessie," Brianna said sweetly, but with a deadly warning.

With a swish of her ample rear, Bessie left the table.

God, she was hungry, but she wanted to eat quickly and leave the public room. Glancing up, she discovered that he was still watching her, and that he was very close.

"Umm, aren't you eating?" she inquired.

He shook his head, his expression curious. "I've eaten, thank you."

Brianna glanced quickly toward the tavern's doors. It was possible that the officers would rush into the tavern, screaming "witch," and drag her back out into the rain-muddied streets. She had to eat quickly.

She did so, taking large sips of her wine in between bites of the stew. The wine was potent and comforting. It helped to blur the rough edges of terror that still gnawed at her whenever she glimpsed the tavern door.

She was startled when the long fingers that had been idly drumming the table suddenly stretched out to cover her hand. A little jolt of heat seemed to flash through her at that touch, and she lifted her eyes warily to meet his.

"Are you through?"

She nodded uneasily. For a second there seemed to be a quirk of amusement in those enigmatic and compelling eyes.

Fears played havoc with her; icy shivers ran along her spine. She was going to have to play her role if she wanted to escape the public room. *Distance,* she reminded herself. *Withdraw into yourself, and he cannot really touch you.*

"Would you like something else? More... stew?"

"No!" she responded quickly. She leaned across the table, reaching out to touch his cheek, to caress the rugged contours of his face with her fingers. Her fingertips seemed to burn at the action; he was very real, male, and disturbing. She wanted to pull away so desperately. "I told you," she whispered. "I'm anxious."

He caught her hand and pressed his lips against it. "Are you really?" He asked softly. "I'll be...anxious...to see this myself. After you're cleaned up, of course."

She did jerk her hand back, but forced her lips into another smile. He lifted a hand to summon the serving wench, but as they waited for the girl, the tavern doors swung open. An old peg leg entered, shouting excitedly. "They're combing the streets out there—a witch-hunt if ever I've seen one!"

Brianna froze in her chair, feeling as if cold fingers had grabbed her by the throat. She lowered her lashes instantly over her eyes in hope of concealing her terror.

But the handsome captain didn't notice. She heard him utter an exclamation of disgust, and her eyes flew open. "Superstitious rot!" he muttered, but he wasn't talking to her, just to himself.

Brianna barely noticed his words because panic was with her once again. She stood, took his hand, and leaned against him. "May we leave?" she murmured. Leave! When they left, she would be running out of time. No, no, she could stall, and play for time once he took her to his lodgings. Fool! She charged herself. How would she play for time then— when she had been telling him how "anxious" she was! Then he would discover that she was not at all what she claimed.

That would still be minutes away, and right now she had to take things minute by minute. She had to get out of the main room of the tavern just in case the searchers did burst through the doors.

One of his handsome black brows quirked up a third time as her entreaty brought him back from private thoughts. "Please," she said more softly.

He inclined his head slightly, a faint smile curving the full and sensuous mouth. "Certainly." He stood, and once again she was struck by his height and powerful size.

Where were his lodgings? she wondered in a moment of panic. If he headed toward the street, she was doomed.

His hand slipped around her elbow and they left the sheltered table behind. The tavern's patrons, listening avidly to the peg leg's account of the witch burning that had taken place in the common, barely glanced up as they made their way toward the stairs.

Bessie, her pert nose still somewhat in the air, stopped them at the landing. Her eyes flashed over Brianna's slender figure contemptuously before boldly meeting those of the man.

"Yer room's fresh and clean, m'lord Treveryan," she said with a little bob. "Ye will call me..." Her voice trailed away insinuatingly.

"Water, Bessie, and soap, please."

"Right away, Lord Treveryan," Bessie said with another bob. She wrinkled her nose toward Brianna, but Brianna barely noticed, she was so intent upon Bessie's words.

Lord Treveryan. Whoever he was, he was of the nobility. He might think witch-hunts contemptible, but he might still be loyal to the crown of James.

She didn't have long to think, for moments later she was being ushered into a small, sparsely furnished room. There was a bed and a dresser, and a plain latticed screen to the far left of the room. They had barely entered the room before Bessie followed them with a washbowl and pitcher. She carried them behind the screen, where there must have been a table, as Brianna heard the pottery click against the wood.

But she did not pay attention to Treveryan or Bessie, because there was a shuttered window overlooking the street below. Brianna walked nervously to the window and cracked open the shutters. The rain had stopped, and afternoon was fast fading into night. Her heart skipped a little beat as she saw a man in the king's uniform stalking down the street.

She almost jumped out the window when a hand came down upon her shoulder.

"What is the matter with you?" Jade eyes bored into hers as Treveryan irritably voiced the question. His hands were upon her shoulders, holding her to face him.

Brianna blinked quickly, and reminded herself that it was her life at stake. "Nothing," she whispered huskily to him. "Nothing at all—"

He lifted surprisingly gentle fingers to her cheek and traced the bone structure down to her mouth. A shiver trailed down her spine as he lightly followed the curve of her lips with his thumb.

His voice was husky when he spoke again, and the velvet within it sent another tingling wave racing along her spine.

"If you do not wish to be here, Brianna, then you must leave."

Leave! Walk out when the king's men were prowling the street!

"No!" she murmured quickly. She forced herself to open her eyes to him again and face him with a dazzling smile. "No," she repeated, softly this time. "I'm exactly where I wish to be."

"Then let's get on with it, shall we?" He said softly. But there was a hint of impatience in his voice—a warning.

He had cast aside his greatcoat and she saw that his shirt was of fine white silk. She shuddered once, just once, and resigned herself to her charade. If she did not please him, she would think of something to say. But while there was breath in her, and while he offered this hiding place, this safety, she would stay with him.

"The washstand," he told her pointedly, "is over there."

"Yes, yes, of course," she murmured, and walked quickly behind the screen.

She hesitated there, just for a moment. If a miracle was going to occur to save her, now was the time.

No miracles occurred. She closed her eyes tightly, then reached nervously to undo her muddied gown. It fell to the floor, and when she stood in her shift only, she shivered fleetingly, then with numb fingers she reached for the soap. Cleaning herself of the mud felt good, but the water was cold, shocking her into a greater realization than she wanted to face. She couldn't do it. She couldn't go through with it!

"Brianna!"

His tone was very irritated. She flinched behind the cover of the screen, finding strength in the hatred for him that leapt to her breast. "I'm coming," she called out sharply, then winced again at her own tone. "I want only to please you!" She called out silkily. Then, she came around the screen and in desperation, hurried to him.

She slipped her arms around him, allowing her fingers to play upon the flesh at the nape of his neck. She felt his muscles beneath her touch and the crush of his broad chest against her breasts. His arms slipped around her and the power and heat that enveloped her made her shiver. She had to go through with it, she warned herself furiously.

But what then? What happened when he was done with her?

She had to pray that darkness would have descended and that the streets would be cleared of soldiers. She could escape back to the forest and then somehow get to the Powells.

She smiled at him, aware that she didn't know what was expected of her. Words, she hoped, would suffice. "Lord Treveryan, truly, truly I wish to be nowhere else," she murmured, the nervousness in her voice giving it a husky, sensual quality.

"I'm glad," he told her in a low murmur. He turned then and sat on the bed to remove his boots. Brianna watched him for several seconds, then turned quickly from him, unnerved by his strange appraisal of her. His eyes moved over her as if he were surprised by her, and oddly pleased. Brianna risked another glance out of the window. Soldiers were still prowling along the street. She felt the coil of fear wind tightly in her stomach, and she stared surreptitiously back at the captain.

He was, she decided objectively, an extremely fine example of a man. Lean, fit, and agile, and yet so sinewed that an attractive play of muscle could be seen beneath the taut fabric of his breeches and beneath the ballooning silk of his shirt-sleeves. His countenance, with the piercing eyes and coal-dark arching brows, was more than handsome; it was ruggedly strong and determined. She could well imagine him as a sea captain, standing solid against the wind, his voice roaring out orders above the tempest of the sea. She had no doubt that each and every man aboard would scurry to carry out his commands.

She suddenly had to clutch her fingers together to keep them from shaking. Her position was a miserable one. She was forced to play a humiliating role before a man who emanated power, a certain arrogance, and a very rugged determination. How she would love to keep her pride before such a man.

His boots hit the floor with a thud.

Her heart was pounding; her limbs seemed frozen. She felt a sudden terror that she would break if he touched her. He moved silently on his stockinged feet, and that silent movement of such a hard and well-muscled man unnerved her further. *You would sell your soul to the devil,* she reminded herself, and perhaps that was what she was doing. There was a heated gleam in his eyes that surely belonged to a devil, and a pulse ticked within a blue vein in his well-corded neck.

No! she thought, this just couldn't be happening. She had to try to stall, to keep praying for a miracle...

She stepped back—eluding his arms.

She saw a frown knit his brow tightly, and then the flame of anger creep into his eyes.

"Lass! I warned you I was in no mood for games. I have to be back aboard ship soon, and I haven't the time for whatever this is that you're playing."

She thought quickly. "Aren't you forgetting something?" she queried with a show of bravado.

"Am I?"

"Payment in advance, Lord Treveryan." Would they haggle? Would it buy her more time?

"Dammit! Certainly—but, so help me, wench, let's get on with this!"

With his words he tossed a handful of gold coins upon the bed. A flaming blush of humiliation crept into Brianna's cheeks and she raised her eyes to meet his; but he was no longer watching her. He had turned with disgust, and now it was he who stalked to the window to stare out to the street below.

Brianna stared at the coins, ready to burst into tears, wishing she could slap herself into some sense. He did not want to hurt her; he just wanted her. She was trying desperately to save her life—but allowing panic to bring her closer and closer to the stake.

"Dammit, girl!" he thundered, and she realized he was watching her again, his eyes flashing annoyance. "I ask you again, is this bargain not to your liking? If that is so, go! I will have no unwilling woman, lady or whore."

She must have flinched visibly, because his voice softened. "If you need the money, girl, take it. But if you wish to leave me, do so now, for I have been at sea a long time, and there are things I would forget for a while in the arms of someone soft and sweet-smelling. It matters not to me who this woman should be, as long as she is clean and shapely and can ease the needs of a man."

Brianna began to speak but couldn't continue. He was being kind, she realized bitterly, offering her pay for services not performed. For some absurd reason it hurt her that he didn't care if he had her or another.

"Make up your mind now," he told her. "You were so anxious before—have you lost interest now? If so, I want you out of this room."

"No!" Brianna protested quickly. Blindly, she picked up the coins. Bitterly aware that she might need them to reach England and the Powells, she slipped them into the pocket of her shift.

With awkward, trembling fingers, she reached to unfasten the hooks at the rear of her shift.

It was then that there came a tapping at the door and Brianna's fingers froze once more.

"My lord?"

It was a woman's voice. Soft, questioning, and it was followed by a husky giggle.

The whore—the whore he had been expecting! Brianna thought swiftly. In desperation she flashed him a quick smile as she hurried to the door.

She threw it open and stepped into the hall, closing the bedroom door behind her and forcing the golden-haired woman with the painted face away from it.

"Who are you?" she demanded haughtily of Brianna.

"The first to arrive," Brianna replied coolly.

"I'm here for the Lord Treveryan," the golden-haired woman said angrily.

"Then you have been misled, for he is already occupied."

"Get out of my way. I was told to come—"

"So was I," Brianna lied, smiling sweetly but with a determined flash to her eyes and a threat of malice. She handed the woman one of Treveryan's gold pieces. "Take this—and yourself—out of here quickly."

"I will not!" The whore protested, narrowing her eyes. "I think I'll just take a look at his lordship myself, love, and see if he wouldn't prefer—"

"I'm much, much younger," Brianna interrupted pointedly. She couldn't let this slut cost her her life!

But pity touched her, and she could really feel no malice.

"Please, take the money and leave be. It will be for nothing."

"You have youth, but I have experience. Perhaps my Lord Treveryan would prefer what I have to offer." She laughed. "He's not choosing a bride, lass, Just an hour's entertainment."

"Brianna!" The voice thundered from the room. At any second Lord Treveryan would stalk into the hallway, demanding to know what was going on.

Brianna took a step toward the woman with new menace and a ruthless determination. "Take yourself from here now! He is mine, and I promise to slit your throat from ear to ear to keep him! Keep this—and go!"

The woman appeared stunned, but still the gold piece was being offered her, and the assurance of that piece seemed more profitable than an assault upon herself. She backed away.

Brianna leaned wearily against the doorframe, desperately wishing it were she with the freedom to walk down the steps.

"Brianna!" The impatient call came out to her, like a noose, tightening about her throat.

Better that noose than the heat of the flames, she reminded herself.

She reentered the room, grateful for the coming darkness that hid her eyes from the relentless green stare of the man, Lord Treveryan.

Chapter 3

Sloan Treveryan frowned as he watched the unusual blue-eyed beauty who had come his way. Her manner was most peculiar—one moment he felt as if he were with the most sensual harlot, and in the next, he felt as if he had come across a most indignant aristocrat.

Brice MacMichael—whom Sloan had met when he docked, and who had convinced him he was in need of casual companionship—had kept his promise to send someone "exquisite." Someone to ease his dark and brooding mood, a temporary haven from the cares of a tragic personal responsibility, and from the tension and danger of his true purpose in Glasgow.

This girl could, he thought with a smile, do all that. She could make him forget everything.

At times it seemed she shuddered from his touch—but she had fought with a fiery temper to keep him for herself. There was a strange sense of innocence about her, yet he sensed in her blue eyes that she could be a tempest of sensuality. He had felt that for some reason she was regretting their liaison, yet when she was offered an out, she strenuously declined to take it.

She had sent away another woman, Sloan reflected with amusement. It was a curious situation. Who was this Brianna—and just what was going on? Had old Brice decided to send him not just one woman, but several?

Brianna was awkward with her hooks, almost

as if she were reluctant to disrobe. Yet she was beguiling as she did so. Her shift came slowly up, baring long, shapely legs that were as lovely as alabaster. She hesitated again with the hem just at the top of her thighs. Sloan realized a bit foolishly that he had held his breath while her fingers hovered there...anticipation created a rush of blood within his ears. He exhaled as she raised the shift again, uncovering to his view firm, rounded buttocks that were as shapely as her legs. Her waist was tiny, emphasizing that subtle and evocative flare of hips, drawing attention to her long ribcage, sleek shoulders, which were proud and square, and the hint of the swell of her breasts that he could just see as she tossed back her rich mane of ebony hair.

Darkness was falling, he realized regretfully. How he longed to light a candle. But he did not, sensing that she needed to come to him in shadow.

She didn't glance his way, but hurriedly climbed into the bed. He caught a quick glimpse of the front of her and he was suddenly aware that his breath was as ragged as the wind. A shudder tore through his body, and he was made very acutely aware of his almost painful reaction to her. His muscles tensed; his manhood throbbed.

A loud shout from the street pierced the web of sensual enchantment that was spinning around him, and he twisted to glance out the shutters once more.

Matthews. That damned raving lunatic!

Sloan had seen him before, finding "witches" in Liverpool by order of King James.

Matthews shouted something again. He and his men turned down the alley. They slowly disappeared.

A slight sound, a shifting of long limbs against the sheets, attracted his attention. He returned his gaze to the bed, and the stunning woman who lay upon it.

Her hair was spread upon the pillow, a dark silken fan against the white linen. Her eyes were closed. His eyes roamed to the elegant length of neck and ivory throat. She was flushed a tender pink, and her luxurious dark lashes swept low over her cheeks.

Just a glance at her, he thought incredulously, *and I feel that I am touched by fever.*

The roaring in his ears began all over again, and thought was swept cleanly from his mind. He wanted his cravings soothed and his mind cleansed. It could happen.

Even in the darkness she appeared pale as new-fallen snow and her enigmatic eyes were as wide as a pair of gold doubloons. But then that look was gone—her ink-black lashes slid lazily over her eyes, a subtle curve touched her lips, and a tremor suddenly riddled his body.

He moved lightly to her. She glanced up at him, blue eyes widening again. He saw a pulse beating furiously at the base of her throat and again he found himself wondering just who was this most unique female? Too fine, too beautiful, for her calling.

He touched a silken lock of her hair. Her eyes

45

stared into his, deep and mysterious, slightly glazed and luminescent. Her lashes brushed over her cheeks and her fingers curled over the sheets. He moved his gaze over her, haunted by the round, full beauty of her breasts, and the valley dipping between them.

He found himself smiling at her, impatient, his rushing blood seeming to come alive with a smoldering fire. Yet he was equally willing to go slow and prolong his own torture to touch and explore all that made up the perfection of her form. He had wanted nothing more than a quick, uninvolved bedding; now he wanted to make love, to tease her senses as he allowed his own to soar.

He knelt down beside her, taking her gently into his arms.

"I need you, Brianna," he whispered to her.

She flinched at his touch but so faintly, he might have imagined it. He began to touch her, savoring the softness of her flesh. She jerked slightly as his fingers grazed the crest of her breasts, then settled between them to find the erratic beat of her heart. She was still as he allowed his fingers to explore, massaging her throat, the slope of her shoulders, the length of her midriff to the curve of her waist. He found the cleft in her back, the slight dimples that shadowed her buttocks just below her spine.

Brianna barely dared to breathe, staring, as if compelled, at his eyes. It had taken all her willpower—and the rampant fear of a burning death—to remain still at his first touch.

It was becoming more than willpower and fear that held her. If there was truly a devil who could lure and seduce the innocent, it was he. Conscious thought slipped slowly but surely away from her. A part of her mind darkened to oblivion; a new part awakened vibrantly. Her flesh came alive, and the heat grew within her, spinning from some undefined center.

She wanted to scream. She wanted to stop him! She wanted more!

"Search! Search every street! Suffer not a witch to live!"

The cry came to them faintly from the streets. Brianna, hearing the words, willed herself not to stiffen. She offered Treveryan her best attempt at a sultry and seductive smile and pressed her nakedness closely against him, slipping her arms around his shoulders, allowing her nails to graze and tease over his shoulders.

"How I want you," he murmured.

"And I you..." she replied, again grateful that the fear in her voice created a huskiness that could pass for sensuality. And she was aflame—torn between the exotic new sensations of his caress and the terror that kept her blood pounding mercilessly through her system.

He was gone suddenly—she opened her eyes cautiously to see that he was stripping away his shirt. He paused then, drinking in her beauty as she lay there, the rouge crests of her breasts provocative as they darkened and hardened in sweet reply to his care, the natural seduction of the curve of her hips, the

47

shadows of her abdomen. One of her knees was slightly raised over the other, creating a haunting and intriguing mystery of velvet ebony where the shapely length of her legs converged.

He lay beside her again, slipping his arms around her and crushing her breasts against his bared chest. Her head tilted backward, her eyes widened as her arms responded instinctively to his hold, slipping around his neck. Despite the fever that gripped him, straining his masculinity against his breeches, he was still too fascinated to hurry his torment to an end. He lowered his head slowly over hers, feeling as if he were drowning a bit in the fantasy of her blue eyes. His lashes closed only as he touched her lips with his, tasting her natural sweetness more potent than wine. With the lightest touch he caressed her mouth, vaguely aware that he had stumbled into quicksand and he would sink farther and farther into a magical abyss of no return.

It didn't matter. He traced her lips with his tongue, and then the fever overwhelmed him and he delved deeply into her mouth, tasting a nectar that drove him wild. He was compelled to consume, and his mouth hungrily ravaged hers, his tongue delving deeper and deeper, demanding all. A soft, strangled moan escaped her, but she was not fighting him. Her lips were forming to his, her fingers threading through his hair.

"Brianna..." he said softly, the word on his lips a caress, "You are, my sweet, a witch..."

48

Her body, so sweetly pliant beneath his, suddenly stiffened. Her eyes widened until they seemed to encompass her face.

"What?" she gasped, a croak that sounded strangely of terror.

"A temptress, my sweet," he assured her, "enchantress, seductress. You have ensnared me in the spell of your beauty."

She took a deep breath and exhaled, and — as she did, the tension left her limbs.

"Oh..." she murmured softly. When her eyes met his again he saw that they were veiled, her cheeks were flushed.

Sloan stood to pull the string on his breeches and remove them. She returned his gaze at first, but when he stood naked before her, the flush in her cheeks became crimson. As if suddenly aware of her own nudity, she closed her eyes with a shudder and reached nervously for the linen bed coverings.

"No!" he cried, startling himself with the sound of his voice. But her action had stunned him. It was almost as if his nudity had frightened her, where her own did not.

Earlier, he could have let her go. Not now. She would not turn away from him. He had offered her every option, but she had insisted on her game, and now he was finding the touch-me-touch-me-not plays to be fraying upon his temper.

He was beside her, wrenching linen from her grasping fingers, pulling her into his arms, beneath his weight, before she could even begin to muster the strength to fight against him.

His mouth found hers. The gentle, seductive quality was gone, but this kiss seduced Brianna no less than the first. It was hungry. It ravaged and demanded and swept her into a tempestuous windstorm she was helpless to resist. His mouth left hers to find her breast, to caress the nipple with lips and tongue and teeth. Again the lightning knifed through her, leaving her trembling, clinging to his shoulders, her nails curving convulsively into flesh. She sobbed out a broken moan, of dismay, of yearning—of something she had never experienced before—the burning ache that blazed from a secret place deep within her.

She was unaware that she tossed her head upon the pillow, back and forth, emitting soft little moans. The world for her had ceased to exist; she was adrift upon a sea of sensation, and he was the sensation that overwhelmed all else. His lips and hands moved down her torso, still hungry, still demanding, and she could do naught but swirl along with him in the vortex of his storm. She wondered vaguely what would have happened if she had had the will to resist him. It probably wouldn't have mattered in the least. He was like the steel of a forge, heated strength, and his limbs, the hard-muscled arms, the lithe, corded thighs, were like the finest blade. He could have subdued her, had he wished, at any time, with the long fingers of a single hand.

A gasp escaped her as his hand spanned over her thigh, fondling, exploring. His lips burned against the shadowed hallow of her abdomen beneath her hip. Unwittingly she tore her fingers into his hair again; he caught her wrists, and laced his fingers through hers, and held her hands at her thighs as his mouth continued to taunt the vulnerable flesh of her belly. His tongue drew moist patterns, following the line of her hips, circling lower and lower until he brushed against the blue-ebony curls that were the frame of her innocence. She should have been shocked at the intimacy, but it was her body that responded now, not her mind. And her body writhed and arched.

A shudder went through her, an incomprehensible cry escaped her. Her fingers tightened, knuckles white, upon his. She writhed to escape him, the sweet glory of the liquid fire that swept her, but he held her hands firm. In seconds her writhing was not to escape him, but to have more and more of him.

His mouth came to hers again; the heat and strength of his body enwrapped her. His chest crushed against her breasts, and even that sensation was intoxicating, as was the shaft of his sex, pulsing powerfully against her. She shivered beneath him, vaguely aware that they had passed a point of no return.

Sloan exulted in her. Her exquisite form heightened his desire unbearably. He had never known a woman to give pleasure so unthinkingly, whose innate sensuality alone could send a man into tempest. He slipped his hand between her sleek thighs, parting them. They trembled slightly, and gave to his touch.

The invitation of her body totally severed the fine line of his control. He groaned aloud as the floodgates of his restraint shattered, leaving him totally at the mercy of his need. He entered into her with explosive force, and was stunned as the scream tore from her throat, shocked at the message that vaguely filtered into his mind.

But he couldn't withdraw from her. Nor would any purpose now be served. Questions would have to come later. She had come to him, and her innocence was irretrievably lost. He could only hope to gentle his approach, coax her along as he would have had he known...

It was too late to ease the pain he had inflicted with his first explosive thrust—it was equally too late to leave her.

"No. Dear God, no! Leave me!" she pleaded brokenly. And then her voice rose in anger. "Leave me!"

She suddenly pitted her strength against him like a madwoman.

Sloan was startled, and then furious. No man was expected to come—to be seduced—to this point and then to withdraw with chivalry. He had given her every opportunity to leave his chamber.

He smiled grimly at the glazed fury in her eyes as she struggled against him. "Mistress," he said softly, "the damage is done."

"No," she denied with a shake of her head; and yet the fury left her eyes and pain replaced it. He eased his hold upon her and gently soothed her hair.

"Shhh..." he murmured to her, able to pause only a minute, but gaining control again. "I will be gentle, Brianna. He moved against her slowly, fluidly. She clasped her arms around him as he held her still beneath him, her teeth grazing into the muscle of his shoulder, her nails lightly raking his back. He felt the tenseness that had seized her slowly begin to ebb, and he whispered to her, promising the pain would go away, that the rapture would come again.

And his strokes within her were velvet and smooth. He was right; the pain did begin to ebb. But when it had come, it had been a slap in the face. It had reminded her what she had done. Where she was. What she had lost.

"Brianna..." His voice was a whisper of air. A husky sound that touched inside her again. As the pain faded away, the fire began to lap at her again. And suddenly she realized that his thrusts were deep within her again, steel and fire.

The smoldering fire became a flame. The flame rose surely to a blaze. And she was holding him, fusing with him. Arching with a hunger all her own. He took her with him, and they were flying.

Then everything ebbed except for blinding sensation. She was gasping for breath, half sobbing as she clung to him, arching, emitting a strangled cry—an echo of the shattering ecstasy that convulsed her body, flooding it with the most wonderful, volatile, delightful sensation she had ever known. For long moments the feeling held her in wonder, and then it slowly began to fade. All that was left was the comfort of the man who held her through it, smoothing her hair, his steel power cooling but losing no strength.

She was alone, naked in bed, with a stranger.

Brianna choked back a cry of pain and fury and twisted from him, stunned and so miserable that she was almost numb. She knew that he was watching, that she was risking his fury— and her own expulsion. She felt so coldly wretched that she couldn't care.

Sloan was watching her. He made no move to touch her, but frowned as he observed her slender shoulders, moist with the dampness of their passion, tremble with emotion.

Why had she come to him, he wondered— irritated and confused. He finally reached out to touch her shaking shoulder. "Don't!" she demanded in a low, cold voice.

Stunned, Sloan felt his anger grow along with the deathly silence that seemed to fill the room. Perplexed, and thoroughly annoyed, he swung his legs over the edge of the bed and raked his fingers through his hair.

A shout, clear and thunderous, rose from outside the window again. Heedless of his nudity, Sloan stalked over to the shutters.

"That damned Matthews," he muttered beneath his breath. "It's a pity the devil doesn't rise up in a wall of flame and consume him."

Sloan heard the sharp intake of her breath and turned back to the bed. She was staring at him now—and her face had gone as white as the sheets she had drawn about her.

He frowned curiously, then added, "I believe he's gone."

She relaxed visibly; a small, soft sigh escaped her.

Sloan's sharp gaze narrowed reflectively. He crossed his arms over his chest and strode back to the bed as she watched him warily, her blue eyes wide with alarm at the speculation in his stare and cynical, knowing half-grin.

"You're the witch," he breathed.

"I'm not a witch!" she protested desperately.

"Oh, you are a witch!" he laughed, "but not the type Matthews is hoping to burn. Are you?"

If possible, her face went whiter.

"Brianna," he persisted, the teasing smile leaving his face. "Are you the woman Matthews is out there searching for?"

She dropped her head hopelessly against the pillow, staring sightlessly up at the rafters.

"Why didn't you just tell me?" he asked softly. "You could have saved yourself the apparent misery of my person."

She swallowed and touched her suddenly dry lips with the tip of her tongue. "I...I didn't dare tell you. You might have..."

"Turned you in? Please, madam! What do I look like? A fanatic like Matthews?"

Brianna bit her lip, trying to weigh her desolate reply. "You're a lord," she told him tonelessly. "You might be a loyal supporter of King James."

He chuckled softly. "I'm a Welsh lord, my sweet. One who does not feel he owes loyalty to James. And anyone who thinks the devil dwells within innocent women, be he Welsh, English, Scot, or Frank, is either sadly misguided or a raving lunatic." He paused reflectively for a moment. "Matthews, I believe, is definitely the latter."

"Welsh," she murmured.

"I beg your pardon?"

"Welsh," she repeated tonelessly. "I had no idea who or what you were. I didn't know whether I could possibly trust you. I don't even know your given name," she added bitterly.

The wicked smile came into play. "Sloan," he told her. "Captain Sloan Michael Treveryan, mistress, Fourteenth Duke of Loghaire. It is a Welsh title, not always recognized by the English. We have been "united" for over a century, but the English still have a penchant for acquiring Welsh lands. Nevertheless, my father was a close friend of the late and well-lamented King Charles, and therefore the Treveryans' fortune has done well of late."

Brianna was amazed to hear herself laugh, but she sobered as he did. He grinned wryly in return, and yet she sensed a tension in him, a bitterness, when he spoke of the English crown. It was apparent that he had loved Charles II, and equally apparent that he did not bear that same love for James. It appeared that he despised James—deeply, personally.

"The question," he said softly, "is, who

are you? Certainly not the girl Brice promised to send."

"Brice?" Brianna murmured with confusion.

"Never mind," he said with a shake of his head. "Who are you? Why is Matthews after you?"

Brianna blinked furiously as tears came to her eyes, her voice breaking as she spoke. "The 'witch' Matthews executed this afternoon was my aunt. She didn't even get a trial. I tried to get her a barrister, but no one would even speak with me! I didn't dare go near her because my neighbor warned me Matthews would take me if I interfered."

Brianna lowered her head, feeling her tears fall upon the linen she clasped against her chest. "Pegeen was never a witch; she was wonderful, and admired, and loved."

Sloan reached out a finger to smooth the tears from her cheek. "Probably too well loved," he answered quietly. "Love can breed envy, and the envious make the most vicious enemies."

The gentle quality in his voice brought her eyes back to his. She was suddenly acutely aware of the strength of character in his face. The long, hawklike nose, the high-arched jet brows, the full, demanding mouth, were ruggedly arresting. Confidence and command were indelibly stamped into them. And, a touch of arrogance.

She furiously wiped her tears away. She withdrew as far as possible from him on the bed as she thought of all that had passed between them. He was a man she might have been able to admire and respect. A man from whom she would have liked to receive admiration—and respect.

But his respect was lost to her now—as shattered as the innocence she would never know again.

Perhaps he read the thoughts in her mind. Or perhaps his own thoughts had simply fallen upon the situation. He crossed his arms over his chest and said softly, "Don't worry, Mistress Brianna. I will take care of you."

A tide of shame and humiliation washed through her. Brianna was grateful for life—but she felt as if her pride lay at her feet like cold ashes.

"Why should you?" she asked coolly.

His eyes narrowed. "Because I'm not fond of seeing women burned at the stake," he replied in a low, warning voice.

"I appreciate your concern," she heard herself murmur, "but I prefer to take care of myself. I'll leave alone."

"Leaving the tavern?" he inquired. "For where, dear lady?" he mocked curtly. "Matthews will seek you out through all of Glasgow—for days."

"I won't stay in Glasgow."

"What will you do? Hire a coach and ride away? That's quite unlikely. The roads will be guarded."

"I'll hide in the forest."

"Forever? I don't believe they'll stop burning witches next month! In time, perhaps, men will know their folly. But that time could be decades away, even centuries. It wouldn't matter either way; you would long be dust in the wind."

Brianna swallowed with despair. His words were true. There would be no sanctuary for her in the forest she so loved. But if she could just reach the Powells, they would somehow manage to shield her.

"I'll have to take you with me," he murmured, more to himself than to her.

Her eyes flew open wide. "Take me with you? No! I've family in England; all I have to do is get to them—"

"And you're talking in circles, girl!" Sloan exploded irritably. "Don't you understand yet? You can't get anywhere without me."

"But I just told you, I have family! I—"

"You have to come with me!"

"And where might that be?" she demanded, her voice rising with fury and desperation.

"I'm not sure yet—" he began, cutting himself off sharply as he suddenly stiffened, his eyes sharp and narrow.

"What—"

"Hush!" he exclaimed.

And then she heard what he had. A commotion growing in the common room below, and the tread of footsteps upon the stairs.

A thunderous pounding on their door.

And the roar of a voice. "Open in the name of the king! I know you're in there, Treveryan, and you harbor a witch!"

Brianna's eyes met Sloan's with undisguised terror. He stood, putting his breeches on, his stare willing her not to make a sound. "Get behind the screen!" he whispered.

For an instant she froze, and then she jumped to do his bidding, shielding herself with the screen and peeking around it.

To her horror she saw that he was about to open the door.

Chapter 4

"What the bloody hell do you want, Matthews?"

The Welshman's voice bellowed angrily within the small room. Behind the screen, Brianna tried desperately to still her shivering, and yet she could not. Her life hung in the balance in these seconds.

Despite the danger she had to peek around the corner of the screen. She could see only Sloan Treveryan, who was clad in nothing but his breeches, while Matthews was in full dress; still, it was the sea captain who appeared the most threatening. Brianna was gratified to see that Matthews took a step backward when challenged by Treveryan.

"You bed with a witch, Milord Treveryan," Matthews stated, his voice rather politer now. "I ask only for the harlot. For the good of your immortal soul—"

"My immortal soul is my concern, Matthews," Sloan interrupted coolly, "as are my bedding habits. Get out of my doorway."

"Milord, I do not care to enter by force—"

"Enter by force and it is your life that will be forfeit," Sloan interrupted once more with harsh assurance.

"I am on the king's business—"

"For a king who sits upon a shaky throne. A king who must now placate his nobles, since the Prince of Orange looks ever toward England."

"Take heed, Welshman."

"You take heed, Matthews. I would cheerfully run you through with my sword; I spare your worthless life begrudgingly. Trouble me no further. I am soundly aware that James wants no nobles—Welsh, Scottish, or English—disturbed. I would take great pleasure in reporting to your king that you barged into my bedroom and most rudely disturbed my leisure activities."

Brianna could see Matthews's face, choked by rage, turn into an ugly mask.

"You are a traitor, Treveryan," he told Sloan. And suddenly Brianna wondered if there was more going on here than she knew.

"Nay—never a traitor to the people," Sloan retorted, "but you, Matthews, are a cold-blooded murderer."

"He who deals with the devil becomes the devil," Matthews charged, pointing a finger toward Sloan's chest. "And witch doth harbor witch! I charge you—"

"I charge you to get your ugly carcass out of my doorway this instant!" Sloan demanded with quiet, deathly fury. Again Matthews took a step backward, his gaunt face with its fevered eyes acquiring a considerable pallor. Brianna swallowed back a gasp as she saw why; Lord Treveryan was now brandishing a cutlass. The finely honed muscles in Sloan's shoulders and back rippled—as if with impatience. "Get out of here, Matthews!" Sloan commanded once more. "And disturb me no more!"

"Leave him be!" Brianna heard the voice of one of the officers standing behind Matthews in the hall whisper loudly with nervousness. "James will surely have you set to the stake if he hears that you have created problems with Treveryan."

"Treveryan is trouble!" Matthews declared.

"Aye, that I am," Sloan said with a soft threat.

Matthews paused only a moment longer, visibly shrinking from the razor edge of the cutlass aimed toward him. "I am going, Treveryan. Take your heathen pleasure with the girl. But know this: I will find her. She is a witch and an affront to God and all men who are holy. I will see that she burns. And I will pray that your soul can be saved from the clutches of the devil."

Sloan threw back his head and laughed. "Don't pray for my soul, Matthews. They already call me the devil, and there have been times in the past when the crown was glad to do so. Pray for your own soul. You seek out this girl for your own lust, Matthews, but I promise"—he paused, the laughter leaving his voice—"she will never be touched by dirt such as yourself. Now, get out of here."

"I'm leaving, Treveryan, but I will get the girl."

"You will get the girl?" Sloan ridiculed. "And then what, Matthews? Will you answer to the law you claim to serve? Will there be a trial? Will you torture a confession from her? Torture is illegal, Matthews, in Scotland as in England."

"Never have I tortured an accused person."

"Never? What do you call it, sir, when you seek your 'witches' marks,' stabbing your victims with your picks until they can feel nothing at all? Declaring when they no longer scream that you have found their devil's mark?"

"That is legal procedure."

"Damn your form of legal procedure, Matthews. And damn you—you make a mockery of justice."

"You know not what justice is! This whore of Satan has bewitched you, and you are her slave."

"Take care that in your determination to have the last word between us you do not discover that the words you speak are truly your last."

Treveryan's voice was quiet once more, and yet the threat was there. Matthews took heed. Brianna was amazed when she saw the witchfinder's lips whiten and his jaw snap shut. He turned and started down the hall with his retainers following him.

Relief flooded through her.

Sloan slammed the door closed. Still amazed that the immediate threat to her life had vanished, Brianna walked around the screen in a daze. Instinctively, she wrenched a sheet from the bed in which to wrap herself. Then she turned to find the Welshman gazing at her in brooding silence.

"You were—incredible!" she acknowledged, clinging to the sheet as she might to a lifeline. She added quietly, with all the dignity she could summon, "I do thank you, milord."

He bowed low. "The pleasure was mine, Mistress Brianna." His eyes became deadly as he added, with gravel lacing his tone, " 'Twould truly have been a pleasure to run the man through."

There was nothing that would have given her greater pleasure, either, Brianna thought, feeling the tautness in her body ease as she came to realize more and more that she was truly safe—for the moment at least.

And yet, as she looked at Sloan Treveryan, the trembling seized her again. Treveryan. He, too, was a man to be feared. And she was in his debt. What price was she going to have to pay?

She had already paid with her virtue, she reminded herself bitterly. She did not regret the cost—but the blow to her pride still wounded her deeply. In less than an hour's time she had become more intimate with him than she'd ever envisioned possible. Already she knew the pleasant masculine scent of him; it was like a sea breeze. She knew the depths of those sea-jade eyes, the timbre of that deep male voice with its soft lilt.

She knew the feel of muscle play beneath his taut bronzed flesh. She knew the strength of his arms, the rough feel of manly hands that could be infinitely tender.

She wished she could trade all the intimacy for his respect. She hurt and felt humiliated to the core of her heart.

Nervously she pulled the sheets more tightly about herself, clearing her throat. A hot trembling riddled through her with the memory of their passion. Her flesh burned from his mere glance and her body recalled the touch of him—warm, secure, steely. She couldn't control these feelings, these automatic responses to his eyes, the handsome planes of his face, the caress of his lips, and the masculine scent that was both earth and sea.

Confusion gripped her. Not because she had paid this price to save her life but because he had touched a part of her that had never been touched before.

But she had lost her pride and honor today and she must resign herself to that loss. Perhaps she had also lost the ability to love—along with her dreams of love, and the adoring knight of her imagination. She was not completely naive. Pegeen had taught her something of the physical expressions of love between men and women, but she had really only learned today.

But what she had learned had not been

love. It was lust—primal desire. Treveryan had proven himself to be a courteous lover, but still, his touch had had nothing to do with love. He had taken her and then defended her because he was, it appeared, a determined fighter. He was smiling slightly. Full mouth curved, eyes ever so slightly mocking that seemed to hold within them a smoldering fire. Truly a hint of the devil.

Brianna straightened her spine and squared her shoulders. A sob was welling within her and she choked it back. The look in the Treveryan's eyes and upon his handsome rakish face spoke desire. There was something totally male and predatory about it. He had saved her, and indeed, he thought that she was his.

In his debt, yes, she decided angrily—but his possession? Never! All she wanted to do was find a place of refuge, time to heal her wounds with her family. Dear God—how she wanted to forget him and the terrible fear and humiliation.

He lowered his cutlass and took a step toward her. She backed away, blue fire snapping in her eyes. "No! Don't come near me! Would you add the gravest insult to one you've injured?"

"Injured?" he thundered. Infuriated, he swept his gaze over her. "Damn it girl, but you're—" He broke off, grating his teeth so hard that she heard the sound. He took a swaggering, taunting step, but only to snatch up his shirt and slip quickly into it. He warned

66

her sharply, "If you are fond of living, Mistress Brianna, I suggest you don your clothing quickly. I have no men nearby to respond to an alarm. Matthews will be back in full force. I assure you that he is carefully planning my demise and even more carefully planning yours. Of course, you will not die quickly. I may be the devil, but the anticipated rewards feeding the fires in his eyes are hardly godly, if you can follow my meaning. If bedding with me so abused your sensitivities—imagine bedding with Matthews."

He had no need to say more. A white pallor touched her cheeks and she dropped her sheet to scramble hurriedly for her clothing. Sloan paused for a second as he watched her, his eyes narrowing. She was, indeed, a beautiful woman. So young and slender, and yet rounded with enticing perfection. She was as fresh and lovely as the coming of the dawn, as ripe for the taking. Watching her slip into her shift and dress and stockings caused his flesh to burn with hunger all over again, despite the circumstances.

He pushed these thoughts from his mind and pulled on his second boot. "Come on," he urged her, slipping into his greatcoat and returning the cutlass to the scabbard at his side. "Let's go."

Brianna hastily finished lacing her left shoe and hopped to her feet, then paused.

"Go where?" she demanded curtly.

"To my ship, of course."

"No—I'll not go to your ship. If I can just—"

"You will go to my ship, you idiot! Don't you understand—"

"Don't you ever listen? I have family in England. All I've got to do is get to the forest, and from there—"

"You'll never get anywhere. Matthews will have you by midnight."

"I'm not going with you."

"And I'm not going through life with your death on my conscience."

"Treveryan, we part ways right here," Brianna cried out determinedly.

"The hell we do!"

"You got your money's worth. I've my life!"

He laughed dryly. "I'm not so sure about my money's worth, and your life will be worthless if you don't listen to me. Oh, the hell with it—there's no time left to argue."

Brianna backed quickly away from him, her eyes warily upon him as he came to her with determined strides. "No, Treveryan," she warned him, but her words were useless. He caught her outstretched hand and ducked low, heaving her over his shoulder while she cursed away at him and furiously pounded against his back. "Let me down. I despise you, I've no wish to go with you—"

"Stop pounding on me and shut your mouth, or I'll knock your head into the wall!" he warned her in a deathly rage.

"You will not."

"Don't test me!"

Where would he take her? Oh, God, she would never get to her family! "Let me go!"

she cried again, slamming a fist hard against his shoulder. He grunted and she felt his palm crack full force against her buttocks, causing a stinging pain. Salt tears of fury and humiliation stung her eyes; she blinked them away, stunned and seething with rage.

"You—" she began.

"Shut up!" he finished, swinging about so that she flounced hard against him and totally lost her breath.

With her as his burden he threw open the door and hurried down the stairs. Liam stood at the landing. "I've a horse ready outside, Cap'n. Godspeed, m'lord."

Sloan nodded his thanks. "Take heed, Liam."

He carried Brianna through the tavern and out into the cool night—oblivious to her muffled curses.

A tavern youth held the reins of a handsome bay gelding. Thrown roughly, over the saddle, belly down, Brianna once again found herself breathless and unable to curse him any longer. With an agile leap he mounted behind her, tossing coins to the boy, and smacking his mount soundly upon the rump.

The horse broke into a gallop. She could do nothing but cling to the gelding and feel the coolness of the night sea breeze as it whipped against her face. The clip-clop of the horse's hooves against the cobblestones was like the hard and trembling beat of her heart. Tossed about by the horse's gait, she barely noticed the shops that they passed and the few stragglers still walking the streets. She was aware only of the strong muscles of the horse bunching beneath her as they reached the docks and veered northward along the berths.

Darkness had descended. The glow of the moon and the oil lamps from the various tall ships that lined the harbor lit their way. Before one of these ships their wild ride through the night suddenly ended. Sloan reined in and leapt from his horse in one fluid movement, then reached for Brianna and swept her to the ground without ceremony.

The second his arms released her, she turned to run.

"Get back here!" he exploded. "I swear to God you're the most stubborn creature I've ever met!"

She cried out as his fingers tore into her hair, pulling her back hard against his chest. She saw pure fury in his eyes as they met hers for an instant—and then she was gasping again because he was tossing her over his shoulder and swearing viciously as he hurried along.

"Paddy!" he shouted loudly, his strides long as he carried Brianna along with him to a broad gangplank.

"Who goes there? Cap'n? Is that you?"

"Aye, Paddy, 'tis me. Rouse the crew and make way to sail."

"Now? Damn, Cap'n, but we weren't *due* to sail—"

"Now, Paddy. I've a feeling in my bones we'll be contested if we don't leave port with all haste."

70

Brianna finally saw the man called Paddy as Sloan jumped to the deck and swung around. He was tall and slender, and a cap covered the shock of snow-white hair upon his head. His face was weathered by wind and sea, but his eyes were a young and brilliant snapping blue.

"Did ye get yerself in trouble, then, Lord Treveryan?"

"Aye, and 'trouble' is with me!" Sloan replied irritably. Brianna struggled to sink her teeth into his back. He cried out sharply, slapping her rear soundly once again. "More trouble than she's worth!" Sloan muttered, further irritated by Paddy's laughter.

"She seems to be quite a woman," Paddy observed with amusement.

"I'm glad you approve," Sloan said with a scowl. "Now, Paddy, cease your prattle and rally the crew. I'll be topside as soon as I've secured Brianna within quarters."

"Quarters!" Brianna cried, trying desperately to dislodge herself from Sloan's hold. "Sir!" she called out, trying to gain Paddy's attention. "This man is abducting me! I don't wish to come aboard this ship! Sir, I've a family! I need help. I—"

"Talkative, isn't she?" Sloan groaned.

Paddy laughed and Brianna realized she would have no assistance from Sloan Treveryan's man. She groaned furiously as Sloan spun about again—knocking her cheek hard against his rigid back. Paddy shouted, and the silent ship came alive. Brianna instantly

71

saw ghost shapes hurrying along as Sloan carried her along the deck, nodding briefly to the men who saluted him curiously. She tried to twist, from his grasp to survey the massive ship, to no avail. Near the aft he stopped before a door and shoved it open with his boot. He set her roughly on her feet, catching her for only a second as she staggered, then releasing her quickly. Brianna found her balance, then raged after him almost insanely, thrashing out at his chest with flailing fists. "You imperious, insolent, arrogant—rogue! I can't go on this ship! I've got to get to my family. Please!"

"Leave off!" Sloan grated out like a whiplash, catching her wrists, then pushing her from him. "Girl, I am trying to keep you alive!"

Brianna paused, gasping for breath, staring at him incredulously. She just couldn't make him understand, and there seemed to be no way to fight his strength.

Seeing her breasts heave as she struggled to breathe, he bowed mockingly. "Sleep well, mistress!"

"I will not be your prisoner, Lord Treveryan," she raged, stamping a foot in her impotent fury.

"Really?" He cocked a rakishly angled brow with amusement, took a long step toward her, and reached out a finger to lift her chin. " 'Tis a far better thing to be at the moment than a 'witch'! And"—his voice deepened slightly to that soft but husky tone she was coming to know as dangerous—"for that matter, 'tis preferable, I would think, to be my prisoner than a lady of the streets. Of course, you would be going out with more experience now."

Brianna jerked from his touch. How grating he was against her fully ignited temper—and her raw misery, and all the horror the day had wrought. It was true that she had no wish to burn, but how she hated him now! He was taking her from her only salvation—the dream of reaching her family, the Powells. She would get away from him; and tightening her lips in white rage, she raised a hand to strike him.

She never got the chance. He bowed again, and withdrew. The door closed upon her uplifted arm. She heard his husky laughter. "Perhaps you should spend the time meditating upon your temper, my love."

The door shuddered as she struck wildly against it, and the next spate of curses he received would have brought a blush to Paddy's face. "Treveryan, you have the sense and manners of an ass! Do you hear me? Open this door!"

"I haven't the time, lass. But it is flattering to know how eager you are to see me! I shan't be a minute longer than necessary."

"Damn you, Treveryan! Open this door!"

There was no answer—except that of his footsteps receding along the planking.

She pulled at the doorknob, twisting and jerking, but to no avail. "Treveryan!" she screamed with rising anger. How dare he make her a prisoner! "Treveryan!" Her fists pounded furiously against wood, but the action was an exercise in futility.

Suddenly the great ship pitched, and she fell awkwardly to her knees. She scrambled back to her feet, but since she had never sailed before, she found even the slightest rocking of the ship difficult to handle. She finally discovered that she could stand and sway with the movement of the ship, and Brianna hung on, listening to the shouts in the night and the pounding of feet along the decks.

How many minutes passed as she clung to the door? she wondered. She wasn't sure, but finally the pitching ship seemed to steady, and she was finally able to survey her surroundings.

It was, most obviously, the captain's cabin. A broad bunk was fitted into the far left corner, with cabinets above and below. A large wardrobe was built into the opposite corner, and a huge desk stood prominently to the right. The cabin was compact, and yet it held all the amenities. A rich Oriental carpet covered the floor, and the teakwood that made up the few furnishings was sleek and simply carved. A large bird in flight was the emblem on the footboard of the bunk and the huge desk. Upon careful examination Brianna noted that the bird was a seahawk.

"Treveryan!" she murmured dryly to herself. He had saved her life, that much she had to admit. But though "Lord" might be his title, the man was no gentleman. He seemed to be an adventurer—fond of action. He didn't own her, though, and he had no right to hold her against her will.

The ship rolled again suddenly and she grasped at the desk for balance. It occurred to her then that they had actually set sail, and her eyes moved instinctively to the bunk and the shuttered porthole above it.

She moved quickly to the bunk, mindless of the neatly folded comforter. The window glass was fogged, and she quickly ran her fingers over it.

Already the coastline was growing dim. The buildings of Glasgow were fading into the glow of darkness, becoming like little miniatures in a shop window. The other ships at dock appeared as nothing more than toys.

A haze was over the city. It joined with the misted light and orange color of distant lamps and reminded her of the fire that had burned earlier the same day. It reminded her that Pegeen was dead.

The pain was like the honed edge of a blade, twisting deeply within her, cutting away a piece of her heart, of her very existence.

Would she ever see Scotland again, her homeland? The heathered hill where she had grown, the slopes and valleys that had embraced her and all the dreams of innocence? Tears filled her eyes and she fought hard not to cry. Yes! Yes! She promised herself. She would escape Treveryan, and she would get to the Powells! It was a promise she made to herself, a vow. It was all she could do to hang on to the shreds of her pride—and her life—and to still the misery in her heart.

And so she continued to stare as the distance

and night swallowed the shore. The pain of her heart began to fade like the shoreline, dimmed by the succor of exhaustion. It was impossible that one day had held so much. Impossible that Pegeen was dead, impossible that her fate was in the hands of an arrogant Welsh lord—whom she had come to know far too well. But he didn't own her! And if he thought she would be waiting for him, that she would ever allow him to touch her again—he was crazy!

A gentle shudder touched her, warm and aching. In all her dreams the man to have claimed her, loved her, would have been of a gentler sort—more determined to woo and please. But he might have stood as tall as Sloan, and he might have had his muscled, agile form. His eyes would have had such a touch of steel—or of fire that made her tremble at their gaze, too weak and stunned to do other than relish his touch.

She smiled, bitterly, sadly. The girl she had been was gone. Her world of independence had crumbled. But she would have it again, she promised herself. She would have it again...

All she had to do was escape Sloan Treveryan. When and where, she couldn't know yet, but she would use her time wisely and well.

Brianna stared out the window again. There seemed to be nothing but clouds, obscuring all vision of land, even all vision of the seemingly endless sea.

Scotland was gone, but maybe not forever.

But Pegeen was dead.

Brianna took a deep, shuddering breath. Tears fell from her eyes in a sudden cascade of loss and misery. They fell, and fell, and fell, and she could not control them. She shuddered and gave up. Perhaps they could cleanse her soul and take away the terrible edge of pain.

I will cry tonight, she promised herself, and then I will cry no more.

She realized that she wasn't afraid anymore. Not of the sea, not of fire, not of anything. She was just weary. Numbness and exhaustion at last took their toll upon her. She slipped out of consciousness rather than into sleep.

Chapter 5

Sloan slowed his footsteps as he neared his cabin. He hesitated, then quietly twisted his key in the lock and silently slid the well-oiled door inward. His tread was silent as he moved toward the bunk, and he stood still again, gazing upon her by the muted light of the moon. She was curled upon the lower section of the bunk with no pillow beneath her head. Watching her, he thought of how he had first seen her lying upon the bed at the tavern. Then, he had been fascinated by her. And he still was.

He bent to see her closer, and noticed the tears that had dried upon her cheeks. A strange feeling of tenderness assailed him as he watched her; how horrible it must have been for her to see one she loved murdered so cruelly, and to know that the same fate awaited her.

Sloan straightened. It was over. She was in his care now and there she would have to stay. She was so desperately fighting him that she could not see her own danger. She didn't realize that she was condemned without a trial. He could not bring her to her family because Matthews would find her.

He sighed and strode the few steps to his desk, where he pulled out the captain's chair, sat, and stretched his booted legs comfortably over the teakwood corner. From the bottom left drawer he drew out a pint of Caribbean dark rum and drank a long draft from it, wincing slightly as the potent brew burned down his throat.

Rubbing his temple, he began to think of his own future, and of the business that had brought him to Glasgow. Ostensibly, he had been selling tobacco. In truth, he had been sent by a London delegation to ferret out the political climate in the city.

The same English lords who had sent him to Scotland had recently sent ambassadors to Holland, inviting William of Orange to invade England—and force James to abdicate his throne.

On June twentieth, James II's wife had given birth to a son. While the English people had tolerated their Catholic monarch as long as they assumed his heir apparent to be his oldest daughter, Mary, a staunch Protestant and the wife of William of Orange, they were not likely to tolerate the possibility of their king's leaving the throne to a Catholic son. There was trouble ahead; of that Sloan was keenly aware. He knew the king. He knew that James would so implement his power that he would enrage his barons, as well as the English people. Sloan also knew William of Orange and understood that he was very ambitious and determined.

Sloan winced slightly. There had been a time when he had liked James. A time when James had been a bold and brave man, a careful thinker, and a fine admiral. But that time was past. James had grown older, and fanatical—unbending, and sometimes cruel. He had executed his own nephew. Over the crown.

James, the Duke of Monmouth—"Jemmy" to his friends—had been the illegitimate son of Charles II. He'd possessed a full quota of Stuart charm; he'd been reckless, daring, and adventurous.

To Sloan he had been much more. When he was ten years old, his father had died—and he'd been sent to live in Jemmy's household. When Sloan was young, Jemmy had been his hero. As he grew older and wiser, Sloan recognized his good points as well as his lack of prudence over the matter of the crown. But knowing his recklessness had done nothing to change the emotions that had grown over the years, and when Sloan heard that Jemmy had lost his head after his fruitless rebellion to gain the throne, he felt the deepest loss and fury. Jemmy had pleaded for his life but James had refused him—and executed him.

Sloan cast his head back and drank another long, long draft of the rum. The things he'd learned in the tavern that day had been interesting. William of Orange had assumed the Scots would be solidly against him. Some of them would be, but not all, Sloan knew now. If William and Mary secured their position in England, it was quite likely that the northern country would accept them too.

He laid his head back, brooding about politics, and then about the ties that bound him to Wales with webs spun of pity and honor.

Then he started suddenly, hearing a rustle from the bed. He had forgotten the Scottish lass in the gloom of his thoughts.

He smiled and pulled his boots from his feet, setting them beneath his desk before stripping methodically and casting his clothing over the chair. Then he stood over the girl again, debating whether to move her to a more comfortable position or let her be.

It was not surprising that she had been labeled "witch"—she was incredibly beautiful. The loveliest ladies were usually marred in some way; minus several teeth, perhaps, or scarred in face or form by pockmarks or the like. This girl was nothing less than perfect. It was easy to believe that a less fortunate person might enviously decide that only a pact with the devil could create such flawless beauty. But that didn't matter now. He would keep her safe. He found himself shuddering slightly, warmed by the thought of her. He wanted to sleep with her again—and again. He wanted her to touch him and practice her brand of witchcraft upon him. He could lose himself so easily within the midnight web of her hair, the soft mystique of her cream-and-rose flesh.

His thinking should have surprised him— perhaps even worried him. He had never before been so enamored of a woman as to worry about their future together. But he thought of permanency when he looked at this girl. And as he was of high-ranking nobility, Sloan possessed the inevitable ego of his rank. He was the Fourteenth Duke of Loghaire and a Scottish country lass should be quite content as his coveted mistress.

Would this fascination last forever? Or would he find, even now, his passions rising for another voluptuous woman?

Men were not sworn to be loyal to their mistresses.

She is a witch, he thought again with a smile as he looked upon her. *So exquisite...*

She inhaled and exhaled with a slight shuddering sob. Sloan bent nearer, but saw that she still slept. He knelt beside her and unlaced her shoes, then carefully slid her stockings from her shapely legs, feeling the heat rise in him as he performed the simple service. Still she did not awaken, and he realized how sorely exhausted she must be. The compassion she brought forth from him worked well to dampen the fires the touch of her created, but he was determined still to undress her for her comfort. Therefore he worked carefully upon her gown hooks without moving her, then lifted her into his arms to attempt to lift the fabric over her head. The muddied gown he cast haphazardly to the floor, making a mental note to purchase her some clothing. They would have to dock somewhere along the English coast—probably at Liverpool—before sailing to Holland. He could shop for her then.

She was slumped against him still, and he tenderly adjusted her weight to wrest her shift from her. It was then that she awoke, her huge blue eyes reflections of dazed alarm in the dimness, her fists instantly flailing against him.

"I am not a witch! Leave me! Leave me! Before God most holy, I am not a witch!"

She pounded against Sloan's bare chest, causing little harm, but one of her blows caught him well in the chin, causing his mouth to bleed where his tooth caught against his inner lip. Grimacing with a bit of surprise at the extent of her power, he secured her wrists and held them tight over her head, breaking, still gently, into her wild speech. "Shhh! You are not a witch, and no man will harm you! Shhh... It is all right, everything is all right."

The wide, terrified alarm slowly faded from her eyes, but still she surveyed him. "You..." she whispered, and it was not with pleasure that she did so.

"Aye, me," he agreed, with a wry bite to his words.

"Treveryan, let me be!" she ordered with quiet fury.

Sloan became keenly aware that she was naked now, as was he. Each of her tense gasps for breath pressed the hard peaks of her breasts more temptingly to his chest; her slightest movement was a brand of her body against his own. To his vast annoyance he found his own resolve faltering; against his will intense desire took hold of his body.

"I've every intention of letting you be," he informed her irritably, further annoyed by the flickering of her lustrous lashes, which signified all too clearly her knowledge of his arousal, her fear that he could not wield control over his own body as he lay with his weight sprawled over hers. "I am but trying to allow you to sleep in comfort," he informed her, scowling darkly.

"If you wish to grant me comfort," she snapped, "leave."

Sloan took a perverse pleasure in the slight tremor that touched her voice. Damn her! They might have been strangers.

"Sorry—this is my cabin."

"Oh," she said. "Well, then, I shall be glad to leave."

To Brianna's vast surprise she was instantly lifted from beneath him and set indecorously upon her feet beside the bunk. Sloan Treveryan surveyed her with idle interest as he stretched his length over his bed, lacing his fingers behind his head comfortably. "My crew will love you," he told her dryly.

Brianna stared at him with uncertainty for a moment, but then her anger exploded like cannon shot within her head. She was instinctively tempted to cover what part of her nakedness she could with floundering hands as he watched her so casually, but she resisted the foolish temptation to reach furiously for her discarded shift, crumpled at the foot of the bed.

Dignity, she reminded herself firmly. He had taken her unawares but now she was ready to fight for her dignity.

"Obviously, Lord Treveryan," she said crisply, "I had no intent of rushing onto the deck unclothed."

Her voice, so cool, taunted and reproached him. He was aware that he was losing something. Her unwavering denunciation of him rankled deeply. For the first time he was completely at a loss as to how to deal with a woman. Confusion ignited his temper, and he was left to fight for control.

Treveryan moved to keep her gown on the floor by placing a foot hard upon it. He smiled with deeper mocking amusement as she inadvertently met his eyes before tugging. "I've a crew of fifty, mistress. Good men, stout-hearted seamen. But long days at sea make a man crave for warmth and companionship. They are controlled by the appetites of the body, rather than the finer qualities of the mind. A bewitching form appearing suddenly to them at sea...well, I believe you know the likely consequences."

Brianna tugged more viciously at the fabric

of her shift in order to fight the desolation that filled her.

"I will cause no trouble," she told him, but could not retrieve her gown. "Sir! What can I suffer that I have not already?" she demanded with a cry of indignity.

Treveryan clamped his hand around her wrist with a painful force that brought her eyes instantly clashing with his flashing green stare.

"Can you suffer worse, mistress? Oh, aye. I do think so. Each man will demand a turn, his share of spoils at sea. Little gallantry will be offered. But then, of course, the choice is yours. I cannot set you ashore, for we are not at dock. But by all means, if my protection is so loathsome to you, feel free to venture out. My lads will not be at fault!"

"Let me go!" she cried. Sloan smiled slowly— far more bitterly than he would have had her know. What had he done to her? Nothing, except save her fool life. Damn! How he would have liked to despise her in turn. But it seemed that she might very well be a witch; the more she reviled him, the more determined he became to win her.

"Nay—I cannot let you go," he told her, and was startled when she bit hard upon the hand that held her.

Treveryan grunted out his pain, relaxing his hold only to secure her chin tightly. She stared at him defiantly, but a small gasp of pain escaped her and he eased his touch as soon as he was assured she would not use her teeth against him again.

She inhaled a long breath and began to speak. "Never think that I am not wholly grateful to you. I would give you any riches if I but had them. But can't you see? If you've truly saved my life, then is it not my own again?"

How could she make him understand? Brianna wondered a little desperately. He was just staring at her—holding her, and staring at her. There was compassion within him, wasn't there? She took another breath, coolly determined to start over again.

"Treveryan, I have been robbed of very much—"

"Robbed!" His exclamation was loud enough to rend asunder the timbers of his ship. "Robbed of your virtue, I suppose." His repetition of the word was softer and more deadly. She found herself swept into his arms and cast down upon the bunk again. His grip was then upon her shoulders as he leveled himself over her, the green of his eyes seeming to shine like the honed blade of a rapier. "I am exactly where I wish to be," he said in a velvet-soft voice, mimicking both the tone and quality of her own, the whisper seeming to caress her cheeks with warmth. And then his fingers were winding into her hair, just as hers had wound into his all those hours earlier. The touch was soft, caressing, and yet very firm, holding her as if in a spell. She could not have fought his grip anyway, nor the breadth of shoulder leaning above her, nor the long, sinewed leg cast negligently over hers. So she merely stared at him, wondering just what manner of man had been cast by fate as her protector. She could feel the tension within him, and yet it was with control that his gentle hands mocked her by their teasing touch. A control that so clearly reminded her of all that she had done earlier that day; her seduction of him. Yes, she had played out a role with surprising expertise.

"How I want you..."

His inflection on each word was exactly as she had spoken it earlier, a mockery that was almost unbearable—and very angry.

"I had reasons!" Brianna protested. "Don't mock me—I had no choice and you know it!"

His eyes, with their wicked gleam of anger, were still upon her. The caress of his fingers, soothing hair and temple now, were still a touch that both lulled and enticed. The intimacy he had so assuredly and casually demanded was still between them. She felt him ever more keenly—his leg, hard-muscled, covered handsomely with coarse black hair, was a brand that burned against her. Her breasts seemed to swell, the peaks harden, against the warmth of his chest.

"I..." she began, her voice catching, "I beg you not to touch my hair."

One brow hiked slightly, and the devil gleam in his eyes increased mockingly. He obediently removed his fingers from her hair and temple, only to rest them slightly below her breast. To Brianna's horror she exhaled a whimper at the touch that made it seem as if her body screamed inside.

"Don't!"

"Ahh...that is right. My touch is extremely distasteful. I learned that this afternoon." The mockery was like knives against her heart. She closed her eyes and tried to close her mind.

He moved his hand slowly, palm and fingers a light massage, cupping the fullness of her breast. His eyes left hers to move over that firm mound, and he watched the result of his thumb's grazing over the nipple. Brianna closed her eyes and swallowed, aware that her body was traitorously giving her away. Sloan Treveryan saw the rose hue darken hauntingly, the peak tautened delightfully to his whim.

She opened her eyes to find his eyes daring her to deny her response. He mocked her; she had angered him, and he was angry still.

"Lord Treveryan, I do not wish to be used by you!" she said.

"I see how fully you are repelled," he replied, amused.

"You are ignoring my words," she reminded him.

"Because they make no sense. When I touch you—"

"I cannot fight you physically!" Brianna snapped, and then she closed her eyes and lay still. "You touch nothing," she said tonelessly.

Inadvertently she moistened her lips, and that slight gesture was an invitation he could not refuse. He moved his lips to hers, barely touching. "What is done, is done, little witch.

There was a time when you might merely have spoken—but it seems that without judgment you've called me 'an arrogant nobleman' and so sealed your own fate. I cannot return what you have lost, but I can care for what I have taken..."

His whisper died on her mouth as his lips at long last touched fully, cajoling her acceptance with the swiftness of his devouring assault. His tongue delved deeply, seeking with ardor the sweet crevices of her mouth. She tried to twist from him but he held her still. She pounded against him but he caught her arms. Her protests became soft moans, her lips began to move against his. She arched slightly, with a natural instinct, filling his palm with the soft but firm weight of her breast. She felt the powerful muscles of his shoulders. Even as she desperately tried to hold on to the will to fight him, she knew he was unlike anything she had ever known. He held a physical fascination for her that wove a magic spell. There was something about his masculinity, something that beckoned a response as if she had been destined for this stranger's arms. Where she was small and slender, he was strong and broad. Their bodies interwove as if crafted by an artist.

No! she thought with horror. She was giving in to him!

But just then, he broke from her—and smiled mockingly, and grimly. "Forgive me, Mistress Brianna," he murmured, unwinding her arms from his back and folding them across her chest. He moved away from her so that his body no longer brushed against hers but was still close enough to touch her. "I must have lost my mind. But as I see how very abhorrent my touch is to you, I will fight the devil that lurks within me when I fall prey to your blue eyes. Do forgive me. I will strive to remember your words in the future."

Brianna was heartily glad for the dimness of night as she felt the blood rush to her face. But it mattered little, for even before Sloan Treveryan had finished speaking, he was turning from her, his manner definitely one of nonchalant dismissal.

"What future?" she demanded heatedly. "You've no right to hold me! I've a place to go—"

He twisted back to her, angry and impatient. "You can't go anywhere, Brianna! Not safely. If I set you ashore, I promise you that Matthews would find you. You can keep your damned chastity, but even if I saw fit to dock tonight, I could not let you off this ship!"

Her eyes fell from his at last. Dear God, he did intend to hold her! He just didn't understand that she was capable of hiding, of moving quickly—of taking care of herself!

When would she ever manage to escape him? She shivered suddenly. How much of this could she endure? She was nothing but a toy to him—a toy with whom he had just played.

Brianna angrily forced herself to lie rigid. He was too close beside her; she must assure herself that she did not touch him in the night. She curled closer to the teakwood planking that edged the bunk, silently hurling every imaginable oath upon his head. She wished desperately that she might pull the pillow from beneath his head and rip out handfuls of his jet hair. But it would be futile to attempt retaliation because she would only receive another lesson from his hands.

I will escape you, Lord Treveryan! she promised herself in an impassioned silence. They would have to come into port, and when they did, she would find her chance. She had his gold coins in the pocket of her shift. They were hers for services rendered in full. Before God! She would get away from this man who had claimed her as casually as he would a new coat, to don and cast aside at his whim and leisure.

Sleep—dear God, she needed sleep. Release from pain, from the tempest of her soul. And though sleep eluded her for a time, it eventually brought her release again.

She saw his eyes as she slept. Deep green, devil-green. Narrowing angrily, glittering with sensual amusement. The planes of his face, the full, mobile line of his mouth and the handsome slash of white teeth against the tan of the seafarer.

The arch of his jet brow.

He would not leave her dreams.

Chapter 6

Brianna awoke with a start of panic to a knock on the door. Then she realized that Sloan Treveryan would never knock upon his own door. She was well swathed in her blanket but still loath to see anyone clad so—within the captain's cabin. She shrugged and lifted her chin—there was no help for any of it at the moment. "Yes?" she queried softly.

"It's just me—Paddy. Captain asked that I bring ye something clean to wear."

"Uh—come in—and thank you," Brianna responded.

Brianna tried to hide her astonishment at the wardrobe carried in for her. Paddy laid out a pile of fine muslins and silks, some trimmed with delicate laces, some with precious furs. Paddy, after spreading the rich clothing out, turned back to her, and noticed the surprise upon her features.

"Uh...an old friend of the captain's used to keep quarters upon the ship, my lady. I doubt she'll be needing these again."

Color suffused Brianna's face along with the rage that filled her. Treveryan! He was giving her the cast-off goods of another woman. Another woman who had apparently had the run of the ship—despite Sloan's men! He had done nothing but lie to her and give her ridiculous excuses about her situation!

Brianna said nothing and fought to hide her emotions from Paddy. Sloan was the one who had wronged her. Her dark lashes swept her cheeks and then she faced Paddy with a slight smile. "Thank you, Paddy."

Paddy had spent his life serving the Treveryans and sailing the seas. He was an old sea salt—a far cry from a courtly gallant. But when she spoke, he felt a gentling toward her, despite the fact that she seemed like nothing but trouble. " 'Twas nothing, girl," he promised.

There was a slight sound at the door, and both Brianna and Paddy looked that way, startled.

Sloan stood within the doorway. Brianna stiffened, expecting some form of mockery at the interchange.

But his expression was unfathomable. "I see that Paddy has provided you with clean clothing to wear. I'll give you leave to dress and return with a meal."

He left the door open behind him. Paddy shuffled his feet awkwardly and then backed toward it, pausing only to grab up the wet pile of her soaked things. "Good day...Brianna."

"Good day," she murmured.

He left her with a bit of a grimace and Brianna followed to close the door behind him. When she was alone she again glanced at the pile of luxurious clothing strewn across the chair. The gowns were stunning—far grander than any she had ever owned.

But fury grew within her again at the sight of them and she stomped across the room and swept them onto the floor with a vengeance.

They had belonged to another woman. A mistress. A woman he had discarded and passed on as easily as he did the gowns.

What would be her fate when he finished with her? Would she be cast aside as easily? Lord, how she wanted to thrash him at that moment! Treveryan! The arrogance of the man! He would never, never cast her aside, because she would never be his to cast. But something within her hurt again; an ache that attacked her stomach and caused her to grit her teeth tightly together.

She sighed—she had to school herself away from both anger and pain. Neither would serve her and the gowns would, since she preferred to be fully clad when she was near him!

She paused for a minute. Had last night meant that he intended to respect her wishes? A shiver first cold, and then warm, touched upon her spine. Or was he baiting her, taunting her, playing with her, as a cat did with a mouse?

How she wanted her freedom! Freedom, and safety, she reminded herself. But anywhere would be far from Glasgow—and Matthews. All she had to do was fight to maintain a remote distance from Sloan—until they docked somewhere. Then she could disappear. Dear God! she prayed silently. It wasn't that she wasn't grateful to be alive—she was, so very, very grateful. But it was becoming increasingly difficult to be grateful to a man like Treveryan. Without fail he had the ability to make her completely lose all control of her temper.

She chose the most modest of the gowns, a deep-blue muslin with a petticoat in a lighter shade of velvet, and dressed quickly. It was a bit loose, and a bit short (as she was tall for a woman), but the fit was far better than she might have expected. She determined to have the rest of the gowns picked up before Sloan returned, but it was when she started this task that she suddenly spun around with horror.

Brianna closed her eyes, remembering how Paddy had picked up the bundle of her own soaked clothing when he left the cabin.

Her clothing, the gold coins—her means for escape were gone!

Brianna raced stupidly to the spot where her clothing had lain. How had she let it happen? "No!" she whispered. And then she screamed the word, stamping her foot down furiously. Panic and anger filled her with a driving bitterness. She had earned that money; earned it with the loss of all innocence and the one beauty that had been hers to give. She had to get the money back, because it was the one means she had to escape Sloan Treveryan.

"Damn!" Brianna emitted in a furious wail, and her temper took complete control of her for a moment of ridiculous vengeance. She swirled about and lifted the new gowns and kicked and tossed them furiously about.

So involved in the venting of rage and misery did she become that she did not hear the door when it opened. It was by pure chance that she raised her eyes to the doorway and saw Sloan standing there, holding a tray, and watching her with curious amusement.

"What is your problem now?"

Brianna stopped cold, staring at him warily while she warned herself to take as much care with the situation as she could.

"My—my own things are gone. I want them back," she told him.

He shrugged. "When they are dried and clean, they will be returned to you." He took a further step into the room, closing the door. "What did you want with them? They are little but rags now."

I've a great sentimental attachment to my own things," she told him coolly.

"Have you, now?"

As he walked past her, Brianna inhaled a delicious aroma that reminded her she was starving.

Sloan paused for a moment, his eyes sweeping the scene before him—the disarray upon his floor, and the rebellious defiance in the stunning blue eyes that rose to his. He successfully hid a smile as he continued on to his desk and set the tray down.

"There's room in the wardrobe for those things," he told her casually. "But perhaps you would care to eat first."

Brianna, wondering how to make sure she got the coins back with her clothing, was startled from her reverie by this very polite side to the devil she had come to know.

"Ah, yes," she murmured, "thank you." She quickly lowered her eyes from his. It appeared he intended to remain polite. She would challenge him, but be polite and distant herself. She would prefer to demand that he give her what was rightfully hers, but she was afraid that any insistence would only make him laugh and keep the coins, knowing she intended to use them for escape.

"Sit," he told her pleasantly enough, "and I'll prepare you a plate."

Brianna sat nervously upon the edge of the bed. Sloan didn't glance her way as he heaped a plate full with biscuits and steaming beef swimming in gravy. He handed her the plate with decorum and no mockery—his gaze telling her nothing when their eyes did meet. Sloan set a cup of tea before her within easy reach before preparing himself a plate. He then sat down upon the captain's chair.

He ate without talking and for several moments Brianna followed suit. But then she decided that he would also be suspicious of her if she did not challenge him. To plan an escape, she had to know where they were heading, and what difficulties she might encounter.

"Where are we going?" she demanded, staring at him pointedly.

His eyes swept from his food to sear into hers. "Holland," he replied briefly.

Brianna was so surprised she almost lost the plate of food that was balanced precariously upon her knees.

"Holland!" she gasped with dismayed amazement. How would she ever escape him in a land so very foreign to her? And though she didn't know much about politics, she did know that there was severe tension between James II and his son-in-law and nephew, William of Orange; a friction that hinted of a coming war. "But—but," she stuttered, "then you are a traitor, Lord Treveryan!"

Perhaps if she hadn't been taken so much off guard, she wouldn't have blurted out the accusation so foolishly. As it was, there was no recourse when she saw his lips compress angrily within the strong contours of his jaw and his eyes sizzle as they narrowed.

"I am no traitor, mistress. I am a Protestant, and a friend to the Parliament James has seen fit to dissolve. I am also a friend to Princess Mary of Orange, and therefore to her husband, William."

Brianna stared blankly at her plate, stiffening beneath his words. "William of Orange—and Mary," she murmured, struggling to maintain her composure while her mind whirled. Holland! How would she ever manage to get back to her family? She wouldn't even be able to hire passage aboard a ship if she didn't get the money back.

Sloan leaned back in his chair and crossed his arms over his chest. His eyes had narrowed upon her, and it seemed that a hint of amusement played about his mouth.

"Of course," he told her, "we won't be heading straight for the Dutch court. We'll have to dock for supplies and repairs."

"Oh?" Brianna nonchalantly picked at a

bit of food. "And where will that be?" Her heart thundered with new hope.

"Liverpool."

Liverpool! Wonderful, Brianna thought. It was a busy, bustling port where a woman could quickly disappear, and close enough to the southwest counties so that she could reach the Powells.

"But then again..." Sloan's voice drifted away. Brianna stared at him sharply once again.

"Then again what?" she snapped impatiently.

He shrugged. "We might dock farther south. Who can say?" he replied with a pleasant shrug.

"Umm. Who can say," she returned, trying not to allow her voice to ring with sarcasm or anger. A silence followed her words, one that made her uneasy. She didn't want him knowing anything that went on in her mind. More for something to say than to really strike a blow at him, she glared at him accusingly again.

"You are tampering a great deal with the law. James is the proper heir to the English throne."

He laughed briefly, a dry sound that cut the air with no humor. "So thought Charles, and yet I doubt that he believed his brother would ever murder his son."

"Jemmy Scott?" Brianna frowned, curious despite herself at the tone of Sloan's voice. "The Duke of Monmouth?"

"Aye, the same," Sloan said, "Beheaded at James's command," he added harshly. For a second he fell silent; then he was staring at

99

her again. "You owe little loyalty to James, my little Scottish witch. It is beneath his rule that you almost burned."

"Do you mean to tell me," Brianna demanded coolly, "that all persecution shall cease beneath William and Mary?"

Sloan wiped his mouth with a linen napkin and, tossing it upon his unfinished plate, stood and stalked the room. Brianna noted that he wore the same clothing of the morning, the fine silk shirt, the fawn breeches that fitted so finely to his form, hugging sinewed thighs and muscled calves.

"I tell you," he said heatedly, "that Charles, libertine as he was often labeled, was still a just and tolerant king. He knew his people and he knew when to give. James has proven himself to be an ineffectual king with a talent for turning even his friends into enemies. Will persecution cease with William and Mary? No, not completely, for people still believe in the power of witchcraft. And," he reminded her pointedly, "there are people who do practice witchcraft. I'm not so sure yet that you're not a witch! But both the Prince and Princess of Orange believe passionately in tolerance, and in Parliament. And I might add that they are the choice of the people."

She set her plate upon his desk. "You'll forgive me, Lord Treveryan, if I know little of the English court or its royalty. Or of the intrigue of politics. I have spent my life in the 'wilds' of Scotland. A country 'witch,' if you will, my lord."

None of it made any difference, Brianna knew. Whatever British port he chose for his repairs, she would find her escape there. But she spoke with biting sarcasm—and curiosity—continuing caustically, "And what, pray tell, do you intend to do with me in Holland?"

He appeared somewhat startled by the question, as if she should know the answer. And then his anger faded with amusement. "I intend to leave you with Mary," he replied simply, smiling at her.

Brianna successfully hid her surprise at his casual reply. Fine! Let him believe that he could safely leave her in the charge of the princess he so admired. She would never have to face Mary—as Lord Treveryan's courtesan or anything else. She would be a memory to Sloan Treveryan before he ever reached the Dutch shore.

Sloan came to her and lifted her chin. "Are you dismayed?" he asked her, his voice suspiciously solicitous. "Don't be. Mary is a kind woman, you will be safe in her keeping."

She pulled her chin from his grasp and met his eyes with a bitter smile. "How do you plan to introduce me to our chaste princess, Treveryan?"

He sighed with impatience. "Have you no comprehension whatever, girl? It makes no difference! I could not, in all conscience, set you ashore! Until Matthews is stopped, you will not be safe anywhere in England or Scotland—or even Wales."

"That's not true! If I went to my family—"

101

"They could do nothing if Matthews found you!" Sloan interrupted savagely. Then he emitted a groan and turned from her. "Mary grew up in her uncle's court. James kept as many mistresses as Charles. She will hardly be shocked."

The argument made no difference. Brianna was certain that he was wrong, and that she could hide for as long as was necessary with the Powells. But she could not help arguing with him and mocking him for his negligent assumptions. "No," she told Sloan with saccharine sweetness, "Mary will merely assume that I am your current entertainment."

"Entertainment?" Sloan queried, spinning to face her once again, his hands tensing over his hips as his anger rose. "Lass, you have been anything but entertaining. You have been a complete nuisance to me. If it will stop your shrewish tongue, I will assure you that I will tell Mary of your predicament—and that I seek to give you asylum only."

She lowered her head quickly, trying to remember that she must keep her thoughts hidden from him, and that to do so, she should learn to control her temper—and her tongue. She spoke quietly to him.

"It will stop my shrewish tongue if you will assure me that you truly wish to give me asylum and ask nothing in return." With the words out she faced him again.

For long seconds they glared at one another. Brianna could almost feel the heat of his anger; it seemed to crackle about him. She quailed within, yet would not allow her eyes to fall from his, nor relinquish her stand. She could not bear the tension that riddled the air, so she spoke, trying desperately to keep entirely calm. There were things she wanted from him—things she wanted back!

"I know you must think me ungrateful. I am not. I do thank you, again, for saving my life. But if you did so, it was, I believe, your own choice. I don't owe you anything, and yet you continue to take from me. I—"

"I continue to take from you?" He interrupted softly—his voice a rasp of silk. "To what are we referring? Your clothing? I did assure you it would be returned, didn't I?"

"Yes, you did," she agreed quietly. "But when will I have it?"

He walked closer to her, as he brought a hand to her cheek. She shuddered slightly at that touch; no matter how infuriated she became, she could not deny the startling heat of his caress and its unnerving effect upon her.

"Oh...soon, I would think," he assured her.

Rather than meet his eyes she allowed her lashes to fall. "Thank you," she murmured demurely.

"Brianna?"

"Yes?" She raised her eyes to his.

He smiled, and for a brief moment she was allowed to feel a little thrill in her art of craft and seduction. But then that victory was dashed as he said simply, "You won't get the money back."

Her smile faded; open hostility filled her eyes and she stepped back from him furiously.

"Why not? It's mine—I earned it!" she snapped, bitterly mocking herself.

Sloan laughed, walking toward the cabin door, then turning back to her and grinning as he leaned idly against the paneling. "I'm not so sure that you did earn it. A man hires a...lady of the streets for her to pleasure him. I don't remember your going terribly out of your way to be the obliging one."

The taunt touched her soul like blazing iron. Without thought or reason she swept across the small cabin, determined to fell him with her furious blows.

She did, at least, force his grin to fade quickly. But that was all. Her wrists were quickly secured behind her back and she found herself pressed hard against his chest, her breasts heaving with exertion.

"When will you learn!" he exploded harshly. "I care for you, little fool, and I will not see you dead by your own folly!"

"My life is my own!" Brianna cried out in protest. "I am not related to fools! I can find shelter. I can remain hidden."

He shook his head, sadly, his anger fading.

"I am not a man known for his patience," he told her quietly. "Don't keep testing it."

She lowered her head. "Let me go," she told him dully.

He released her, stepping back. None of the tension left his strong and resolute features, but when he spoke, it was with a measure of patience once more.

"Brianna, what has happened cannot be

erased. I cannot give back what I have taken. I haven't forced anything from you, nor will I. You must stay in this cabin, for you are not safe abovedecks without me—and I am far too busy to worry about your effect upon the men. You must sleep in that bed, for there is nowhere else where you may safely sleep. Whether it is a palatable situation to both of us or neither of us, you have become my responsibility—and must remain so, for the time being."

"You are a liar, Treveryan!" she charged hotly. "What of the woman whose clothing I wear? She had her own quarters—and, I would assume, the run of the ship!"

There was a furious tick of a pulse against his throat, yet he remained in a deathly calm control. "I had a smaller crew when she was aboard. Sleeping arrangements have changed."

"I don't believe you."

"And I don't give a damn what you do and do not believe! This is my ship, I am the captain, and so help me God, you will follow my orders. Do you understand?"

"Oh, I think I understand too well," she replied bitterly.

"Just so that you do," he warned in a chilling whisper.

She lifted her chin and spoke softly. "How long will we be at sea, Lord Treveryan?"

He shrugged. "Three to four weeks, depending upon the weather."

"And you suggest that I not leave this cabin all that time?"

He sighed. "I'll take you out for a stroll on deck each afternoon. But you will have to find a way to entertain yourself for the greater part of the day. The panel behind the bed slips open, and you'll find a number of books. Do you read?" At Brianna's nod he continued. "Should you happen to do anything so useful as sewing, and not find the task too distasteful, I've shirts within the wardrobe which could use the tender touch of a needle."

She didn't reply. Sloan noted that she stood very straight, but that the sweep of her lashes hid the blue flames of her eyes.

"Good afternoon," he told her cordially, sweeping her a very proper bow—and allowing a wicked grin to filter across his lips in the midst of it.

As he closed the door behind him, Brianna was very much tempted to throw something after him.

The days they sailed south upon the Irish Sea were long ones.

Sloan did not come to his cabin until late at night, and when he did arrive, Brianna feigned sleep. She had found a nightgown among the clothing given her by Paddy, and she wore it each evening, grateful that it was modest.

He unfailingly stripped without a shade of self-consciousness before stretching beside her. But he did not touch her. Not once. And it seemed that she heard his even breathing almost instantly when his head touched his pillow.

He was always gone when she awoke in the morning, but he returned to the cabin in the midmorning to breakfast with her. He spoke to her very courteously at those times, as if the nights did not exist, and as if they had never been lovers.

Often, in the late afternoon, he would escort her about the ship. Within days she had learned a great deal about the *Sea Hawk*. He brought her to the cargo holds and showed her where the guns were placed. She learned the names of the numerous sails, and she met the fifty-man crew one by one. They ranged in age from youths to graybeards, and just as widely in social standing. Younger sons from noble families sought their fortunes at sea, just as did the strapping sons of commoners.

Some were rough and quarrelsome, some quiet and genteel; but they all seemed to share one common trait—an intense loyalty to Lord Sloan Treveryan. She knew that their respect for their captain kept them all cordial to her. Yet she often winced when they passed a group of the sailors, for she felt the gazes they raked over her form. They knew that she slept in the captain's cabin—assumed her to be "his"—and perhaps envied him.

Brianna had seen Sloan roar out orders with the severity of a fire-breathing dragon; she had also learned that service and valor were rewarded, that double portions of rum were doled out each time the crew brought the

Sea Hawk through a storm or treacherous shoal.

Although she came to know the ship and the men, it was all for show. The promise of escape was the hope that she clung to. Every day she plotted her escape; how to slip the lock should it be turned, which passages to take, where to dive from the ship to the sea, should that prove necessary.

She awoke slowly one morning to realize that she was becoming accustomed to the sounds of the sea—the wind as it whistled through the rigging, the waves as they lapped and crashed against hull and bow. And as she closed her eyes once more to savor the gentle sounds of morning and close out the brilliance of the sunlight streaming into the cabin, she realized unhappily that she was also becoming accustomed to Sloan Treveryan.

Although he was distant, as if his mind were far from her, their life aboard ship had assumed a certain domesticity. Boredom had taken its toll upon her, and bit by bit she had come to keep the cabin impeccably neat; she even mended his shirts. More often than not they shared their meals. And every night she waited for him. Waited to feel his heat as he slid his long form beside hers. He always smelled so cleanly of salt air and the sea, he exuded a masculine strength, and despite herself, she longed to curl against him, to be held, to touch him. It was agony to know that she must despise him and escape him— when she could not, inside herself, deny his allure. When she could not pretend that his arms were not those of a strong and fascinating man, that he was not arresting, that his eyes did not touch her all the way to her soul. And so she lay awake wretchedly, sometimes barely breathing, sometimes praying that he would shift and slip his arm around her, stroke her hair, edge closer to her—and then praying fervently that he would not.

She could not deny to herself that she was falling beneath his spell. Perhaps, falling a little bit in love. Sometimes, she allowed herself to dream. To envision that he might marry her, love her, and cherish her.

It was a sweet dream, a bitter dream. Yet it went on. She wondered if he could love her; and in that wondering, she could not help but think that he was a man to do what he chose to do, rather than follow convention.

If he loved her, he would marry her.

It was a dangerous fantasy. Very dangerous. Sloan Treveryan was a lord, and a man as fiercely independent as she longed to be. She urged herself strenuously away from dreams and fantasies, and set herself firmly to remember that she must maintain her distance from him—and escape him as soon as possible.

Before she lost more of herself to him than she already had. Without malice he had taken her innocence. She grew ever more terrified that if she did not cling to outrage and fury, he would also take her heart.

Chapter 7

Sloan's temper had been growing shorter and shorter during the endless days, until his control over it was almost nonexistent.

He had been polite, he had been reserved. He had escorted her unerringly. He had been certain that she would begin to bend—and then yield. They lived together, damn it!

But she didn't bend—and she didn't yield.

He knew she was awake— when he entered the cabin at night—and each time he heard her relieved sigh when she assumed he was asleep, he wanted to pounce upon her like a tiger.

But he couldn't. As he lay beside her, unable to reach out, feeling the light fall of her every breath, the curve of her body so close, his muscles would constrict, sweat would break out upon his brow and he would remember her so vividly that he bit into his lip until he drew blood to keep from groaning out in the depths of an agonized shudder. Finally, he would sleep.

Their battles—for the most part—had abated. She had ceased to rail against him. She kept a cool distance, answering his every question, speaking civilly, even caring for his clothing and cabin. And yet she was more untouchable than any queen. Always it seemed that something simmered beneath the surface, a brooding tempest that seemed destined to erupt.

"Damn witch!" Sloan muttered, staring portside to the coast of England. The sun was shining brilliantly and everything that surrounded him, the fresh sea air, the warmth, the sound of the waves, was beautiful. But the beauty of the day did nothing for his mood, and he sighed. He had been avoiding his own cabin and Brianna this morning.

"Paddy—take the wheel!" he called out.

"Aye, aye, Cap'n!" Paddy returned, hurrying from a task at the rigging to take Sloan's place. Sloan felt that his mate was amused as he gazed at him—which further irked him.

He paused before ducking down the steps that led to his cabin. They were at last nearing Dover. Tomorrow, he decided, they could put into port, where the ship could receive her minor repairs and take on fresh provisions.

He hesitated before his cabin door, about to knock. Annoyed, he reminded himself that it was his cabin, the captain's cabin, and twisting the knob, he entered.

He found her still in her nightgown, reading by the light from the paned window. Sloan entered the cabin slowly, feeling the familiar tension creep through him. Her hair was a tangled enticement upon the pillows, a fan of deep and rich billowing black. The perfection of her features was enhanced by that raven frame. Her skin so like ivory contrasted with the darkness of her hair. The lace of her modest nightgown edged about her throat, but still he could see the rise and fall of her full, firm breasts.

She hadn't noticed him there, he thought with annoyance—she was involved in her book. And the cabin was a mess! Clothes strewn here and there, the bed tousled and with her still in it!

"Lass," he exclaimed irritably, ripping the bed coverings, "it's nearly the noon hour and time you should be up and about!"

Her eyes, wide, startled, and resentful, met his. Sloan turned quickly from her, determined that she not realize he was angry.

"When one is a prisoner within a cabin," she responded calmly and quietly, "it seems to matter little how the day is spent!"

Sloan sat behind his desk and finally brought his eyes to hers. "You are not a prisoner, Mistress MacCardle, merely a well-tended guest. Yet it ill befits such a guest to while away the hours with no purpose. Women who grow fat and lazy and indolent are considered most unattractive."

He had wanted to anger her, to get some reaction from her. But when he was met by her blue gaze once more, it was annoyingly cool.

"Lord Treveryan, I would of all things hope not to prove myself indolent, so I suppose I must rise. Perhaps you would be good enough to leave the cabin again so that I might dress."

He rested first one booted leg over the edge of his desk, and then the other over that, leaning comfortably back in his chair as his brows arched high in disapproval. "Nay, lass, I'll not be asked to leave my cabin so that you may dress, when the sun is already in the middle of the sky. You'll have to make do with my presence."

He expected to see the fires burn in the depths of her eyes. She would try to hold her tongue, but she would not be able to, and soon she would be tempted to scratch out his eyes. But she only shrugged, as if he were indeed an annoyance and nothing more. She rose from the bed and turned her back on him, and as she did so, the brilliant daylight clearly showed every curve of her body. She moved to the wardrobe and chose a gown, and with graceful dignity loosed the nightdress from her shoulders and arms, yet held it about her hips as she slid the mauve velvet over her head. It was a difficult procedure performed well—too well. He was given a long glance at her bare back, the gentle curve of her spine leading to the dip and swell of her buttocks. He could see a hint of the fullness of her breasts, and it was a merciless taunt to his senses.

He could not see the sudden smile that tinged her lips, nor the mischief that seized her. Brianna was weary of boredom, weary of the solemn role in which she had cast herself— and she was very weary of the silent torture she endured night after night when he lay down beside her. There was only one more day at sea. She had seen how closely they traveled to the coast and she heard the sailors talk about Port Quinby. She decided, quite abruptly, that it was time for him to suffer. She had done well, maintaining a polite, very remote distance from him. Today, with so little time left before she would escape him for good, she was determined to play a different role—one that would thoroughly taunt and haunt him, and leave him as miserable as she had been as his prisoner all this time!

His feet suddenly hit the floor with a thud and he stood and paced the small confines of the cabin as he finally bellowed out at her, "Have done with the primping, lass. If you've trouble with the hooks, come over to me."

"I have no trouble at all," Brianna replied sweetly, securing the last of her petticoats and turning to face him.

"I haven't eaten all day, Brianna. If you wish a meal, come along now."

She was startled by the freedom offered her, and so swept by him quickly. But whereas she usually took great care not to touch him, she did the opposite this day, passing him so that her skirts brushed his thighs, turning as if in apology so that the fan of her hair teased his chest and chin. "Excuse me," she murmured primly, and continued down the hall, bowing her head as she walked to hide her smile. She had clearly heard the grating of his teeth as she passed him.

Her smile faded as he gripped her elbow roughly, jerking her around. The scowl that tightened his sun-bronzed features gave her pause for a moment; a shiver rippled through her. She knew that she was playing a dangerous game. She felt reckless, ready to explode, and she could not help herself. She felt as if her flesh were scorched where his fingers touched her.

"Since it is my ship, lass, and since I am the one with knowledge of the whereabouts of the galley, I think that I should lead."

She offered him a dazzling smile. "Forgive me, Captain," she murmured, extracting her elbow from his grip and slipping her arm through his. "The thought of leaving the cabin for a breath of sunshine left me so exhilarated. Please, do lead, Captain."

Her sweetness left him wondering bitterly at what mockery lay beneath it, and did not ease his temper. Nor did her pleasant proximity. Her hair smelled faintly of light summer flowers, and he thought dryly that she had bewitched Paddy as she had himself. Apparently Paddy had been daily supplying her with a tub of heated water for bathing and the best of the French toilet articles contained within the hold of the ship. The hall was narrow until they reached the deck, and she was pressed against him. The mauve gown she had chosen displayed an ample portion of ivory bosom, and that was continually crushed against his arm and chest as they walked.

Moving topside toward the bow did little to ease his irritation, for the men all stopped at their tasks to salute him and bow to her with deep smiles. He saw wistfulness and envy—and hunger—in their eyes.

She smiled in return, replying sweetly to their good-days.

He wanted to slap her.

"You're rather charming today, aren't you?" He queried her suspiciously.

"Am I?"

"More so than usual."

"Ah! But it's hard to be charming when you continually pursue your prison tactics! Today, My Lord Treveryan, I am seeking to turn the other cheek."

Sloan laughed. "I don't believe you'd ever 'turn the other cheek,' Brianna. But we'll see, shan't we?"

He had never brought her to the galley before. She was surprised by the elegance of the crew's dining quarters within a ship designed for cargo and speed—and warfare. Ol' John, the cook, seemed as startled to see her as she was to be there, and he prepared her a plate of fish dressed in herbs and ringed by lemon rinds.

Sloan led her to a planked table and sat across from her, eating his meal.

He didn't speak, but she felt his eyes upon her as she ate, and so she looked at him and questioned him curiously.

"How is it that you, a Welshman, have become so familiar with the Prince and Princess of Orange?"

Sloan hesitated for a moment, then shrugged.

"My father was a friend to Charles II when he roamed in exile. Sons are often sent from their homes to be tutored in other households. I spent a great deal of time with Charles in the English court."

"And yet you turn from his brother," she said softly.

"I've reasons."

Brianna touched his hand where it lay idly upon the table. "There is a passion in what you say that goes beyond politics," she murmured to him earnestly. "Did James wrong you?"

"Nay..." Sloan replied slowly. His eyes were upon her fingers as they rested lightly upon the back of his hand. They were very long, and they appeared very delicate and feminine. He twisted his hand so that their palms met, his engulfing hers, and he idly rubbed his thumb along her fingers—and to the center of her palm.

"James did no great wrong to me. But he did to Charles after his death. He had Jemmy beheaded."

Brianna frowned, more curious than ever, and yet greatly distracted by the simple touch that made her blood grow warm and race through her. "You knew him well?"

"Very well."

"Oh," Brianna murmured, absurdly longing to smooth the frown from his brow. "Sloan," she reminded him quietly, "Monmouth was a bastard—a pretender to the throne. He fought against James, declaring himself the King. It was treason."

His touch upon her ceased; the hand was withdrawn. He stood abruptly. "I have no time for your prattle. I'll return you to the cabin."

"But I haven't finished."

"Then you should have eaten rather than spent time voicing opinions over matters of which you are ignorant."

She was hurt and furious, but she controlled her temper. Obviously he had cared deeply for Jemmy Scott—but he did not care to talk about it with her. Because she meant nothing to him! He was quite talented at hurting her, but she was learning she had her own weapons to wield. *Treveryan,* she fumed silently, *you will learn what it is to hurt.*

She would be so very sweet and he would be entirely off guard when she did escape him come the morning!

She stood, keeping her eyes downcast, and when he came around the table, she meekly took his arm. She thanked the cook, and when they crossed the deck, she was careful not to speak to the men, but equally careful to give them all brilliant smiles. Holding lightly to his arm, she felt each ripple of muscle beneath his shirt, and the leashed power within him—and she felt his tension.

In the hall she swayed close to him, gaining satisfaction and a sense of power with the knowledge that she did indeed have an effect upon him. The sea-jade eyes that lit upon her were hard and brilliant, and his mouth was sternly compressed. He could not possibly understand her sweetness and humble obedience, but neither could he condemn it. And neither could he force his touch upon her, for he had stated he would not.

She almost laughed when he at last led her into the cabin. But she did not. She turned to him and said simply, "Thank you, Captain

Treveryan, for your time and the outing. Both are greatly appreciated."

He barely replied to her. The cabin door slammed in his wake, and she did laugh. She had discovered she could play the game—and her desire to win was strong.

But as the day passed, her excitement waned with bitterness. The afternoon came and went, and Sloan did not reappear. She had run out of shirts to mend, the cabin was spotless, and she could not clear her mind to enjoy the volume by Chaucer she had found in the hidden bookcase.

Evening came and daylight faded from the cabin. Paddy brought her water for a bath. He tried to speak with her cheerfully, but could not ease her mood.

"Paddy," she demanded of him, "whose clothing do I wear?"

He hesitated uncomfortably. "I told you, lass, a lady who was a friend to the cap'n."

"His ex-mistress, you mean. Or perhaps she is still his mistress."

"Nay, lass," Paddy muttered, "he'll not be seein' her again."

"Did she hurt him, Paddy? Is that why her things were not within his cabin?"

His startled eyes met hers. He chuckled. "Nay, lass. The captain broke the relationship. Her things were not within the cabin because he's never shared his quarters before. Now, lass, I'll be getting back to me work and ye can enjoy your privacy."

Brianna mulled over his words once he had

gone, wondering at the pleasure they gave her. Then she reminded herself that it did not matter in the least. Tomorrow she would be free. She would find her family—and once again she prayed she would know what it was like to love and be loved in return. The Powells, she knew with a warming certainty, would want her and welcome her lovingly.

Brianna stayed in the tub until the water grew cold and she feared Paddy would return. She had barely dried herself and redonned the mauve gown when he did, and she thanked him sweetly. When Paddy had left she combed her hair to a glossy shine and waited for Sloan once again.

But still he did not come, and as her agitation and hunger grew, her temper soared once again.

He had barely allowed her to consume half of one meal, and now it appeared that he was too busy to offer her dinner.

For another half hour she paced the cabin, cursing him profoundly under her breath. Then she decided that meekness be damned. She knew the location of the galley, and she had befriended the cook. If Sloan was angry that she had left the cabin, all the better.

The Cornish cook frowned his disapproval when he saw her, but he prepared her plate with special favor once again. She was standing before him, waiting for her meal, when a young seaman with whom she had spoken briefly a number of times approached her.

"Mistress Brianna, you should not be here.

The captain would be furious, and you place yourself in grave jeopardy."

Brianna smiled. "It seems that Captain Treveryan is very busy tonight. And I was very hungry."

"You shouldn't move about unescorted."

"Then perhaps, sir, you would escort me."

He flushed deeply with pleasure, but then took her plate from the cook with a nod and led her toward the back of the galley, as far as possible from the crew members who were taking their meals.

"Tell me"—she thought furiously to remember the youth's name—"George, where is your home?"

"The north country," he told her pleasantly. "I'm the third son of Lord Percy, and therefore, not in line for much of an inheritance!"

"Ahh," Brianna murmured, chewing a morsel of food before speaking again. Dinner was fish once more, but she was truly ravenous, and so it mattered little. Also, it was nice to be in the company of this youth so near her own age, who was so cordial and obviously pleased to be with her.

"I shouldn't worry, George," she told him. "You seem a bright and able young man and I'm sure you'll make your own way in the world."

He beamed at her words. "Oh, I do think so, Mistress Brianna. Being a younger son has its advantages. It gives me a certain freedom. I can work where I will, and love where I will. My brother must make a marriage advantageous to the family, while I..."

His blush became very dark. He stuttered for a moment, and then began to speak once more. "Should you ever find yourself alone, Brianna, I would be honored to marry you."

She was both stunned and touched—and ashamed at the implication. If the captain tired of her and abandoned her, he would be there...

"Thank you," she managed to choke out, but before the startling conversation could go farther, they were interrupted.

"Seaman—what goes on here?"

The purser, Gyles Brill, a dark-eyed Welshman, stood behind George's shoulder. He was close to forty, Brianna imagined, but a man still in his prime and confident with himself. He smelled faintly of rum, and the gaze that he gave Brianna made her distinctly uncomfortable.

"I am escorting the captain's lady while she has her dinner," George mumbled swiftly.

"That's not your job. Get on deck, seaman, the winds are shifting."

"I'll take Brianna back to her cabin."

"You needn't. I'll do so."

"You haven't the rank."

"I outrank you."

"Eh, look, mate, will you!" someone suddenly rang out. "The dandies are fighting over the captain's whore!"

Brianna blanched, but the horror had just begun. Young George was suddenly on his feet, hurling himself across the room to find the speaker. Shouts rang out all over, until the galley was in bedlam. The dining area had turned into a brawl, a cacophony of grunts and curses and flying fists.

Brianna leapt to her feet in horror as a man came flying across the room, crashing into her table. He gazed at her with a crooked smile upon his face, and then shot like a cannon back into the melee. "I'd brave the plank for a touch of her silk! For but a minute with the captain's whore," someone yelled, and Brianna wondered briefly who would uphold what was left of her honor, and who would be ready to take it. Chairs, plates, and tankards flew. "Ye'll not call her a whore!" George raged, and others joined his bellow. "Let me to her!" The words came wrapped in a licentious chuckle, which ended in a loud wallop and a groan. Her effort to flaunt Sloan had created the disaster, and she realized that her wisest course of action would be to disappear—lest the winners of the brawl include the man who would walk the plank for his chance with the captain's "whore."

She turned to flee, but as she did so, she crashed into something that felt more impregnable than the ship's panels. Something, however, that radiated heat and steel, strength. A man's chest, clad in light-blue silk.

She looked up to his face just as a pistol was fired into the ceiling—silencing the melee into instant sobriety and stillness.

Sloan was not looking at her. He was staring

123

with utter fury at the scene before him—his men bloodied from their brawl; the galley a shambles. His eyes gleamed his wrath with a devil fire.

She had seen him angry, but never like this.

For a moment of cowardice she was ready to slink to the floor and crawl away to avoid him. But she was not at fault! she cried to herself. She had been hungry and he had ignored her to a point where she had been forced to take action.

"I warrant you, gentlemen," Sloan said coolly, hands upon his hips, legs spread and feet firmly upon the ground, "that it is easy for men to come to blows at sea. I'll warrant that you've even had a certain provocation." At this point he glanced briefly at Brianna, and she wanted to slap him. There was nothing but a raging venom in the gaze he gave her; cold and contained. He did not defend her, he accused her.

"But you've all jobs to do for which you're all well paid aboard the *Sea Hawk*. And at this moment, lads, we are sailing for the Princess Mary. Clean up this mess and report back to duty. If the perpetrators of this brawl do not report to me, you'll all be on half rations until we reach Holland."

George stepped up to Sloan immediately. He was trembling, but he stood with dignity. "I started the actual fighting, Captain," he said.

"I suppose I needn't ask why," Sloan said dryly, and again his deadly gaze lit upon Brianna, who had no choice but to remain before him.

"A night in the brig," he said dismissively. He turned around to speak and Brianna saw Paddy following behind him. "There are others who created this fiasco. See that they step forward as George did. Those responsible can make their peace in the brig till we make port in Dover tomorrow. Then the matter will be forgotten."

Brianna had been listening to him—but still she was taken completely off guard when his hand clamped upon her shoulder and wrenched her toward the door. She wanted to remain calm, to tell him scathingly but clearly just what she thought of his treatment. It was impossible.

"Treveryan, you disgraceful sea-scum, you are hurting me! I insist that you release me."

"Hurting you!" he exploded. "I'd like to whip you black-and-blue. You were told not to leave the cabin alone. You deliberately defied me, and thanks to you half my crew will spend the week limping and losing their teeth!" They reached his cabin, but even when he slammed the door behind them he did not release his grip upon her.

"Defy you! I owe you no obedience," Brianna protested heatedly. "I was starving, and since you were too busy to care, I was left no recourse except to seek something to eat."

"Does it give you pleasure to see men brawl for you, lass? Did you promise that fool boy special favors to defend you?"

125

With a strength that amazed her she broke his grip and whirled on him, raking her palm and nails furiously across his face. "Noble bastard!" she hissed, too incensed to care that she was adding fuel to his fury. "That boy should never have had to come to my defense! It is because of you that I was called 'whore'—'the captain's whore.' As I am forced to sleep in your cabin, milord, it is difficult to blame them for labeling me so."

"You little witch!" he replied in a whispered quiet that frightened her. He went tensely still, bringing his hand to the scratches that welted red upon his face. "Were you not with me, mistress—the captain's whore— they would have their fun with you. But *whore* is not the word I would have used. *Slut* is more applicable for a woman who flaunts herself and enjoys taunting men." He took a step toward her and she felt as if the blood were draining out of her.

"Slut!" He hissed venomously as she backed away, seeking the shield of his desk.

"That accusation is laughable, milord. And, no, Captain Treveryan, I promised George no favors, but I would! He is a man who at least cares for me, who is at least a gentleman, who is there when I need him, willing to defend me. He does not ignore my needs."

"So your needs have been ignored, mistress, is that it?" That he spoke quietly did not fool her. His steps were calm and unhurried as he came toward her. Her heart beat erratically, for she felt the tension leaping and crackling like lightning, and the fury that, still leashed, was as combustible as a storm.

"Was that it, my sweet innocent? You've taunted each and every one of my men to blows because you were ignored? The beguiling smiles, the gentle, bewitching speeches? You've seduced them all."

"I have not!"

They faced each other across the desk, but then he began his stealthy walk once more and Brianna was forced to counter him. "George has simply been kind to me, and I have—"

"Played your act upon him, as you have on me? A light touch upon the arm, forced nearness in a narrow hallway? Pressing close..."

"No!" He was moving toward her again. In desperation she clutched the logbook from his desk and threw it at him. It grazed off his shoulder, and she shivered as she saw his eyes narrow and his lips compress still further.

"I did nothing!" she cried.

"No? I think you have done much. Take this morning, my little Scot. That lovely little charade when you dressed before me with such modest allure."

"You refused to leave."

"Aye—I played right into your hands!"

He was staring at her, his eyes cold and challenging. "Don't come any nearer to me!" she warned, and nervously continued. "And I understand, Lord Treveryan, that other women have sailed in this ship—with their own sleeping quarters. I demand—"

"You demand?"

"Yes!"

He offered her a subtle grin. "You demand, Mistress MacCardle?" he repeated softly, brows arching as he rounded the desk and seized her with a lithe movement that was too quick and too agile for her to counter.

"No!" she shrieked, wrenching about in panic. She kicked and bit at him and struggled like a wild tiger, only to exhaust herself as he parried her every movement. He held her shoulders and jerked her so that her throat arched and she was left to meet the full fury and tension in his grim features. "Aye, my lass, I'd like to whip you black-and-blue, cure you of your scratching and throwing. But you've been demanding all day— and fool that I am, I didn't understand. Worry yourself no longer, my Scottish love, for I'll take care not to ignore you."

His fingers sank into the hair at the nape of her neck as his mouth lowered to hers. She brought her hands against his chest, but it was like pitting a straw against the wind. Warmth filled her, a touch of hot flame; yet she fought that warmth as she fought him, furiously, wildly, fully aware that if she lost the battle, she lost all.

"No!" With desperate effort she at last twisted her head from his, gasping for breath, praying for strength.

He did not release her, but his hold eased and he pulled her head to his chest, where she could hear the rampant beating of his heart. His chin rested over her forehead as he massaged her back.

"I've tried," he murmured. "God knows I've tried. Don't play games of chance, my love."

Brianna realized that after all, he intended to keep his word. He was going to let her be. Her system was alive with tumult. She wanted to beat against him in fury, and yet she was sorry for her actions.

She tilted her head to meet his eyes, wanting to say something, to tell him somehow how it hurt to be called whore, that she was sorry she had played foolish games. But as she gazed into his eyes, where passion still smoldered and anger still lurked, she couldn't find the words. She simply shook her head. She had won, she thought bitterly. She had won her game. He wanted her—he wanted to strangle her—but he wanted her.

The victory was bitter. And for some inexplicable reason she had to ease the tension that again reigned. She stood upon her toes and kissed him, meaning the gesture to be the apology she couldn't voice. She had no thought of malice; she wished only to make amends. She did not realize the portent of her simple actions, nor did she think of danger when he lifted her against him to close the short distance to the bed. She did not realize that she sought a peace that could not be. She just kept whispering his name.

He didn't make a sound to alert her to his change of intent. She felt his hands upon her gown and heard the rip of the material as it failed to give to his impatient hands. Apology instantly faded from her mind. Where she had been penitent, she was freshly enraged.

"No!" She attempted furiously to pull from his hold. But his hands about her were firm and strong, his glare scornful and resolute.

His voice grated harshly to her. "Lass, I may be a fool, but never a saint. You cannot jerk the strings of a man as you do a marionette."

She was stunned as he rose and tossed her upon the bed, and yet she saw that he truly believed she had been beckoning him on further to test her power. She stared at him stunned—and then gasped in outrage as she saw that he was stripping with a ruthless determination that assured her she had indeed tested him too far.

She began scrambling for the torn fabric of her gown. His boots hit the floor, his shirt was cast aside, and still she scrambled to pull on her clothing. She fumbled to her knees upon the mattress, drawing her bodice together, yet he blocked her exit from the bed. And when she attempted to rise, he relentlessly pressed her back.

"Sloan—wait—damn you—I didn't mean... don't you dare—"

"At this moment, witch," he murmured, bringing her wrists to the bed in a vise and leaning near to whisper, "I will dare whatever I choose. I have had it! All day you have taunted me, and when I would still uphold my promise, you choose to test me further. The strongest man has his breaking point. You have discovered mine."

She struggled wildly but soon he had her naked in his arms. Still she fought him, furiously, then desperately, until her strength failed against his indomitable will. Then his kiss, the lightest caress, touched upon her forehead. And then upon her cheeks...and finally upon her lips. She lay still, mesmerized by the tenderness within that gentle assault, such a contrast to the tempest of anger that had exploded between them. Again his kiss was searing, delving, commanding all, but now the hunger was tempered by a yearning that sweetly seduced. Her hands, still bound into fists above the bonds of his grip, slowly relaxed, and when he drew his lips from hers, he kissed the palms of her hands, vulnerable then, weakening to his will as she was.

She could not deny the pleasure of the sweet fire ignited within her at his intimate touch. He wrapped his arms around her, savoring the touch that melded them then, giving them a moment of intimacy that was completely tender; an eye within a storm, a brief interlude of sacred peace. A broken sob escaped Brianna. "I did not want this."

But she did want him. She was in love with him.

His pain-filled whisper brushed and caressed her hair and her ear. "Always you refuse me too late, my love. For I must be with you. Please let me love you. Touch me, have me..."

She couldn't speak, and yet she answered him by winding her arms more tightly about his back, by kissing the hollow of his shoulder.

Her teeth grazed against his flesh with the passionate craving that wound deep within her.

He pulled away from her and lifted his weight from her and spread her thighs. He slid his hands lovingly over her breasts, along her hips to her legs, lifting them high around him. And then he came back to her, fusing his lips to hers as he gently claimed her, shuddering as he filled her and received her embrace. His strokes were slow, and his whispers reassured her. She arched to meet him, and he enveloped her within his arms and allowed his passion full rein. Her soft moans and the sensual undulation of her hips against him fed the fires of his hunger to an all-consuming flame. He heard her cry out and shudder beneath him, and all the passion within him burst in an explosive moment of pleasure so great that he trembled again and again as his limbs slowly relaxed against hers.

He wanted to speak to her but could not. And when he finally said her name, she shook her head and buried her face against his chest. He held her and, in time, rose to extinguish the lamps that still burned, and then lay down beside her once more.

There was a spell to the night, and as long as it was not broken by words, it would endure. Within that spell and the enchanted darkness he could make love to her again, slowly... nurturingly...teaching her new beauty. In turn, his witch truly taught the devil what heaven could be.

His brooding eyes were upon her when

morning came. She rested upon his chest, her cheek a gentle warmth against him. His arm cradled around her shoulder and back and his hand rested upon the sloping curve of her hip. He reveled in her beauty, and the light brush of his fingers that idly massaged her spine spoke of tenderness, and not of passion.

For he was torn by a deep sense of shame, and he did not know how to face her; he was convinced more than ever that he could never let her go. He had to mask his feelings and stiffen his resolve, for when she awoke, the magic of darkness would be gone.

He would have to defend himself; yet he felt his guilt and so would have to shield himself with declarations of right. He would do so, for he could never promise to keep his distance from her again.

He felt suddenly a difference within her, and realized that she, too, had been pensively lying awake. He tensed, expecting her tears or her anger. Then he twisted above her, green eyes hard as they stared into hers, but what he found was far more difficult to bear than fury or tears.

Her blue gaze echoed a depth of misery that clamped about his heart. She offered no reproach, only the pain of that sadness.

Instinctively he moved to pull her close, to offer the comfort and security of his strength and warmth. But she pulled away from him and drew the bedcovers about herself, smiling ruefully and shaking her head.

"I did not—" he began.

"Sloan," she interrupted with soft dignity, "I charge you with no fault. I did not seek to cause trouble with your men, but I did think to taunt you and cause you misery. It was a foolish game to play, milord; your strength should not be tested. Perhaps I...I did want... what happened between us. I did not know it... nor am I glad to know it now. And so I beseech you, please release—"

Rising on his elbow, he cupped her chin in his hands. "Do not ask me to give you up, for I cannot." He fell silent for a moment, searching her eyes. "I need you," he told her, with fervor and conviction. "I swear, Scottish witch, that I need you as I have never needed another woman in all the years of my life."

She returned his gaze, and he felt her shivering. "I cannot be your mistress," she said painfully. "I cannot bear it when your men shout 'whore' at me—and know that they speak the truth." She continued in a whisper, "If it is true, my lord, that you need me above all others, then give me the freedom to be there for you. Marry me."

The cold shield that covered his eyes was instantaneous, and the hands that touched her grew stiff. He stared at her a moment longer and then turned from her, rising to dress with smooth efficiency. He glanced her way only once, and Brianna knew the man who had loved her with both tenderness and burning, passionate demand was gone.

"I cannot," he said simply, as he pulled on his boots. It was not only his words that ripped her apart as if a blade had pierced her; it was his chilly flat tone. "You have no choice but to remain aboard the *Sea Hawk*," he told her harshly.

He turned on his heel and stalked toward the door, the captain of his ship, the unfathomable, cold, and authoritative lord.

"We dock today for supplies and repairs, Mistress MacCardle. Do not seek to leave the ship. Paddy will remain aboard, and he will see to your needs until we set sail again." He hesitated a moment and continued. "You needn't fear being called 'whore' again. The men would not dare anger me a second time."

Brianna began to laugh, yet sobered quickly. "Milord, you cannot punish them for what they see, and for what is truth!" It didn't really matter, she thought dully. Once they docked, she would be gone. More than ever, she had to escape him.

"You will not hear the word again," he said curtly.

He walked out the door, and she heard the slip of the bolt. Still, she was too numb for tears. Surely the pain of burning at the stake could not equal the agony of loving this man and knowing that she must leave him. If only he loved her. Cherished her. Wished to marry her. But he had never said that he loved her.

For a moment she closed her eyes tightly against the pain. Then, rising from the bed, she dressed methodically, glad of the numbness that sustained her.

The door had been bolted, but she would

find a way to escape him when she was on English soil. It would be her last chance to save her heart—and her soul—from this devil of a man with whom she had so foolishly waged battle—and lost.

Chapter 8
Port Quinby

From the high ridges of the cliffs, a troop of men looked at the *Sea Hawk* as she glided smoothly into harbor at Port Quinby. Three quarters of her massive sails were furled, yet she still appeared majestic as she skimmed the light waves before her shirtless crew brought her to dock.

Matthews, clad as always in black, stood with a booted foot cast arrogantly on a high rock, his elbow resting upon his knee as he watched the scene. That the *Sea Hawk* had now docked made the misery he had endured to reach this squalid port town well worth the effort.

He had barely slept as he pushed himself and the troops, given him by the crown, to the limit of human endurance. He had been certain that the storms at sea would force Treveryan to seek harbor. He had traveled over fifty miles most days, and Matthews had remained certain all the while that God was guiding him. Never had he pursued a witch with such a vengeance, but never before had he met quite so frightening a witch. The girl had power; she had haunted him, she had come night after night to torment him in his dreams.

Oh, bless God, who was about to deliver the enemies of heaven to his feet!

At last Matthews turned to Lord Darton, commander of the troops. His eyes held a fevered gleam that made even Darton uncomfortable.

"You see, Darton, that devil traitor does seek harbor, as I prophesied."

Darton shrugged. "Luck has been with you, Matthews."

"Luck? No, never luck!" Matthews exclaimed fanatically. "It was the Lord who sent him to my snare! The Lord, Who will suffer not his witch to live, nor allow that messenger of Satan himself to draw breath upon the morrow!" He had not known that he would catch Lord Treveryan in southern England, but he had prayed fervently each and every evening that he might do so.

Darton appeared startled. He was a military man, accustomed to battle, and to the law. He knew that village hags who dealt with potions and the like were sometimes executed for witchcraft, but to accuse a man such as Treveryan? It seemed most implausible. "You cannot mean to burn Treveryan, sir! I do not doubt that witchcraft exists, but I cannot believe that Lord Treveryan consorts with the devil!"

Matthews looked at Darton long and hard, then sighed. "They hang witches, here, sir, and

I do, indeed, intend to see the man hanged. Be not fooled, my Lord Darton, by the appearance of the man! He has been bewitched, and has fallen to the devil himself."

"I have known Treveryan," Darton said stiffly. "He is a powerful man with a will of steel—and the courage and strength to pursue his will."

"Strong men are ever better tools for their master, the devil. Satan is clever and cunning. You must understand, Lord Darton. Satan has imbued his servant with the power to seduce even such men as yourself. I tried to save Treveryan, but the Scottish witch delivered him into the arms of the devil. And see! See how he comes to me now. God has given me the power to seek His vengeance. It is His will that I cast those sinners this day into their rightful place in hell!"

Matthews waited for Darton's response.

"I will not see Treveryan led to a noose without a fair trial—if," he reflected, "we are able to bring him to trial." He glanced sternly at Matthews. "I do assume you intend fair trials for Treveryan—and the girl?"

"I will prove her a witch! Do not be seduced by the beauty of her face; she is the devil's own mistress," Matthews vowed earnestly. For she was a witch. He saw her day and night when he dared to close his eyes. She had cast a spell on him and he knew his only release would be through her death. He turned abruptly and sought his horse. "Come. We will pay our visit to the lord mayor of Port Quinby and set our trap for Captain Treveryan."

Darton followed suit, but not at all happily. Treveryan was a better man to call friend than enemy. The man did not need the help of any devil to be a formidable foe.

Within fifteen minutes Matthews stood at the doorway to the lord mayor's attractive brick residence. The serving girl who answered his pounding greeted him nervously, informing him that the lord mayor was at breakfast.

Matthews pushed his way through the door and stalked through the house until he found the portly lord mayor, a jovial man, about to savor his second serving of kidneys.

"What is this interruption?" he demanded in a fluster, and not without a certain nervousness, as Matthews in his raven-black and ten of the soldiers filed into his sunny breakfast room.

"King's business!" Matthews bellowed, tossing a document before the man's nose. "The sea devil and Welsh traitor finds port here today. It is known, Lord Mayor, that you have a fondness for the man. He will come here today, and if you value your own health, my friend, you will be ready to welcome him—as my men will be."

The lord mayor nodded slowly and set down his knife and fork as ten swords were drawn and angled toward his neck. Matthews did not notice that the lord mayor gazed beyond him—to the girl who had opened the door.

The lord mayor's nod to her was imperceptible to the others. She slipped out of the house just moments before Matthews's boots rang clearly upon the cold stone behind her.

"Darton—I leave you in charge. See that Treveryan wears chains as soon as he enters. Remember that he is the spawn of Satan—and a dangerous man."

"Aye, I'll remember," Darton replied broodingly. He was well aware that Treveryan was a devil—with a cutlass at least—and he feared for the lives of his men. He was not happy about arresting one of his peers, especially when it seemed that Matthews was sure of conviction before the trial. How Darton despised this duty to which he had been assigned! He sighed. How he despised Matthews. The gleam in the man's eyes—it was almost as if he were not quite right in the head. And yet few men were qualified to deal with matters such as witchcraft, and Matthews had been given his commission by the king.

Matthews was leaving. He called a division of twenty men to follow. "Where are you going?" Darton demanded, irritated that he had been set to such a task by a fanatic not willing to be a part of the bloodletting sure to follow.

Matthews halted in the entryway and faced Darton with red-rimmed eyes that seemed to gleam with greater fever. "To seek the girl," he said with a smile that was so chilling that Lord Darton felt fear ripple along his spine.

He would be glad when this day was over.

When they had docked, Sloan left Paddy with only a skeleton crew aboard ship. Port Quinby was a friendly town. Trade with the Continent and sailing men of many nations had given her a worldliness lacking in many a larger city. Her streets were full of markets, taverns, and brothels.

His men, Sloan decided wryly, were well in need of an afternoon in the company of women. Some good strong ale would be in order, and a little revelry to ease the tempers that were too quickly rising.

Those left behind were to have liberty as soon as their tasks were completed. Sloan expected no trouble in Port Quinby, but he had ordered the men to choose between two neighboring taverns for their sport. He had learned in his travels it was always wisest to band near—and to keep one's cutlass always at one's side.

George followed him about with an expense ledger as Sloan first paid a visit to a number of merchants, ordering shipments of fowl and dried beef, vegetables, and several crates of provisions. At last all purchases were complete, their delivery in progress. Sloan glanced up at the sky. It was cloudless. The beauty of it somewhat eased the darkness of his soul.

"What now, Cap'n?" George queried. If he had felt any rancor toward Sloan for his night in the brig, he gave no sign.

Sloan shrugged. "Enjoy yourself, George.

The Wild Boar Tavern offers good stiff drink—and round, cheerful maids!"

George shuffled his feet. "And what of you, Cap'n?"

"I should see the lord mayor—"

"And if I may suggest, Captain Treveryan," George interrupted a little nervously, "you should drink a pint with the men." George blushed as Sloan stared at him, startled by this familiarity. "It's been rough sailing, lately, Cap'n," George continued, trying not to stutter. "I just meant to suggest—I mean, you've a loyal crew, Cap'n, but they enjoy the sight of you, the feeling that you are one of us."

Sloan burst out laughing and clapped George affectionately upon the shoulder. "George, my boy, if you ever get over that stuttering, you're going to make one hell of a sailor! Come along, and we'll definitely down a pint or two!"

Or three or four, Sloan added silently to himself. He would love to get roaring drunk. Maybe he could clear his head that way and convince himself that there was nothing special about the lass who had so captivated his heart. She was a woman like any other; arms, legs, breasts, hips. In the darkness it was all the same.

But it wasn't. No other woman had eyes so beautifully blue; no other had skin as soft as Oriental silk. Limbs so wickedly long to move against him, breasts so full yet so firm to tease his fingers and chest. A voice that touched his soul with a whisper.

He scowled as he walked beside George, thinking that bedding wenches was a seaman's sport—each offered the same, and each offered something new. Joan had been his mistress, yet he had never owed her loyalty, and every port offered a comely lass willing to ease a captain's needs. Brianna she was just a woman.

He sighed softly as they reached the boisterous tavern, unaware that George was watching him and guessing curiously at his thoughts. What was it about her that tied him in knots of longing and guilt? He had stripped her of her purity, but that had truthfully not been his fault. He could not have left her in Scotland, she would surely have died. And now...now he could not bear the thought of her with another man, without feeling a blinding rage.

"Captain Treveryan!"

He smiled as he was greeted warmly by his men within the tavern. Tankards were raised high to him and one was pressed into his hands. Toasts rose in his welcome. "To the finest rogue ever to sail the seas—be he a lord at that!"

Laughter filled the room. Sloan raised his tankard in return. "To the scurviest lot of rowdies e'er to crew a ship!" he returned. "And—the finest!"

He turned to the innkeeper—a man who had entertained his crew often. "Master Lawton, the drinks are on me. Just see that they all manage to stumble back to the ship by nightfall! And"—he pulled George around by the

143

neck of the shirt—"see that my friend here, young Percy, has the finest time the place can offer!"

Loud guffaws and cheers followed the announcement. George blushed furiously but didn't object when a pretty and very buxom wench took up the cue and slid her arms around him.

"Master Percy!" she murmured, "L'il Annie will promise to see that you have the finest time available...."

Sloan chuckled as Annie led a wide-eyed George up the stairs. He took his tankard to a table and stretched out his legs, continuing to banter with the men about the education George was sure to receive. The ale he drank finally began to relax him and lighten his mood. He would, he promised, drink until he could forget her.

"Please! I must see Lord Treveryan!"

Sloan glanced up as a young girl rushed awkwardly into the tavern. It was obvious from her simple dress and that she did not frequent such places, and yet she was anxious to see him.

Sloan stood, frowning. As he appraised the nervous young girl with the flaxen hair, he dimly remembered having seen her before. Then he recalled where. She was a servant within the lord mayor's household.

"Here I am, girl. What would you have of me?"

The tavern fell silent as she wound her way through men and tables toward him, nervously wringing her hands. "Lord Treveryan, you are in grave danger." She fell silent, staring about her.

"Speak freely, girl. These are all my men," Sloan said.

She began to speak again, fumbling for her words. "A man has come with king's troops. His name is Matthews and he awaits you at the lord mayor's house. He is in black, and his eyes burn. He—he—intends to put you in shackles and—and hang you!"

"Matthews?" Sloan repeated incredulously. How the devil had the man moved overland so quickly? He moved forward and gripped the girl's shoulder gently. "Tell me, how many men has he?"

"I—I don't know. Perhaps fifty. Perhaps a hundred. They are split. Some await you at the lord mayor's house. Matthews himself has gone to your ship. He wants a girl." Sloan's face whitened.

"To the ship!" a man roared.

"Nay!" Sloan thundered, raising a hand. "We are outnumbered, my lads, and therefore we must outwit Matthews. Robin!" he called to the sailor who had harassed him. "Come with me to the grain merchant. We will don wigs and capes and go to the *Sea Hawk* as delivery boys. We will find out if they have boarded her. Geoff—you take command here until I return. Be prepared for my word when I know what we must do."

He smiled at the gentle young girl who had risked her life to bring the warning to them.

145

He kissed her lightly on the cheek. "And see that our young lady is rewarded well."

The bawdy drunkenness and laughter of the men had ceased. Each crew member placed his hand upon his sword hilt and awaited with sharp attention what would come as Sloan and Robin left the tavern.

Sloan was puzzled when he and Robin at last reached the *Sea Hawk* with their heavy loads of grain. Paddy challenged them when they would board, and then laughed heartily at their disguises.

"What ye be up to now, Sloan?" he demanded.

"Paddy—has no one come to accost or question you. Have you seen no troops, or king's men?"

Paddy scratched his chin. "Come to think of it, I did see some men in uniform idling about the waterfront shops."

Sloan threw off his cape. "Give me the glass, Paddy. I'm going up the crow's nest."

Sloan quickly shimmied up the mainmast to the lookout point. Carefully he scanned the dock and the waterfront shops. Aye, the uniformed men were scattered throughout.

Why, he wondered fleetingly, hadn't Matthews stormed the ship? Probably because he didn't want a battle with the crew. Sloan's men were known as fierce fighters.

No, all Matthews wanted was Brianna—and himself. But how else could he get Brianna unless he came aboard ship?

A cold terror suddenly gripped his gut so that

he shook, and sweat broke out in furious beads across his brow. He clutched the mast with the muscles of his thighs and shimmied back to the deck. "They are still about," he told his confused first mate quickly. "Paddy— when did you last check on Brianna?"

"Oh, not more than an hour ago, Sloan. I'd never leave the lass longer than that with you not aboard."

Sloan tore across the deck to the bow and down the short flight of steps to the hallway that led to his cabin. He crashed the door in with his shoulder, and the terror that had gripped him found full substance.

She was gone.

Brianna had listened throughout the early morning hours to the shouts and movements of the crew as they brought the *Sea Hawk* into dock. She had not cried, but sat numbly, waiting. And then, when the scurry of footsteps overhead had grown silent, she had stood and carefully inspected the lock upon the door.

Sloan's desk provided her with a scrap of parchment, which she carefully wadded in her hand—and held until Paddy came to deliver her breakfast tray. She chatted as he set the tray upon the desk, meanwhile backing silently to the door, and stuffed the tiny wad into the keyhole, praying that it would keep the bolt from sliding again.

She managed it, folding her hands behind

her back just as Paddy turned to offer her his kind smile. "I've work to do, Brianna, but I'll not leave ye all day! I'll be back fer yer tray—and to take ye topside in the afternoon to see the dock. Ye'll be okay till then?"

"Oh, aye, Paddy. I'll be just fine!" Brianna promised softly. "I've been reading a book. I'll finish it this morning."

Paddy nodded, pleased and relieved by her apparent complacency. "I'll be about me business, then, and should ye need me, give a loud shout."

"I'll do that, Paddy."

She held her breath as she heard him twist the lock, and then forced herself to wait until the sound of his footsteps had faded down the hallway. She heard him shout an order, and slowly released her breath. She approached the door and twisted the knob.

A shaky weakness swept through her when it gave way, and she had to hold to the paneling of the door to stand.

This was it—the time to escape him! The opportunity she had prayed for. She had nothing but her faith in herself, and yet with that she was determined to leave. She would work her way across the country until she could find the Powells. She now believed that Sloan sincerely thought she would only be safe away from the British Isles. But he just didn't understand the Powells, or the ways of their Puritan society. They knew she was not a witch and they would fight with her against the world, if need be. But who would ever find her in a small, seldom-visited village?

It was what she wanted, for she could not be his brief passion. Not according to the morals imbued in her for a lifetime, and not when she loved him with such intensity. She had longed to be free of him but now that it was time to leave, she was sadly realizing that all along he had been her knight in shining armor. He had rescued her, and swept her away, far from danger.

"Because I love you," she whispered out loud, tears sliding silently down her cheeks, as she looked about the cabin for the last time. His desk, where they had shared so many meals in both hostility and peace; his bed, where she had slept beside him, and learned that she desired and loved him.

Brianna swallowed and approached his desk, where a gold coin and several silver pieces had been cast. She bit her lip, knowing she would be a fool to leave without the coins. Hurriedly she made her decision and pocketed the money within her dress—bitterly remembering that she had "earned" his coins. Sloan would not care about the money—that she knew. She picked up his quill and scratched out a quick note upon his blotter—asking him not to search for her, if he cared for her at all.

Then she left the cabin, closing the door quietly but firmly behind her.

Brianna hesitated as soon as she reached the deck. She would never manage to walk smoothly off the plank to the dock. Paddy was guarding the *Sea Hawk*—no one would come or go by that avenue without his challenge.

She nervously ducked partway down the steps and watched the few crew members still aboard as they mended sails or attended to other tasks. She noticed that a hemp ladder had been rigged portside for the men to work upon the *Sea Hawk*'s hull. If she could just cross the deck...

She waited, barely breathing. Finally the deck cleared except for Paddy, who lounged against the mainmast, arms crossed as he relaxed in the warmth of the sun. She took a deep breath and sprinted the width of the ship on her toes and, taking a firm grasp upon the ladder, vaulted over the side in one fluid movement.

She paused and took several deep breaths then, trying to still the erratic beating of her heart. Looking down, she saw that the water was well below her—even falling from the end of the ladder was going to be quite a distance. In her dress and petticoats, she would sink deeply into the sea.

But she had learned to swim well in the chilly lochs of Scotland, and she wouldn't have far to go once she surfaced. She would emerge wet and cold, but that would be a problem to deal with once she reached the bustling docks.

She scrambled down to the end of the ladder and convinced her unwilling fingers that she must let go. The fall was not as bad as she had expected. The icy clutch of the water embraced her immediately and she plunged downward... downward...until she feared that her lungs would burst. The saltwater stung her eyes, but she forced them open, knowing that if she saw light, she would make it. The water seemed to release its hold, and she jackknifed her legs strongly, reaching upward for the light. Seconds later she breached the surface, gasping for air. Her skirts weighted her down terribly and so she did not hesitate, but began clean strokes eastward of the *Sea Hawk* where the small boats found dockage. There she could climb an area of jutting rocks to reach the dock and then the street.

It was too late to wonder what passersby and fishermen would think of her rising from the water. She would have to pretend that she had veered too close to the land's edge and fallen.

But she was never to have a chance to explain. Just as she found a foothold upon land and struggled to her feet, panting with her exertion, a horribly familiar shout riddled the air about her.

"Witch! Good people—see how her master the devil embraces her and carries her through water! Take her—this day she will hang, and sleep with the incubus in the fires of hell!"

It couldn't be. It couldn't. Shock held her immobile. She didn't even shiver as she stood there dripping seawater—and staring at Matthews's fanatical eyes as he waved his walking stick at her. She had lost her mind and impossible visions were filling her head.

"Take her!"

"No!" The protest at last ripped from her throat in terror and agony as she saw beyond Matthews a dozen men in uniform. She tried to stagger back to the sea, but she tripped upon her soaking gown and crashed to the rocks instead. A sickening pain speared the back of her head; darkness spread its wings across her eyes and she drifted into oblivion as rough arms wrenched her from the earth.

"Damn her!" Sloan raged as he read the note scrawled upon his blotter. "Damn that little Scottish witch to hell!"

Paddy, who had followed him, halted in the cabin doorway, knowing that the hammer of rage was about to fall his way. He didn't care—he had never known such a sinking panic himself.

"She must be aboard, Cap'n—I swear by me life she never walked off the ship."

Ledgers, papers and quills went flying from the desk in a furious sweep. "That wench is more trouble than she's worth! I'll have to search the town and hope I find her before Matthews does."

"Captain!"

The shout sounded from topside. Sloan stalked past Paddy and up the steps to collide with Robin upon the deck.

"They've got her, Captain. They've got her!"

"Calm down, Robin. Who's got her? Where?"

"Matthews!"

"How do you know?"

"A town cryer just passed by. They're trying and hanging a witch in the town center sharp upon the noon hour."

"Trying her—*and* hanging her?" The pain that pierced Sloan's insides was so great he almost doubled over. No! His rage and pain were explosive. He could not lose her, by God, not to Matthew's sick fanaticism! Not now, not when he had discovered how deeply he...

Loved her. Loved her more than the vast ocean, more than the *Sea Hawk*...more than his own existence....

He forced himself to draw a ragged breath, stiffen his spine, and clear the darkness from his mind and think.

"Captain?"

He waved his hand for silence. "Here's what we do. Robin, get back to the tavern. I want all hands on deck except for ten men. I'll need horses for myself and those ten. Give me Pickens, Beaufort, and Gest—they're best with crossbows. And Miller and George—they can hit a bird's eye with a pistol at a hundred feet. And—"

"I'll be with you, Captain," Robin said staunchly.

"Me bones may be old," Paddy offered, "but they still sit astride a horse just fine."

"No, Paddy. I need you here. The *Sea Hawk* is going to have to be able to sail at a second's notice. We'll need the guns manned, and the men aboard will have to be ready for hand-to-hand combat. Robin, get going. I'll join you at the tavern as soon as I've laid out my plan for Paddy."

Robin nodded grimly. Still in his disguise, he walked to the dock and onto the street unaccosted. Sloan exhaled a shaky breath and turned to Paddy. "Call whoever of the crew is aboard. Tell them what we're up against, and tell any man who chooses that he may go ashore and not be forced to this battle, for I am labeled a criminal now, as well as a traitor. Association with me will guarantee a rope around a man's neck if we lose. The guns must be discreetly set at the ready to fire—and the sails prepared to unfurl."

Paddy shook his head dolefully. "Aye, aye, Sloan. That I kin manage fer ye—and I warrant not a man will step ashore, though I'll give them all yer offer. But how will ye manage with just ten men to save the girl from the hangman's noose?"

"Surprise will be my main weapon, Paddy. And my prayers that the devil will take the hangman."

He gave Paddy a few more instructions, and then he, too, slipped away unobtrusively back to the tavern, where further meticulous plans had to be formed.

Chapter 9

Brianna was already drifting back to reality when a booted toe slammed painfully against her ribs. Stunned by the blow, she cried out, squeezing her eyes tightly against the pain. Her sea-dampened hair was plastered about her face, as was her clothing to her body; she was miserably stiff and sore and cramped—and horribly, horribly afraid to open her eyes to the terror of what was happening.

"Up, witch. Now."

Rather than receive another cruel blow to the ribs, Brianna forced herself to open her eyes and willed her cramped legs to raise her up off the cold stone floor.

She was alone with Matthews in a small room crudely furnished with a wooden desk and high-backed chair. The room had spun when she stood, but she gritted her teeth against nausea and faintness. Beveled glass windows overlooked the town center, where she could see workmen constructing a haphazard gallows.

"Am I already tried and condemned, then, Matthews?" She challenged the witchfinder, amazed that her voice was strong and not filled with the tremors that she felt.

He did not reply. He waved a hand toward the door. Brianna followed his direction and saw two very dour matrons standing there, heavy women with faces hardened by years of harsh toil, or so she assumed. Their shoulders were as wide as those of many men, their hair gray, and from her distance Brianna could see no color at all to either woman's eyes. Their mouths were turned in sullen frowns and they did not gaze at her at all, but looked to Matthews, as if for instruction.

He stood very straight by the desk and nodded grimly toward the women. Brianna kept her gaze sharply upon the women and began to back away along the wall. There would not be far to go, and her heart was pounding fiercely. They moved slowly toward her, but with determination. Brianna turned her stare to Matthews. He smiled, or rather his lips twisted into a sickening grin. "We must find the proof of Satan upon you," he told her simply. It was then that she noticed a tray on the desk behind him filled with strange instruments, the likes of which she had never seen before.

"Torture is illegal!" she blurted out wildly. "Even I know that, Matthews. I know the law. Torture is illegal!"

"Girl, I know the law," Matthews said, and he turned to the matrons once again. "Strip her," he commanded.

"No!" Brianna cried. Good God! That this man would kill her was horror enough, yet Christ had promised that death brought peace and solace. That they should be allowed to strip and humiliate her, bring agony to her flesh and senses, was beyond all realms of justice and humanity.

Was this what Pegeen had endured? Dear God. But her fair aunt had been a braver woman, and Brianna might have wept and raged for her all over again now were she not in such mortal terror herself.

The women were upon her, and she screamed again, trying to evade them first, but found herself backed into a corner. Then she lashed out with all her fury, but neither woman uttered a sound of pain, and they were two very sturdy specimens against just one. Her vicious fight against them came to a quick halt when Matthews stepped forward, stunning her with a hard blow to the cheek. She fell limply against the wall, struggling against unconsciousness, grasping desperately at the material of her gown as it was roughly wrenched from her. Tears stung her eyes, but she would not cry. She could not give up, not while her heart still beat and breath was in her body.

But no matter how wildly she fought, the end was the same. She was left there, naked and vulnerable, dizzy and ill. Gray mist seemed to swirl all about her, and at first she was barely aware when Matthews came at her again—with a long steel pick from the tray on the table. She heard his cold words. "We will find her devil's mark," he told the women, and they nodded, each gripping one of her arms.

"You are vile! You are loathsome—you are a viper!" Brianna told him, hating that he would touch her, that she could do nothing to stop him. She gritted her teeth, praying to keep her courage, but she screamed when he stuck the pick into her shoulder, drawing blood. Blinded by her tears, she stared into his eyes. They swam dizzily before her, gleaming pools with no mercy.

"Not even God could forgive you, Matthews!" she cried.

"God has given me this task," he answered her, and she was quite certain that he was totally, utterly mad. Why didn't others see it?

The pick struck again, upon her back. She screamed in pain, and the pick fell again, and again. When it struck again, at her left breast, she fell to the floor screaming with the pain. Matthews paused. Brianna lifted her eyes, filled with tears and pain—and hatred—to his. "God's mercy, Matthews!" she cried. "Christ himself would confess beneath your hands."

Matthews did not reply with words. He compressed his lips and brought his knee to slam against her jaw. The world seemed to recede—and then, though she felt the touch of the pick again, she could not even draw the breath to scream against the agony.

But she heard his excited words. "We have found it! There— see how she feels no pain when I touch that mole. It is her witch's teat, and there she suckles her familiars—and Satan!"

She was going to die. There would be no help for her this time. No Sloan Treveryan—no, heroic knight—to come along and save her from Matthews's hell. Sloan would find her note, and he would rage against her, and then he would sail away as they slipped the noose about her neck.

"Confess, witch!" Matthews commanded.

Naked, soaked, and miserable, and left to huddle against the wall on the floor, Brianna felt hysteria rise again. She laughed, harshly, bitterly. She stared at Matthews, and wondered desperately what manner of demon lived inside the man that could make him so totally, ruthlessly cruel. She shook her head, unable to fully comprehend that this man could so eagerly bring her such agony.

"You're insane, Matthews," she whispered.

"Confess!"

"Confess? To what? I am no witch, Matthews. I have no 'familiars,' I have harmed no one. And one day, when God judges us both, it is I whom He shall find innocent of malice."

Matthews knelt down beside her, wrenching her face to his by jerking her hair. "I've charges that Pegeen MacCardle of Glasgow did bewitch and kill one Mary Corcoran with herbal concoctions, made with the blood of infants. That—"

"Mary Corcoran died by her own hand!" Brianna cried out in protest. "Pegeen only mixed herbs to soothe fevers and gout! Never would she have harmed an infant! You murdered a good woman!"

A scream tore from her throat as he pulled her hair again. "Brianna MacCardle, I bring charges that in the forest you did knowledgeably and willingly consort with the devil in the form of various animals. Confess! Save your immortal soul. Cry out now to the Lord, and admit your guilt, and He will find the mercy to allow you to enter His Kingdom."

She was in shock, barely able to fight a flood of laughter, the charges were so ridiculous.

She spat in his face.

"You cling to the devil still!" Matthews cried, wiping his face with a white handkerchief and rising. He jerked his head at the two matrons. "Go now. With God as my witness I will drive the devil from her that she may enter God's grace with death!"

Misery hung over Brianna so darkly that she barely noticed the women leave the room. The will to fight was being sapped from her. The room seemed to drift into light, then shadow, and back to light again. It was not the room, she realized, but the way she perceived it.

There was silence, a silence that allowed her to think and feel, and she wished she could do neither. She realized her state of abject humiliation, naked on her knees before this hideous creature, her hair spilling over her shoulders in tangles. She clutched her arms around her like a shield.

She thought of her battles with Sloan—of the many times she had feared him. She knew now that Sloan would never have harmed her, and that even the days of being vulnerable before him had been a time of beauty. But Sloan was a normal man, possessing all the best qualities of character and heart that could

160

create a man. Matthews was not normal. And beyond her pain and fear and terror there was also the misery of feeling unclean, tainted and fouled by his very nearness.

He came to kneel beside her again, threading his fingers through her hair once more, and yanking at it so fiercely that tears sprang to her eyes.

"Confess your sins, girl. Confess to me now. Tell us of your fornication with Satan. Else we'll leave you here. The shackles can be tightened about your ankles until they bleed. You'll be bound and cast into the water again."

"Bind me, cast me—I care not."

He stood, and walked across the room. Her head was spinning, and she shivered with the severity of the cold that remained from the chilly waters, and from the damp room. She closed her eyes. When she opened them again, Matthews was before her, holding his lethal pick. "Confess!" he ordered. "Or, by God, I'll find more of the devil's marks upon you, until you bleed out your love for Satan."

Sight of the pick brought her staggering to her feet, clutching the cold stone wall behind her. "No!" she cried, reaching out with her hands only to feel the merciless strike of Matthews's hand across her cheek again, a blow that sent her sprawling back to the floor.

Torture was illegal by English law! she reminded herself dully, but "Pricking" a witch for the devil's mark was not. Ah, the law! How it was twisted for those who knew how to manipulate it. She had seen what they had done to her aunt. She had heard, even in Glasgow, what ghastly torments had been inflicted upon the poor wretches in Newgate prison. And now Matthews, she knew, one way or another—within the gray area of the law—would find a way to see that she confessed.

She hadn't any more strength to fight him. He would prick her until she was a mass of blood, and he would hang her anyway. Tears stung her eyes, and panic rose within her. Then a weariness settled over her.

"If you would have me be a witch, I am a witch. I consort with the devil. He comes to me every night. I expect him to arrive any minute in a burst of fire to slit your throat and save me from your touch. Were I truly a witch, I could certainly demand that he do so. Now leave me be. Hang me! Have done with it!"

Exhausted, her eyes closed, she leaned against the wall, huddled there, naked. She expected him to call for the soldiers to take her away. But she heard nothing; instead she sensed him beside her, kneeling. Then he touched her hair, and she opened her eyes with new alarm.

"I can save you, girl." His voice was very low, but held a ring of passion.

"Save me?" she whispered. What new manner of trick was this?

"Hold me. Hard, and close, and I will take the devil from the weakness of your body to the strength of mine!"

Brianna stared at him, incredulous, desperately trying to think with her pain-ravaged mind. His arms came around her. She felt his bony fingers over her breast, and she fought the raging desire to slap him and the nausea that almost overwhelmed her. It came to her with a sense of absurdity that almost sent her again into bitter gales of hysterical laughter, that he wanted her. Matthews—the great seeker of virtue and enemy of the devil—would save her if she would "fornicate" with him—rather than with the devil.

As his hands moved over her, she felt as if she were being touched by a creature so vile that she would never rid herself of his filth. Then she felt his touch no more, as she became numb, reverting to a distant place far within her mind. She hated him, loathed him—but enough to die?

The door was suddenly flung open.

"Matthews!"

An officer, bedecked with the ribbons and jewels of the nobility, stood in the doorway.

Matthews stiffened, dropped her as if she were fire itself, and rose. Then he fell to his knees, his hands clasped in supplication. "Almighty Father! Bless this, your servant!" He crawled to the officer at the door, kissing the hem of his cloak. "Darton—thank God! For this confessed witch hath almost taken me from His glory. Man—you have saved me."

"Confessed?" the man inquired with a skeptical edge to his voice.

"Aye, confessed!"

163

The officer was looking at her, but Brianna could no longer see. The blows to her head were causing everything to swim before her eyes. She wanted to speak, to retract her confession, and swear that the charges were absurd. But she could not make her lips move. All she could do was lapse in and out of consciousness, and pray that death's embrace would be as gentle as this gray place, easing her from pain.

"Find clothing for her," someone said, "and bring her before the court."

When they brought her before the court she could not stand. She should have been fighting, declaring her innocence, but she could not speak. Dimly she heard the matrons give testimony to her "devil's mark." From a different world of mist and blackness she heard Matthews tell of how she had murdered—in consort with the condemned witch, Pegeen MacCardle, and Satan—one Mary Corcoran of Glasgow.

They will not believe it, Brianna thought through the haze that surrounded her. Surely good people could not believe the things of which he accused her. Matthews continued to talk, his voice rising and falling, and with each word Brianna realized that he longed for her death with a passion. She opened her mouth to deny him, but blackness descended on her and she swayed to the floor. Someone held her up, and for a moment she could not even remember her name, or where she was.

Then it was over. She was condemned, sentenced to hang by the neck until dead.

She was taken to an empty cell to await her execution. It was then, pitifully, that she came to full consciousness again. Her merciful world of mist and gray left her. She was doomed to die totally aware—when she had not been so to fight for her defense.

In that little room she sank to her knees and folded her hands. She asked God's forgiveness for those sins she had committed, but she could not, even in her prayers, accept defeat with true Christian fortitude. Over and over again she asked in silent supplication how God could allow Matthews to live.

She prayed for her family and for Sloan. She begged God not to allow Matthews to take Sloan. That he should die for having rescued her seemed entirely too great an injustice.

Time passed too quickly. Men came for her again, despite her protests, and dragged her along an arched hallway that led to a street on the common, where the townspeople were milling. They stared at her; some with curiosity, some in horror, some with indignation.

It was like the day her aunt had been killed. There were many who would have protested, but they feared for their own lives as this insanity surrounded them.

"I am not a witch!" she screamed. "This man is the creature of the devil! He is not a man of God. God does not condemn without trial! God does not torture innocents—"

Her arm was twisted so viciously that she broke off her speech with a cry. The assembled crowd began to murmur and shuffle about uneasily, but despite this she was dragged up the steps to the gallows. She noticed that the sky was a brilliant blue and that the air was crisp and cool and beautifully clean.

Her executioner jerked her hands behind her back and tied them despite her struggles. "Good people, don't let them do this to me! You will be next! You—"

"In the name of His Royal Majesty, James II of England, Scotland, and Ireland, you are condemned to die for the ungodly crimes of witchcraft and murder!"

Matthews's voice rose above hers. The noose was slipped over her neck and she felt the rough fiber of the rope against her throat.

She was about to die and all she could think of was the beauty that had been so briefly hers with Lord Sloan Treveryan. Life. It was so very, very wonderful. And she had only seen it so clearly when it was about to be taken....

"Recant to the people, witch! Confess before them your sins and die in the grace of God!"

"I am not guilty! You are guilty, Matthews, of the murder of countless innocents! Cold-blooded murder—"

"Executioner!" Matthews ordered. "Pull the lever!"

"No!"

Fragments of her life flashed through her mind, but above it all desperation shrieked within her. No! This could not be the end. Not for her. She could not be about to die.

Not now! her soul cried out in terror. Not

now, not when she had just learned what love was! Sloan! Tears stung her eyes. She had left him not knowing life was to be so short. If she had but an hour now...but the moment of death was at hand.

Her mind registered the sounds around her. She heard the crank of wood as the lever for the trap door was pulled, and vaguely heard a peculiar whistling through the air. Strange, but, she knew that whistling sound.

"Die, witch! To the devil goes your soul!"

Matthews's voice rose high over the crowd, a chant that compelled and jerked at the emotions, calling on fear, on the terror that lurked within the souls of all men.

What did a whistling sound matter? she asked herself. Matthews had not heard it; his voice had risen above it. Perhaps she was only imagining she'd heard something.

"The trap!" he raged.

She thought she saw an object fly through the air.

The trap door beneath Brianna's feet snapped open beneath her and gave way to the void of death. She was dying. She felt the coarse rasp of the rope against her neck and tensed instinctively with final, desperate horror, awaiting the merciless jerk of the noose.

But miraculously, the rope tightened for barely a second—then hardly at all. She did not choke, nor did she stop breathing. The rope broke—cleanly, completely. She kept falling and falling, until she lay sprawled on the dusty ground, stunned and incredulous.

A voice rang out from the crowd, loud, strong, and scornful, riddling the air with its forceful timbre.

Sloan's voice!

"I charge *you* Matthews with crimes against God and humanity! And I promise you sir, that this will be your day to die!"

Sloan! Tears filled her eyes in gratitude and disbelief. Sloan was there for her again, when all had been lost, when she'd known no hope....

The whistle she had heard had been that of an arrow, sent soaring through the air with a cunning and uncanny marksmanship, severing the rope.

He, courageous as the wind, she thought with the greatest pride, had come to challenge the lethal shadows of injustice. To challenge the crown—and death itself.

Chapter 10

The dirt, which created a gritty feeling within her mouth, assured Brianna that her rescue from the portals of death was not a dying dream, but incredible, wonderful fact.

She had little time for anything but that realization, for all hell was breaking loose upon the earth.

She scrambled to a crouch beneath the scaffolding of the gallows while the sharp whistle of flying arrows continued to sound as music to her ears and the cacophony of pistols fired at close range set her ears ringing. Before her, the man who would have been her executioner dropped to the dirt.

All about her the people were shouting and screaming. For several seconds Brianna held very still, wondering in awe how Sloan had managed such a swift and sure attack upon the witchfinder and the forces of James II.

At last she crept from beneath the gallows, ripping the noose of hemp from about her neck. She froze at the sight of a king's man approaching her, then exhaled as a shot was fired and he spun about like a marionette jerked by strings, and fell. Brianna gazed at him for a second of horror as his eyes glazed not inches from her feet, then crawled again to rise outside the scaffolding.

She raised her eyes to see that Matthews alone remained alive, standing on the gallows. He shouted orders furiously, but already a good fraction of his men lay dead while the rest fought the crowd to find their attackers.

Only Sloan could be seen. Mounted atop a gleaming roan, he charged through the crowd, who cheered him on and eagerly made way for him.

Matthews drew a pistol as Sloan approached. But the witchfinder panicked at the cold relentlessness of the man bearing down on him, and his shot went harmlessly into the ground. He was shaking too badly to reload, and cast the pistol aside, drawing his saber instead.

"Captain! The girl!"

Brianna saw that the warning had been shouted from the roof of a nearby smithy by Robin, one of Sloan's young crewman. And then she gasped, realizing the cause of his warning—more of Matthews's men were barging their way to the gallows. One burly soldier was almost near her.

Sloan was at last upon them—but his purpose changed radically when no other course was open to him. He had wanted to kill Matthews—God, how he had wanted to kill him—but Brianna was vulnerable. And the king's forces were closing around her.

The roan pranced and shied to the steps of the gallows. Sloan kept one eye on Matthews and shouted. "Brianna! Run, girl, run to me!"

A soldier came toward her with his sword raised to strike her.

She ran to Sloan. He reached for her with one hand, commanding, "Jump, lass—now!"

She gripped his hand and leapt with all her strength and energy, throwing herself in front of his saddle. She felt the deadly tension of his arm as it swung, and his cutlass flashed in the air with deadly purpose. The soldier screamed and fell. "To the ship, lads! To the ship!" Sloan shouted.

Sloan's arm came around her, securing her to the saddle with his vital strength and warmth. "Hold tight, lass!" he compelled her. The roan reared and bolted and took off in a mad, erratic gallop.

The crowd, now alive with excitement and

frenzy, thundered out their cheers, parting to allow Sloan and the scattered sailors to escape. Matthews shouted orders in their wake, and as they clattered their way furiously down the cobblestoned streets, the soldiers were hard on their trail.

Merchants' stands of fruits and vegetables crashed and careened around them as the sailors raced their way to the *Sea Hawk*. Several of the horses were forced to leap a hay wagon, yet they continued on. The streets swept dizzily by until they reached the dock—and the berth of the *Sea Hawk* where the horses snorted and shrieked in protest as they were jerked to rearing halts.

Brianna found herself thrust into Robin's arms from her seat atop the roan. "Take her below!" Sloan ordered, sliding the mount himself and swatting the animal's rear to send it skittishly racing away.

"Come!" Robin urged her.

His arm was about her and she followed his lead to the gangplank, but twisted to look behind her. Sloan was hurrying his men along, and shouting orders. "Slash her ties, men! Raise the sails!"

And beyond him the king's troops were coming, Matthews at the lead.

"Robin!" Brianna shrieked as she saw an arrow sail through the air. She dragged him down with her, in time to save them each from a mortal blow, but too late to avoid a hit, as evidenced by Robin's agonized screech as the arrow tore into his thigh.

"Leave me!" he commanded Brianna, gritting out his words painfully between clenched teeth.

"Nay, I cannot!" she cried in horror, locking her jaw together for strength as, placing her hands beneath his arms, she dragged along. The task was almost beyond her and she was moving terribly slowly.

"Brianna!" Robin hissed. "Go—seek shelter."

Salt sweat fell from her forehead in slender rivulets into her eyes, and she gasped for breath and tensed again to pull his weight along. "We shall make it, Robin."

But they wouldn't. The king's men were almost upon the *Sea Hawk*. A cannon suddenly boomed from the deck of the ship, slowing the tide that swarmed upon them, but not ceasing it. There were still more men.

The thundering repercussion sent Brianna sprawling to the gangplank, coughing and choking from the powder that filled the air. She struggled to her feet, tears falling as she reached desperately for Robin's arms again. She would not make it. Already soldiers were engaging in hand-to-hand combat with the sailors upon the gangplank. They drew nearer. And nearer. She stared with horror, then screamed aloud as a bearded soldier bore down upon them, his sword gleaming as it caught the golden rays of the brilliant sun.

"This way, gent!"

It was Sloan's voice, and his cutlass teased the steel armor upon the man's back and forced him to turn with a growl. "Soldiers should fight armed men, not defenseless girls and wounded boys!"

The soldier bellowed and charged at Sloan, who sidestepped him with agility, swiftly parrying the assault with a slash of his cutlass. The man let out a hideous shriek and careened over the plank to the water below.

Then Sloan was sheathing his bloodied cutlass and hunching down beside Brianna. "Get aboard!" he ordered her, ducking to take Robin himself. He grunted, and hefted the heavy seaman over his shoulder. Brianna coughed and whirled to obey Sloan. He followed behind her, shouting as they leapt to the deck, "The gangplank—drop the gangplank!" The men were all aboard, but so were more than two score of the soldiers. The bow of the *Sea Hawk* was alive with the curses and screams of battle, the clash of swords, the thud of steel.

Sloan propelled Brianna before him as he hurriedly carried Robin to the shelter of the forward companionway and deposited him there.

"How is it, lad?"

Robin grinned through his pain. "Not so bad, Captain. Not so bad."

Sloan nodded grimly and patted Robin on the shoulder. He glanced briefly at Brianna. "Get yourself to safety, girl! Into the cabin, now!" he railed.

She could not seek out the cabin—not with Robin upon the stairs and the men who had so valiantly fought to save her locked in mortal combat. Sloan, assuming she would obey him under the circumstances, had already turned from them to join the fighting.

If he dies I shall not be able to bear it, she thought.

A groan from Robin reminded her of his presence—and of the tearing wound within his thigh. She dropped down beside him, ripping shreds of material from her dress. "Robin!" she whispered to him. "I'm going to take the arrow out."

"No." He groaned. "The blood…"

"I can stanch it," she assured him, trying to smile her assurance even as she heard the groans of the men fighting just feet away. "Trust me, Robin," she encouraged him. "I swear I'll not let you die."

She clenched her teeth and studied the arrow. Fortunately, the shaft had not fully penetrated the flesh. Brianna breathed a sigh of relief. No major blood vessels had been severed, she was certain. She placed her left hand upon his thigh and her right upon the arrow shaft, tensing with her determined effort to bring forth all her strength. The arrow stubbornly refused to give; she just as stubbornly refused to allow it to remain.

It gave so suddenly that she keeled backward. Robin screamed, and she scrambled back to her knees swiftly to wrap the wound in the fabric from her dress, pressing upon his thigh firmly and pulling her bandage tight to stanch the flow of blood.

Robin opened his pain-glazed eyes. "I'm the one who called you 'whore' " he confessed with whispered shame.

Crimson splashed over her cheeks and she lowered her eyes, then raised them quickly to smile at him. "It does not matter," she said softly, "and you must not try to talk."

He gripped her fingers with hot, dry hands. "It does matter," he whispered. "It matters, for I wronged you. You are not a whore, but an angel."

She was stunned. Witch, whore—and now angel. The pity of it was that she was just a woman, a terrified woman now as the hand-to-hand combat continued just steps away upon the deck.

A scream caught in her throat at the sight of Sloan. As he engaged in swordplay with a soldier, a black-clad figure was creeping toward his unwary back.

"Sloan!"

Her horrified scream rose above the din of steel and men.

Sloan ducked and spun just in time to allow Matthews's blade to find its mark in one of his own men. With a stunned gurgle the soldier gasped, gripped his gut, and fell to the deck. Matthews's eyes lifted from the dead man he had accidentally killed, and fell upon Brianna, who hovered within the shelter of the companionway. She returned his stare with wide, mesmerized eyes. She saw the mad hate in his eyes and she knew he would readily sacrifice his own life to take hers.

Sloan shouted the witchfinder's name from his perch upon the boom of the mainmast. "If you would face me, witchfinder, do so now!"

Matthews's eyes turned to the man who hovered near him with catlike agility, ready to pounce between him and his intended victim. "Son of Satan!" Matthews raged. But he spoke no more, for Sloan Treveryan bounded from the rigging to land before him, his deadly cutlass raised.

Transfixed, Brianna watched the swordplay. Her heart seemed to rise to her throat and constrict her breath as the two men parried one another again...and again.

And then she saw that Sloan's grim features held a lethal grin. His eyes were narrowed and hard...glittering with deadly vengeance. He had been playing with the man all along.

The cutlass made a high sweep into the air—and then descended.

Matthews—the witchfinder—stood still for an instant. An instant in which he stared incredulously at Sloan, and at the stream of blood that stained the white of his shirt beneath his black coat. Again his eyes fell upon Sloan.

And then he fell to the deck.

Brianna let out a shriek. Forgetting Robin, she stumbled to the deck. He was dead. She felt waves of heat engulf her, then a rampaging cold that tore like ragged ice against her spine. By God's grace, was it decent to feel such a joy at a man's death? No longer could he hunt her; no more could he aim a finger at the innocent and bring down agony and death. He was dead—and with or without God's forgiveness, Brianna was so grateful and glad that she felt she could die herself with the shuddering power of her relief.

And Sloan...Sloan was still alive!

There truly was a God. Justice had come at last.

But the battle was not yet over. Even as Brianna stood at the top of the stairs, she heard a whoosh of sound, and instinctively ducked. A sword, caked with blood, had swerved unnervingly near her throat. With glazed eyes she looked around her. Sloan was engaged in a deadly duel again, and right next to her George was fencing with a very young, frightened soldier. Both of them, so young, the fear of death in their eyes.

She thought that she would scream again. Scream and scream and scream because she was the cause of it. So much bloodshed!

"Surrender, Darton!" Sloan shouted, and the king's man paused. She thought she had seen him before, but she was too dazed to remember when.

All action aboard the ship ceased. There were no more sounds of the clash of steel. Only the ocean could be heard, the waves lapping peacefully, lullingly, against the hull. All the men stood still, breathlessly waiting as Sloan and Darton stared at each other.

At last, at very long last, Darton lowered his sword. He held it out before him; then, lowering himself with an unassuming grace, he laid it at Sloan's feet. Still there was silence, and as the two men stared at one another, it was obvious that they had met before—as friends. Sloan's voice was low when he spoke again.

"Lord Darton, in surrendering to me, you surrender to William of Orange, and cast yourself into the midst of what —with God's grace—will be a peaceful revolution."

Darton sighed. "I've heard it said you were an Orangeman, Treveryan. So shall it be. I ask that any of my men not willing to serve in such an army be sent back to shore."

"Agreed," Sloan said, and with his words it seemed that the others were given leave to breathe once again. The clatter of fallen swords could be heard all about the planking, and a subdued murmur arose.

"So be it," said Darton.

Brianna vaguely understood that these king's men were about to swear allegiance to another lord, but it mattered very little to her. All that she could comprehend was the state of the ship: the decks had been washed with blood. Men had fallen everywhere.

She brought the back of her hand to her mouth and bit down, totally unaware as she did so that she had begun to take small, jerky steps toward the mast. How many dead? Her mind raged in silent, agonized reproach. Bodies were tangled everywhere. She paused, ready to scream in mindless grief as she looked down at the body of the *Sea Hawk*'s cook, fallen arm-in-arm over the rail with a uniformed graybeard. So many...

Men were beginning to move, to tend to the dead and the moaning wounded. Brianna's eyes swam with blinding tears. Through a thick haze she saw Sloan. His eyes were on her. She stood in blood, was covered with it, and she felt a horror that far surpassed any threat or pain inflicted on her by Matthews.

She had brought it all about. Dear God, not by malice or intent. But simply by her existence. She had crossed Sloan Treveryan's life, and because of it his brave, fine men lay dead and dying all around her.

A sob welled in her throat, choking her. The breeze swept by her and the sun was shining fiercely upon her with all its warmth, all its brilliant life...

But her scream was not one that could be released; it was within her, and would stay with her forever. It was too much; she could assimilate no more of the pain. The breeze, the gentle balmy breeze, swept all around her, embracing her. She could see nothing but mist, and the mist darkened and darkened.

She saw Sloan's eyes again for just a moment, then that striking jade, too, blended with the gray. Merciful, merciful succor came to her. She slid to the deck, unaware that she had fallen, unaware of the day or the sun—or the death about her. She fell like death itself; consciousness deserting her at last, bringing her to a peace she might never find again.

She awoke alone—and mercy was gone, for she immediately recalled her image of the deck with its bloody carnage. A low wail escaped her; she struggled to sit, but as soon as she raised her head, pain seared through it and her stomach twisted in a miserable heave. Her fingers clutched the sheets to fight off the pain, and she looked down at her hands, and at the bed. Sloan's bed. She was back in his cabin.

Brianna closed her eyes again; but then she heard a sound and struggled fiercely to raise herself to the window. There was nothing but the sea, but she did hear men's voices and slowly realized that they were chanting in prayer. Then there was a flash of white going past her, and a startling splash upon the water. For a moment she frowned, puzzled, then what color had returned to her face fled once again. She had awakened only to witness the burial detail. Voices rose again; another white-shrouded body fell, to be accepted by the sea.

Brianna fell back onto her pillow, praying that God would strip her of consciousness again. Mercifully, he did. But dreams tormented her, dreams in which the dead came to her, their wounds bleeding, and accused her of taking their lives to preserve her own.

It was Paddy's dear and grizzled face she saw when next she opened her eyes.

"Paddy?"

"Aye, lass, 'tis me."

"Thank God that you are well."

Gruff Paddy discovered that he had to swallow fiercely; he felt her pain and the overwhelming vastness of her depression.

"Girl, ye've not been well. I've broth, and ye must drink it, lest we lose you too."

"Oh, Paddy," she whispered. "Perhaps I should have died, should die...." Her eyes had closed again, as if she were willing them to remain that way.

He took a deep breath. "Would ye have it, lass, that their lives were given in vain?"

"Nay, nay, but—"

"The lads we lost were fighters. 'Twas their choice to do battle. 'Twas their right as men to rage against such foul injustice. They died with their honor."

She allowed her eyes to close again. "Paddy?" she asked, then hesitated.

"Aye, lass?"

"Sloan—was not injured, was he?" she whispered.

"Cap'n's fine, don't ye worry 'bout that one, now. He's a cat with nine lives—and 'e always lands upon his feet." Paddy paused but a moment. "He has much on his mind, now, girl. We hover off the coast, as the ship must have certain repairs made afore we can set sail for the Netherlands. There is a need for haste, as William of Orange has long been expecting him. Yet he must take grave care with his choice of port now, lest we find ourselves engaged in battle again."

"I don't understand," Brianna murmured. "Matthews is dead; I saw him fall. Where is the danger now? Dear God, am I forever to bring about death and misery?"

Paddy sighed. "Nay, girl—you are no cause of this, except as victim. In killing Matthews, Sloan became an outlaw himself—but only as the law stands now. Wise men, when given the full facts, will know that Matthews was no true seeker of justice, or firebrand against true witchery. I believe myself that the man was grievously ill, and death his only release. He did not uphold the law, but only time will tell this true. There are many across the land— the firm and pious Britains of many persuasions—who believed Matthews to be an animal, and they would cheer his death by Sloan. But My Lord Treveryan is known to be ardently in favor of James's abdication. The Papists would not welcome him. Therefore, we must assure ourselves that we make port in a community of those who are staunchly Protestant, and looking toward Holland too."

The girl sighed softly, and Paddy was glad, for it seemed that her conscience had been somewhat eased. But then her eyes met his again and they were stricken with misery.

"What of Robin, Paddy?"

The old seaman had been sitting at the foot of her bed. He rose and shuffled about uncomfortably.

"Robin...well...uh..."

"Paddy! Please, don't lie to me or hedge about! Tell me, is his wound healing, or not?"

"He's fighting a fever," Paddy said simply. "We know not if he can best it, as it ravages fiercely. But you must not be downhearted, for his chance at life at all comes from your quick thinking to remove the arrow."

"Dearest God!" Brianna moaned, and she thought to rise.

But she realized then that the covers upon the bed were all that clothed her, and with a puzzled frown, she thought, too, that her flesh was not grimed by salt or grit, that her scent was rather one of soap and something else—something sharp and medicinal. She glanced at Paddy, her puzzlement obvious. He cleared his throat.

"Girl, you carried frightening wounds yourself. Holes upon your back and breast, matted with blood. I seek not to embarrass you, but we had no choice but to tend to those wounds—"

She smiled, so wearily that Paddy thought his heart would break. "I'm grateful, Paddy. And you mustn't worry that I feel shamed or humiliated. I don't believe anything could cause me shame again...." Her voice trailed for a moment. "Not after Matthews," she continued softly. She met his gaze. "That friends should have cared for me warms my heart. Yet, how long have I lain so, out of touch with the hours?"

"A day, no more."

She nodded gravely, then said, "Paddy, I would see Robin."

He shook his head. "You must eat the soup. When morning comes, if you are strong enough, I will take you to Robin." He rose, trying very hard to smile cheerfully. "If you wish to be strong, then you must eat the soup."

His ploy worked. She nodded slowly, then reached for the broth. He left her then, certain that she would comply.

Brianna did comply. She ate the broth, but she could not rouse herself from lethargy. She lay there, finding that not even her thoughts could torture her to feeling. She was numb, and nothing more.

When morning came again, though, a natural mechanism forced her to rouse herself. She tried to crawl from the bed and discovered that the cabin careened crazily when she did so. She fell back to the bed, astounded by her weakness. But then she tried again, and very carefully came to her feet, found clothing in the wardrobe, and dressed herself.

She sat on the bed then, clasping her hands together, accustoming herself to an upright position. A dull pain beat against her heart as she wondered why she hadn't seen Sloan. It seemed highly likely that he had at last decided she was not worth one tenth of all the trouble she had caused. Perhaps it was best. He would cast her from him now, surely. For now, she prayed with ever mounting fervor to remove herself from his life. Not for honor—after her time at Matthews's feet she was not sure she would ever know the meaning of the word again—but because of him. Her love for him had grown and multiplied until it seemed entirely a part of her; but surely he despised her, and if he did not, he would grow to. It was, once again, very strange. Life was the greatest gift, but in its receiving, she had discovered again that it was a gift that must be lived by the heart, soul, and mind. She was alive, and being who she was, she could not be the man's mistress—or his whore.

Paddy came to the cabin as she sat there, and seemed distressed to see her up and gowned. "Ye do not take care—"

"You said that I might see Robin."

"But the surgeon says that there is naught which can be done fer young Robin that he is not doing already! The lad must fight the poison with the strength of youth and, lass, ye've just opened yer eyes after a fair injury and bout with the devil of yer own! Ye haven't the strength."

"I must see him. I will do so with or without your help," Brianna said softly but firmly.

Paddy muttered under his breath, certain that Sloan wouldn't approve one bit. But the captain was closeted in the hull with Lord Darton. The military man was telling of the latest developments in London regarding the coveted crown and the mood of the people.

"All right, lass. We'll go see Robin, and then ye'll come back here with me like a little lamb and take yer own rest again."

"Agreed, Paddy," Brianna said, but then, strangely, she hung back.

"What is it, girl?" he asked her.

She shook her head. "Nothing. I am ready. I was just thinking that—that surely the men must despise me."

Paddy stared at her in surprise, and then shook his head as he gripped her arm to escort her. "Nay, lass. There's none who despise ye! Those lads are crowing like a pack of roosters with their victory! 'Tis nothing they enjoy so much as routing the likes o' that black-hearted murderer!"

Brianna didn't quite believe him, but she said no more as he led her through the ship.

He brought her to a section of the *Sea Hawk* where she had never been before, a deck below the galley and the guns but above the cargo hold. It was composed of dual stairways and countless small cabins; the cabins were for the officers, the dual stairways were a quirk of Sloan's which he had demanded when the ship was built. Sloan, Paddy said, had been but a youth when Charles II had fought the Anglo-Dutch wars, but he had never forgotten the cries of his mates trapped in their burning ship. Regardless of the expense, Sloan had ordered that the *Sea Hawk* offer her men every possible means of escape should the majestic lady ever catch fire.

Brianna nodded vaguely as she noted a man exiting the cabin door toward which Paddy was leading her. It was the gunner, Geoff, a man of mature years with heavily muscle-bound shoulders but gentle brown eyes.

He had been frowning, but when he saw Brianna, he smiled with swift pleasure. "Ah, Mistress MacCardle! How fine it is to see you up and about!" He clutched her hand and kissed it with warmth and respect, leaving Brianna feeling a bit awed and vastly cheered by his tender emotion. "We feared for you, sweet lady!"

"Thank you, Geoff," she murmured "Thank you so very much...you, and all of the crew."

"Ah, 'twas our sweet pleasure to battle the

likes of Matthews! Seein' them slip that noose 'bout your lovely throat, 'twas enough to make devils o' the lot of us, lady!"

"Bless you," she murmured. Then she asked worriedly, "Were you with Robin? How is he doing?"

Geoff looked past to Paddy. "I was on my way to find the captain and that surgeon of Lord Darton's. I'm afraid that poor Robin's fever grows. Paddy, if you will stay with him—"

"We will stay with him," Brianna said.

"Nay, 'tis not a sight for a lady."

Brianna swept by Geoff, placing her hand firmly upon the door. "Then it is well that I am 'Mistress MacCardle,' and not 'Lady,' for I do intend to be with Robin."

She awaited no word from either man, but pushed her way through to the cabin. It was much smaller than the captain's cabin, and it was sparsely furnished with just a bunk and a small chest of drawers. The stench within the cabin was grim, yet the 'sight' that Geoff feared would be too much for her tender senses was not strongly repellent.

Robin lay twisting upon the sheets, mumbling in the throes of his fever. He was shirtless, and his breeches had been slashed upon his thigh. The arrow wound had obviously been treated beyond Brianna's efforts, and a smoothly constructed bandage cradled the injured leg, giving credence to the careful talents of the newly acquired surgeon.

No, it was not the appearance of the carefully tended wound that was tearing upon the heart, but the strain and agony in the whitened features of the youth. The poison, causing the wound to fester beneath its clean linen covering, was permeating Robin's blood.

Brianna knelt beside the lad and found the damp cloths with which Geoff had been cooling the boy's body. Tenderly she smoothed the tawny hair from his forehead and bathed his face. "Paddy! Come and help me! We must cool his back as well as his front, or the fever will merely settle!"

Paddy hurried to her side. Geoff watched them for a moment, and then murmured something about finding the captain.

For once, Brianna was not thinking of Sloan Treveryan but of Robin, who was raving.

"The lad is delirious, Brianna," Paddy said sadly. "Are ye sure we're doin' right? Shouldna we be coverin' the boy up?"

"Not when he's this hot, Paddy. He is burning inside and out and his mind will be damaged if...if he lives and we cannot cool him quickly. Lift him now, so that I can cool his back."

Tirelessly, Brianna and Paddy worked over their patient. Brianna kept talking to Robin, soothing him, though he did not hear her. So involved was she that she did not notice when the cabin door opened once more and Geoff returned —with the weary surgeon and Sloan.

She was startled when a gaunt and weary white-haired man knelt down beside her, placing his hand upon Robin's brow. He looked to the boy first, but then smiled at Brianna.

"You're doing quite well with the boy, lass. Perhaps he is at last fighting the fever."

"I'll move, sir, so that you may get to him."

"Nay, girl, for you do more than I can at this time."

Robin's eyes suddenly opened; they were glassy with fever and pain.

"It hurts!" he cried. "Dear God, it hurts like fire! It twists in me like a knife. Please, God, let me die...."

A furious spasm suddenly riddled his body, and then he stiffened, shuddered violently once more, and lay still. His youthful heaving chest rose no more.

The surgeon rose. "I'm afraid, lass, that there is nothing more any of us can do."

Brianna could not believe that Robin— brave, cocky young Robin—had died. She sobbed out his name with the pain of it and leaned forward to clasp his body, willing it all to be a mistake.

But it was not. Even as she sobbed, George and Paddy caught hold of her and hauled her away; the surgeon draped the covers over Robin's ravaged face. Still Brianna did not see Sloan, for her face was buried in Paddy's chest, the old man comforting her as best he could. Sloan watched the scene silently, his sorrow for Robin deep, his heart a tempest for the woman he loved. Paddy was looking to him for help, Sloan knew, but he felt entirely helpless. She had almost died to escape. Better to leave her with Paddy, who had earned her caring and respect.

Paddy, nodding to Sloan, led the sobbing girl from the room.

Sloan paused only a minute at Robin's side. "You were the best of seamen, the best of men, my young friend."

"He rests in the hands of God," the surgeon said quietly.

"Aye, surely he must," agreed Sloan, and turning, he left the cabin. They were at anchor that day, and half the crew were on guard. There was little for to do, since he and Lord Darton knew it would be best to allow a few days to pass before leaving for another port.

He could not return to his own cabin. Perhaps he had to find his own peace before he could even attempt to console her. That night he found his peace in a bottle of rum.

When Robin's body was cast into the sea, it was Paddy, Geoff, and young George who stood beside her. And even as Sloan ached for Robin, he was seared with an envy that he despised. He could not help loving her, but still he could not go to her. Paddy later informed him that George and Lord Darton had tended to her like two mother hens, escorting her to the galley for a meal, returning her to his cabin. Paddy looked at Sloan very reproachfully as he talked, but then Paddy was aware that he had been spending his nights in the chartroom since Port Quinby. But Sloan had nothing to say to his first mate except that he chose to be left alone. Paddy did not leave the chartroom quickly enough, and so Sloan departed himself with an angry exclamation.

He hurried along the hallway. His boots clipped crisply across the flooring as he sought the companion ladder to climb topside. He needed time to feel the sea and the wind, to watch the great sails of the ship billow proudly against the velvet night sky. The wind had always been his true mistress, the unpredictable sea his tempestuous love. Perhaps they would reclaim him, or at least fill him with new strength. Work their form of magic upon his soul...and return to the staunch guise of indomitability that was the trademark of Sloan Treveryan, His Grace, the Fourteenth Duke of Loghaire.

The "devil" master of the swift and cunning *Sea Hawk* and a man so enamored of a blue-eyed lass that he trembled beneath a clear sky, searching for answers within the stars.

Matthews was now dead. Brianna was going to assume that made her safe, that she had every valid reason to demand that he set her free to reach her family. But she wouldn't be safe until William was king, and her records could be swept clean of the witchcraft accusations. She was an outlaw, just as he had become. She was going to have to stay aboard the *Sea Hawk* and he was going to have to tell her so.

He emitted a loud oath, suddenly furious with himself. Then he gripped his ship's rail and exhaled a long breath. He was Lord Treveryan, the master of his ship. He had twice wrested her from the hands of a true devil. He could command her, for he was a man who had rightfully and unquestionably made her his.

But he did not seek to command. He sought to be loved. And to give her his love. But he could not give her the one thing she so heartily desired. He could not give her his name.

Chapter 11

"Ah, Brianna, it was not my choice to be assigned to the likes of Matthews," Lord Stuart Darton said as he sat opposite Brianna in the galley. "I am a soldier, a fighting man. I've little knowledge of the law." He shrugged, then stared up at her. "Odd, though, I did not doubt Matthews's ability. Not until he accused Sloan. I could not believe Lord Treveryan of all men to dabble in wizardry!" He shook his head. "It did not seem plausible. And yet I am convinced that Matthews believed you both truly to be the devil's representatives on earth."

Brianna stared at Lord Darton curiously. He was a tall, muscular man with snow-white hair, and a face wrinkled with the years. And he had been very kind to her.

Robin's death was a cruel blow to her heart. Sloan wanted no part of her, and that increased her heartache. She had not even been able to thank him for risking his crew and his life to save her. For long hours she had lain in the cabin thinking that she would have welcomed death in Robin's stead. Lord Darton and

George had brought her back to an acceptance of living. But she stared at him now, curious to know his true feelings.

"Lord Darton," she said at last, "truly, I am not a witch." He smiled slightly and drank a long sip of his ale.

"I believe you," he told her, leaning slightly across the table so that his fading blue eyes seemed to touch hers. "But do not judge the law too harshly, girl, for witches do exist."

"Do they?" Brianna asked skeptically.

"I've seen them," Darton said simply. "Six months ago in Norwich we did bring to trial one Anne Gilligan. She argued with a neighbor, then told him he would die that night. The poor man did. When the warrant was sworn out, Anne Gilligan's house was searched. She had fashioned a doll of straw and stuck numerous pins into it. She confessed to the murder and she was quite proud of her craft."

Brianna lifted her hands helplessly. "But, Lord Darton, you tell me of one woman. I know that I am not a witch, and therefore I must believe that many are falsely accused."

There was a sound of dry laughter beside them and Brianna smiled slightly as George slid onto the bench at her side. "Ah, Lord Darton! You should hear Captain Treveryan on this subject! He is very opinionated! Sloan says that it is not witchcraft that kills or injures, but the very fear of it."

Darton shrugged. "Perhaps. I know little of the matter."

"Ro—" George broke off quickly, looking

at Brianna. He exhaled a long breath, then decided to speak. "Robin also had strong views on the subject. His grandfather was hanged as a warlock."

"He was?" An ache grew in Brianna's heart, and yet she was glad that George was telling her this.

"Aye. When Cromwell defeated Charles I, a witchfinder named Matthew Hopkins became the scourge of England. Thousands died at his hands." He hesitated. "Robin was quite willing to do battle with Matthews."

"But the devil does exist!" Darton exclaimed. "If we, as good Christians, believe in our God, we must know of the devil."

"I believe in God," Brianna said. "And there might well be a devil. But I know, too, what it is to be innocent—and persecuted."

"Persecution was once much worse," George told her. "They say that James I, back in 1598, had been threatened by a wizard. To extract confession, the wizard was tortured. His fingernails were ripped out and he was beaten unmercifully. Nor are we English alone the barbarians! In one German city, nine hundred witches were executed in one scourge."

Brianna's face paled and her stomach heaved. "George!" Darton cut in sharply. "Take care of your speech, seaman, I charge you."

"I'm sorry," George said quickly. "Brianna, I did not mean—"

"I'm all right, George, truly," she assured

him. But though she had long ignored her own draft of ale, she smiled a little painfully and consumed half of it. Lord Darton was quickly changing the conversation. "Young George, have you heard? Lord Treveryan and I have decided upon Upsinwich as the port in which to berth."

"Upsinwich? 'Tis a Puritan community, is it not?"

"Aye. Men who may not be fond of the Church of England, but who surely stand against the Pope."

Brianna almost choked on her ale. "Puritans?" she inquired.

"Aye," Lord Darton said curiously. "Why do you inquire so?"

"I—uh—I have family of the Puritan persuasion," Brianna murmured. They were not from Upsinwich, but they were not far inland.

She noticed then that both men were staring at her curiously. "What is wrong?" she asked them.

"Oh, nothing," Darton answered quickly.

George hesitated, twisting his jaw. "Brianna, this Matthew Hopkins who executed so many witches with such zeal was a Puritan."

She stared at George, then laughed, a thing she had thought she might never do again. "George! The Powells are my family! They are kind and good and wonderful, I promise you."

George shrugged. "I'm sorry, Brianna. It's just that I do find their leanings to be strange." He finished his ale quickly. "I must be back on duty. Brianna—may I take you to your cabin?"

She did not get a chance to answer. Darton was sighing and rising. "I, too, must meet with the men who were under my command. George, you will see to Brianna?"

"Aye, aye, sir!" George said respectfully, and Brianna went with him back to the lonely cabin.

But at least now she had something to think about other than grief. If they came into Upsinwich, she would have the opportunity, possibly, to receive news on the Powells. And since it seemed quite obvious that Sloan no longer cared...

She stood still in the center of the cabin, knotting her fingers together in her lap as she fought a wave of surging depression. When he had come for her, when he saved her...

Somehow she had dreamed that he would sweep her into his arms and hold her as if she were a fragile flower, a precious gem. And he would whisper that he could not have stood it had she died, that his life would have no meaning without her; that he would tell her he would ignore all obstacles, all barriers of class and nation and creed—and make her his wife.

"Fool!" she whispered aloud, yet she found herself racing the short distance across the cabin to hurl herself on the bed, and though she had been certain that she had already been bled dry of tears, she cried once more. All the while she tried furiously to tell herself that surely she had learned that life was the most wonderful gift, and Sloan owed her nothing more, for twice he had granted her that gift. Whatever her future held, she was blessed to be alive.

Her tears at last dried and she rose numbly to pace the cabin and at last to stare blankly upon the wardrobe. Sloan's treatment of her was all for the best, for she must find infinite strength if she was going to be able to offer him her most heartfelt gratitude—yet plan to leave him still. Quietly. She would never risk a recurrence of what had happened at Port Quinby, though such a thing could not happen again, Matthews being dead.

But her life still remained a question—one with little hope of a decent answer. And she was worried now that she could bring trouble and heartache to the Powells.

Her thoughts and the beat of her heart seemed to cease simultaneously as she heard the rasp of the door. She did not turn, but she knew that Sloan had entered the room. His presence was as dominating as his character; his masculine scent of clean air and sea wafted about her like a breeze.

She turned, facing him. He had come to her at last. It was wrong, but she knew the greatest joy.

"My lord?" Her query was breathless. She could not read or understand what his tensely drawn features concealed. He closed the cabin door firmly behind him, and then leaned against it, arms staunchly folded across his chest. He opened his mouth as if to speak, but no words came. He cleared his throat impatiently, and when his words came they were husky and harsh.

"Girl, if you ever pull a stunt again such as that one at Port Quinby, I'll tie you to the mast!"

Brianna winced painfully and stared down at her fingers as she swallowed and breathed deeply. Still, her voice was barely above a whisper. "I can never tell you how sorry I am that I caused so much trouble and grief. I put not only your life in danger, but the lives of your entire crew. I brought about so many deaths."

"You did not, Brianna. Matthews did."

She lowered her head, wishing not to dispute him in her heart. "Sloan, twice you risked your own life for mine—"

"Damn it! It is not my life that worries me, and although I readily admit that the lives of my crew are dear to me, those men are fighters trained and ready—and quite pleased when given an excuse to wage war against the likes of Matthews. Brianna, you made me half insane with worry. What if Matthews hadn't been there? You didn't need a fanatical witchfinder to bring you to grief! Port Quinby is a dangerous town for a girl alone. You might well have found your way to the slave marts of the East!"

"I could never thank you adequately—even if my life were to stretch a century—for all that you have done for me! When that noose was about my neck I was certain that I would die, and never, never could I have known how precious life is—until that instant. Never can I repay that!"

"Brianna!"

His voice silenced her, and she at last allowed herself to look up into his eyes, which held such turmoil that they frightened her.

"Brianna," he repeated more quietly, "when I knew that Matthews had you I was ill. I wanted to tear him limb from limb. I swore that if he had touched you, done you harm, I would sever into bits. Dear God, you little fool! I would battle any man for you again and again, peasant or king."

"Sloan—?"

"Hear me out! I meant what I said. I would kill for you. I would die for you. But so help me God, girl, don't go dancing into the hands of the enemy again! Don't think to defy me so foolishly!"

"Sloan, please, you don't understand."

"I am not sure that I care to," he said violently, pushing away from the door to stalk toward her. "But then maybe I do already. Do you find a gentler man in young George? Or perhaps Lord Darton's staid age is to your fancy?"

"George! Lord Darton?" she repeated incredulously, and then her anger rose. "You come to me now with vile accusations? Nay, I seek neither of them—as husband or lover. All I have ever sought from you is the freedom to find my own flesh and blood! How dare you, Sloan! When I was shocked and bereaved, when I despised myself for the death of poor loyal Robin, they were there, to help me, when you were not!"

"But you did not want me! How many

times, mistress, have you made that abundantly clear!"

"I did long to tell you of sorrow—and gratitude."

He turned from her, sauntering to his desk and turning about to casually take his chair. He swung his boots atop the desk and laced his fingers behind his head.

"Sloan, Matthews is dead. Now I must leave the ship."

"Leave!" He raged suddenly. "Are you insane? As I am an outlaw, so are you! I pray that we can reach Holland in one piece."

"But—"

"Brianna, that is the sorry state of it. Under William's rule I can see your name cleared. But until then... Tell me, Mistress MacCardle, just what would you have me do. You must understand why I cannot set you off the ship."

"I..." *Foolish man!* she wanted to scream. *I would have you marry me, I would have you love and cherish me with death itself the only thing to break the bonds of God.*

"Ah, yes, lass, I know. You still cannot be my mistress. It is not enough that a man is willing to lay down his life."

He sounded bitter.

She held still, afraid to move. Still he used the word *mistress*. She knew how she loved, how she longed for him. Yes, he would fight for her, as he would fight for his ship, for his men, for the Prince of Orange and Princess Mary, to whom he had sworn his fealty.

She met his eyes and lifted her hands,

200

encompassing the cabin. "You are the master of the ship; you are the captain, Lord Treveryan. You are His Grace, the Duke of Loghaire. The commands are yours. You spoke the order, and I reside within your cabin. The strength is yours. The power is yours. You commanded, and I was yours."

"Brianna! I never—"

His voice was a warning, a threatening growl; his boots hit the floor and he was back on his feet.

"Stop! Please, I beg you!" She lifted her hands against him, and the sudden entreaty in her voice held him still.

"You did not ravage or rape me, Sloan, but perhaps what you do is worse, for you seduce me, when you know it is not my will to be seduced! You say that I want you, and, aye, Sloan, that is true! That I cannot pretend to deny! Just as I want to thank you for the gift of my life with my arms about you, to hold you, cherish you. But, Sloan, for God's sake, have mercy! Oh, don't you understand yet, you fool!"

He was staring upon her so curiously, so gently, and now she understood what emotion had been in his eyes: it was pain. He took another step toward her, so that they were almost touching again, so that she could too clearly feel the strength and heat of his muscular form, too dearly wish to reach out and touch the sinewed cords of his neck, the thick dark hair that feathered coarsely at the opening of his silk shirt.

"Sloan!" Her voice was a sob as she backed away. "Don't you see, Lord Treveryan, it is no longer my honor at stake! In all that has come to pass that has been truly brutal and cruel, I am most painfully aware that my loss of innocence at your hands was a gentle thing—never truly shameful, for in Port Quinby I came to discover true shame. I watched men die for me, and what then was my honor? But, Sloan, as I live, I must seek to save my soul! I cannot afford to need you further than I do! Sloan, you are a gallant man, but the day will come when a new maiden takes your fancy, and it will be she whom you will desire! And then I shall be lost. I cannot be your mistress, for the fact is that I do need you and there is nothing you can do or say to change that."

"Is there not?" he asked her quietly, taking that last step so that she was crushed into his arms and held tenderly. She felt the beat of his heart and the touch of his hands on her hair as he cradled her against his chest, and then he pulled away from her and led her to sit on the bed. He sank to one knee before her and kissed the palms of her hands with gentle reverence. "Dear God, Brianna, can you not love me, can you still deny me, even knowing that I love you with all my heart and soul, my strength and purpose?" he whispered, seeking the answer within her eyes.

"What?" she murmured.

"I love you, Brianna. I swear, before God and all that is holy. I swear upon my life that

I love you, and will love you all the days that I may live."

Tears slid down her cheeks. He lifted his thumb to brush them tenderly away. She threw her arms about his neck and held him, marveling at the simple beauty of holding him close. He loved her. And love...love could conquer anything!

"Nay, Sloan," she whispered. "I cannot deny you. I love you." She repeated his name with tender love and reverence, but couldn't summon words to describe the depths of her emotions. There was so much of him she wanted, so much of herself she yearned to give.

"Beloved, beloved witch..." he murmured in reply.

Her eyes rose to his, filled with the sweet beauty and promise of her heart. The last rays of her tears glistened upon the deep blue of those glorious pools, and Sloan realized that never before now had he known the simple wonder of such an overwhelming love. At long last he managed to speak, and his voice rang with conviction. "I swear to you, that I will never for a moment forget you, that I will care for you always."

She felt dizzy with the incredible delight of his words. He loved her as he loved his life; he would make her a part of his life. He would never for a moment forget her. They would marry, have a fine home filled with the laughter of children, and forever they would love each other. Perhaps it was wrong to find such happiness in the wake of tragedy, but she could not believe that anyone could begrudge her this love when she had learned so much of the terrors of life. She could barely think; all she could do was look at him trembling with wonder.

He caught her fingers and massaged them with his, then kissed each individually. Desire, warm and delicious, began to sweep through her like the relentless push of the tide.

She shakily extracted her fingers from his and began to undo the buttons of his shirt, her eyes upon her task. She felt the rush of his breath when her fingers touched his bare chest.

His arms swept around her and his lips crushed hers hungrily, devouring with need and tenderness. He drew apart from her again, trembling as he held her away. "Sweet witch, your magic has more strength than my will. This is a temptation that I cannot deny...."

Again his mouth came to hers and his tongue parted her lips and elicited the most tantalizing elixir of ardent response. For a long while they kissed deeply, holding each other in a passionate embrace. But at last he broke away from her, peeled away his shirt, and when his chest was bare, she had to explore the thick dark hair that covered its expanse, her eyes following the touch of her fingers with fascination. She noted all wonderful things, the tensing muscles beneath her fingers, the clean line of his collarbone, the hard rounded sinews of his arms and the curling trail of hair which became so slender as it narrowed to his breeches.

She set her hands upon the drawstring,

and again delighted in the force of his shudder, the catch of his breath. The tide of yearning washed over her again, leaving a fire that blazed and wound within her abdomen and sent her quivering.

The string about his breeches gave under her questing fingers. Her feminine wiles were quickly igniting him to excitement unlike any he had felt before. Her fingers slid over the tensely knotted firmness of his hard-muscled buttocks. Each graze of her nails sent his senses spiraling to a higher pinnacle of arousal, each movement of her lips against his sent him deeper under her unique bewitching spell.

This was no cunning seduction game for Brianna. She longed for him and she needed to touch him. Her lips traveled over his chest and she paused at his hard nipple feathered with dark hair. She grazed it with her teeth, nipping, tasting the salt spray and his intoxicating maleness. Her hands and fingers moved caressingly, and as he stood, she slowly lowered his breeches down his trim hips until she knelt to peel them from his strong legs. She was overwhelmed with the wonder that he was hers, that she was free to love him so, that she could create the racing of his blood and incite his desire.

"Dear God!" His husky groan touched her heart and thrilled her senses. "You *are* a witch, you love me as no other..."

He broke off with a gasp as she slid her hands over his legs, luxuriating in their strength. With the innocence and curiosity of

Eve she pressed the moist heat of her kisses along his calves and then moved upward, to his knees, and to the tightly wired muscles of his thighs.

"Brianna!"

He was down beside her with his hands on her shoulders, holding her. She met his flaming eyes, and then his lips were on hers, ravaging, and yet tender. He ripped away the flimsy material of her gown.

Then he froze, and abruptly withdrew from her.

"What is wrong?" she cried, wondering desperately what could have overtaken him with such horror.

Then she felt his hands on her again, gently touching those spots where the pick had broken her flesh. "Damn fate that I cannot kill that man a thousand times again!" he swore.

She clutched his head to her breast, breathing a sigh of relief. Her fingers moved through his hair and she brokenly assured him, "There is no pain, Sloan; that is in the past. Please, don't leave me! Your touch is the greatest balm."

"I would not hurt you—"

"Then love me, and let him come no more between us."

So tenderly did he touch her, his lips were a cooling breeze to every small hurt. She could not bear to go slowly, and pleaded that he set his passion free. He responded to her entreaties and allowed the leashed desire of many cold and lonely nights to unfold and soar.

She was lifted high and the remainder of her clothing impatiently drawn from her. He laid her down on the bed, and she met the blaze of his eyes with yearning invitation, her slender arms outstretched. The heat of anticipation that raced through her could mount no higher, and intuitively she shifted her long legs to receive him; but he smiled as he knelt beside her and brushed a kiss against the column of her throat.

"Not yet, my beloved witch...not yet. Magic is eternal...."

His hand moved to the juncture of her thighs and she gasped out his name as she convulsively arched to him. He smiled at her, his ravenous needs drawing his features tight, yet still he waited, watching her, reveling in the undulation of her form, hips writhing, breasts arching.

"Sloan..."

His kisses muffled her words as he touched her, and his mouth followed his expert and reverent fingers, knowing the swell of her hip, the dip of her belly, the slender length of her thigh, and the flowering of her deepest desires. His name was not a whisper when it gasped from her throat, but an ardent cry. And she could no longer lie prone, but twisted to rise and meet his embrace. He buried her face against his neck. "Now, my love," he murmured.

He lifted her chin and their lips melded, fiery and sweet. When he at last brought his body to hers, their joining was as smooth as a silken embrace, and velvet strokes became a tempest of nature, a maelstrom of wild, shuddering ecstasy. Rapture soared to sun-drenched peaks, and soared onward yet again, his rhythmic, pulsing strength demanding the ultimate triumph while ever seeking the ultimate intimacy, as if he could touch her soul and truly make them one.

Their rapture at last reached its shuddering pinnacle and burst with volatile brilliance. A thousand golden snowflakes littered the warm air about them as they lovingly, tenderly clung together and allowed the satiation of love to still the mad beating of their hearts.

He buried his face in the damp web of her luxurious hair. "Glorious witch," he murmured. "Beautiful, beautiful witch. Ever more you entice me, ensnare me, until I feel I am not whole unless I can experience your touch and see the love in your eyes. Ah, Brianna, never have I known anything so sweet as your love."

Brianna smiled, wondering if her happiness could ever be greater. It was as great as the rapture he created in her. For a moment, a chill passed over her heart. She became afraid, for the rapture of their lovemaking flew so high and crested so intensely, swathing her with pleasure so great it was almost unbearable.

And then it ebbed. Gone, until it should be nurtured again.

Could happiness, could love, follow that same sweet route? Growing ecstasy, a moment's wonderful glory—and then a fading as irrevocable as the yearning for release.

No! She stopped her silly, fearful thoughts. No! For the rapture between them did not end with that release; the moments after, when he held her, were just as dear, just as awesomely sweet. Her happiness, her love, would also soar and peak and crest. It would find calm and it would find storm, but always it would be nurtured.

She curled into his arms, forcing the chill of fear to leave her and savoring the repletion of her body and soul. "I love you so much, Sloan," she murmured, limbs entangling naturally with his. "You are a part of me, milord, the part that is my heart."

He loved her. He loved her. He would make her his wife, and she would happily follow him anywhere until the end of her days.

Chapter 12

For Brianna, the early morning was as full of wonder as the night. The sun rose gently, creeping through the starboard window like a silken pink mist. Bathed and shrouded in that tender glow, she curled against Sloan, her fingers against his chest. She did not seek to wake him; she was happy just to lie there, basking again in the knowledge that he loved her. And at his side she could learn to live again—forgive herself for all that had occurred, and learn to forget the horror of Matthews's touch, the feel of a rope about her throat, the scent of death in the roar of a fire.

He was not sleeping. He stroked her hair until she tilted her head and looked upward, smiling a little shyly into his eyes.

"I love you," she whispered.

"And I you." He returned her smile, and his arms held her tightly but tenderly. Then he drew away slightly, for he longed to look at her, to bask not only in her beauty but in the warmth of her smile.

She nuzzled closer to him, pressing her cheek against his chest once more. She sighed softly, a contented and yet sorrowful little sound that shook her.

"Oh, Sloan! If only Matthews had not somehow chased us to Port Quinby. If only Robin and your other fine men had not died."

"Hush," he told her, frowning as he stroked a lock of her hair over the healing wound on her shoulder where Matthews had stabbed her with his pick. "He wanted my blood as much as yours."

"But it was my fault he wanted it to begin with," she said mournfully. "Had I not stumbled upon you in Glasgow, you would now be peacefully on your way to your prince. And Robin and the others would still be alive."

"You can't punish yourself for what happened, Brianna. We are a crew of men trained to fight—be it pirates, or even the king's forces, should they not accept William."

She twisted her head upward once again and

saw that he was staring out the window, watching as the pink light of the sun suddenly flared with a stroke of gold and crimson. There was something tense about his face, which was not unusual, except that last night... last night he had seemed to lose the hardness of his countenance; he had seemed younger, lighter of heart and spirit than she could remember. He was not a solemn man, but he was stubborn and determined, and ever sure of his course of action. Last night she had seen the lines ease, and laughter come to him again.

"You truly hate King James with all your heart, don't you?" she asked now.

His gaze came quickly from the window to her. "I don't know anymore," he said, watching her with a small smile. "He executed a man who was committing treason in his eyes; what I cannot bear is that Jemmie was his own blood, and that he pleaded for his life and lost it anyway." He paused, noticing how she watched him, aware that in the blue depths of her eyes there was a longing to understand everything about him. He stroked her cheek. "I cannot tell you what it was to have grown up with Jemmie Scott, Brianna. When I was a lad, he was everything. At times, my only friend. So like Charles. Willful—but generous of himself in every way. He knew he was his father's son, and he knew the English people did not want a Catholic succession. He was young and very brave and, with the right guidance, would have made a very fine king.

The only thing that stood between him and the crown was his bastardy. When I heard of the execution, I despised James. I longed to kill him with my bare hands. Yet now—I think I pity him. I've searched my soul over this, and I can now say that I join William and Mary because I believe they will be best for England."

Brianna raised herself up, planting a light kiss softly against his lips. "You are truly," she told him, "a knight in the most shining armor!"

He burst out laughing, rolling over to pin her beneath him. "A knight, eh? Nay, love, a salt-ridden man born to a title, nothing more. But I am deeply gratified to hear you call me so, for it is far kinder than anything you had to say when first we met!"

She laughed, too, delighted that life could remain ever more sweetly beautiful with the coming of day. And then she was laughing no more, for the tenderness in his eyes did take flame and she felt her flesh heat with his desire. He brought his lips to hers, kissing her slowly, and soon their arms and limbs were entwined with the eager passion of their love.

Later, feeling wholly languorous and as satisfied as a sleek black cat, Sloan sighed and dragged his legs over the bed, stretching before he stood. Brianna watched the muscle play of his back and quivered a bit, wondering that she should be loved by such a man. But she did not doubt that she was, and that, too, touched her with wonder.

He pulled on his breeches and reached for

his shirt, wishing fervently that the ship did not need repairs so he could order Paddy to take command for a day of leisure.

" 'Tis very hard to leave you," he told her.

"Is it?" she asked him.

He dropped his shirt and knelt down beside her, curling a lock of her hair about his finger with abject fascination. "Aye. 'Tis so hard that I can barely do it. So easily could I climb beneath the sheets again, between the silken embrace of your bewitching thighs! Forgetting all, lamenting not. Forgetting that we are outlaws and prime picking for a navy of hangmen."

Alarm jumped to her eyes. She shoved at his chest. "Go! Get about your business—lecherous swain that you are!" She was teasing him, but she was not. He shrugged and rose, still regretfully. "The situation is not that bad," he admitted. "We'll make port for our repairs, and I believe we'll find cordial welcome. I've come often to Upsinwich," he assured her. "We will make out well, I'm sure."

She stretched out lazily again, closing her eyes with a smile.

"Eh, girl! None of that!" Sloan admonished her with a firm swat upon the derrière that rose temptingly beneath the sheet. "If you would set your feet on land with me, you will get yourself ready now!"

"You'll take me ashore? Is it safe? Not for anything, Sloan, would I cause bloodshed again!"

"You didn't cause bloodshed—and aye,

I'm quite certain it is safe. The town would warn us long before a battle could arise. And I've anchored here these several days to give belief to any enemies that we are halfway to the Orangeman's household."

She was out of the bed before he finished speaking, excitement giving a high flush and beauty to her cheeks and lighting up her eyes like the summer sky beneath a dazzling sun.

"Wear something demure, my love. You're likely to dazzle the steadfast morals of these pious folks as it is!"

She tossed her head back imperiously. "I'll have you know, Lord Treveryan, that I'm well acquainted with the Puritan faith! I was raised in it for many years." She noticed the smile that twitched about his lips and queried him sharply.

"What, my lord, is that smirk for?"

"I am not smirking. I merely find it difficult to think of you as an innocent Puritan maiden, that is all."

"Hmmph!" she sniffed, and turned her back on him once again.

She slipped her gown over her head, yet before she could secure it she was struck with a sudden thought, and even as she fumbled with the gown, she was crossing the few steps to him, clasping his arms in high excitement to gain his attention.

"Oh, Sloan, I was thinking! I know that we're entering a Puritan town, but surely, we could find a minister of the Church of England—and we could be married today!"

The smile faded from his features so suddenly and completely that she was stunned, and felt as if she had been covered in ice. His eyes clouded, and she saw the hard jade once again, rather than the verdant warm green of a forest.

"I told you once, Brianna," he said, his voice suddenly harsh and raggedly pained, "I cannot marry you."

Had he viciously slapped her, he could not have given her a crueler blow. Her hands fell from his arms; she backed away from him and stared at him, seeing the implacable set of his face. All thought of laughter departed; it seemed that perhaps a storm cloud had passed over the sun, for neither did the day remain brilliant, but appeared to grow as gray as the pall that had come between them.

Brianna moistened her lips to speak. She did not recognize her own voice, it was so cool and distant. "I do not understand. Last night you promised that you loved me. That you would do so for life. Is your word so light, then, so completely without honor?"

His eyes closed briefly as he struggled with himself. He stepped toward her, reaching out a hand. "No!" she cried, and she feared that she would burst into tears if he touched her. "No! Explain yourself to me!"

"I said nothing that was not true. I love you. I love you with all my being, as I had never thought to know love. From now until my dying day, I swear that I will love you. But I never promised to wed you, Brianna. I told you long ago; I cannot marry you."

"Why?" she shrieked, furiously battling her tears. "Dear God, sir! I cannot understand! Aye, you've risked your life for me, yet still it seems I am lady enough for the sport of your bed but not to bear your name under God."

"Brianna." He came to her then, grasping her arms. She twisted her head from him and tried to fight his grip, but he was firm and would not release her. "Brianna—I am married."

"What?" The word was both cry and whisper. She no longer fought him, but stood dead still, staring at and refusing to accept the finality of what he was saying.

"I am married, Brianna," he said quietly, trying to soothe her, to hold her.

She did not want to be held, or touched, or soothed. She pulled away from him, shaking her head furiously and fighting tears. "Don't, oh, don't! Sloan—"

"Brianna!" He tried to interrupt: she would not allow him.

"How could you, Sloan? You have a wife, yet you determined to keep me too? You had no right—"

"You do not understand!"

"I could never have been anything to you but a mistress!" She was dangerously close to tears. "Never—there was never any chance! Oh, all my dreams! I believed that, yes, you did love me! That there could be a future—"

"I never lied to you!" Sloan charged, clenching his hands into fists at his side, fighting the urge to reach for her, grab her, force her to listen. "If you'd hear me out—"

"And what of your wife? Oh, poor wretched lady! She sits at home, always alone! Wondering, waiting, anxious—while you! A whore in every port!"

"Brianna!" His voice had taken on an edge of warning. She could not take heed; she could not care. Oh! It should have been so obvious! She should have realized. But she had not, and the fantasy had so recently soared. She did not know if she wanted to scream and shout, or dissolve onto the floor in tears.

"How could you?" she repeated. "How could you have done this to me? Surely you knew, you knew that I was falling in love with you, and you did not care! You knew that nothing could ever exist between us, and still you led me on—"

"Brianna!" He was aching so desperately for what was slipping between his fingers that he could barely think. He came to her again, catching her shoulders, holding her fiercely against all her struggles, even when she pounded his chest with futile vengeance. At last he shook her, firmly, and her head rolled back, her eyes met his—stark with hopelessness and bitter resentment. "Let me go, Sloan. Fool that I am, I really did not know."

"I cannot let you go—now or ever!" he thundered to her, shaking her once again. "For the love of God, will you listen to me?"

"To what end?" she demanded heatedly.

"It is not what you believe."

"What I believe? You have just told me that you are married."

"I am married, Brianna. But—"

"Let me go, Sloan!"

"Nay, because I cannot!" Despite her protests he swept her into his arms and pinned her to the bed. He had to make her understand.

"No, Sloan!" she shrieked, her voice breaking.

"Brianna—there is a future. I love you."

"What of your wife?" she demanded, ceasing her struggles, to stare at him with blunt accusation.

"If you would but give me leave, I would explain."

Bitterly, she answered him. "I've no choice, it seems."

His hold on her eased. She plummeted to the depths of despair, and he knew well that her fury came from the misery he hadn't the power to erase. He could only try desperately to make her see, to hold on to what they had.

"Her name is Alwyn," Sloan said, and then he swallowed. To say her name, the woman he had only alluded to, was perhaps one of the most difficult things he'd ever done. "Alwyn does not care—"

"Does not care!"

"Cannot care," Sloan said, ignoring her interruption. He did not know how to plead; he had never pleaded before. But God help him, he had to make her understand. "Brianna, we were wed fifteen years ago. Our estates adjoin. The match was arranged when we were both just infants and we were wed before my twentieth birthday. I was not against the marriage, because I had known Alwyn all my life.

As a girl she was very lovely, and very gentle."
I am not saying the right words, Sloan thought
in anguish. She was so stiff in his arms.
Already, he thought, I have lost her. "Brianna!
You have to understand!"

"Understand, My Lord Treveryan?" she
asked coldly. "I understand quite well. You
are married. You wish me to remain with
you—as your mistress—while you leave a
gentle wife behind."

"Nay! Your tongue is ever sharp!"

"Show me where I am in error!"

"She is mad!"

Brianna held very still for a moment, aware
that his voice and the tension in his body, in
his very hold about her, betrayed a misery deeply
akin to her own.

"Mad?" she whispered.

"Quite," he said bitterly. "Alwyn was always
frail. She trembled at the sight of me once we
were wed. I was ever gentle with her. I let her
be, and I wooed her as graciously as any man
ever wooed his wife. There was a time, when
we were very young, when I came to have
great faith in a fruitful and happy life reaching
out before us. But then—we had a child. A son.
He did not survive three months in this world.
And when he died, all that had been happiness for Alwyn died also. Slowly she began a
retreat from this world. And now..."

"Now what?" Brianna asked him, aware
that his eyes stared unseeingly across the
cabin, that he was watching something a long
way off. He shrugged.

"She barely knows me. She lives in my home, but all she knows is the forest and the pond of the estate where she finds peace. She is cared for by her old nurse, and she keeps cages of exotic birds. She loves to hear them sing, and to watch them fly. When I am at home, I allow her the fantasy that we are children again, and she believes that our fathers are visiting, and that we are together to play—as children."

He stopped speaking, his eyes returned to Brianna's. He wanted her to speak as she longed to do so. Yet it all swirled within her mind and wrought painful constriction in her heart and throat, and she could find no words.

He released her and stood, pacing the cabin. Finally he paused again, leaning against the doors.

"I have not touched her in a decade, Brianna."

Brianna inhaled deeply. "Sloan, I—"

"You must understand," he said, and his features were taut as he searched her countenance. "She is my wife. I never loved her—not as I have learned to love you—and yet she does hold a part of my heart for all that we once were. She is mine to care for, Brianna, and that I do. I beg you not to despise me, for I have come to need you just as I love you."

She had never heard more earnest speech nor seen a man more fraught with pain. She felt no more anger against him. She longed to reach out to him, but could not.

"Sloan," she whispered at last, "I am sorry.

So very sorry, for I believe with all my heart that you do love her. And I believe that you do love me. I—I don't know what to say to you, or what to do. Oh, Sloan! I just can't be your mistress! Taken about from port to port, displayed to the world, with no home, no life, no future...."

"It would not have to be like that!" He came to her then, falling to his knees before her, taking her hands feverishly in his. "Ah, Brianna! Do you think that I would not care for you, that I would not silence the world if—"

"No man can silence the world, Sloan. Not even you," Brianna told him wearily. "But it is not the slights of any that concern me. Sloan, I just don't know that I could bear it; that I could ever forget Alwyn, or"—she paused, searching out his intent and blazing eyes—"Sloan! Have you forgotten how you decry the plight of bastards? Jemmie Scott, dying in his quest for a crown denied because of his birth. Sloan, it frightens me."

"Nay! Brianna, once I swore that I would not inflict such a fate upon a child. But I love you; I long for our child. Brianna, I will leave no legal heirs! Our child—?"

"Will be a bastard," she interrupted simply. "You cannot change that."

"I swear that he will never suffer...."

She smiled at him, feeling numb and exhausted. "Sloan—it is not right. I am an adulteress, and perhaps because of it, we are cursed. Oh, Sloan, look at all that has befallen!"

"I do not believe in curses!" he cried to

221

her passionately. "Nor can you! Brianna, I love you. I would gladly lay down my life for you a dozen times, and a dozen times again."

"I believe that you love me," she whispered.

"But that is not enough?" he demanded bitterly.

"You don't understand—" she began, but before she could say more there was a pounding on the door.

"Approaching port, Cap'n!" Paddy's voice called out.

Sloan lowered his head. "I must be topside," he murmured, and then he was staring at her again, intently. "Brianna..."

"Nay! What can be said? You must take command as we go in."

"You will not leave, me!" he commanded her, and Brianna stiffened regally. "I am not your property, Sloan."

Angrily he dropped her hands and rose. "Nay, you are not property. Is it property you seek? You have my love, and my life, should you require it. All that I deny you is my name, yet for that you would scorn me. Are you no better than the whore I thought had come to me in Glasgow? Is it the position you crave, the titles and the land? On that account, dear girl, you need not be concerned. I always pay well for services rendered—or have you forgotten?"

She leapt up to face him, slashing out hard with the palm of her hand, driven by the fury and the hurt. He caught her wrist hard, twisting her arm behind her back, and bringing her body to his. The angry tension within him frightened her. "Sloan," she gasped, for his hold stole her breath, just as his eyes made her tremble with sudden weakness. She fought it, and challenged him. "Sloan! That you can say such words to me belies all the love you claim for me!"

He lowered his dark lashes. His hold eased and then tightened as he cradled her to him. "Forgive me," he said simply, and she felt the quivering of his hard form.

How dully her heart ached! For all her shattered dreams she could not stop loving him.

"You must go topside," she whispered miserably, pushing away from him.

He nodded, and for several moments his throat was too thick for speech. "Are you coming ashore with me?"

"I—I do not know, yet."

His eyes narrowed. "You must not plan an escape. Matthews is dead, but the danger for you is not. There is always another to take Matthews's place."

"I'm not planning anything."

"We have not finished with this discussion. Before God, I tell you it is not safe for you to run. Brianna! Think of the dead!"

Her face paled, and he was sorry; but he could take no risks. She lowered her head. "Go! You know I will not risk more lives!"

For a brief moment he continued to watch her, but she would not look at him. He turned and quit the cabin for the deck.

*   *   *

An hour later things were going well beyond all expectation in Upsinwich. They'd been welcomed by the workmen at the docks so enthusiastically that he'd felt no apprehension when he was invited to the home of the lord mayor.

The man was a firm member of the Church of England, and Upsinwich proved to be not only a Puritan stronghold, but that strange place, wonder of wonders, where all sects were living in tolerance and peace. By law a Puritan could not hold Lord Patterson's office, yet Lord Patterson seemed beloved by all, if the cheerful words of the dockhands were any true indication of town affairs.

They were barely docked when Sloan received an invitation from Lord Patterson requesting they meet for lunch in a public tavern near the *Sea Hawk*. Barely had Sloan sat down before the lord mayor was lowering his voice to say that he was quite certain his people were expecting the Prince of Orange any day—and would welcome his arrival. But Sloan could give scant attention to Lord Patterson, because Brianna had not come with him, and he could think of nothing but her.

Ah! Not long ago, politics had filled his thoughts. He had been eager for Holland to bring William and Mary to the throne and to see James brought low for his crime of murder. Still he would fight; aye, if Princess Mary and William needed battle, he would gladly go into battle for them. But he did not feel the tearing sense of revenge that had once been his. For all of the tempest between them, Brianna had given him a sense of peace. He wanted her to be most important in his life, to rule his every move.

He was so very afraid. He had never meant to hide his marital status from her. He had told her that he could not marry her and he didn't know that she was dreaming of being his wife. Perhaps it was saddest of all that she seemed to understand about Alwyn. She had not demanded that he seek an annulment or a divorce, and she would never—as his London mistress, Joan, had once done—suggest that Alwyn might be hurried from this life. Nay, Brianna would never do such a thing, because she had learned the wonder of life.

He sighed, though, unable to cease his brooding. She had accepted his situation, and she had promised not to attempt to escape. But he had wrung that promise from her cruelly, he did not know if she had decided to accept him.

"My Lord Treveryan!"

Startled, Sloan gave his full attention to the jovial, red-cheeked man before him. Patterson was short and squat with twinkling blue eyes, but gave the appearance nevertheless that he would be a determined adversary if crossed.

"Your pardon, sir!" Sloan said apologetically.

"Ahh, no pardon needed, sir!" Patterson replied, raising his tankard of ale. "I know you've grave matters of state on your mind! I was saying that the men have promised to give your *Sea Hawk* their most fervent attention. I assure you that no one will come near the town without your knowledge."

"I thank you, sir. But what if you are challenged for harboring outlaws before William arrives?"

Patterson chuckled. "Challenged? But how, sir? I'm a busy man. How would I know what ships come to port? This is England! We have our freedoms, sir."

Sloan chuckled and drank his ale, first lifting his tankard high to Lord Patterson. But for his life he could not keep his mind fully upon the conversation—brooding came to him today as naturally as breathing.

Brianna spent the first hours he had gone, sitting upon the bed. She tried to think and reason, but she could not. All she could do was sit, and feel the dull pain in her heart.

Ah! If only she could hate him! But she believed every word, and her heart and soul ached for all of them. Poor Alwyn, stripped of her child and mind. Poor Sloan, caring for her, denied both the heir he surely craved, and perhaps the possibility finally, truly, of finding love. She could picture his Alwyn, pale and frail, seeking only the company and solace of her birds!

Nay, never could she deny she loved him still. Perhaps she loved him more. But could she stay with him? She trembled slightly, sitting there. She knew that, for him, it was all quite simple and easy. To the eyes of Lord Treveryan there was no hardship in being his mistress. But try as she might, Brianna could never forget that he had a wife. And he was, like all men, a fool. He thought that he could protect her from scandal. He did not realize that she would never be accepted in his world. That should she conceive, their child would be an outcast—shunned, just as his dear friend Jemmie had been shunned. Even King Charles had not been able to protect his son, and Sloan was not a king.

She sighed and began to pace the cabin, barely aware, as she passed back and forth, that she was lovingly touching things. His desk, the bottle of dark rum upon it, the chair behind it. The bedding, the pillows they had shared.

She did have to leave him. Not as she did in Port Quinby—never would she risk others' lives again. But there had to be a way, and tomorrow she would find it. She sat down again, shaking and weakening. Leaving him would be like cutting out her heart. It would be so much easier to stay.

But, dear God, what would happen if he ceased to love her? If the strain of all that lay between them ate at their love until there was nothing left but bitterness? That would be far worse than going now, when at least she could cherish the memory forever.

Paddy had come to tell her that the *Sea Hawk* would remain in Upsinwich for at least two days. Since it was a Puritan community, perhaps she could find word of the Powells—and, with them, a firm bulwark. Not against Sloan's strength—against his love.

But that would be tomorrow. Tonight, tonight she could not leave him. She wanted to hold him and cherish and give him all her love—one last time.

Sloan didn't know what to expect when he returned to the ship. And so he paused outside his cabin door with his heart pounding, his head reeling. He was so afraid she would be gone.

When at last he opened the door, the cabin was dark. Then slowly he realized that a single small candle was burning upon his desk. He stood still, blinking to adjust to the muted light. His heart rose to his throat in anguish; she wasn't there.

But then he heard a slight rustling sound from the bed; his fingers, upon the door, began to tremble. He heard her voice, as soft as the muted candle glow, as sweetly welcoming.

"Close the door, My Lord Treveryan."

He did so, leaning against it, finding that the trembling had spread from his hands to his limbs. He blinked once more, and then he could see her clearly, slowly unwinding her slender body from her curled position on the bed. Her only garment was the sheer white thin shift which barely hid her slender curves. As she walked toward him, he knew he had never seen such a heavenly vision. Her hair was a regal display of gleaming black, curled and waved over her shoulders, playing provocatively over her breasts. Through the gossamer fabric he could see the sway of her hips, the beautiful clean line of her legs, and the fascination of all the secrets in between.

When she came at last to stand before him, he saw her eyes, teal-blue and shimmering in the candle glow. Her knuckles grazed his cheek as their eyes met. He caught her hand, so fine-boned, so delicate. He brought it to his lips and kissed her palm.

She led him to the bed. He followed her, trembling. And he continued to tremble, all through the sweet tempest of their love-making.

When at last they both lay still, filled with their love, he kissed her forehead in reverence and knew that should he die upon the morrow, he had already received the greatest glory on earth. He'd known sensual pleasure before, a good deal of it—but never like this. Because the difference lay in the loving, in the aching to touch the heart as well as the body; in the vast depth of longing to be completely united.

She stirred against him, and he touched her chin to raise her eyes to his. The tenderness he felt for her then was overwhelming, and he was stunned by the sadness he found in her eyes.

"What is it?" he asked her, and she shook

her head. "By God, you must know how I love you!" he told her vehemently.

"I don't deny it," she said softly. "And forever will I be grateful for it." She paused. "All that touched my mind was that it didn't seem right that a the wonder between us should be wrong."

"Ah, my love! Before God I feel that our love is sacred. Brianna, believe what I say now: I would give anything to make you happy. My ship, my land, anything that I hold. You already know that I'd give my life, should you require it. Brianna, the only thing that I cannot do is harm in any way—"

"Hush, Sloan, oh, hush!" She turned to him, fighting back the tears she could not shed. "I could not love you so if you would hurt your wife, who is sick and who bears no ill will to others. Sloan, let it lie. I beg you. Hold me, and talk no more of it."

He did. He held her as he would the most precious thing in his life, for that was what she had become.

Chapter 13

The morning was glorious, and Sloan was convinced as they walked, arm in arm, from the *Sea Hawk* that Brianna had never been more beautiful. He intended to be very discreet, of course. He would not cause her discomfort for anything in the world. But she had been anxious to come ashore, and he had been happy to bring her. He felt that they were safe here. He trusted these people implicitly, because they were determined to go William's way. He would introduce Brianna to the lord mayor as a lady of humble means, traveling to be a companion to Princess Mary of Orange. And, in fact, wasn't that to be the truth?

He smiled at her; she glanced at him, and quickly returned his smile. Sloan frowned then, wondering why she seemed so nervous, for it had been her idea to come ashore. He assured her that he would not have her on shore if he weren't convinced of the wisdom of it. She merely flashed him another smile, and asked him some question about the port town.

She was somberly garbed in forest-green wool, and he watched her with affection as they moved along. Her footsteps seemed tiny today, very ladylike. She had dressed modestly for the Puritan community. He smiled secretively; it was very difficult to equate the demure maid of this morn with the wanton temptress of the night. Her hair was tightly secured at her nape and the neckline of the green gown was at her throat. He lowered his eyes a little unhappily, shivering at an unexpected flash of foreboding. What could be wrong? he wondered. Then he carefully weighed his position again, and came up with the same conclusion. They were quite safe. Perhaps it was just her nervousness—and that terrible sadness he caught in her eyes when she wasn't aware of his scrutiny—that was touching his soul. Yet she loved him, and he her, and in that they were complete. In time she would cease to reflect upon the things that could not change. He would see that she did. By his honor, he vowed silently, he would do everything in his power to make her happy, to give her peace. To let her know that she was cherished as few wives could ever be.

In the tavern the lord mayor became quickly entranced with Brianna, as did a young man joining the party, a very solid sort of citizen in a black coat and black breeches, and a tall black hat, introduced as Luke Farley. As a casual discussion ensued, Sloan quickly learned that he was one of the Puritan leaders.

"We do quite well, here, that we do!" the lord mayor boasted proudly. "We bring about the England that the late Queen Bess, and even His Majesty Charles, did so intend. We don't persecute our people for any religious belief!" He nudged his companion. "Ah, but Luke here is longing to set forth for the Massachusetts Bay Colony—to one of the Puritan towns there! But they are not so tolerant as we, eh, Luke?" He leaned across the table, his merry eyes twinkling. "They send those who are not 'God's chosen' away from God's towns!"

Luke Farley flushed and his fingers tightened a little nervously about his tankard of ale. Then his eyes rose to Sloan's, and he shrugged. "Surely, Lord Treveryan, you are aware that the condition of the Colonies cannot last long. Our charter was rescinded, and even now, we have representatives at court trying to regain it!"

Brianna glanced curiously at Sloan as he answered the young man. "I'm aware of the difficulties, sir. But I'm afraid it will be a long while before the new charter is obtained. James is busy with other affairs now."

"Aye, that he is," Luke Farley murmured, and then again he shrugged. "I do not expect to hear of a charter until William and Mary come to England."

"You are confident of their success?"

"And equally confident that our charter—when it is obtained—will not be the same." He gazed at Brianna. "Forgive me, Mistress Mac-Cardle, for you appear confused by our conversation. Previously, the laws were such that only those of our profession—our religion, as we term it—could hold public office. Perhaps we have been intolerant of others. But please understand that those of the Massachusetts Colonies battled the sea, death, and great loneliness—when they were under persecution!"

Brianna smiled—this was her opening. "Mr. Farley, there is little you need explain to me. I spent my childhood in a Puritan household. In fact, my family are not far from here. Perhaps you know of them. The Powells?"

"The Powells?" Luke questioned her, rather sharply. But Brianna did not have a chance to answer then, for Paddy suddenly appeared at the table, his old hat in his hands as he begged their pardon for the interruption.

"It's sorry I am, Cap'n, to disturb you, but the carpenter wishes to consult with you before doing certain work upon the hull."

Sloan appeared surprised, but not annoyed. He glanced at the party at the table with a grimace. "You'll excuse me, gentlemen, Brianna?"

"You, sir, we must excuse!" The lord mayor laughed. "But I pray, do not deprive us of the company of this lady."

"We will guard her with all our honor," Luke promised solemnly.

"I will return quickly," Sloan promised.

Brianna noticed that he whistled as he left the taproom. In fact, she noted every little thing about him then, the breadth of his shoulders, the assurance of his gait, the darkness of his hair. Everything. With her eyes she followed him until he had left the tavern, and she felt when he departed as if everything that was beautiful in life left with him. She weakened. Tears brimmed on her lashes that she feared she would not be able to blink away, and she brought every rationalization she could think of to the fore of her mind. She could not leave him, she had been a fool to think that she might. But even as she stared after him, her heart seeming to bleed from the pain, Luke Farley was speaking the words that were to sever her from Sloan.

"Mistress MacCardle, you were asking after the Powells. I know them quite well. A number of the family are planning a move to the Colonies."

"Ah, your pardon, sir?" Brianna forced herself to swallow and turn to him.

"Yes. They're leaving in a matter of weeks. If all goes well, I, too, will be a member of the party. In fact, it is quite a coincidence that I should meet you at this time."

"Oh?"

He smiled and leaned toward her. "Dear lady, if you were to rise now and walk to yonder corner, you might find yourself most pleasantly surprised."

Brianna frowned uncertainly. She felt the oddest tingling sensation in her body, as if she should be aware of something that she was not.

"Please," Luke said with a grin, and then he turned to the lord mayor. "Sir, would you—"

"Excuse you, too?" The lord mayor asked a little tartly. "By all means, boy. If the girl has kin here, she must see them."

"Here!" Brianna gasped.

Luke laughed. He was already on his feet, helping her to hers. "Come, please."

The tingling sensation had become such that she would not have managed to rise without Luke's assistance. In the far corner was a group of men, all somberly garbed in deep browns and grays, their heads bent to their conversation. They ceased as she was led to them, and then she stood dead still herself as the slimmest of the men lifted his head, and saw her.

Oh, he was so very thin and fragile in appearance. But his deep, dark eyes were dearly familiar, as was his compassionate face, the wisdom of his gaze, and the dark hair that hung to his shoulders. So familiar! So loved, and so well remembered!

"Robert!" Brianna gasped out. "Robert Powell!"

He stood quickly, and Brianna instantly fretted that he appeared too pale as well as far too slender, and she was shocked by the fierceness of his hold when he came to her, hugging her with a look of joy.

"Brianna! Where—what—"

She smiled very sadly, and not knowing anything at all about the others present, she spoke very simply. "Pegeen is dead, Robert."

He was studying her face intently, thumbs and fingers touching her cheeks and chin as he assured himself that she was real—and well. "I'm so sorry, Brianna, so very sorry for thee! She was a dear woman, and surely sits with God our Maker."

"So I am sure," Brianna murmured.

"Ah, but you have grown!" Robert said, shaking his head as he clutched her hands next, standing back to take in her full appearance.

"I should hope so! I was but a child when last we met!"

His touch was so gently warming, and she felt that seeing Robert, she had come home. It was all she could have hoped for; it was what she had longed for when she had first left Scotland.

But that was before she had fallen in love with Sloan. And now, no matter how great her pleasure in seeing Robert, it was bluffed with pain. Things couldn't have worked out any better! She didn't have to go through any difficulty at all to find the Powells—she had found Robert without lifting a finger.

Suddenly, in her heart, she was praying that she hadn't found him at all. She still wanted a way to stay with Sloan.

She lowered her lashes quickly, frightened that she would begin to cry. "How is your mother, Robert? And your father? And—"

"Everyone is fine, Brianna. We have aged, as is God's way, but we do well. But you've no thought of leaving without seeing mother and father, have you?"

I've not thought of leaving at all, she replied in silence, wincing against the pain when she thought of leaving Sloan. She raised her eyes to his. "Robert, I—I have longed to reach you and your family since Pegeen died."

What had happened, she wondered then, what had she said? Nothing, nothing at all. But something must have slipped into her voice, something that echoed all the heartache and agony she had endured, for her cousin's arms were suddenly around her, holding her, and his slim fingers were gently soothing her hair.

"Thou art with us now, dear cousin, and while we breathe, none will hurt you again."

Don't! Oh, don't be so terribly kind, she wanted to cry out. She was trying to stand on her own feet, but he made it so very easy to lean against his shoulders! What would he think if he knew the whole story; that she had been condemned as a witch, that she had earned her passage by playing a whore.

That she loved a married man with all her heart and soul, and now needed protection against herself, rather than him.

Someone cleared his throat; Brianna and Robert both started to see that Luke and the lord mayor were standing quietly to the left of them.

"My dear girl!" the lord mayor said, perplexed. "What is going on here?"

Brianna forced herself to laugh lightly. "Oh, sir! Meet Robert Powell, Luke's friend, and my dear cousin."

The lord mayor raised a white eyebrow. "Cousin?"

"Ah, don't perplex the man further, Brianna!" Robert said, bowing slightly to the lord mayor. "Our mothers were cousins, sir. Brianna spent part of her childhood in my household."

"And—" Brianna hesitated. She knew she must speak, and convincingly, and yet she couldn't. It would be so easy to wait for Sloan to come back. To sail away with him, and forget all that she knew about right and wrong. But she could not. He was married; he had a wife, before God. He could never love her completely, and in time the pain of it would tear them apart, and she would hold nothing. Before God, she would be an adulteress, and willingly so.

"Oh, dear sir!" she exclaimed to the lord mayor. "You must explain to Lord Treveryan for me that I have found my family, and that I am going with Robert to join my own kin."

"Brianna—" Robert began, and she didn't know what he was about to say, so she discreetly stamped on his foot, cutting him off.

"Will you do that for me, please?" Brianna finished.

"Well, I—I—" the lord mayor stuttered, his cheeks turning red, and Brianna was sorry that she did not dare meet Sloan again herself.

"He will be most pleased to hear that things have worked out so well!" she lied.

Luke stepped into the conversation, believing her every word. Perhaps his heart was so staunchly Puritan, so trusting in goodness and the truth, that he didn't think to doubt the situation. He was, perhaps, such a man as to consider it unthinkable that she had spent her voyage as the Lord Treveryan's mistress.

"Praise God!" said Luke, smiling as if a miracle had indeed occurred. "That you have sought your kin, and found them here in our midst!"

"Amen!" Robert said, and suddenly all Brianna wanted to do was leave the tavern before Sloan could walk back in. If she saw him again, she would never be able to leave him.

"Robert, forgive me. I'm feeling a little faint...."

"Ah, poor child! Come to the bench, I'll call for water and salts."

"No, no!" she pleaded, lifting a hand. "If I could but have some fresh air..."

"Of course, of course!" Robert bowed slightly to all assembled, then, gripping her elbow, hurried her outside the tavern.

"Do you wish to sit?" he queried gently. "What shall I do?"

She smiled wanly. "Get me out of here, quickly, Robert, please."

"But should you walk—"

"Yes, oh, please take me home. I do not wish to disturb your business, but I am desperate! I cannot stay here."

She would never know quite what he understood at that moment, but he tarried no longer. They hurried across the road to the small stable where his horse was lodged, and he apologized that they must ride together, for he had no other. Brianna assured him that it didn't matter in the least. Finally, when she was mounted behind him, she pressed her face against his back, willing herself not to cry out, not to jump from the horse and race back to Sloan.

As they rode he told her about the family. There had been many births over the years and there were babies always about the house, to his mother's delight. Then he started saying something about the Colonies, but she didn't hear. With each tired plod of the old workhorse's hooves, she realized that they were going farther and farther away. She could no longer smell the sea, nor hear any sound of waves or surf, Each of those hoofbeats kept time with the dull thud of her heart; she was leaving Sloan, she was leaving him, when he was all that she loved in the world.

"Ah, Brianna, despite the problems, it is a new world. A wonderful new world. Far away.

A man may hold all the land he craves, and all his neighbors are of like persuasion! Think of it! It is a special place for God's chosen...."

She didn't know what he was saying, although she fully heard the drone of his voice. It meant nothing. Nothing at all.

Suddenly, in the haven of a green forest cove, she burst into tears.

Robert drew the horse quickly to a halt and slid from the saddle. Vaguely she felt his arms, the slimness of him, and the rattle in his chest, and fearing for him was perhaps the best thing for her at that moment. She stiffened, determined not to lean, and she tried to wipe the tears quickly from her cheeks.

"Brianna, what is it?"

"Oh, you're not well."

"I'm fine! I'm fine!" He told her impatiently, and, his arm set about her shoulders, he walked her to a spot of rich and splendid green beneath a gnarled oak, and pressed her to sit. He disappeared, and was back, offering her water. She took a sip, then leaned back against the tree, staring upward to the sky. The leaves played over the fall of sunlight, one minute shadowing, the next breaking apart to allow a dazzle of golden light through.

At last she looked at her cousin and she felt ridiculous, for she was trying to smile while great liquid drops which she could not prevent fell from her eyes and dampened her cheeks.

His face, that gentle, caring face from her childhood, touched now with lines of age about his eyes and mouth, was taut with worry.

"You are so very good," she whispered.

"You must tell me what hurts you so," he returned quietly. "Please." He hesitated just a moment. "You would not have my mother see you so distressed, would you?"

"No, no," Brianna said, lowering her head. She plucked a blade of grass from the ground and shredded it between her fingers. Laughter bubbled in her throat, although nothing at all was amusing. Then she stared at him and blurted out, "I am a witch, Robert. Did you know that?"

"Brianna!" His dark brows knit in a stem frown. "You must not say such a thing, even jokingly."

"But I am—"

"If you have been practicing witchcraft, white or malefic, you must cease immediately You will be hanged, and far worse, you will cast your immortal soul into the pits of hell!"

Staring at him, she began to shake her head. "Oh, Robert! I never practiced any form of witchcraft! But that is why Pegeen is dead, Robert. They—they—burned her. Oh, Robert! There was a horrible, evil man, I swear it, who claimed against her, and she was innocent. He brought me to trial also, and I was almost hanged. I—"

"Stop! Stop!" Robert interrupted her. "Slowly, Brianna, tell it all to me slowly."

She did. She drew in a great shivering breath and began to tell him part of the story, leaving out most things about Sloan, except that he had twice saved her from the clutches of "the law." And at long last she ended with "But I am innocent, Robert. I swear it to you."

"I believe you." He sighed, leaning against the tree beside her. He was silent for several minutes, and when he spoke, it was thoughtfully. "This all seems to be for the best," he said. "In a matter of weeks we will be gone from England. No one will know what went before, and in the Colonies we will start over."

"The Colonies?" she murmured.

"Aye." He set his arm around her again. "Brianna, if you escaped, as you say, you are still guilty before the law. Only the king could give you a pardon, and he certainly would not. Brianna, I would not spread this story farther than it has gone, for people who do not know you would think you guilty of the crime."

He paused again, then asked quite suddenly, "Why did you start to cry so?"

"I—I just told you."

"Nay, you told me a tragic story, but not why you were so very anxious to leave the tavern. And why did you burst into tears as we left the sea behind us without taking proper leave of the man who saved your life?"

She couldn't find words, or her voice. At length she shook her head and whispered, "I could not."

"You are in love with him." Robert said gravely.

She lifted her hands, not willing to dispute him, and not able to lie. She remembered that the greatest sin among Puritans was to tell a lie. Truth was precious to them.

"He is married," she said flatly, and when he replied with a very soft "Oh," and held her to his shoulder, she knew that he understood.

A leaf, deep green and summer verdant, fell from the tree and drifted down beside her. She felt the stir of the breeze, a ray of the sun streaking through the blanket cast against the sun by the tall branches of the tree.

The sky, the earth, the wind, and all beautiful things were hers now—because of Sloan. And yet leaving him was the only thing that she could do.

"Will he come for you?" Robert asked.

"I don't know."

"He will."

"Oh, I pray that he does not. For I do love him with all my heart and I ran from him today because I am afraid that I haven't the power to stand against him."

"God will give thee that power, Brianna."

He was sure, so positive in the simplicity of his faith. Robert stood and reached down a hand to her. "Come, cousin. I will take you home. Our love will be always with thee, strong against temptation."

She accepted his hand and rose—even though she felt she knew much more about temptation than Robert. But now she must trust him and the love of her family, and cling to them for strength to hold fast to her resolutions.

They rode in silence for some time. "It is unlikely," Robert mused at last, "that Lord

Treveryan could find you tonight. But he will come. I'm convinced of it. When he does, you must meet him, and convince him that he imperils your immortal soul."

Brianna closed her eyes and wondered if she'd ever forget what it felt like to live with this horrible, aching pain? To breathe, and breathe in loneliness and despair.

Yes—she would be going to a new land. She would no longer be an outlaw, a condemned criminal, for none would have heard of her crime. She had to keep believing in the new land.

Chapter 14

The Powell home was a small two-storied cottage that was cared for with great love. Begonias grew in profusion about the entrance; bright clean curtains hung at the windows. When Robert pushed open the door, wonderful cooking aromas filled their senses. Hook rugs adorned the simple floors, and precious candles burned brightly from a well-polished dining table.

"Robert?"

There was surprise in the dulcet tones of the plump woman's voice as she came toward them. Brianna blinked, for Margaret Powell, her mother's cousin, did not appear as if she had changed a wit in all the years gone past.

But evidently Brianna had changed some-what herself. Margaret stopped walking, absently pushing back a still-black wing of hair, and stared at her with a curiosity that was not rude, but rather a bit stupefied—as if she should be able to place the girl on her son's arm, but could not. Then, quite suddenly, she let out a little gasp and rushed forward with a smile as radiant as the sun.

"Brianna! Oh, Brianna! All grown up! Oh, child, child, come in, come in!"

At last she was being crushed by safe and loving arms. Explanations could come later; for now, there was only the bliss of being cher-ished. Tears had filled her eyes by the time Robert's father came to hold her too. Tall, slim, and weathered, he said her name gently, and she knew that they would give her all the support she could find in this world.

By nightfall the Powells had been given a sketchy version of all that had happened. They did not judge her, nor did she even know what they really thought. Ethan said solemnly that they would stand by her—and that surely God would too.

To her amazement she slept soundly that night. Sleep was a respite from anguish. A blessed respite, for the morning brought all that she had feared. Margaret woke her with calm warning. "Brianna, he is here."

"Sloan?" she gasped out shakily.

Already? It was too soon, she was barely awake. She wasn't strong at all.

"Aye, Lord Treveryan."

She closed her eyes again. Had he thundered into the house? Demanded that she be returned? If he displayed the arrogance of his class, she might well find it easier to despise him; to find some shame that she desired him enough to forget that he was wedded to another in the eyes of man and—and God.

"Did he...did he..."

"He came as courteous as a man might, my dear. I thought to loathe for the dishonor he has brought you to, but I cannot, for even if he stands like an oak and is as sound in mind and body as any ship, his eyes harbor such a tumult that he must not be despised. Deal gently with him—but firmly. You must not go with him."

Brianna nodded miserably. She rose quickly and dressed, and with shaking fingers knotted her hair firmly at her nape. Her palms were damp, her throat was dry.

At last she opened the door and came to the parlor.

Sloan was there, by the fire, one hand upon the hearth, his head inclined toward it. Seeing him, she felt that she wanted to die, quite truly, rather than watch him walk out the door. When he turned to her, his features were strained, but his eyes were vividly, brilliantly green against the redness that marred them. She thought that he had not slept at all, and she desperately wanted to run to him, to hold him tight, and ease the deep-set furrows from his brow.

But Ethan and Robert stepped beside her to walk with her to the parlor.

"I would have you come back with me," Sloan said, and his voice was harsh and hoarse, and ripped at her soul.

She opened her mouth, but no sound would come. She hated herself for being such a coward, and finally found the words to speak.

"These people are the family I have so craved to reach, Sloan. My place is here, with them. I beg you, leave me where I am loved—and respected." Her emphasis on the last word was soft, and yet it was clear, so that he would truly understand.

Then he appeared angry, and in her heart she was a little glad; she did not want to forget his anger and his touch of arrogance, for they were a part of him that she loved; his determination that he could always best the world.

"Brianna—"

Robert set an arm about her and stepped forward slightly. "My Lord Treveryan, I will speak frankly here. You cannot give Brianna that which I can. Think my lord! What would her life be? Access to port upon port? And what of your loyalty, sir, to the prince you serve? There is hardship ahead, war and battle. Would you see her brought to danger or left behind to suffer scorn? My lord, we are her kindred, and we must protect her life and soul. We are grateful to you for saving her life, but, my lord, we are her male protectors; we must guide her life. Sir, I must tell you that

248

Brianna and I are betrothed. I will marry her, my lord, and give her that station which you cannot."

Sloan's incredulous exclamation covered Brianna's own gasp of shock.

"But you cannot!" he exclaimed in a fury. "You are cousins."

"Nay, sir, our mothers were cousins. And I might remind you that the Prince and Princess of Orange are first cousins."

For one terrible minute Brianna feared that Sloan meant to draw his sword and slay Robert on the spot; she had never seen such a fire in his eyes. He seemed indomitable as he stood there towering over them all, fierce and bronzed—and beautiful still to her eyes.

"Sloan!" she cried out, stepping forward. "Please, I beg of you! If you care for me—if ever you have loved me—leave me here, in peace."

He turned away from her, striding back to the mantel—he could not look at her. Her words rang in his ears, an echo of reproach. "If you ever loved me..."

If? He didn't think that he could walk away, that he was capable of doing such a thing. He wanted to rip to shreds this man who was claiming Brianna. But Robert Powell was aware that Sloan could kill him with little more than a blow—and held quietly to his stance anyway.

And Brianna...

There had been such pleading in her voice. Dear God, he did love her. So much that he couldn't wrench her away, no matter what his own feelings were. He'd go through hell for her; he would face a thousand Matthews. But he couldn't fight her. Not now.

He could give her almost anything in the world, but not the most important thing. He could love her with all his heart—but he could not make her his wife.

Neither could he bear being here longer thinking that she would wed another man. And he could not despise Powell, for even though he appeared as gaunt as birch branch, he was not without courage.

Sloan longed to fight for the woman who was his. But he couldn't. Brianna had begged him to leave her, and because he did love her, he had no choice.

But he made one last protest, his voice so harsh that it was a crude rasp.

"Have you forgotten? Brianna MacCardle is an outlaw here—until William of Orange marches into England. Only then will I be able to clear our names."

"My Lord Treveryan," Robert Powell said distinctly. "I am aware of that. I intend to take her far from England. The *Lady of Bristol* sails in three days for New England. We will be on her."

Sloan nodded. His heart seemed to be ripped from his chest, and sink bleeding to his feet. He stared at her then, determined to memorize her for a lifetime. The beautiful blue of her eyes, radiant now, dazzled with liquid tears. He must remember her face, her form, her fiery pride and rages, the melody of her laughter, and the parted curve of her lips when she anticipated his kiss.

Sloan took a step forward, dredging up everything he knew of gallantry.

He knelt at her feet, took her hand, and lowered his head over it. Slim and delicate—he would never forget the touch of her fingers.

"Peace and happiness, to you, then, my lady. Godspeed to you both."

He kissed her hand and rose, bowing sharply to Robert and Ethan Powell.

Then he quit the small cottage, allowing the door to slam shut behind him. Holding back a man's tears, he jumped upon his horse and sent his heels flying against the beast's flanks. He rode until he came to a cove in the forest, where he dismounted, finally realizing that the animal did not deserve to be the brunt of his turmoil.

Sloan sank to the grass. For once in his life he had wanted some one thing... someone...more than anything else in the world. And he could not have her, simply because he did love her so much. He ached as though mortally wounded. He did not know what to do, where to turn, and so he thundered his fists against a tree, and when his hands were bloody, he fell to the forest floor.

Morning passed; the sun rose high above him. And suddenly he screamed out—screamed out in rage, in loss, in frustration—and in love.

Finally his voice went hoarse. He stood and patted the neck of the horse he had run so ragged. He found a stream and let the animal drink, next he splashed his face again and again with the cold water and cooled his battered hands.

Then he mounted the horse again and started back toward port. He wanted to reach the sea; she was his mistress, she would heal him, she would give back his reason and passion for life.

And he would reach Holland. He would be there for William and Mary; he would fight with fury and vengeance, cast himself into the tumult of battle and fray. He would then go back to Loghaire. Perhaps he could not love his wife, but he would try to be her friend. God, how he pitied her now, for she could never know just what beauty God could give—and take away.

His eyes carefully following the movements of his fingers, Robert Powell knelt beside the chair he had almost completed. His file moved quickly and fluidly in his hands; he touched the hard wood with an almost loving reverence.

Long ago—when he had been a very small child—he had learned that he did not have the strength or energy of other men. While his father labored with heavy hauling and planting, and his brother split logs, and his sister helped with the birthing of the farm animals, he had been sent to help in the kitchen. Even there he had been given the lighter tasks, peeling apples, plucking feathers, washing the family plates.

He had been teased mercilessly by the boys his own age, and because they declared him less than a man, he had determined to prove them wrong. He had struck off for the farmyard with a vengeance, hacking at a full cord of wood with his father's weighted axe. Barely had he begun the task before it seemed that the blow of an anvil struck against his chest. He heaved with bitter desperation for breath, but could get no air. Ultimately he fainted.

He was very, very sick when he opened his eyes again. His mattress had been dragged before the fire, over which his mother had a kettle boiling, the steam redolent of herbs and precious mint. He could just barely breathe, and knew from the tears in his mother's eyes that he had come very close to dying.

Getting well had taken a long time; hours and hours in which to brood, in which to wonder why God had cast such a fate—actually to berate God in his mind, even though he knew and feared the blasphemy of such a thing.

He had also had time to stare out at the beautiful summer mornings, to see the birds flit about the trees, and to watch the way the rising sun played with and glittered over the dew in the fields. He realized that he loved life and that he was grateful to be living. That there was so much to see, so much to be experienced, even if a man were to have his limitations.

Somewhere during that time he came to terms with his God. Having come to peace with himself, he knew he would never again need to prove anything to others. As the years passed, he became an avid scholar and writer.

And he learned to carve. Furniture and toys, utensils, and frames, beautiful things, sturdy things. Wood became creation in his hands, and his usefulness to others was further established.

But now as he labored over his task with infinite patience, he did so with a heavy heart. Brianna was still in the room where she had run with a little cry when the noble seaman had left them.

She would be left alone today, he knew. His parents were giving her this time, for her life had been hard of late. They were not without pity, but pity was not an emotion fostered among his faith. Treveryan was imperiling her immortal soul, so he had to be severed from her life, and it was quite that simple. Hard work would cure her of her ills; perhaps her heart was shattered, but it was a young heart, and mendable. And they did not live in a world that could be ruled by the heart, anyway. In time she would meet the proper man, she would stand beside him before God, bear his children, and raise them in the Lord's way. Happiness was not a promise, it was a blessing that sometimes came like spring rain—and oft departed as quickly.

Tomorrow Brianna would be set to work. Hard toil and labor that would send her to bed exhausted and too bone-weary to bear any anguish in the night for what could not be.

Robert felt her pain and longed to soothe it. He did not believe that she would forget her sea captain—ever. And he knew that now she would be thinking that she did not care about right or wrong, or even her immortal soul. She would be thinking herself the greatest of all fools for having cast away everything in life that mattered to her.

He smiled to himself suddenly, thinking that she was like a summer's breeze to his life. She had been a beautiful child and she was lovelier as a woman. Just to see her was one of those special gifts that made life worth living. He wished to hold her in his arms and give her what tenderness he could; and he thought then that he loved her himself, and was heartfully sorry for Treveryan—a man who deserved her love, but by God's will could not have it.

"Robert?"

He started at the soft hesitancy of her tone, but also seemed warmed by its very utterance. He turned to see her, slim and lithe, a silhouette in the doorway, framed by the luxurious colors of the waning sun. She stepped into the barn, and her features became clear.

There was no sign of tears about her face, but she was pale and drawn. Her eyes told of a woman decades older than her age. She was very calm and very still—just so very weary- and empty-looking.

He tried to smile for her. "Come in. Do you like my chair?"

"It is beautiful, Robert," she said, and she came forward to touch the wood, smoothing it.

She looked at him and there were still no tears in her eyes. Something had settled over her that afternoon, as surely as a cloud of gray—of mystery and steel.

"I wanted to thank you, Robert. Without you I would not have managed to be here still."

"I did nothing," he said, simply, and rose.

"But you did," she murmured. "You stood between us...you told him that we were betrothed." She stared at him incredulously. "I know that you never lie, Robert!"

"Ah, but was it a lie? For, this afternoon we shall say that we are betrothed!" He walked by her, glancing back over his shoulder. "Brianna, we have little time to prepare and get back to port to sail. That we must get you from England quickly is one of the greatest truths I have ever spoken."

He felt her tremble even at his distance and he knew that she was not all right. "Imagine, Brianna!" he told her then. "A new land, a different land, far, far across the sea. Something emerging, growing—and we shall be a part of it!"

Two days later they set sail. He stood by her at the ship's rail, and they stared at England. "Glasgow, and now Upsinwich," she murmured. "I feel that I am always sailing away."

"New beginnings," Robert murmured, squeezing her fingers. "Don't look back."

She turned away from the rail. "No," she promised softly. "I will never look back."

But every sane person aboard did think to look back as the days at sea passed while terrible storms whipped and raged about them. Traveling was total misery. Brianna had no cabin in which to sleep. She was down in the hold with fifty other women, with only canvas sheeting separating them from the men. There were rats and lice, and always a stench of sickness. Brianna had learned something about sailing, so for the first week, no matter how the ship pitched and swayed and threatened to break apart, she was all right.

But on their ninth day at sea, when the sun suddenly rose brilliantly to crest atop a teal-blue sky, Robert found Brianna alone at the stem of the ship, ghastly pale and gray and wretchedly sick. She tried to wave him away, but he wet a cloth in the barrel of drinking water and returned to clean her face. Her eyes were full of confusion and tumult as a spasm struck her again. She had thought herself a fine sailor.

Robert didn't say anything to her then; he brooded over her illness for the next few days as it continued.

When they had been out for two weeks, Brianna knew it was time to speak to him.

"Robert," she said quietly, leaning weakly against him as the shuddering spasms of nausea subsided, "I am expecting a child."

"I wish to marry you—in truth," he told her.

She stared at him, stunned. And he thought that she would cry, there was such a crystal glistening of moisture in her eyes.

"No!"

"You do not understand. Everyone on this ship knows that you have no husband."

"I have endured too much to care what people think or say about me."

"But what about your child?" he asked her, and her eyes dropped, and she shuddered.

"I can't marry you." Then she smiled ruefully. "I love you too dearly as a cousin to marry you. I could never love you as a husband." The spark left her eyes and she whispered, "And I carry another man's child."

He put his arms around her and held her close. "I do not care."

"I could not hurt you so!"

"Nay, feel no guilt! If we married, I'd not be used, but rather you would be! We must not fool each other. I never try to fool myself. I am not the man Treveryan is."

"We are sailing to a new land and I have set my heart on starting over! I will not think of him."

"You must, just for these moments. He is a good man; he loved you. And you should love his child, with no threat or worry. I am not strong and healthy, and, compared with him, I am a poor excuse for a protector. I can give you almost nothing, but I will love you, and your child, with all that is within me. Can't you care for me, just a little?" He stepped back. "Brianna! I am sorry. Of course, you are young—you will love again, you will find another—"

He broke off because she was laughing and

shaking her head. "I do not want to love again. Never. Robert, I seek no lusty youth. I don't believe I want to live with a man."

"Even one who asks nothing from you?" Robert interjected softly, and she stared at him again, very confused. He cleared his throat. "Brianna, I—I ask that we live as friends. I—I... Lord! Don't you understand yet? My heart is weak and my lungs are worse. The sea has helped, but I'm often bedridden. Perhaps in time I will grow stronger. Perhaps in time you will love me enough to want me. But for now... You are with child. Can't we, the three of us, create a life together?"

She did cry then. She leaned her head against his chest and cried.

They were married that evening, just as the sun fell from the sky. It was a calm night, without a breeze. The sea was entirely peaceful, as if content.

And the old world was fading behind them.

Interlude
November 1691

The waves that roared and crashed along the coast were not a pleasant blue. Here, against the rugged coastline, they were gray, ever roiling with great ferocity, as if they promised death from the sea.

It was a lonely place—forlorn, many would say. Grass did not grow like velvet over the rocky mountains and plains—growth here was tenacious. The mauve shrubs and occasional weeds that grew high were stubborn and tough, as were all the coastal inhabitants of this stretch of Wales, Sloan mused as he stood on the high and ragged cliff and stared out broodingly over the ever-changing sea. Then he closed his eyes and shuddered.

He had long ago learned not to think of her. He had schooled himself to follow his quest, to pitch his thoughts and strength and mind into battle. But today, today he could not help but think of her with longing. Perhaps it was being home, perhaps it was staring out at the tempest of the sea. Whatever the reason, she was in his thoughts today, filling his heart with nostalgia and pain.

She was well, he knew. Well, and fine, and

happy. He knew because friends of his had been to the Bay Colony, and they had carried tales home. She was so extraordinary lovely that no man who had seen her had ever forgotten her.

"Aye, I know of her," old Captain Ben of the *Inverary* had told him when last they'd met outside Dublin. And his eyes had taken on a faraway look; his parched and weathered lips had twisted to a smile. "She lives in the village, she does—Salem Village, that be. I saw her at the tavern near the dock; they had come for wool. Brown wool, and unadorned, but—"the old man shrugged—"I heard her name, and it seemed to linger on my lips. For in that very plain garb she was more beautiful than a woman fully adorned. When she walked, it seemed she floated; she was soft-spoken and sweet and her scent was one of flowers. She seemed happy, and yet sad..."

The old captain had gone on. About her husband—"A rail of a man, he was, but e'er gentle to the woman and the boy. Did I tell you of him? Ah, he's not more than a year or so in age, but hale and hearty, with a look o' the devil about to catch your heart and bring a smile to your lips."

Sloan stretched his hands out before him and saw that they were trembling. She was happy. And if the child was his, he had no right to interfere. As it was then, so it was now. If he loved her, he would stay away.

He sighed and turned from the sea to stare up at the great gray pile of mortar and stone that was Loghaire Castle, his home. It was drafty and cold; the foundations dated back to long before the coming of William the Conqueror. But as forbidding as the gray stone walls could be, it was home. It was beautiful to him. The land, the sea, and the rugged castle rising like a natural butte against the terrain. When he'd fought the Irish under the Prince of Orange's command, it had been here that he had dreamed of; his land, a place of solitude and peace.

William had quite easily walked into England. It had been all that Princess Mary had envisioned it might; a glorious, "bloodless" revolution. Her father had been forced to flee; the crown had been offered to William and Mary by the people.

But a number of Scottish lords had rebelled, and they had been crushed. Worse still had been the battles in Ireland. War had seemed interminable there, and through every victory Sloan had felt nothing but sorrow and pain. The Irish had stoutly defended James, even after he had fled. The Battle of the Boyne had brought about the end of the conflict, but even there Sloan had known no triumph. A multitude of fine, noble Irish lords had chosen exile rather than bow down to William. The death in Ireland had wrought fiercely against Sloan's heart, gnawing at his reason. He had fought hard, but no longer for vengeance; he had fought only for loyalty, and perhaps, out of a flirtation with death.

Sloan suddenly clasped his hands to his

head and sank down among the pebbles and the weeds. He wanted so badly to forget Ireland, and the screams of the dying and the wounded. A shudder ripped through him, weakening him, and he took a deep breath and stared out to sea.

He loved the sea. It seemed to beckon to him.

But then he pivoted on his heels and once more stared up at the castle. He couldn't put out to sea again. Not yet.

Alwyn had been very strange. When he had first returned, he had taken great care that she not see him in his battle garb. He had spent long hours bathing, and dressing to please her. But when he had tried to bring her a present of fine Irish linen, she had screamed so at the sight of him that he had quickly left her chambers and had spent the next days keeping himself out of her sight.

Then one morning she asked to see him; she recognized him again as her childhood playmate.

It was strange, yes, very strange, to play hide-and-seek and chase his wife of a decade around the rosebushes. But her physicians had recommended that he indulge her in her whims, and he was very grateful to see her smile, and hear her laughter.

He loved her, yes: loved her as the child she sought to be.

Sloan stood, straightening his shoulders. Brianna was a dream denied him; Alwyn, sweet Alwyn, was his responsibility. He was all she had to shield her from harsh reality. He owed his wife his loyalty and care now. In time he would sail again and find his soul cleansed with the cool sea breezes.

She, too, stared out at the water at Salem Town, where the great ships brought news and supplies from the Mother Country. They had come today because the *Marianna* was due in—with news on the progress of the ambassadors the Puritans now had in the court of William and Mary.

The Massachusetts Bay Colony was still without her charter, and Increase Mather was working hard to convince the new sovereigns that the charter revoked by Charles Stuart must be regranted.

Brianna did not care much about news of the charter. The Puritans were anxious that those who were not of their faith be forbidden to hold public office, but Brianna could not care much about such things. She thought it an intolerant attitude for a people who had long sought toleration, but she kept her thoughts to herself. She was getting along admirably well. Perhaps there were no highs to her life, no days of excitement, no nights of...

Love. Dear God! Would she never forget him?

She had carved out a life for herself. Robert was, if not all that a husband could be, her friend, and a dear, dear companion. He was Michael's father now, and at that he excelled. He had given her a home, and he had given her respectability. And he gave her, every day, his devotion and care. If they did not have passion, they did have a form of love. There was always work to be done, and if the sermons delivered in the Salem Town parish were a little strict to Brianna's mind, it didn't matter, because among these staid and God-fearing people—His "chosen," as they called themselves—she had met good friends. They did know how to laugh, and to care. Some were gossips, and some were dear. "God's Chosen" or not, they were people with the frailties common to all.

The breeze picked up from the harbor. From where she stood in the field across from the docks, Brianna felt it lift her hair and cool her cheeks. The salt smell of the ocean was rich today. And though she had long ago steeled her mind against fancy, the scent of the air brought with it a sharp pain that wound tightly in her abdomen and seemed to reach up and place a stranglehold about her heart.

She closed her eyes, feeling the breeze sweep by, praying that it would ease the pain it had brought.

Time...time should have eased the loss, and the longing. His face should long since have faded from her memory, but it would not. She could see him as clearly today as she had when she had faced him last. His eyes, with their searing, haunting gaze. The height of him, the warmth of him, the strength when he had held her. In her mind's eye she could reach out with her fingers and feel his face—the contours of his jaw, the sun-bronzed skin of his cheeks, the thick dark brows that arched over his eyes. Reach out...and touch him, and in turn, he would clutch her hand, and bring it tenderly to his lips...

"Mama!"

The spell was broken. She opened her eyes. The sky was a dull gray today, for winter was coming. The grass was flattening in the field, and out on the sea the great sails of the ships coming to harbor were blown out wide and full.

She turned around. On sturdy little legs Michael was racing to her. His long dark hair was clubbed neatly at his nape, but tendrils were escaping to the wind. He smiled as he neared her, and his eyes flashed in the sunlight, as rich and radiant as the verdant field. He wasn't quite two and a half years old, but he was already tall and sturdy and vital and wonderfully bright.

"Rabbit!" he told her, catapulting into her arms.

"A rabbit, darling? How nice."

She embraced him, lifting him even as he protested her crushing hold. He pushed his hands against her shoulders and stared down into her face with those beautiful green eyes that could wrench her heart. Michael squirmed out of her arms, and she set him down on the ground, taking his hand.

"I want to tell Papa 'bout my rabbit!" he said.

"Yes," Brianna murmured.

Michael was tugging her toward the street, toward the tavern where Robert was awaiting his friends from the ship. She was ready to

267

follow, but she paused without thinking, staring out to sea again.

What held her there? Tears burned suddenly and hotly in her eyes. There were just times...when she missed him. Fiercely. Incredibly. Times when she could not stop the dreams of what could never be. Times when she longed for him with an ache in her heart that could not be brought under control.

The war in Ireland was over. That, at least, she knew. She had prayed, night and day, that he would live. She had promised God that she would cease to want him—if only God would grant that he would live. But it was not an easy promise to fulfill.

"Mama?"

Michael pulled at her hand, staring up at her with curiosity—and a strange look of understanding that was very unusual for one so young. He was concerned; he did not know what hurt her, only that something did.

She gave herself a little shake and stared down at her child. Her love for him suddenly seemed to pour out of her like the rush of a geyser, and she picked him up again, cradling him tightly to her heart.

Life was good. She could not have Sloan, but she had their son. She had Michael. And as long as she had him, she had everything.

And she had Robert, as kind and gentle a man as had ever walked the earth. They had a good life. She was content.

As long as she kept her eyes from straying to the sea.

January 1692

A cold wind blew in from the sea. Winter had come that year with a chilling blast, as if the season itself had life and menace. He stood on the cliffs with the wind whipping around him, watching the terrible power of the sea and feeling powerless himself.

Alwyn had taken ill. Even now she lay in her beautifully adorned chamber, tossing with fever. No matter what the physicians tried, she slipped daily. She was so very thin now, blue veins were bright against the pathetic delicacy of her hands, her coloring had gone ashen. Like gossamer or silk, she became ever more elusive.

How he longed to give her his strength, to hold her, to give her courage. But the fever had brought delirium, and though he held her hand, she seldom knew he was there. No matter how he longed to help her, he could not. And it was a hard lesson to learn that no matter how strong a man might be, he hadn't the power of a single gust of wind, or of a single wave that might crash against the shore.

"Lord Treveryan! Lord Treveryan! You must come, quickly."

Sloan turned and seized the horse's reins as the steward, an old man long in his service, dismounted.

"What is it, then, Gerald?"

"She asks for you, my lord. My lady asks for you."

Sloan frowned. "She calls for me by name?"

269

"Aye, my lord."

Sloan had nothing more to say. He nodded briefly, taking the steward's horse, and turning the mount for the castle. He raced the rock-strewn cliffs and clattered across the bridge, and the garden, void now with winter's death.

At her door he paused, for her ladies were all around her; but she saw him. She looked at him across the expanse of the room, and she smiled at him, with eyes brilliantly clear. She lifted her free hand to wave the others away and beckon him. Still she was smiling at him, as she might have years and years before. A smile that welcomed; that recognized; that saw him as a man, and not a friend or brother!

He swallowed sharply and hurried to her bedside, sitting there and taking her hand—alarmed by its heat.

"Sloan," she said, reaching to touch the wings of his hair.

"Lie back," he urged her hoarsely, "save your strength."

She shook her head. " 'Tis too cruel, is it not, Sloan, that now, when I must leave this world, it is all so clear to me! The mists are gone now, and the flowers and the birds and all that I thought were my world. You are here. Oh, Sloan, hold me!"

He did. He felt her bones, and her burning flesh, and the gold cascade of her hair, beautiful still as death stole away all else that was lovely in life.

"Hold tight to life, my wife," he urged her. "Hold me, and I'll give you strength."

Against his chest she smiled again, wanly now. "Nay, my love, for I am weary." She was silent for long moments, and then she spoke again, brokenly. "You must live well, my dear Lord Treveryan! For never did you seek to disown me, to see me locked away beyond convent walls. So much I denied you...the heir you so craved."

"God denied us, Alwyn. And there was nothing that I craved."

"You lie, my lord, but I bless you for it."

She inhaled a long, shaky breath.

"Easy, Alwyn, be easy, and fight for life."

"Just hold me, Sloan. For these moments, let us know love, as once we did."

He held her all through the night. He whispered soothing words to her, and he forced her to take water. But when morning came, she was gone. She did not convulse, nor was her last breath different from any other. He spoke to her many, many moments after she lay dead, and it was one of her ladies who came gently to tell him that his lady had departed this life to rest with her Creator.

He took to his chapel then, staying there for hours in the pew before the altar. He did not know if he was plagued by guilt, or simply by loss. In all his light trysts, he felt that he had taken nothing from her.

But when he had loved Brianna, he had loved her fiercely and intensely, with all his heart. Somehow, that hurt him now; and yet, he could not feel guilty for that love. The emotion had been something pure, and very,

very beautiful. And so he did not understand what haunted and twisted so in his heart, unless it was simply the sadness of what might have been, had Alwyn found the strength in life that she had found in death.

With her passing, the winter winds seemed to rise with greater vengeance against the castle. January came, and with it ice and snow.

Sloan at last left the darkness of the chapel to come to the sea again. Not the wind nor the ice nor raging gales could keep him from staring out to sea, and at last he knew where his salvation would lie.

He could go to the Colonies. Carry letters, woolens, and goods.

She lived there. With her husband, he reminded himself. And her child. She had a home, and a family. But he longed to see the child he felt was his. What man would not?

With an aggravated and anguished oath he clenched his fists to his sides. He would put to sea again, but he would head for Boston, or New York. He would try with all his strength to stay away from Salem Town. If he went near it at all, he vowed to himself, he would do so in secret. He would allow himself to see the child, and then slip away. And if he saw her...?

"You will do nothing!" he thundered to himself aloud, and the wind picked up the cry and carried it about, mocking him.

He had to go. The sea beckoned to him, as did the wind. As did his desperate need to see the child.

And Brianna. Even if he did not speak to her; even if he just stood and watched her walk, or whisper to the child. He had to see her, or he would never be free of the memory that haunted him.

2

The Devil in Salem

*"You tax me for a
wizard; might as well
tax me for a buzzard!"*

George Jacobs, Sr.

Chapter 15

Always poor in health, Robert did not fare well during the height of winter. And now that large quantities of snow had alternately melted and frozen to create constant slush, he was doing even worse. When the service had ended on Sunday, Brianna had wanted to do nothing more than get home and set Robert before the fire with a cup of warmed ale.

But now it was Monday morning, no longer the Sabbath, and there was work to be done. Wood had to be chopped for the hearth in order to bake the bread and warm the house. Brianna did not want Robert cutting wood, and so, when he insisted he must go into Ingersoll's Ordinary to meet Liam Hardy and work out a deal to purchase cattle, she was happy to see him go. It was better than having him working outside, chopping the wood.

As soon as he'd left, Brianna bundled Michael into layers of clothing. She set him in a patch of white snow, and he laughed with pleasure, making snowballs while she split logs. When enough was accomplished, she gave Michael a twig to carry each time she made a trip to the woodshed, then carried what was necessary back to the house. She stoked up the fire, heated the oven, and measured out a portion of their dwindling grain supply to make bread. For a while, Michael played happily with a set of wooden soldiers Robert had carved for him, and when he tired and began to fuss, Brianna brought him into the bedroom and put him down for a nap.

By then her bread was ready for the oven, and when it was in and baking, she boiled water to make herself tea and sat down at the high-backed pew that faced the fire and guarded its warmth from leaking out the rear door.

It was Eleanor knocking at the door, Brianna realized as she rubbed the fog from a windowpane and looked out. With a delighted cry she threw the door open, and quickly pulled the bundled Eleanor inside.

"Eleanor! How wonderful. I must admit, I was just sitting here feeling a little sorry for myself. Robert has gone to town and Michael is sleeping and I was just having tea. You'll have some, of course? I made a few pastries along with the bread; and we've honey, since Robert did so well with his bees last summer!"

"Wonderful," Eleanor murmured, following Brianna to the fire. She drew off her heavy coat and ran her fingers lightly through her head of tawny curls. "I'm afraid that I was bored with my own company, too, Brianna." She sighed. "Dear Lord! Will this dreary weather never cease!"

Eleanor sat and Brianna gave her tea. For a while they spoke of all the hardships that winter had brought, but they were both young, and able to laugh at some of their own ridiculous efforts to cut corners on their work. Eleanor then told Brianna happily that she and Philip Smith might be married by April, as he had spent the winter chopping and hauling wood for others, and had put aside the money to buy a house in the Village.

"How is Robert?" Eleanor asked then, and Brianna admitted that she always worried over his health.

"I thought that was why you hurried away yesterday," Eleanor murmured. "You missed the excitement."

"The excitement?" Brianna queried, and Eleanor set down her tea to wander about the room. She grimaced at Brianna.

"There's quite a furor going about—but I supposed you've not noticed, for you two do keep to yourselves. A number of girls have taken severely ill, the Reverend Parris's daughter and niece among them. Seems the doctor can find nothing wrong, but Abigail and young Ann Putnam fell into fits as service ended yesterday that were a true terror to behold."

"Fits?" Brianna queried.

Eleanor lifted her hands, a little helpless for an explanation. "Fits—convulsions." She sat again, staring with confusion into the fire. "Mercy Lewis too," she murmured. "But Ann Putnam was the worst. Her limbs contorted so that when her legs crossed, they were locked like bars of steel. Her tongue was so glued to the top of her mouth that her father was frightened she would swallow upon it, and choke."

"The poor child!" Brianna exclaimed, then asked, "And the doctor could find nothing wrong?"

"Nothing of the flesh. Dr. Griggs told Reverend Parris that he must look to prayer. The doctor said that the devil had plagued the girls—he suspects that malefic witchcraft is at work."

"Witchcraft!" Brianna mouthed, stunned and stricken.

And Eleanor's eyes came to hers, suddenly full of sorrow.

"Oh, Brianna! You must not be concerned. There will be no insanity such as you met with in Britain. We've laws here, and wise and learned men who love God with a passion! The matter will be solved, oh, certainly!"

Brianna said nothing. Fear had begun to creep along her spine like the blade of a knife.

"Brianna, Brianna!" Eleanor bent down before her. "Oh, I am sorry! I shouldn't have spoken, yet you would have heard sooner or later. But truly, we are in the Massachusetts Bay Colony! Men take grave care here."

It was then that Robert returned, but Brianna could not even rise to greet him. As he removed his coat and hat, he looked at Eleanor with inquiry and reproach, wondering what she had done.

When Eleanor tried to explain, Brianna knew from Robert's expression that he had already been aware of the events. He moved to the fire, angrily, to warm his hands as he spoke.

"The whole thing," he said harshly, "has been caused by that Carib slave of Parris's. Tituba! She spent the winter telling those girls that her ex-mistress in the islands was a witch!" He sighed. "John Proctor has been saying that a good whipping would cure the girls of their fits, and I've a mind to believe he might be right."

"Robert," Eleanor reproached him, "I—I've seen them! They are truly grievously ill!"

"Aye," Robert murmured, "and encouraged to be so, as it appears!" He paused, then turned to look at Eleanor with his eyes very dark against the gaunt contours of his face. "Four children were taken so in Boston not long before we arrived here."

"Aye," Eleanor said unhappily.

"What happened?" Brianna demanded.

"They were—cured. The eldest was taken into the home of Cotton Mather, and eventually, she was cured."

"And a woman was hanged," Robert said harshly.

Eleanor threw up her hands in defense. "Robert! She was stealing articles of the children, brewing up potions, making dolls to torture—she admitted to witchcraft!"

Robert laughed dryly. "She was Irish, and spoke far better in Gaelic than in English! Who knows what defense she might have had?" Robert turned from the fire in distraction. "Where is my son?" he demanded of his wife.

"S-s-sleeping," she replied.

He strode for their bedroom door, but before he entered he turned back suddenly, practically shouting at her. He who never sought to command was suddenly giving out fierce orders. "You will stay away from the Village center!" he told her harshly. "You will not say a word, you will not become involved in this, do you hear me, wife?"

She could not reply.

"Brianna!"

"Aye, Robert, aye!" she replied at last. He went into the bedroom; the door closed like thunder.

"I'm sorry," Eleanor said bleakly. "Truly sorry."

Brianna shook her head. "Don't be. He will not stay angry long. He's just worried."

"Brianna, don't be alarmed. Really, in all the time that we have been here, I believe that there have been but four executions for witchcraft. And they were carefully judged and weighed in courts of law!"

Brianna nodded. Eleanor saw that she was still distressed and longed to ease the torment she had unwittingly caused.

"Ah, Brianna, I forgot to tell you! There is another new excitement for us!"

"There is?" Brianna tried to smile.

"Aye! A ship has come in from England bringing letters and wares! And the most handsome captain—even our most stalwart matrons are talking about him!"

Brianna barely heard her words. She gave Eleanor a wan smile, but she still worried about the things she had learned. Oh, it was true that these people were ardent on justice! But it was true, too, that they believed deeply in damnation, that man was created in God's image to fight the devil all his days.

"—that he comes to us from King William's war in Ireland. A fighter, they say, fierce and dangerous, and yet with a stature and cast of the eye that could seduce at will. He's courteous, yet remote. The girls might well swoon in his path, but he wouldn't notice, which makes him all the more fascinating."

"What?" Brianna said at last, brows furrowing, eyes narrowing, and her heart seeming to cease its beat with a single careening thud.

"You haven't been listening to a word I've said!" Eleanor laughed, glad to see that she had at last brought her friend's mind from the scare of witchcraft. "I was telling you about the captain newly in! I've heard he's a duke. 'Tis amazing that he breached the weather to make it here at all! Lord Treveryan is his name. Philip met him—and was most impressed. He was ready to set to sea himself—"

She broke off. Brianna had risen; her cheeks had gone as pale as new-fallen snow.

"Brianna? Are you all right? Oh dear, my Lord, what have I said now? Robert will be ready to take a stick to me!"

"No, no!" Brianna said quickly. She tried to breathe, in and out, in and out. "I'm fine, I'm fine. I was just a little dizzy."

"Dizzy. Ah, Brianna! Perhaps you and

Robert will have another child—a brother or sister for Michael!"

Brianna had no desire to discourage such a belief. "Ah, perhaps, yes, that might be it." She forced herself to move, to stir the poke at the logs in the fire.

Eleanor went on to chat excitedly about her forthcoming wedding, and then at last she paused, saying that it was time she went home, for her mother would need help with dinner.

Brianna kissed her good-bye, and thanked her for coming.

But she stood in the rear doorway, out in the harsh weather, waving far too long. It was as if she had been frozen there.

He had come! Here. Dear God, why?

He had let her go once. He had watched her at Robert's side, and he had let her go. Her heart had forever shattered as she'd seen him walk away. But now he was here. Why?

She began to tremble. He could not want her anymore. And she was married; her life was set. He would not think to interfere. At the height of their love he had turned away to give her the peace and honor she could receive from Robert.

Maybe he had come for his son.

She began to shake in earnest then, and it seemed that the blood drained from her body, leaving her incapable of standing on her own, clinging to the open door. He would not could not, take Michael.

No, no, no! She must fight against such

thoughts. There was nothing to fear. She would not see him and he would not see her. She would cling to the knowledge that Robert loved her, and that he had given her everything, a home and the honor of being his wife. He had taken on the role of Michael's father with all goodness and the same loving devotion he had given to her.

But she could not stop trembling.

Brianna had not even known that it was a leap year, but there was to be a February twenty-ninth that year, and no one in Salem Village would ever likely forget it.

She knew the date, and the events of it, because Robert came in late from Ingersoll's Ordinary—late, and very solemn, and mumbling beneath his breath that it was February twenty-ninth.

He removed his hat and coat, and asked if Michael was sleeping. When she replied that he was, he nodded and sat; and when she continued to move about the room—she had been making candles all day, and they had cooled enough to be brought down—he grasped her hand and dragged her down beside him.

"They've issued arrest warrants today," he told her, convinced that he must speak frankly to make her understand what position they had to take.

"For witchcraft? Against whom?" she demanded.

"Tituba, Sarah Good, and Sarah Osbourne."

Brianna drew in her breath. Tituba was the Carib slave who had been telling tales to the girls, so it was not surprising that the magistrates had decided to question her. Nor was it surprising that, if someone wanted a scapegoat, they should point to Sarah Good. The woman was of an indeterminate age, a typical hag, with worn clothing and the unladylike habit of continually puffing upon an old pipe. But Sarah Osbourne was a woman quite well off. She kept to herself, and as far as Brianna could see, brought no harm to anyone.

"Sarah Osbourne!" she exclaimed. "Good God! Why?"

Robert did not look at her but stared pensively into the fire, and then shrugged. "The girls cried out against her."

"The girls cried out against her..." Brianna repeated incredulously. "Oh, Robert That is no reason to drag—"

"Stop, Brianna!" he charged her. Her hand was upon his shoulder; he shook it off and stood and walked to the fireplace to lean against the mantel. He stared at her long and hard. "Brianna, you will not say anything—anything at all—to anyone! Sarah Osbourne has not been to church for over a year. She lived with Osbourne long before they legitimized the union with marriage. She—"

"She is a witch because she lived with a man?" Brianna interrupted furiously.

"Nay! I am merely telling you that those being brought in for questioning are not of respected character—"

286

Brianna was on her feet. "And for that they should be hanged? Robert! Don't ever say anything so ridiculous to me, of all people..."

"Brianna!" He charged her, and she saw then that his fingers were twitching where they touched the mantel—and that he was very frightened by the turn of events.

She turned away from him, wanting something to do, and suddenly feeling very disoriented in her own home.

He came up behind her, taking her shoulders, pulling her back close to him. "Brianna, I do not understand what is happening here yet. Perhaps these women will be questioned and freed—and that will be the end of it. The initial exams will be on Tuesday. March first," he added, as if in afterthought. "We will be there because the town will be there and I am afraid not to go. But, Brianna, you will not speak. You will not cry out that they cannot be guilty. They will think that you blaspheme if you deny the devil." He turned her around slowly. His dark eyes were a tempest against his long hollow face as they stared into hers. "Brianna, I mean this, as I have never meant anything before in my life. Defy me, and I will beat you—the same method Proctor suggests would cure the girls!"

She might have laughed—or wept. Robert had never even laid a hand across Michael's bottom to chastise him, nor did he ever take a whip to their horse, or to their mules. Never before had he even spoken to her so harshly.

She lowered her eyes quickly. She did not

know if she could keep silent. But he was her husband; perhaps she was the stronger of the two, and perhaps theirs was not the normal relationship, but she would not dishonor him now by a show of disobedience.

"It will be as you say, Robert," she told him quietly. But she knew that she lied. Having known the stigma of the accusation, she could not bear to see it cast toward others.

Not only had the village come out for the day, but the roads and Ingersoll's Ordinary were filled with populace from Ipswich, Topsfield, Beverly, and Salem Town. It was, Brianna reflected, for Salem Village, a very grand occurrence. Drumbeats could be heard in solemn dignity and pennants waved against the chill of the air. The examinations were to have taken place in Deacon Ingersoll's great chamber, but the crowd that thronged about was so vast that the meetinghouse was opened up for the occasion. The Puritans were waging battle against the devil—and that battle would be fought in the open.

Brianna had never before seen either of the magistrates from Salem Town. Robert tensely pointed out that the fellow with the stern face and fiery eyes was John Hathorne, and the man with the more tormented expression was Jonathan Corwin. Brianna felt a certain pity for Corwin because he appeared to be miserable with his task. But Hathorne...

Hathorne had a look of fanaticism about him.

A look in the eye that was frighteningly familiar to her. It reminded her of Matthews.

Michael was at Brianna's right side. She suddenly picked the little boy up and hugged him close, furious with Robert that they were here, and that they had brought Michael. But she needed to clutch him then, feel his heartbeat and the warmth of his flesh, feel his little arms curl about her neck. She was frightened.

The afflicted girls were there in positions of importance, near the front, where the pulpit had been removed and replaced by a table. As Sarah Good was brought in—between two heavyset constables—they immediately began to cry out and writhe. Brianna gasped as she watched them, for what she had heard was true. They were ill, or possessed—or something! Ann Putnam fell to the floor; her tongue protruded in a grotesque fashion and none could doubt that the child could not do such a thing of her own volition.

Hathorne conducted the investigation. And he was a fierce questioner. But Sarah Good had something of a swagger about her; she denied all charges with a vigor that pleased Brianna, since Brianna was quite positive that while the old crone had her share of sins, she was not a witch.

Yet it seemed the "witches" were determined to damn themselves. When asked who did torment the children if it was not she, Sarah Good pointed her finger at her fellow prisoner. "Goody Osbourne doth afflict the children!"

she cried—and it was then time for Sarah Osbourne to face Hathorne.

Sarah Osbourne claimed that she had not been to church because she had been ill. "It is more likely I would be bewitched, than be a witch!" she cried, and went on to say that a black man, possibly an Indian, had visited her in her dreams, viciously pulling her hair and pinching her neck. She denied acquaintance with the devil.

Tituba came to the stand. The old heavyset dark Carib's eyes rolled—with fear, Brianna was certain. The room seemed suddenly to go insane, the girls shrieked and screamed and convulsed with such vigor.

Tituba decided to "confess."

She talked of a tall man who carried a book; she said that there had been many witches' sabbaths, and that the tall man brought her there through the air. Her tale was such a good one, told with such a mystique—with such conviction of a frightened, cornered mind—that the room sat quiet and spellbound. And by the time the session was ended for the day, Brianna knew that the village was in trouble indeed. Everyone knew that it took twelve to have a "coven." Where, then, were the rest of the witches?

Outside the meetinghouse the March wind was chill and it seemed to howl about the building. Hushed voices offered greetings to her, but when Brianna did not respond, Robert pinched her hard.

"We will go to Ingersoll's for a drink with

the others," Robert told her, and that was when she rebelled.

"No!" In the middle of the street she wrenched herself from his grasp. There were others about, so she kept her voice low, but she could not go into the tavern room and listen to more accusations.

"Brianna! Do as I say!"

She couldn't help but defy him. She turned, and pressing Michael close to her heart, she ran down the street. She did not know that they had been observed, nor did Robert.

But the man who watched them from the window of Ingersoll's tavern did so intently, and he missed nothing. Not the fear—or fury—in her eyes. Or the anger and command in Robert's tone. Watching from the ordinary, Sloan knew, too, that Robert was very, very frightened—and miserable.

"Only the wind has power, my friend," Sloan whispered. "Only the earth and sea can move mountains."

He left by the rear, before Robert could enter from the front. Though he longed with a physical agony to go after the woman, he did not. He turned his horse southward, toward Boston.

His flesh was hot, his heartbeat erratic. He had told himself he only wanted to see the boy—and he had done so. But when he had seen the child, nestled in his mother's arms, he had felt his resolve crumble like dry, leaves. The child was his—beyond doubt. He was very tall for his age, and sturdy. His hair was as dark as the night, but while his hair could be his mother's, his eyes could not. They were a deep, dark green, with no hint of Brianna's blue—or Robert's deep-set brown. They were large eyes, heavily fringed with lashes.

Damn! Sloan thought, pounding a fist against the pommel of his saddle. How he had yearned to run to her and snatch the boy from her arms. He had never experienced such emotions as now tore through him...

He frowned then, trying to turn his thoughts from the longing he could not appease. Robert Powell had certainly had good reason to be concerned.

Sloan himself was quite certain that the place had gone mad. It wasn't as frightening yet as the European witchhunt. People were not being snatched off the streets to be dragged to nooses or set to the flames, but it was a bad situation nevertheless. So far, it appeared that the Puritan fathers were doing nothing more than conducting examinations. But Sloan had read some of the Puritan literature. He knew the magistrates had carefully been studying such works as Burton's *Kingdom of Darkness* and Baxter's *Certainty of the World of Spirits*. To judge from the gossip in the tavern, these people believed that the Carib slave Tituba had gone to black sabbaths through the air by the vehicle of a broomstick. He had heard by loud discussion that they had determined that such measures as "swimming" a witch were archaic and unchristian— but that they had resolved that the "witch's teat" would be considered evidence, and the devil could not take the form of an innocent person to do harm.

It was not going to be a good place for Brianna. Even if none of her neighbors knew of her past history, it seemed unlikely that she would hold her tongue.

Was there anything that he could do? he wondered in frustration. In Glasgow he had readily kidnapped her and never regretted the decision, but this was different. She was married now to a man that Sloan could not despise. If Robert Powell beat his wife, if he were cruel, such action could be justified.

But under the present circumstances it could not. Even if Sloan could forget the man entirely, Brianna would never come to him. He knew that as surely as he felt that he still knew her. No passage of time could change that.

He sighed deeply. He would have to play for time, and hover in the background. He would be there if she needed him. And, he thought bitterly, this time there would be no payments. No services bought or rendered. He would just be there—because he could not leave.

Suddenly as he rode, he was angry. As angry with her as he had ever been. She should have come to him already. Surely she was aware that he was in Salem. If she'd ever cared at all for him, she should have known how very badly he wanted to see his child, and she should have offered him the joy of holding the boy, if nothing else.

Damn her—damn her, a thousand times over! He groaned aloud and his body shook. How could she have left him? How could she have married?

Because he'd had a wife. The answer was so simple, and yet so bitter. And all the more ironic because he knew what it was like to love one woman—and owe his name and protection to another.

In her simple woolen garb she was more beautiful than ever. She had matured in the more than two years that had passed. Her face had sharpened, but beautifully so. Her figure was fuller, yet she still moved as though sailing from place to place. She seemed quieter, perhaps wiser—but still her eyes could snap with blue fire, and she would fight heaven and hell to have her way.

He fed on his anger. It was good, if only because it helped to assuage the pain of knowing he could not touch her. She owed him—she owed him the courtesy of seeing his child. If he had only known...

He never would have left her, Alwyn or no; Robert Powell or no. Neither the devil nor God himself could have convinced him to leave her—not even when she had begged him herself.

He laughed aloud suddenly, and spoke to the wet and frigid March air. "She is a witch, friends! The kind to beguile a man beyond reason, to taunt and torment him to the end of his days, no matter where he goes, or what he does!"

His horse pricked up its ears and Sloan

laughed again, dryly, as he patted its neck. "Sorry, old boy. Ah, perhaps it is best that she does not come near me. I would want to beat her senseless for keeping him away from me. For leaving me..."

He sighed deeply. He was a fool. He was going to stay around here—torturing himself—while his crew spent all their profit in Boston. Letting his anger and desire simmer and brew until it was a powderkeg just waiting for a spark. He was going to stay and hope that she'd come to him—before he went mad and burst into her sanctified little Puritan household.

Brianna was baking bread again when Robert returned to the house. From the way she pounded into the dough, Robert knew that she longed to pound into the magistrates—probably Hathorne.

"Well," she demanded tartly, "what did you learn in the ordinary?"

Robert ignored her and went to Michael, who was sitting on the floor playing with pewter tins. "Want to come for a walk with Papa, Michael? A thaw seems to be truly setting in, and we'll start plowing up the fields soon. Perhaps your Mama has a carrot or two we might spare for the mules."

Michael happily lifted his arms to Robert. Brianna glanced up and bit her lip, then quickly looked back to her work. Michael was getting too heavy for Robert to hold. And Robert did not look well. She believed that the things going on were disturbing him perhaps even more than her.

Robert walked by Brianna. "You will see; things will return to normal. Seems we have found our scapegoats," he said bitterly. "After Tituba's story the other two would do best to admit their guilt—so that our good people can start saving their souls—and let them live out their mortal lives!"

"A confession will save them?" Brianna demanded.

"Aye—from the rumor that I hear."

She smacked the bread soundly. Maybe there would be justice here—if it was true. She knew these people, and the truly pious would rather die than "belie" themselves, for they believed that God would eternally damn them for a lie. Yet she did not want to trust Robert's words, because it was quite customary anywhere to execute a confessed witch.

He touched her hair then, and bent to kiss her forehead. "I do not think that we have anything to fear." He smiled wanly. "Ingersoll's was most interesting. John Proctor was there, quite disgusted. 'Come to fetch his jade,' he said. Mary Warren is his servant, you know. Her fits did cease, he said, when he thrashed her. He is a man of good standing in the community and he is sick of the nonsense. 'Spectral evidence!' he snorted to me. And old George Jacobs calls the girls 'bitch witches.' It will end, Brianna." He turned away from her, cradling Michael's little face close to his shoulder. "Brianna, do not run from me again. I cannot help but be afraid. None know of you but Eleanor, and she would never harm you.

But if someone did hear something, they could so easily accuse you!"

Brianna swallowed miserably. "I'm sorry, Robert."

"I know how you feel," he murmured. "Well, young Michael, we shall go for our walk. Where has Mama put your coat?"

"I'll get it!" Michael cried happily, shinnying from Robert's arms. He took his coat from the deacon's pew, and Robert helped him into it. Then Robert rose and his dark-brown gaze caught hers again, opaque and troubled.

"There was other talk at the ordinary," he told her, pausing a second. "Lord Treveryan was there right before I came."

"Oh?" The single word caught in her throat. She tried to keep her eyes level with Robert's; they refused to stay so.

"He sailed in a week ago."

"I had heard."

"Had you?" Robert seemed surprised. "Why do you suppose that he has come?"

She shrugged, feeling half blinded as she started to pound into the dough again, trying to reply blithely. "He is a sailor. He captains his own ship. Such men must sail the seas, or so I suppose."

She waited for Robert's answer. It was slow in coming.

"We will talk later, when Michael sleeps."

Brianna nodded and Robert and Michael went out.

The rabbit she cooked that night was tough and stringy, and improperly seasoned. Her bread burned. When she attempted to set the table, she dropped the forks and knives.

Each time she felt her husband's eyes upon her, she wanted so badly to be able to pretend with assurance and bravado that Sloan's being near meant nothing to her at all.

And yet when Michael was at last in bed asleep, Robert's stand regarding the situation was not what she had expected at all.

"One of us must bring Michael to see him," Robert told her. Again he stood at the mantel gravely surveying her.

"I beg your pardon?"

"Brianna," he said very softly, "the child is his, and he will know it when he sees Michael, if he does not suspect so now."

"How can you say that?" Brianna cried, rising from her chair. "Who is to say that he knows we are here or even that there is a child at all?"

"He knows," Robert said. Then he sighed. "His presence here does not make me happy, yet it cannot be denied. He is no fool, we both know that."

"No, Robert! I do not want him to see him! Michael is our son. There is no reason—"

"There is every reason. By the law Michael is mine. But by blood he is Treveryan's. We must trust him—"

"Trust Sloan Treveryan!"

Robert paused, shocked by her outburst. Each word he uttered cost him dearly, and yet he knew that he was right.

"He does not deserve that. He saved your

life not once but twice, and for that I am eternally grateful. When he came for you in England, he could have taken you. You told him that you wanted to be with us—and he respected your desires, rather than his own. There is no reason to believe he would harm you now in any way. But for all that he did for you, he deserves to be shown his son."

Brianna stood, shaking her head, her mouth going dry. "Robert," she said at last, and the sound took great effort, "he cannot care. Our lives have gone separate ways."

"If you choose not to see him, then I will do so."

"No! If we leave it alone, he will sail away again!"

He smiled at her. "Are you afraid to see him?"

"No! I—I don't know. Please, Robert, our life is set. We have done well here. I—"

"Let's go to bed, shall we? It has been a very long day, full of tumult, and I am very tired."

She lowered her eyes and swallowed fiercely at the lump that rose from her heart to her throat. She nodded.

Hours later she still lay awake. She did not want to see Sloan. She was afraid of him. Not that he would harm her but he might destroy all the resolutions, all the contentment she had at last learned. While awake, she became aware of the sounds around her. The wind tore around the whitewashed frame of their home, howling and moaning, rising and falling.

She frowned, and twisted in the bed. Robert

was sleeping, but was tossing about. She lowered her head to his chest but quickly withdrew with dismay, for it was not just the wind that she heard. His wheeze was terrible and he was gasping with each breath he drew.

She was worried, and wondered whether to wake him or let him sleep. She gnawed upon her lip with concern, then pulled her own pillow from beneath her and carefully lifted his head to set it higher. He mumbled something, and turned again. His forehead felt feverish, and so she climbed out of bed and hurried to the water basin, squeezing out a cloth to set upon his forehead. She did not go back to bed that night, and did not sleep.

In the morning she dressed with the first coming of light, bundled Michael into warm clothing, and went out to find the doctor.

Dr. Griggs came back with her and shut her out of the room while he examined Robert. He came out to the kitchen looking grim.

"A fever it is, not uncommon with this winter we've endured."

"But what can we do? He cannot go on wheezing like that!"

Dr. Griggs sighed—and Brianna remembered that this was the same man who had diagnosed "witchcraft" as the cause of the girls' illnesses.

"For a stronger man it would not be so serious. For Robert you must take great care. I've a physic to prescribe for him, and keep him still and in bed and never flat—he must be raised upward as he is now. He needs complete rest."

"Yes, Yes. I will see that he gets it," she said.

Griggs wrote out his prescription and left her—anxious to return to the meetinghouse where the magistrates planned to continue their examination of Tituba. That morning Brianna could not be worried about the proceedings. She was too concerned about Robert.

The days passed slowly and torturously for her. There was Michael to tend to, and now Robert. With Robert in bed all the tasks on their small farm fell to her. The land needed to be readied for the spring planting, and fretting about that made Robert wheeze worse. Brianna had to be a cheerful whirl of energy, convincing him that she wasn't burdened at all.

Eleanor came by on the seventh of March to tell her that the examinations seemed to be over, the "witches" had been sent to jail in Boston to await their trials, and with any luck it would all end.

Brianna breathed a sigh of relief and went back to the task of single-handedly coping with things. She wasn't sleeping well, for she heard the labored sound of Robert's breathing all through the night. And when she dozed, she was horrified to discover that she had dreamed of Sloan, and she was almost gladder to live with exhaustion than to endure such dreams.

The witchcraft tumult had died down; Sloan would sail away, and all would be well.

Toward the end of March, Robert began to show improvement. When Sunday morning dawned on the twentieth of March, he smiled at her, then gravely suggested that she take Michael and attend church services.

"I don't feel right about leaving you alone," she told him, so glad that he was smiling. But he had lost even more weight, and his cheeks were terribly hollow. His eyes seemed enormous.

"I want you to go. You haven't been out at all—and for the both of us, I want you to be there."

She promised that she would go to the afternoon meeting.

Brianna arrived a little late and rushed into a full meetinghouse to find her place upon the bench. Deodat Lawson, from Boston, was at the pulpit. Brianna noticed that the people seemed uneasy, and she wondered what might have occurred during the morning to cause such a thing. But she didn't think about it long, for she was glad to be at the meeting; never had she felt the need for prayer so deeply in her life.

She needed to pray that she stop dreaming of Sloan, imagining herself in his arms again.

Suddenly a shout rang out—high over the drone of the minister's preaching.

"Look! There sits Goody Cory on the beam—suckling a yellow bird betwixt her fingers!"

Brianna's eyes, like those of all others in the congregation, turned to Goodwife Martha Cory. She was a sound churchgoer and upright pillar of the community, and Brianna was astounded at the words cried out by Abigail Williams. Someone would discount them, surely! Martha Cory was a stout and hale elderly matron, a solid farm woman to the bone. She sat stiff and straight on her bench, looking neither right nor left at the accusation.

Then Ann Putnam, Sr., was on her feet, shouting that she, too, could see the specter of Martha Cory on the beam.

No one else spoke. Ann sat again, and the service went on.

Brianna was trembling when she gripped Michael's hand, and hurried out when it was over. Eleanor was behind her, calling out her name and asking if they might ride home together.

As they headed for home, Eleanor began to tell Brianna what she and Robert had missed in their seclusion.

"It was a week or so ago when the girls first cried out against her," Eleanor said of Martha Cory, very distraught. "No one wanted to believe it at first—she is so staunch, you know! But Edward Putnam and Ezekial Cheever rode out to warn her about the accusations and first they asked Ann what Martha would be wearing—and Ann said that Martha knew they would ask her, and had blinded her spectral visions. Oh, Brianna! Do you know what happened then? Martha was at her spinning wheel when they arrived and she welcomed them as if she knew they were coming. She actually asked them if they had spoken to Ann about her clothing! She said that there was no such thing as witches and she was sick of the scandal going on!"

"Good for her!" Brianna proclaimed heatedly, pulling Michael closer to her on the saddle.

"No, no—don't you see, Brianna? To deny witches is to deny the devil, and that is to deny God! It is atheism!"

"I do not believe in witches!"

"But you must never, never say it! Brianna, since Tituba's confession, the magistrates and ministers are convinced that they've barely scratched the surface of some heinous conspiracy. They believe that there is a 'black man' in Boston with a whole host of servants. They will be hunting and probing, seeking out crime!"

"What is being done is the crime," Brianna said stubbornly.

"Please, Brianna, keep quiet. When Martha comes to trial, she must prove her innocence."

Brianna didn't agree, but neither did she argue the point. She had to worry about Robert before anything else—including the fact that Sloan might well still be near.

They reached home, and Eleanor came in for a minute. They did not mention Martha Cory to Robert, and he seemed very glad of the company, so Brianna was happy.

As happy as she could be at that time of her life.

But by the beginning of April she was feeling the birth of a new panic. Eleanor came to see her with another friend, Sarah Ingersoll, the spinster daughter of the people who owned the ordinary.

Robert was still in bed; Eleanor put her

fingers to her lips and urged Brianna to close the door.

"Oh, Brianna, Sarah has come to warn you—she hears everything in the taproom, you know."

Sarah bit her lip and nodded unhappily. "Brianna, Rebecca Nurse was arrested and brought to investigation."

Brianna's eyes darted to Eleanor's and were riveted there. Rebecca Nurse was a grandmother, the matriarch of a wonderful Christian clan who worked the land and loved their God with all goodness of spirit and complete charity. If Rebecca was practicing witchcraft, then God might as well be too. But she didn't echo those sentiments out loud.

"They can't be serious!" she protested.

But both women nodded unhappily.

"It's worse than that," Eleanor told her. "The Proctors have been arrested, both John and Elizabeth. John roared like a bull, I can tell you, but it did no good."

"And Rebecca's sister, Sarah Cloyse, was arrested."

"They're all being sent to Boston to await trial."

"Oh, God!" Brianna gasped, sliding to sit in the deacon's pew.

"There's been talk, Brianna," Eleanor said.

"Talk?" She looked sharply at the two.

"You have not been cried out against, but your name has been bandied about. They say that you do not believe in witches, and you think the whole thing a travesty."

305

"That much is true," Brianna said bitterly.

"You need to leave here," Sarah suggested. "For now, anyway."

Brianna lifted her hands. "We cannot! It would kill Robert to try and ride away now."

The two women sat with her and commiserated with her. No—she could not leave. Robert was too ill to undertake a journey.

Brianna promised to stay close to home and talk to no one.

By the end of April, Sarah and Eleanor were back. Mary Warren, John Proctor's servant girl, had tried to withdraw her testimony against John. No one would accept her retraction as truth. She had tried to talk until she had become so harassed and confused that she had gone into one of the most violent fits ever seen.

The list of arrests was growing longer. Old Giles Cory, a man almost eighty, had been taken, among others.

"Brianna—you must do something. They say that one of the girls muttered Robert's name."

"Robert's!" Brianna repeated, stunned.

"Is there nothing that you could do? What about taking a sea voyage? Perhaps that air would be good for Robert."

"That Captain Treveryan still lingers near. Maybe you could go on his ship."

Her heart slammed like a heavy weight against her chest. Sloan was still there. Sloan—who would understand.

She couldn't see him; she couldn't do it. She just couldn't.

But what kind of a fool was she? The finest people in the community were being arrested on the flimsiest of evidence. If they came for Robert, what would she be able to do?

"Thank you for coming," she whispered to Eleanor and Sarah.

"What are you—"

"I'm going to try to leave Salem," Brianna replied, wincing miserably. "I'll go and see that—uh—Captain Treveryan and ask for passage."

Chapter 16

It was not to be as simple to see Sloan as Brianna had hoped. It would be a week before she could do so. Eleanor knew that he was staying in the neighboring town of Lynn, but not exactly where. Sarah found out at the ordinary that Lord Treveryan was a guest at the home of Lord Turnberry, a man of inestimable means—and Brianna brooded that she would probably not get past the front door if she didn't get a message through to Sloan first, asking if she could see him.

Sarah came to her rescue again. When a delivery boy brought mail to the ordinary, Sarah saw to it that he brought Brianna's note requesting an audience back to the home of Lord Turnberry.

Brianna spent a miserable night wondering

if her request would be answered. It had been more than two years now since she had seen Sloan. Was it possible that he had forgotten her?

But Eleanor arrived at the farm before noon; she quickly gave Brianna a warning glance, called out a cheerful greeting to Robert—then stuffed an envelope into Brianna's hand.

Eleanor hurried past Brianna to the bedroom door, asking Robert if he felt well enough for a visit. Brianna heard her husband reply quite pleasantly that he was always glad to see a caring friend.

Brianna ripped the envelope open, her fingers trembling. She was almost afraid to read his fine looping scrawl. What if he refused to see her?

She couldn't think that way. She forced her eyes to focus on Sloan's reply.

Goodwife Powell, I shall be available this afternoon at the home of Lord Cedric Turnberry if you've business with me.

There was no signature. The paper seemed cold to the touch, as cold as the words. It was beginning to seem possible that he had forgotten he had ever known her.

Brianna sank down by the fire and sighed. She had to go. Increase Mather had at last returned from London with a new charter and governor—a New Englander named William Phips. Phips was setting up a court of oyer and terminer to preside over the ridiculously large number of witchcraft "criminals" beginning to fill the prisons not only in Salem Village, but in the Town, and even in Boston.

She shook and her fingers moved to her throat. It was impossible to forget the feel of the scratch of a rope.

She was going. She would beg and plead, and Sloan, because he was a decent man, would take them somewhere. But why should he? she taunted herself. She couldn't pay him for passage. Or could she?

She wanted to die with her own thoughts. She was horrified! Did she want him to make demands on her, to suggest a form of payment so that she could be the martyr, believing that she would do anything to keep them all alive?

Her eyes darted to the bedroom door. She could hear the low murmur of voices, Eleanor's, Robert's—and occasionally, Michael's laughter. She gritted her teeth, then walked to the entrance.

I will not betray him, she mouthed in silence to herself. Then she smiled, catching Michael as he waddled over to her knees and lifting him into her arms. "Michael, you must stay with Papa. Eleanor, would you mind if I went out for a bit? Robert? I—"

"You mustn't fret for me so," Robert interrupted her. "I would make out fine, were Eleanor here or not."

She didn't want to dispute him, but neither did she want him left alone with Michael—who could tax his strength.

Eleanor spoke up quickly. "Robert, I'd appreciate the company, if you've no objection. My parents are distressed, and it seems that we all snap at one another over all that is happening. May I stay?"

"Eleanor, you are always welcome," Robert assured her sternly.

Eleanor cast Brianna a quick glance. Brianna nervously tucked a tendril of straying hair back into place at the knot at her nape, and she smiled a little uneasily at the two of them, kissed Robert's forehead, and left the room.

For a moment she stood shivering by the fire. She thought that she should comb her hair, that she should change to her Sunday best. Then she cried out softly, impatiently—and with shame—found her cloak, and hurried out back to saddle the mare.

Lord Cedric Turnberry—Rikky, as he was known to his peers—was a few years short of Sloan's age. He was a slim man, with a dry wit and a cynical view of life, ever quick to see which way the wind blew, and ready to bend to it. But he was a shrewd man, fond of amusement, and charitable to his fellow man in a way Sloan found appealing. Rikky had moved to the Colonies, made a fortune in shipping, and regained prominence with the ascension of William and Mary to the throne.

He was fond of elegance and now sat in velvet and silk in his drawing room, sipping port while he watched Sloan Treveryan pace.

Treveryan stopped at the window, looking northward, stared broodingly at the day awhile, and retraced his steps to the mantel once again.

"I would not wish to pry into your business, Treveryan, and yet I must admit to curiosity. Why is it that a message from a simple Puritan goodwife has sent you—the demon of the seas—pacing my poor home like a caged tiger?"

Sloan grimaced and poured himself a goblet of the port. "She is an old acquaintance, Rikky."

"And is she," Rikky queried shrewdly, "the reason you have come here, dallying while you send your crew to recreation in Boston?"

Sloan studied his port. "She is."

"But married now."

"Aye." Sloan breathed bitterly.

Rikky lifted a brow over sharp gray eyes. "But she comes here this afternoon. Why?"

Sloan walked back to the window and stared out at the afternoon. The wind was blowing and the sky was a somber color. Winter never seemed truly to become spring here. "I'm not quite sure," he murmured to Rikky. He turned then, curiously, to face his host. "But I'm concerned myself; I don't like what I see happening here."

"This witchcraft business?" Rikky asked, scornfully waving a hand in the air. "A petty vengeance, if you ask me, nothing more. All those poor souls in the prisons! Men running around praying and fasting! Bah! 'Tis a farce."

"A farce that seems to be getting out of hand," Sloan commented. He frowned. "Turnberry, I was at Ingersoll's tavern on the day of one of the first examinations. It was most peculiar. They were suffering. I do not believe that I have ever seen such contortions in my life. I'd be ready to call it a grievous show myself—except that something does ail those girls."

Turnberry shrugged. "The power of suggestion, my friend! And you must understand the history of our little communities! First, while you were marching into England with our beloved William, these people were busy ousting their hated governor—Andros. All bloodless, of course—but they were still without their charter. Once upon a time the Puritans had a guarantee that they would rule themselves, but that changed with the loss of the charter. Men of the Church of England began coming in, encroaching on Puritan territory. Then there were the Quakers, of course. Ghastly quarrels erupted between the two factions—I promise you, more have hanged for being Quakers than for being witches! But onward with my theory. Three years ago or so, when the people of Salem Town and Village were one parish, there was a split in opinion about bringing in a new reverend to tend to the chosen of the Village. Our Reverend Parris was the subject of much dispute, and the Putnams were the ones to insist on his being instated. Note that now the witch trouble started in the house of the Reverend Parris—and that Ann Putnam has become most respected as a 'seer of witches'!"

"You say she is just a vicious child?"

"No, I do not," Rikky corrected. "She hears the names of her neighbors bandied about with hostility and she fears for her existence, or her family's place in the neighborhood. Then we take a slave from the Caribbean telling tales to the children that her old mistress is a witch, and voilà, you have a child slipping steadily into fits—created by the mind, and not by witches!"

"A good theory, Rikky, but these good people are convinced, it seems, that they harbor a host of the devil's disciples. And I might warn, you—they cry out against those who disdain them."

Rikky snorted. "They would not dare to touch me! I am a servant of Their Gracious Majesties, William and Mary."

Sloan grinned. "I might remind you that Our 'Gracious Majesties' do not doubt the devil or witchcraft. They are tolerant and insist on firm proof, but they would not disapprove the setting up of a court for proper trial."

Rikky laughed. "You know damned well, Treveryan, that you do not believe in witches!"

"Not per se, Rikky. But I believe people practice black arts. In old King Louis's court there was a particularly heinous case—quite well covered up, since the king's mistress was involved. A woman called 'La Voison' was selling potions, a number of lewd priests were in with her, and they were creating devil altars out of the bodies of nude women. They used the blood of infants in their rites—and poisoned numerous people. Poison does kill—so if the practice of 'witchcraft' includes murder, it becomes a crime. But cases like that are rare and I believe what you say, that all this in Salem is a matter of spite complicated by hysterics."

"Aye, that I do believe," Rikky mused somberly. "Our problem here is that a number of the fools give such ridiculous evidence against others to save themselves that they make it all appear very real." He sighed. "They'll try Bridget Bishop first. The woman has quite a reputation for malice, you know, 'cursing' her neighbors and the like. She's been brought to trial once for witchcraft already. The most damning evidence against her will be the dolls stuck through with pins found in her house. It is a sad thing that she will go first, for I believe that she will hang."

Sloan swallowed his port in a gulp, and shuddered. What could he do here? he wondered. The place had gone insane!

There was the sound of a horse clipping along the road. Sloan took a deep breath and realized that Rikky was beside him. "Ah, your Puritan enchantress comes! I'll make myself scarce."

"You needn't—it's your home."

"Oh, I'd like to meet the lady, sometime. But not today. I think I'll go down to Salem wharf and hear all about the witches! I'll be careful to stay gone for the day, and you remember that my servants have learned to be painfully discreet!"

Sloan was about to reply sharply, but Rikky was already gone. Sloan was all alone, waiting, wondering what they would say to each other after all this time.

She should have come to him long ago...

She was afraid to see him, yet she longed to see him. Since she had known he was here, she had been almost physically ill with the craving just to look at him again.

She was a wife now, she reminded herself. Robert's wife. And by God, she owed him everything. He had been kindness itself; he had loved her, cared for her—and she loved him. Never in the exact way she'd loved Sloan, but every bit as deeply.

Brianna forced her feet to carry her to the door. She knocked, and the door opened.

A liveried black butler bowed deeply to her.

"Miz Powell?"

She nodded. The door opened further. "Come in, please, ma'am. Cap'n Treveryan is awaiting you in the drawing room."

With a very correct bow the young butler turned, expecting her to follow. There was not far to go to the double doors that apparently led to the drawing room, but in those few short steps, her heart and mind began to whirl again.

He could not be the same. She would see him, and she would be all right. It would be gone, the "thing" between them—the attraction, the passion, and the love. Perhaps it had always only been illusion...

It had been so long since she had seen him. Almost a lifetime.

The butler threw open the doors and stepped into the room. Brianna froze at the entrance.

His back was to her. He was in tight-fitting fawn breeches and a white shirt with a minimum of ruffles. He wore no wig, his hair was still as dark as the night, as sleek as the night, and knotted at his nape. Just as it had been that first time she had seen him...

He was very tall, and very straight, and his shoulders were as broad as she remembered. And when he began to turn, she almost wanted to scream.

Nothing had changed. Nothing.

"The Goodwife Brianna Powell, Lord Treveryan."

And then suddenly she was ushered into the room. The butler was gone, closing the door behind him, and Sloan turned.

But he had changed. His face was as bronzed as ever, contrasting with the sharp jade color of his eyes, but there were new lines about those eyes, and his cheeks seemed more gaunt. Perhaps it was his expression that had changed. He seemed both tired and worn, even more so than on the day they had parted and she had seen how deeply anguish could etch itself into a man's features.

He held his hands still clasped behind his back, as if keeping them there to exercise the most stalwart control. His eyes moved over her slowly, and she could read no emotion in them. Nor did his features alter—he might have been surveying a stranger.

"Brianna," he said at last. And then he turned from her, and walked to the window. What he watched out on the road she did not know, but it had his attention and she did not. Her mouth was dry, her body quivered.

He turned back to her quite suddenly. "May I get you something to drink?" he inquired politely. She shook her head, somewhat stricken as she watched him turn from the window, his gaze never leaving hers.

"Come, have a glass of port with me."

Still she could not leave the safety of the door. He walked to the rear of the comfortable room, to a sideboard containing a crystal decanter and matching glasses. Into the glasses he poured the ruby-red liquid, and then his long strides brought him disturbingly near.

He handed her a glass. With trembling fingers she reached for it and felt again the full scrutiny of his gaze. But then he moved inward again, sweeping his arm to indicate the settee.

"Sit down, Goodwife Powell. I'm anxious to hear the purpose of this visit."

She was not sure that she could walk, and yet she did. Lowering her eyes, she swept quickly by him, reaching the settee none too soon, else she would have fallen. Her hand clutched the crystal wine goblet as if it were her salvation. Once she was seated, she very quickly took a sip of the liquid, so very grateful that it moistened the dry tinder of her throat.

He did not sit, but stood instead behind the green velvet chair that faced the settee.

He lifted his glass, and a hint of his old arrogant smile curled the corners of his mouth.

"To you, Goodwife Powell. To...past associations.

She could not raise her glass again. He shrugged and tossed back his head to drain his own. Something about him changed then, as if he were a night-stalker tiring of an unexpected chase. Had she forgotten that his eyes could gleam like those of a wary cat, hard and cold as marble? That his tension, unleashed, was like the portent of a storm within the confines of a room?

"Why have you come, Brianna?" he demanded sharply, and his tone, both husky and brushed with fury, stole her breath away. "Why?"

She winced as if lashed by his words, and suddenly her plea came rushing from her. "I need your help."

"For what?"

"I—I wish to leave Salem, Village and Town. I—"

She broke off, because he was bitterly laughing. "Why are you still here, madam? Of all women, you should know that when a witch-hunt begins, it does not end until countless innocent souls are laid bare to bleed."

"We couldn't leave." She swallowed, tightly clutching her port. "Robert cannot travel the roads in his condition. His lungs cannot take the dirt, nor would his heart sustain such a journey."

His expression did not change or falter; he continued to stare at her, until slowly he smiled. "I see. You have come to ask me for a favor. For passage for you and your husband. And that is all."

She did not want to meet his gaze; her eyes refused to fall at her mind's command. "Yes," she whispered.

He picked up his glass again—and she started when he sent it flying across the room to crash against the hearth and fall, shattered, into the ashes. His fingers, as taut as talons, gripped the rich velvet upholstery of the chair.

"That is all?" he grated hoarsely. Before she could do more than emit a startled cry, he was around the chair and beside her on the settee, catching her chin in his hand, studying her eyes with a blazing anger and something quite close to hatred.

"My *son*, Brianna! That child is my son, my flesh, my blood! And you did not see fit to allow me to see him, or even to tell me."

Brianna wrenched her chin from his grasp, got up quickly from the settee, dropping her wine, and ran to the door. He caught her forcefully by the shoulders, spinning her around, then holding her to him. But it was not a lover's caress; it was not longing she saw in his eyes—just fury leashed with a hard and cold demand for explanation.

She tossed her head back angrily to meet his assault. "Michael is not your son, Sloan."

"Liar!" he charged her with a furious shake.

"He is not!" she railed in reply, heedless of his anger. "Robert is his father. Robert married me and gave Michael his name and a home—and his presence and his love! How dare you—"

"Bitch!" He was so angry then that he pushed her from him, not at all certain that he wouldn't strike her if he remained too close. "Never did I desert you, Brianna, never did I leave you! You sent me away without even telling me!"

She stood still, the blood draining from her face. God, they had become bitter enemies! But still she could only think of all she remembered about him: his scent, fresh and male and reminiscent of the sea and storms and waves and radiant sun and musky darkness; his face, so familiar she could feel again, without touching him, her fingers over his cheeks, his mouth; his eyes, that sizzle of jade, cold stone, burning fires. If he reached for her, she would know exactly how to fit into his arms, she would know the giddy, heated feel of her body when his pressed to it like steel. If...

They had become strangers and enemies, she reminded herself.

"I did not know when you left!" she cried out.

Sloan sank suddenly down on the settee, placing his booted feet on the small table before it. He cast her a dry glance of contempt and she shivered at his tone.

"Am I to believe that?"

"I don't care what you believe," she snapped out, spinning around to leave.

He was no longer on the sofa. She was suddenly staggering back and he was blocking the door, rigidly standing with his legs wide apart as if sailing the ship, his hands upon his hips and his eyes seeming to rip through her like green blades.

"Not so fast, Goodwife Powell. Since you are here now, I think we have a few things to discuss."

"There's nothing more to discuss. I came here for help and I can tell I shall get none." She tilted her head to the side, determined not to cry, or beg. "Don't you recall?" she taunted him politely. "I remember a day when you told me I might come to you if ever I found that I was in need."

"Ah," he returned in mocking kind, "but I loved you then. Fool that I was, I loved you."

Her lashes fell, her heart felt as if it were slowly crumbling. She had been the fool, to love on when love had been lost.

She raised her head again. "Could I please step by, My Lord Treveryan?"

"I've yet to hear what you have in mind."

Brianna took a step back, narrowing her eyes while her breath seemed to catch and rasp. "What game are you playing, Lord Treveryan? I told you—"

"You told me that you wished to leave Salem. Am I supposed to drop everything and take you away—you and your husband, and *your* son—is that it?"

His tone was too polite; she had not seen him for a long time, but once she had known him well, and his quiet tones were still, it seemed, his most dangerous.

"Yes—and you've refused me, so let me by."

He backed against the door, crossing his arms over his chest. "Oh, I've not refused you—yet." He lifted an arm toward the settee. "Sit, Goodwife Powell."

She turned, and sat once again upon the settee. Sloan went down upon one knee to pick up the remnants of the glass she had dropped. She stiffened, feeling his dark head near her knees.

"How is Lady Treveryan, my lord?" she queried with quiet and caustic rebuke.

"Dead," he answered bluntly, not looking her way.

Her heart seemed to catch in her throat. "How convenient for you," she murmured.

He jerked up, swinging an arm back with such murderous loathing in his eyes that she cried out, scrambling to the edge of the settee. Dark lashes fell to conceal his eyes; his arm dropped to his side and he walked to the hearth and tossed the fragments of crystal into it.

"I—I'm sorry," Brianna said at last, miserably. She did not turn to look at him.

Silence came between them and then he spoke again. "Well, madam, I can't say that I quite understand why you are here. There are other ships."

"I cannot pay for passage."

"Can't you?" he queried cruelly. "I seem to remember that you are not averse to hiring out—in desperation, that is."

She rose again, her heart and mind a tempest, wishing she could tear him limb from limb. She stared at him then, watching his casual, negligent stance against the mantel, clenching her fingers into fists at her side to keep from lashing out.

"Or," he persisted, "did you come to me specifically knowing that I just might be an easy mark?"

The taunt was more than she could bear. She flew at him, her clenched fists flying hard against his jaw and chest as she sobbed out furious curses.

He caught her arms, locking them with his own behind her back. She struggled with little success, then leaned against him, cheeks dampened by the futility of her action, by her rage, by the wrenching agony of seeing him again.

His hand came to her throat and her cheek, gently caressing as he raised her eyes to his.

"I could demand it," he told her raggedly. "I could tell you that, yes, I would take you away, but that you must pay for the passage. And by God, if you did not agree, you would be a fool, for this place is quick becoming a cauldron of insanity. You would do anything to save your child and your husband. It would make things easy in your heart and mind."

"No," she whispered. She could do no

more. Staring in his eyes, feeling the fascination, the pulse and heat of his body pressed so naturally to hers, she could do no more.

His lips twitched into a bitter and pained smile. His thumb continued its tender graze over her throat and chin, and the soft flesh of her cheeks.

Then his mouth slowly lowered to hers, taking it, softly, in gentle exploration. But that touch was like fire, burning, melting her. His mouth fused to hers then, hot and demanding, sending desire, pulsing and vital, raging through her. His arms wrapped around her, his palms found the curve of her breasts and her hips; his fingers found the pins in her hair and flung them aside until the dark mass, rich and luxurious, cascaded all around them.

Brianna choked out a cry, and turned her face from his. She vaguely heard him draw a hesitant breath and his hand fell tenderly to her head. Ah, how easy it would have been! She had not forgotten him; she had not forgotten how they had loved. Had he forced his bitter taunt, she might have been his again, here, now, upon the clean-swept floorboards of Lord Turnberry's elegant drawing room.

But he could not. She was married, and not—as some ladies of the courts often were— oblivious to such commitments. If she did love him now, she would despise him if he forced her, no matter how deep her need. A woman like Brianna would live with the torment of the damned for her betrayal. Nor would she be wrong in suffering, for Sloan still could not deny that she had married a good man, weak in body but strong in heart.

Holding her gently, he smoothed back her wild display of midnight hair. "Don't fear me. I ask nothing of you. I never would have. I just needed to hold you again, and believe that you still loved me. Forgive me."

She could stand no longer. She slid along his length to sink to the floor at his feet, sobbing softly. He knelt down beside her, pulling her work-worn hands from her face, clutching them tightly in his own, swallowing back his misery.

"Sloan," she whispered, not raising her eyes to his, and speaking with anguish tearing at her every word. "I do love my husband. Not as I...have ever known love with you. But he is a good man. He does not deserve this from me. Sloan! I am so frightened!"

He set his arms about her again; this time with no passion, and no heat. "I will take you from here. You and Robert—and Michael. He will never know that you came to me, I swear it. I will come to your home and speak to him."

She couldn't seem to stop crying. He rose, refilled her port glass, and forced her to drink. And kneeling again before her in front of the hearth, he tried to smile, although the effort was bitter and weak. "I had to see Michael. I don't believe that I can ever reconcile myself to not being able to call him mine."

"You couldn't take him from Robert! Please, Sloan!"

"Nay, love," Sloan said bitterly, "I wouldn't." He rose slowly, painfully. He made her rise then, too, brushing the tears from her cheeks. "I will take you to New York. The governor is a friend of mine, and though the city is in English hands now, it still retains some good Dutch practicality. There is no talk of witches there." He paused, swallowing fiercely. "Go home, Brianna. I will send to Boston for my crew, and I will come and speak with Robert."

Brianna nodded slowly, and walked woodenly to the door, as if each step were a great effort. Once there, she turned back to him. He felt her stare, but he couldn't look at her. He gazed into the fire, afraid that if he saw the haunting blue beauty of her eyes again, he would cry out and race to wrench her into his arms again.

"Sloan...thank you," she said.

He lifted a hand, not sure that he could speak.

She gave out a little gasp, then cried, "I do love you."

The door swung open and then she was gone.

By the time she neared her farmhouse, she was composed. She had indulged in an orgy of tears on leaving Lynn, but by now she had dried her eyes. She squared her shoulders, and was practicing a composed, peaceful smile.

She could never let Robert know where she had been, or the tumult that she had suffered. Tomorrow night they must both be surprised; she must play the very meek wife while she let Sloan and Robert discuss their future—and their flight.

As she turned down the path to the house, she began to frown. It seemed unusually dark, as if no candles were burning inside and the fire had almost died. And the door stood ajar...

Brianna leapt from the mare, heedless of where she might wander. She tore through the front door, calling out Robert's name, then Eleanor's, then Michael's. No one replied.

A gust of wind slammed the door behind her. An eerie gleam of stunted gold and burnt orange from the dying fire was cast about the house as she stared in shock, then raced to the bedroom.

Panic struck her as she continued to call out names and hurried back to the main room and kitchen. *"Robert! Michael! Eleanor—Where are you?"* The wind howled in reply. Then she saw the parchment. Before she touched it, she knew what it was, but she forced herself to sit and focus her eyes on the page.

> *To the Marshal of Essex County or his Deputy or Constable;*
> *You are, in Their Majesties' names, hereby required to apprehend and forthwith secure, and bring before us, Husbandman Robert Powell on Tuesday next being the thirty-first day of this Instant month of May, at the house of Lt. Nathaniel Ingersoll's in Salem Village, who stands charged with having Committed*

327

*Sundry acts of Witchcraft on the Bodys of
Mary Warren and Abigail Williams and
Ann Putnam to their great hurt and Injury,
in order that Robert Powell may be examined
by us. Relating to the premises abovesaid, fail
not.*

    Dated Salem May 27, 1692
      John Hathorne
      Jonathan Corwin   Assistants

Brianna read the warrant several times over.
Then she dropped it and started to scream.
But there was no one to hear her, only the
wind to carry her screams to places unknown.

Chapter 17

Sloan barely had time to reflect on the promises
he had given Brianna before the door burst open
again. He turned, somehow expecting her, yet
not knowing what good it could do if she did
return.

Rikky was back, not Brianna, and agitation was evident in his gray eyes and his quick
stride.

"She is gone?" he asked Sloan.

Sloan nodded, frowning.

Rikky crossed the room, grabbing his arm,
leading him from the room as he spoke. "Go
after her. She will reach home to find that her
husband has just been taken."

"What?" Sloan demanded, drawing back. He stared at Turnberry, eyes narrowing. "What are you saying?" he demanded harshly.

Rikky shook his head with impatience. "Listen to me, please! I heard at the wharf that a warrant had been issued for her husband, Robert Powell—and that it was about to be served. Powell has been arrested by now, and there is nothing you can do for him had you a mind to. But you must get to her! If she creates trouble, I promise you that there will be a warrant out for her by tomorrow."

"They can't—" Sloan began incredulously.

"They can!" Rikky assured him. "It's mad—but legal! The magistrates have been assigned by the royal governor! This isn't James anymore, it's William and Mary! Legal procedure, legal warrants, legal examinations—and public trials to come!"

"I've got to get her!" Sloan rasped out.

"Aye, aye," Rikky agreed, but he was grasping Sloan's arm in a desperate attempt to keep him back. "But you must use great sense and discretion! There are ways to get people out—jailers who can be bribed and the like. Let me work on it, Sloan. If you lock horns with the government now, it can never be reconciled."

"I don't care."

"You have to care, Sloan, for the child."

Sloan went dead—still, startled that Cedric Turnberry knew about Michael—and that he himself had forgotten.

"Very well," Sloan said, exhaling a long

breath. "I'll be discreet. But if they come for her, Rikky, I'll say damnation against William and Mary as well as James." He inhaled deeply, then took Rikky's hand. "My thanks, good friend."

Rikky smiled. "My horse is outside. Go."

He went, riding like the wind that had arisen—a wretched, cold wind that chilled the bones. Before he reached the path to the Powell farm, Sloan slowed his gait, narrowing his eyes against the darkness. There was a woman moving along in the darkness at a hurried pace; a woman clutching a child who whimpered, and fought her hold.

It was not Brianna. The moon glowed down on hair that was very blond. He nudged the horse forward; she turned and saw him and started to run.

"Wait!" Sloan cried out. His heart was hammering, for the child she carried was Michael. "Wait! I swear before God, I am a friend!"

She paused, clutching the child very tightly. He cried out in protest, trying to beat at her breast with chubby fists. "Papa! Papa! I want Papa back! Where is Mama, 'Leanor? Let me go!"

"Hush, Michael!" The woman commanded distractedly. She looked at Sloan nervously while he dismounted from his horse. He came to her, and she shrank away. "Who are you?" Her eyes raked over his clothing, which was clearly not the simple fabric of their Puritan homes.

"Treveryan, girl. My name is Sloan Treveryan."

Her eyes, large and dark and very lovely, widened. "Lord Treveryan! The ship's captain!"

"Aye, and who—"

"Did she come to you, then? Did you see her, Brianna Powell? Oh, it's too late!" The girl wailed, hugging the child. "They came today, with a warrant for Robert. I told them he was too ill, but they would not even leave him in his home until the examination! Robert would not protest; he was anxious to leave with Brianna still gone!"

"Where did they take him? Salem—or Boston?"

"Salem—they do not transfer prisoners to Boston until they have been examined. Oh—oh, dear Lord!" she said, and then she burst into tears, which started the little boy crying too.

Sloan stepped forward to grip her shoulders around the child's quaking body. "Stop, lass, you must," he said quietly. "We will do something. But first, where is Brianna now?" He longed to wrench the boy—his son—from her. It was good that the situation was so urgent.

"I don't know. When they took Robert, I ran with Michael. They've arrested even a five-year-old, you know. I wanted to bring him home, to do something. You don't know where she is?"

"No," Sloan said worriedly. "Could you two have crossed one another without meeting?"

"Yes, yes! I came through the woods. Our property adjoins"

"I'll find her," Sloan promised, and he leapt back on his mount. He couldn't believe that she could have outdistanced him so completely, and started for the farm at a gallop.

He had not gone far along the path when he saw her. She was mounting a haggard old mare.

"Brianna!" Sloan shouted, moving to block her escape.

She didn't seem to recognize him, as her wild eyes seemed to look through him. "Give way!" she demanded hoarsely.

"No!" He twisted his mount about and caught the mare's reins. "Stop this!" he commanded her.

Some flicker of recognition flashed through her eyes, but was quickly gone. Her jaw hardened. "Give way. I've got to get to town."

She wrenched so hard on the reins that the horse neighed and she broke Sloan's grasp. The nag took off.

Sloan chased her. It was not difficult, because his mount was stronger. He reached for her reins but could not grasp them. He was forced to lean forward and pushed her from the saddle. He leaped from his horse as she rolled into slush and foliage, the breath knocked from her. Their horses, unattended, ran away.

"Damn you!" Brianna raged, staggering from the mud. "Damn you! You don't understand. They've taken Robert!"

"And damn you for being an idiot!" he charged, trying to hold her. She was wild; never had she fought with such ferocity. He realized that she was beyond reason.

"Brianna—" he tried one last time. She leaned her head forward, biting deeply into his arm. He swore, shaking off her hold. He knew that if he was to help Robert, he had to do it alone. Brianna would only complicate the situation and possibly put them all in danger. He had to stop her. Hating himself, he waited until she raised her head again, then locked his hand into a fist and struck her jaw.

She went limp, falling into his arms. He picked her up and carried her back to the house.

It was a small place, he discovered as he pushed open the door with his boot. A main room with a hearth and a side room. The door to that was open and illuminated by the dying blaze in the hearth. Sloan went through it with her, and laid her down on the large trundle bed. He sat at her side, running his fingers through her hair.

He should take her away, he thought dully—let her scream and despise him. It might be better than what would come.

A sound alerted him and he stood, ready to fight. It was just the woman he had seen on the road, holding the now-sleeping child. Sloan relaxed.

"Is she—is she hurt?" the woman asked worriedly.

"I've hit her. She should awaken soon,"

Sloan replied tonelessly. And then he saw that the blond girl looked as if she, too, were about to fall. He came to her, at last having a chance to hold the child.

"Let me," he murmured, taking the boy from her. She gave him over easily, and as Sloan held him he felt both warm and shivery. This was his son—his own flesh, his own blood.

He closed his eyes and felt the child's little fingers close around his. Then he placed him in the small bed at the foot of Brianna's bed.

"I'll bring you some ale," the girl said dully. She left the darkened room. Sloan stared down at his son. He gently touched the pitch-dark hair and could not help touching his lips to the small forehead. The child sighed. Sloan was shaken.

He went to Brianna's side. Her cheek, when he touched it, was cold. Sloan pulled the covers over her and tried to see her jaw. She would have a small bruise. It hurt to see his own handiwork, but he'd had no choice.

"Come, have your ale."

Sloan looked to the doorway and the blond woman stood there. She turned, and he followed her out to the main room, where she indicated the deacon's pew. He sat and accepted the tankard she handed him.

"I'm Eleanor, Lord Treveryan," she told him, and he nodded at her, drinking deeply of the ale, which made him feel much better.

Eleanor had prodded and fed the fire. Now it burned brightly, and there were two lanterns on the table. She was studying him nervously by the light.

"You knew her before, didn't you?" she asked.

"Aye."

"She never said so," Eleanor said. Her eyes came to his again, dark and troubled. "She did tell me that she had been condemned—and saved."

He grimaced and shifted his body on the pew. He felt suddenly tired, and too old for his years.

"What will you do?"

"I don't know yet. Wait, I suppose. They haven't had any trials yet. Perhaps all the wretches caught up in this will be released."

Eleanor shook her head, fighting back tears. "I do not think so. They took my betrothed today too. He had been a constable. He resigned his post, saying that he could not serve such warrants any longer. As soon as he resigned, he was accused."

"Easy, girl," Sloan said, not sure he could console her.

"If they've taken Robert, they will take anyone."

Sloan drank his ale and handed her the tankard. "I'll have some more. Is there nothing to eat here?"

She filled his tankard and handed it back. "Yes, I'll find something."

She found bread, cheese, and dried fish, and as she placed them on the table, she spoke more calmly.

"You're a friend of the king. You must be

able to do something. This has gone too far. John Proctor said at the very beginning that the girls would make devils of the lot of us! One of them even admitted that they had first called out his wife's name for sport. John was so right! As soon as he stood by his wife, he, too, was accused. He can be a harsh man—he is a great brute of a fellow—but if witches do exist, they can't be the likes of him! His servant, Mary Warren, is one of the girls afflicted, yet she tried to deny what she had said, and when she did, they brought her forward for examination! Again and again—until she 'confessed' that John had come to her, demanding she sign the devil's book. Yet"—Eleanor paused miserably—"you mustn't judge us Puritans too harshly, for we truly wish only to do God's work."

Sloan smiled dryly. "I do not judge you harshly. This is not a consequence of your creed, it is part of our time." And, he wondered silently, was there a way to escape it?

Eleanor paused as she set the food on the table. "Sarah Osbourne died in prison; she, too, was ill when they took her."

Sloan came to the table. "I cannot clear the prisons," he told her quietly.

She lowered her eyes and sat opposite him. "But you will try to free Robert and—"

"Your young man. Aye, I will. I've a friend with better connections than mine who can help."

Eleanor chewed nervously on her lower lip. "Those who are cleared will be in such horrible debt. Few have much money, and none will be freed who cannot pay their prison costs."

Sloan reached out a hand. "Eleanor, times like these bring out the worst in men—and the best. There will be help from other sources."

She nodded slowly. "We can only pray."

Sloan rose, rubbing his temple. "I'll go to the jail, and find out what I can do for Robert—and I'll see to your young man too. What is his name?"

"Philip Smith," Eleanor replied quickly. "He met you in Boston, when you first came."

Sloan nodded and rose. "Now, get me some blankets and clothing for Robert and your Philip."

Eleanor hurried to do his bidding. Sloan took the things and came out to the yard. His own horse had apparently run back to Lynn and a feedbag, but Brianna's wretched mare was in front, nosing the ground for grass. He caught her easily, and packed the clothing and food on back of the saddle. He saluted Eleanor and left.

Sloan had no problem reaching Robert Powell. The jailers were stout fellows and solemn men, but seemed grieved by the overflowing of their cells. The elder of the two brought Sloan along the drafty facility never intended for this type of scourge, commenting reasonably on the course of events.

"We had Mary Warren here, for a spell,

we did. And when she was left alone, she was calm, swearing that her Master Proctor was no wizard. Yet the magistrates came again, and before long she fell down in fits the like of which could have twisted the hardest heart! It's a sad thing, it is, the devil here in Massachusetts!"

Sloan heard continued clinks of metal. "They are shackled?" he asked the man with a frown. The light was dim, but it was still apparent that most of the weary wretches resting on the cots were old men and women—except that it was shocking to see children here also, many no older than ten. "Official orders, Lord Treveryan. Seems that witches' specters can fly and torture their victims unless they be bound."

Sloan spat out the word "Rubbish!" The jailer cast him a glance, but did not dispute him, for Lord Treveryan was a duke and a personal friend of their Majesties, William and Mary.

"There's your man, Powell," the jailer told Sloan, clanking his ring about to find the proper key. "Now, sir, I mean no disrespect by this, but by the law I must ask. You've no files there, knives, or the like?"

Sloan answered wearily. "No—I've no knives. Blankets and ale and clothing, and nothing more."

The man nodded and locked the door behind Sloan.

Sloan blinked for several minutes before seeing the figure on the cot. There was a clink of chains, and he saw the figure rise.

Sloan moved to him. Robert Powell looked

like death itself; his coloring was gray, his cheeks were hollow, and his great dark eyes seemed sunken in his face.

"Treveryan?" he whispered hoarsely.

"Aye, Powell, 'tis me." Sloan hunched down by the cot, spreading out the things he had brought, finding the spiced ale. Robert watched Sloan as he accepted the drink, and when he had swallowed it, he continued to stare at him with no malice.

"Get her away from here," Robert said simply.

Sloan lifted his hands. "She won't come without you, Powell."

"Make her."

Sloan rose and walked about the cell. "I can't do that—yet. I've some powerful friends and we're going to stand and fight this horrible madness."

Robert started to laugh but then started to cough. Sloan thumped him on the shoulders and the fit ended. He sobered quickly. "Treveryan, I do not believe that anyone can stop it. And I would rather see Brianna and Michael safe."

Sloan emitted a slightly impatient oath and with renewed determination came back to sit on the cot. "Powell, I'll be damned if I'll let you sacrifice yourself! You've not been examined yet or brought to trial. There is no evidence against you."

"Imaginary evidence."

"And what is that?" Sloan demanded.

"Everything—or so it seems," Robert replied dryly.

"Listen! If you go to trial, we'll do our best to free you."

"And when they condemn me anyway?" Robert queried politely.

"Then you confess. They are not even planning trials for those who confess first."

"Only so that the confessed may testify against others."

"Damn you, Powell! Take an interest in your life."

Robert sighed and offered Sloan a weary smile. "I cannot confess to witchcraft. It would be against all that I believe. Perhaps it would be an answer to the court, but there is a far greater judgment. And who would answer unto God for my lie?"

"God in His heaven, Powell! Where is your sense, man? Surely the Almighty sees what is happening!"

Robert lowered his eyes and shook his head. "I will stand trial—and fight for all that I am worth. If you would help me, Treveryan, take my wife and my chi—Michael—far away from this madness." He paused a moment. "I assume you have seen Brianna. I have been terrified since they brought me here that she would come, so wound and wild in my defense that they would lock her away, too, without bothering for a warrant. Where is she?" He came to his feet, gripping Sloan's arm with a surprising strength.

Sloan eased the grasp from his arm, pressing Robert back to the cot. "She's fine."

"But she can connive, that one can! If she's

promised to stay behind, she will follow anyway."

Sloan could not help but grin; it seemed they both knew her well. "Powell, she can come nowhere. I knocked her unconscious."

Robert stared at him in wonder and actually smiled humorously. Then he closed his eyes and murmured, "Thank you."

Sloan noted how the shackles were grating against the man's wrists, and he winced. He tapped Robert's knee. "Take heart, Powell. There are things that can be done; I'll see to it that you are cared for. And when the time—"

Powell's dark eyes opened. "I'll not take your charity, Treveryan. Just take my wife—and go."

Sloan sighed with exasperation. "It's not charity, Powell—and I won't take your wife. We will fight—and if all legal venues fail, then we'll revert to the illegal."

Robert, in return, shook his head with vast exasperation. "Treveryan, never have I thought you an idiot! She has always loved you. Make her go with you. Tie her, beat her, cage her— but get her away!"

Sloan smiled slowly, aware that he could have no greater adversary than this man he would never fight. "You're wrong, Powell. Your wife loves you. I'm but in the sidelines of this. And I'll not let them hang you—because she does love you."

Sloan turned to bang for the jailer to come and release him; but Robert called him back.

"Promise me one thing."

"What?"

"I'll fight. I would do so no matter what, for I am not wizard or witch! But...if things should go badly, if it should become necessary—will you take her away, no matter what her protest?"

"Aye," Sloan said slowly, "that I will promise you."

He tried to give Robert an encouraging smile, then said "I'd like to get the boy away now. Would you object to his being sent to New York?"

Robert closed his eyes again, casting an arm over them. "I would bless your efforts," he said simply. Sloan nodded and called out sharply for the jailer.

Before he left, he saw Philip Smith and promised the bitter young man that he would do his best. He managed to leave him a more hopeful, if not a more cheerful, fellow. Then he paid the jailers the price of a week's stay in the prison for the two and added a generous sum to see that they, and the other wretches in the place, would receive the best care.

He almost raised a fist against the younger of the two guards when he was asked to pay for the very shackles that were rubbing the flesh raw at Robert Powell's ankles and wrists.

But he cooled his temper and paid the price. Whether Powell and Smith were proven innocent or not, they would be responsible for their stay—and all materials, including the shackles.

He did not want to make enemies with these men. Sloan knew that there could be no escape here such as they had ventured from the wild streets of Port Quinby. To pull off a jailbreak here he would have to bribe the guards and coerce their cooperation.

Before he left, he warned the jailers that Robert was ill and that his health was in their hands. He didn't need to threaten, for he was quite sure that his reputation with a blade had preceded him.

It was near dawn when he finally returned to the farmhouse. Eleanor had been dozing in the deacon's bench. Brianna, awake and furious, was pacing the floor. He approached her, ready to reassure her, but was given no opportunity to do so.

"Damn you, you bastard! How dare you do this! You are not husband or father to me, you are not anything to me!" She lashed out at him then with the strength of her frustration, fear, and fury. Her nails caught his cheek; her fists, his throat.

And he was far too tired and dispirited to take it from her. "Bitch!" he seethed in return, struggling for her arms. Eleanor awoke, concerned. From the bedroom Michael could be heard to whimper.

"Please," Eleanor began.

Sloan did not feel like fighting before an audience, nor did he want to wake or upset the child. With a deep-throated rumble of fury he caught her wrists with a steel-tight grasp and dragged her along behind him, back toward the door.

"I've a few things to say to Goodwife Powell, Eleanor, and if you'll excuse me, I believe I'll say them outside, where perhaps the cool air will keep me halfway sane!"

"Eleanor, stop him," Brianna gasped out, aware that she had provoked him past a reasonable point. But Eleanor did nothing.

Brianna stumbled along behind Sloan's furious strides until they were out the door and she was suddenly freed—sent flying to land indecorously and ironically in a patch of wild and beautiful lilacs, so recently sprouted from the slush and snow. Gasping for air and dignity, Brianna looked up to see that he was no less furious now that he had released her. His face was severe with tension.

"Madam, perhaps I am nothing to you, but your good husband just gave me his full blessing to beat you black-and-blue!"

What was there that made her lose all reason? Perhaps it was his power over her. Perhaps it was because he had come back into her life and he was, once again, the greatest threat she had ever known. He had, in the space of hours, erased all the time that had passed between them. She thought herself good and decent, and resolved to her life, but when he stood by her, the air became charged and her blood boiled.

She couldn't help herself; madness directed her words and actions as she lashed out at him.

"Get away from me, Lord Treveryan. I'm sorry I came to you. You are eager for his death! God knows you might take any woman, and yet she whom you cannot obtain holds a fascination. You wish that he would die!" Shredding the lilacs through her fingers, she pushed her way to her feet. "You think to take his son. Well, you will not do so! Dear God, how I despise you!" Her voice was rising, shrill and laced with laughter. She barely saw his features, the whiteness that touched his flesh beneath the sea-bronze or the constriction of his jaw. She didn't even realize that despite the cruelty of her words, he was calm—as if he knew something about her she did not know herself.

"Dead, dead, dead!" she screamed. "Dead—as your own wife!"

One step brought him to her, and he slapped her a stinging blow across the cheek. There was no power behind the slap. It only stung, but had, perhaps, exactly the effect she needed. She became silent, stunned by the torment in his eyes. He stood not a foot away, this tall, broad man who had battled against the injustices of the world. She was miserably ashamed of the things she had said.

Her shaken fingers rose to her cheek. "Sloan, I am so sorry," she whispered. "I didn't mean any of it. I just don't know what to do. He cannot endure much hardship. He will die! Sloan, I have to see him! I have to let him know that I'll not desert him, that—" She ran out of words because there were no words to explain her feelings of absolute desperation.

He lifted his hands hesitantly, as if he were afraid to touch her, but he enveloped her in his arms, and the vibrant warmth of his body did give her comfort. "Be calm, my love," he told her. "Brianna, be calm. You're wrong. I do not seek his death." He pushed her away gently, looking down into her eyes. He smiled slightly. "I know, as well as you do, what it is to love in different ways."

She trembled slightly. She could not ignore the strength of his arms. He, too, felt the tension building between them and released her, offering her his hand. "A truce, milady? Then we might be able to help Robert," he said in a light and teasing tone, and she was reminded of the buccaneer who had kidnapped her long ago to save her from peril.

"A truce," she replied.

He led her back to the house, and his speech became that of the ship's captain—the man who brooked no opposition to his orders. Eleanor, sitting by the hearth, jumped to her feet and surveyed them both anxiously, decided that they had done no harm to each other, and sat again. Sloan brought Brianna to take a place beside her and spoke to them both.

"Robert and Philip both come up for examination in a few days' time. Then, beyond a doubt—since no one seems to escape unscathed—they will be returned to prison to await trial. Brianna, once that is done we can have Robert removed to better quarters. The right sum of money, it seems, can buy a certain freedom. He'll be under guard, but you'll be able to care for him. Eleanor, I'm afraid Philip must wait in the jail because he is young and healthy, and nothing I say can change that." He continued, "You both must realize that we are playing a game where rules of reason do not exist. I don't suggest that we behave as cowards—when it is possible and reasonable, within the law, we'll all speak. But to shout out, to fight, will do nothing to free them. Understand?"

Both women nodded gravely. Sloan eyed Brianna skeptically.

"Do you understand?" he repeated.

"Aye!" she stated again, irritably, and he smiled, because though he did not like her hysterical, he did not like to see her beaten and hopeless either. "I'll take you to see your husband tomorrow," he told her softly, "as soon as we've seen Michael off."

"Michael!" she gasped, and was then on her feet again, facing him. "You can't—you said— you wouldn't..."

He placed his hands on her shoulders and pressed her back to the bench. "No!" he said harshly. "I'm not stealing the child! Would you have him be here for this?"

She shook her head, and he saw that she was swallowing back tears. "He'll be safe in New York, Brianna."

She stared down at her hands.

"Now go to bed, both of you, for what is left of the night."

Brianna looked up at him with surprise. "Go to bed?" she queried blankly.

A smile tugged at his lips. "And sleep. The days will be long from here on out."

"You're staying?" Brianna queried.

"Aye—I've spent nights in worse places than upon a floor before a warm hearth. Now go."

Eleanor obediently walked into the bedroom. Brianna followed her, then turned back. He had an elbow rested on the stone mantel; his fingers moved over his temple in a slow, taut rub, as if his head were splitting. He suddenly realized she was still standing there. "Go to bed!" he snapped to her. She hesitated, thinking there was something that she should say, but there wasn't really anything that could be said. She went on into the bedroom, closing the door behind her.

Eleanor was on Robert's side, already stripped down to her shift. Brianna removed her shoes and stockings and dress, but before she crawled into bed, she picked up her son— and brought him with her, curling his little body to her own. She needed him there. She didn't think that she could send him away, but she knew that it would be best. And yet she was afraid. She was handing her child over to his natural father—a man who longed for a son.

Eleanor shifted suddenly, saying in a fervent whisper, "Whatever he asks of you—do! Robert and Philip have a chance because of him. Please... I'd have a hundred men myself, if but one of them could do something."

Brianna went very tense and swallowed. "Eleanor, he is asking nothing of me."

The bed heaved as Eleanor twisted about. "Then how long do you think he will stay?" she demanded. Her voice was touched by anger, fear, and the hysteria that came easily these days. "I will pray that you rot in hell if you let him leave, Brianna! I will pray that you will rot!"

Brianna could not be angry in return. She understood too well the meaning of fear. "I won't let him leave, Eleanor," she promised.

Chapter 18

In the morning she found Sloan shirtless and shaving over a pitcher in the kitchen, wincing as he nicked his chin—and scowling when he saw her there. A fire burned healthily in the grate. Brianna gazed at his naked torso, lowered her eyes, and stepped by him. "I've tea and honey," she murmured. "The bread will be stale, but—"

He caught her arm. "It matters little," he said.

Eleanor came out. Silence reigned over the room while Sloan finished with the razor and donned his shirt, and the women laid out a meal. Then Michael appeared in the doorway, rubbing his eyes—and staring at Sloan curiously. She heard his voice as he went to the little boy.

"Michael, I am a friend. My name is…Sloan."

Brianna did not turn around, but she sensed what she would see if she had: Michael, very uncertain and wary as he surveyed the stranger suddenly in his home. He would be about to rush past Sloan and race for the protection of her skirts.

"Michael," she said quickly, cheerfully, "Sloan is going to help your papa. Go with him and let him help you dress." She held her breath for a long moment. Eleanor touched her arm and she turned at last to see that the two had gone to the bedroom.

She could not eat. Then they heard Michael's laughter from the bedroom and Sloan's deep voice droning something that they could not understand. And then Michael's delighted laughter again.

At last the two reappeared. Michael crawled up on his mother's lap. "Like him!" he said, pointing to Sloan. Sloan didn't sit; he inclined his head toward the room.

"Get his things," he told Brianna. She nodded and set the child down to eat, and went to do as she had been told, fiercely fighting off tears as she packed the tiny garments she had sewn so lovingly.

In time they were ready. Having only the one horse, Brianna put bridles on the ornery mules. They rode first to the jail. Sloan did not go in, but remained outside with Michael.

Despite all her promises Brianna cried out when she saw her husband.

"Oh, Robert!" she cried, sinking to his side.

He smiled at her. "My wife," he murmured, and he touched her hair, his eyes surveying her. "Brianna, don't look at me so. Have faith in God."

"I do," she lied. Since Pegeen's death it had been difficult to have such faith. "Oh, Robert..."

He pushed himself up and caught her chin between his hands, his eyes dark and serious as they stared into hers. "I do not want you here, Brianna. Treveryan can take you away; and as your husband, I order you to go."

She smiled and shook her head. "In anything else, Robert, I would obey. But at your trial I can testify in your defense." She hesitated. "I am sending Michael to New York today."

He winced, and his pain touched her deeply, but as regarded the child's safety, she knew they were both in accord. "Thank him," Robert muttered, and she knew he meant Sloan. "Let me hold you," he said, and they leaned against the cold wall.

He was very warm, Brianna thought worriedly. But it was true that he seemed to have everything that could be provided here. Blankets, water, ale, and the crusts of his breakfast remained on a tray. The bread and the fish smelled fresh.

In time he slept. She kissed his forehead and left him.

On the street she could find neither Eleanor, Sloan, nor Michael. Eleanor, she assumed, was still with Philip. But where had Sloan taken her son?

At last she hurried to the taproom of the ordinary. Sloan was alone at a table, a tankard of ale before him. With rising panic she rushed over to him and demanded, "Where's Michael?"

"I've sent him on."

"With whom? You didn't let me see him, you didn't let me say good-bye, you didn't—"

He caught her hand and pulled her down to sit opposite him, his eyes flashing a warning as he indicated that others were discussing the witchcraft arrests and the coming trials.

"And what would that have done? You would have wept and he would have gone off in tears, fighting all the way! Your friend Sarah Ingersoll took him to Rikky's."

"Rikky's?"

"Lord Turnberry's," Sloan explained impatiently. "Rikky will take him on to Boston. In Boston, he'll find Paddy and the *Sea Hawk* will take them on to New York and Lady Eastwood, Rikky's aunt."

Brianna stood, eager to rid herself of his presence. Michael was gone, and she knew she was going to cry, and she didn't want to do so in front of Sloan.

But as soon as she was on her feet, he was on his. She had barely reached the tavern door before he caught her hand, shackling her wrist with his fingers. He tipped his hat to a passing stranger as he led her back to the mules.

"Leave me alone!" she insisted.

He shook his head. "I'm afraid I can't. Tomorrow at Robert's examination, I will be at your side—ready to throttle you if you create a disturbance."

"You act as if I had no sense!" Brianna cried out, shaken. She couldn't bear him so continually by her side. Alone.

"Nay, Brianna. You have sense. But it can too easily be lost these days."

"I need to go home alone," she rasped out. Again he shook his head and spoke bitterly.

"I promised your husband I would let no harm befall you," he told her. "Look—here comes Eleanor. We will ride back to the farm and wait for tomorrow."

Somehow, the night passed.

The crowds were out for Robert's examination, but then he wasn't the only "witch" being examined that day.

Philip English, a very wealthy sea merchant, did not hold his temper well. When questioned by Hathorne, he demanded to know, "Where, then, is your toleration?" His preference, all knew, was for the Church of England, and such a thing might well have stood against him.

Martha Carrier was brought in, and remained in total fury throughout the proceedings. She brought her garrulous voice high over the ear-splitting screams of the girls. "You lie! I am wronged!"

Though she was an unpopular old woman, Brianna quite believed that she was.

Then it was Robert's turn.

Brianna, sitting between Sloan and Eleanor, knotted her fingers into her palms in such a tight clasp that she dug holes in her flesh, and only later noted the blood she had drawn.

Hathorne began the examination.

"Why do you afflict these girls?"

"I do not," Robert replied calmly, and the girls, from their place of importance near the front, began to scream. Brianna could not see which, but two of the young girls and one of the older teens fell to the floor in wild convulsions.

"How can you deny it?" Hathorne's voice boomed out.

"As Christ is my witness," Robert replied, staring straight at the magistrate, "I deny it."

"Oh! He pinches me! He pinches me!" someone cried out—Abigail, Brianna believed. Then that child, too, was on the floor, so contorted that her head snapped back to touch her heels.

The room began to swim before Brianna. She had known it would be this way but she had prayed for strength. She couldn't bear it...

She hopped to her feet to defend her husband.

But before she could, Sloan was dragging her out.

"Listen, little fool!" he raged to her. "You'll do nothing here but get your own name on a warrant! When the trial comes, we'll be there—calmly, determinedly, and legally—to save him. Brianna, I swear to you by God and my own life, I will not let him die!"

Brianna looked into his eyes, so intensely brilliant today. She smiled then, sadly, for the cast of the swashbuckler still sizzled there—and she believed him, and God alone knew why he stood by her...

"Why don't you sail away?" she asked him.

"Because you are a witch," he said lightly, "though we mustn't let these people know. Because you've cast your spell on me. I cannot touch you, but I'd die a thousand times over for you. Neither time nor distance can change that."

"It's...it's my husband we are fighting to save."

Sloan sighed deeply and shook his head as if he were a bit puzzled himself. "I don't know if it is because you love him—or because I have come so to respect him myself. It doesn't really matter, does it?" he asked her, his tone suddenly bitter.

She shook her head, lowering her eyes. "Everything that you want is out there now, Sloan. William and Mary sit on the throne. Your home awaits you. You are free to find a woman of noble birth—young and beautiful, willing and able to give you an heir. But here you stay beside a Puritan goodwife who has brought you nothing but heartache, death, and misery since the day you first saw her."

"I am a fool, aren't I?" He tried to grin. "Before God, Brianna, I beseech you to stay silent! Right now, all you can do is be strong for him. Trust in me that I will take action when the time is right."

The afternoon brought no surprises. Along with the others examined that day Robert was to return to prison to await his trial. Because of his health and Sloan's money, Sloan was able to obtain a mandate giving

Robert the privileges usually reserved for the very prominent. He was to reside in rooms in the center of the village under guard, but Brianna could nurse him so long as his shackles were in place and he did not attempt to leave the building.

They moved into those rooms on June second, the day of the first trial. Bridget Bishop was found guilty, and on June tenth the sheriff brought her to Gallows Hill, and she was hanged.

Robert and Brianna spent the days in tension and misery, with Robert beseeching her to leave before her name could be brought forward.

Sloan divided his time between Robert's guarded rooms and the jail, for he had promised Eleanor he would support Philip Smith. Cedric Turnberry maintained his social status with the magistrates and justices, reporting all the news to Sloan as he obtained it.

The prisoners were distressed at the news of Bridget Bishop's execution, but they weren't without hope. There had been physical evidence against Bridget—the dolls stuck with pins. She had been condemned on more than the say-so of a group of hysterical girls.

Robert was to have come to trial on June twenty-ninth but he was too ill on that particular date to stand; so the magistrates took mercy and postponed his date.

Brianna did not attend any trials, though she had set her hand to a petition stressing that old Rebecca Nurse had been a kind and charitable neighbor who could not possibly be a witch.

Sloan did attend the trials and was horrified at the evidence presented. Rebecca was such a pillar of the community that even Hathorne doubted her a witch. When sent out for deliberations, the jury came back with a verdict of not guilty. But the magistrates asked them to resume their deliberations, for when another of the women on trial, Sarah Good, had come in, Rebecca had muttered something about her "being one of them." She meant that Sarah was a fellow prisoner, Sloan knew, but the court was obsessed with the belief that she meant a fellow witch. Being old and hard of hearing, she had not answered when asked about her reply.

But Sloan did not need to protest on her account. Rebecca had a large family and they meant to do something.

One of the women tried that day, Susanna Martin, had quite a reputation for maliciousness. She was condemned for having bewitched a man's oxen and for having appeared in a number of men's bedchambers to taunt them into signing the "devil's book."

Five women were condemned in those days. Sloan longed to do something—even if Susanna Martin was a nasty old woman, she did not deserve to hang for such a thing. Two of the matrons had been pious and calm and soft-spoken, no matter what ridiculous thing they were accused of. Like Robert, they absolutely refused to "belie" themselves—

they believed in a far greater judgment than that which they would find on earth.

Sloan wrote to the king and queen, yet knew it would be a long time before an answer could come, much longer than these women could wait. They were scheduled to die on July nineteenth.

When Sloan came to tell Brianna the news, he warned her in hushed tones that they should try their escape soon.

She looked horrible, he decided that day. Too, too thin, and pale. "I'm afraid," she whispered to him, closing the door to the bedroom. "I don't think we can move him at all now! Since those nights he spent in jail he can barely breathe!" she told him.

Sloan watched the grief in her face and could barely stand it. "Brianna, I'm going to Boston, to bring the *Sea Hawk* to Salem in readiness. We cannot wait much longer to leave Salem."

"We must! They haven't tried Robert yet, Sloan." But then she sank into a chair and rested her head tiredly against the wall. "Rebecca Nurse! How could they condemn her?"

"Her family is still trying for a reprieve. Perhaps the governor will grant one. I plan to see him myself, but..." He hesitated. "Brianna, I can not stand much more of this. I can't get too heavily involved, or anything that I say will be discounted when it matters." He hesitated a moment, then said angrily, "When I return, you will be ready to leave!"

He saw the stubborn set to her jaw, and left her.

He didn't attend the executions on Gallows Hill, but Cedric did. "Rebecca went like a lamb to God's fold, a prayer on her lips, an awesome dignity about her. But Sarah Good! The assemblage was shocked, for what Christian dies with a curse on her lips? Sarah promised the Reverend Noyes that he would die choking on his own blood!"

"Good for the old pipe-smoking hag!" Sloan exclaimed.

Rikky chuckled dryly. "I'd not make that sentiment well known, Treveryan. Even those kindly reverends of Boston who do not trust 'spectral' evidence do most assuredly believe that old Goody Good was a witch! But not Rebecca Nurse," Rikky said softly, with a gentle reverence. He glanced at Sloan and grimaced. "I believe you've made a crusader of me, too, friend. Do you believe that I, a lord of the king's realm, plan to spend my evening with the relatives of that lady? Deep and dark at night we will go to Gallows Hill and dig up her body to give it proper burial."

"A toast to you, Rikky!" Sloan said, and the two shared a glass of Irish whiskey. "I'm riding to Boston tomorrow," Sloan said then, "to pull my crew together and try to prevail on some sane ministers to make their thoughts more fully known to the magistrates." He paused. "Keep an eye on her, will you, Rikky?"

"Aye, that I will," Rikky said, a droll humor in his eyes. "The lady must truly be virtuous if you trust me to watch her."

Sloan laughed. "Why, Rikky, you know as

well that I could take you with a blade in seconds and we both know full well that you would never put me to the test! Besides," he added more soberly, "she is virtuous, not to me, but to her husband."

Rikky raised a skeptical brow. "You are not—"

"Lovers? No."

Rikky suddenly became thoughtful and serious. "Aye, Sloan, I'll watch her, and guard her, with all the power I have."

Sloan left for Boston in the morning. When he arrived, he easily found Paddy in a tavern on the wharf. Paddy was tired of inaction and totally impatient with the situation around them. "Blimey, but this is scary, Cap'n! Listening to the talk hereabouts. They argue nothing but witches night and day!"

"Aye, and I fear we're up to more of it. Tell the crew they'll not be endangered this time; we'll oil some palms well and depart with the night."

Paddy eyed him curiously. "We don't mind action, Cap'n. Weren't we with you in Ireland, Sloan, every last jackanapes of us?"

"Aye, that you were. But I'm tired of losing men, Paddy. And I'm getting tired of hangings."

Paddy shook his head and leaned over his ale. "It's a strange world, that it is."

Sloan clapped him on the shoulder. "I've got some men to see, so I'll meet you next in Salem. How's the *Sea Hawk*?"

"Ready to go, Cap'n. Oh, and Cap'n! I've

got something for you"—he produced an envelope—"from Lady Eastwood in New York."

Sloan pocketed the letter. "Thanks, Paddy."

He saw a number of the members of the Boston ministry who were critics of the proceedings, but he learned nothing that could help him. After two days he returned to Salem, determined to make definite plans for escape.

Chapter 19

Sloan found Brianna with Robert. She was growing as thin and pale as her husband, he thought dispiritedly.

He sat with the two of them, speaking about the events taking place in Boston. Robert listened, nodded, and pretended to believe that things could get better. Brianna tried to speak lightly. It was Robert, Sloan thought, who was the stronger. They were trying to find a hope to cling to, but Robert was resigned to whatever life might bring, his faith being stronger.

At length Robert yawned discreetly and agreed that he was tired. He asked Sloan to take Brianna out for a breath of air. Sloan remembered the letter he carried from Lady Eastwood, and added pressure to Robert's insistence. The letter was about Michael's adjustment, and Sloan did not believe he could produce it or discuss it with Robert present—no matter how much he had come to admire the man.

The guards allowed them to exit, and Sloan led Brianna far along, determined to be alone. She didn't seem to mind. Perhaps she needed to feel far away from her husband's prison, if only for a while. They found a wooded cove, gently fit by the moon. A fallen tree trunk served as seating. Sloan gave Lady Eastwood's letter to Brianna and watched the color suffuse her cheeks as she read it.

"Michael is doing well," she murmured to him, and he knew the color would come to her cheeks anytime she thought of their child.

"Paddy is bringing the *Sea Hawk* up from Boston," Sloan said a little harshly. "It's time to leave."

"Robert is not well enough," she began, paling.

"Whether he is or isn't, they might bring him to trial. The wind is blowing both ways in Boston. Some are saying that too many of the accused are escaping justice through protestations of illness, and some are furious that they have not had a mass hanging for the 'confessed' witches. Brianna, more trials are being set and more executions will follow. We must flee."

She nodded and said vaguely, "Soon."

Sloan sighed, and decided he'd have to talk to Robert Powell himself. He couldn't bear to see her so unhappy. He smiled and very gently brushed her cheek with his hand. "All will be well," he whispered.

She tensed at his touch, but then sighed softly, and he tenderly sat her on his lap. "Look at the coming fog," he murmured. "So soft and magical. It blurs harsh edges...ah, Brianna. There is still good magic in the world. Things of grace and beauty..."

Beauty, yes. Like the night that encompassed them. Magic. They might have been alone in the world.

They stared at each other. Her head tilted slightly as if in expectation, her eyes beckoning like the eternal depths of the ocean. Looking down at her, he ached with the need to know her again, to hold her. He could not remember why she had ever left him. And he could not, God help him, remember at all that there was any reason for them to be apart. She was his, and had been since the first time he had taken her, yet he had been the one forever and fully seduced.

The air was fresh and clean, the moon blessed with an ethereal glow of beauty. He brought his palm gently, tenderly, to her cheek. She clutched his hand, and pressed her lips to it, then slowly looked to him again.

He touched her mouth with his, feeling his blood and his life suffused with a warming fire. He savored the taste of her, he caught her to his heart, and felt the erratic thunder of her own. Moon fever, he would think of it later—a touch of madness—but it was only the hunger of knowing that he loved her and needed her. His hands began to move over her, gentle and shaking, then fevered. She was soft and feminine, she was the dream he had dreamed so long. He slid from the tree trunk on one knee, carrying her down, laying her down in a bed of clover and pines.

Her eyes were on him, wide and dark. Her lips were parted, her breathing ragged. He leaned beside her and tasted her lips again, then brought his palm along the length of her, caressing her with reverence. He found the hem of her skirt, and slid his hand along her calf, over her hose, until he reached her thigh, and the erotic fire of her bare flesh. He wanted her naked in the clover—coming to him, touching him, his at last again! He wanted to touch her, drown in her, die with her forever in a sea of verdant green and swirling mist and the sweet smell of summer wildflowers...

But he could not.

What stopped him he would never really know. Her eyes closed suddenly, and she shuddered, and despite the mist and magic he paused. There was a Robert Powell—and Sloan had told him he did not intend to steal his wife. It seemed like a vow, and in his heart he silently cursed the man he could not despise.

Brianna shivered, and opened her eyes, and it was as if an awakening of painful reality had come to her too. "Oh, my God!" she gasped out, and then she was struggling against him, trying to rise. "Damn you...don't, please, don't touch me or come near me again!"

"Wait a minute!" he said harshly, angered

at her condemnation of him. He would not let her rise, but pinned her there, hands to the ground, a knee cast over her legs. "Don't you ever think to blame it on me, Milady Virtue! My God, yes! You were here, you made no protest! If you remained faithful tonight, it was by my accord."

"I really do believe I hate you!" she cried as she strained against his hold.

"Do you? You have a strange way of showing it, my love."

"Sloan! Let me be!"

"Oh, aye, I'll let you be. And why, I do not know, for we both know that what I crave I might have taken."

"No...yes! Yes, you're right! And that's why I hate you, don't you understand! Please..."

He didn't shift, but stared into the night. "I wonder if he wouldn't even give us his blessing."

"What did you say?" Brianna stared at him, puzzled, glad of his weight against her, glad of his hold—desperately aware that she had to break it. "Robert!" she exclaimed, realizing where his brooding thoughts were taking him.

He stared down at her again, ruefully. "It's true, isn't it? He trusts us both. Oh, God, but that's the pity of it! How to bring hurt to such a man! Were he but strong and healthy, a fool or a swaggering bastard! Were he anything other than what he is, I'd care not that he was your husband. I'd take you away, I'd fight, I'd duel—I'd kill or die, but I'd have choice and reason and action to take! Why, in

God's mercy, have I come to like that man? My promises are not to you—they are to him!"

"I cannot see you again. I can't. I still must beg for your help, for I am still terrified. When Robert gains just a little strength, he must be moved. I cannot repay you..." She pulled herself up.

He interrupted her bitterly. "You paid in advance, remember."

She went silent for a moment, then squared her shoulders and stiffened her spine. "Well, if I have paid, then there is nothing to collect."

He gripped her arm and practically dragged her along. "I'm taking you back."

"I can go alone."

"No!"

Soon they were almost at their rooms and Brianna tugged against his arm. "Sloan, you don't need—"

He spun on her, furious—with her and with himself. And suddenly he was out of control again.

"Oh, yes, I *need*. What do you think you have here—steel or stone? I am neither! You will go home to your husband, and I cannot find fault or blame with that. But I love you—and I will never leave you. When you call on me, I will be there. But this...this I can bear no longer. You will stay on your pedestal, Brianna, always. A goddess whom fate has made me worship from afar. But I am flesh and blood, lady, and flesh and blood desires what you cannot give! Women are not hard to come by for lords and gentry, Brianna. I can no longer send you back to another man and toss my way through the night."

Brianna stepped back from him and a cry of realization and dismay escaped her. It was so evident, so very obvious, that she could not ask him to live a life of celibacy. And yet...she had wanted to believe that he was. It was right that he should seek out another; it was right, but it hurt with a wrenching agony. Before she knew it, she was speaking. "You go to another? But you know that—"

He crossed his arms over his chest, his lips twitching with irony and sadness as he interrupted her. "I know that your husband is ill; that you go home to care for him and nothing more. I—" He broke off, emotion flashing quickly through his eyes, as if he had come across some hidden knowledge. His voice was a little harsh, a little incredulous, as he spoke again. "That's the way it's always been, hasn't it?"

"What do you mean?" She breathed uneasily, stepping away from him. "I—I don't know what you're talking about."

He came to her. "You—and Robert. It's never been a real marriage. You've never lived as man and wife."

Furiously she ripped away from him. "We are man and wife!" she cried. "You know nothing—and I want you to stay away from me!" Dismay filled her voice. "He married me—I am his wife! Go where you will!"

She stared at him tumultuously for a moment,

let out a little cry, then shoved at his chest and raced past him.

Returning—to Robert.

Sloan stared after her for a long while. At length he turned and walked down the street. He headed for the wharf and spent the night staring out to sea.

The special court of oyer and terminer met for the third time on August fifth. Sloan did not go to the trials, but Rikky kept him informed. Paddy had brought the *Sea Hawk* up to Salem, and Sloan was busy conferring with him and trying to find a doctor to take aboard to care for Robert Powell. There was nothing he could do at the trial; nor, for that matter, had there been anything Rikky could do. Lord Turnberry was well acquainted with Chief Justice William Stoughton—a man as hard as nails, as strictly puritanical as was possible to be and determined to cast his rising political star into the hands of the majority clamoring to see that the devil's disciples met the hangman.

Rikky returned from the affair very subdued.

"John Proctor was condemned today. His wife is spared because she pleads her belly." He grimaced bitterly. "An unborn child cannot be condemned—even if he is the child of a 'proven' wizard and a 'proven' witch." He continued. "I saw Proctor after the trial. He is still fighting mad and he asked to see me because he thought, as I was a lord, that I might have control somewhere. He told me that two of the boys who 'confessed' and gave evidence against him had been tortured into their confessions—tied head to heels in horrible contortions." He paused. "I had time to voice an objection with Stoughton, but it seems the man is deaf. The town has gone insane, with crazy things being said—witches' sabbaths, rides through the night on poles, devil's rites! What has come over these people? They join their accusers in pure lunacy!"

Sloan was silent for a moment, his thoughts on Robert Powell with an understanding he wished he did not have. Powell refused to add to the very lunacy of which Rikky spoke. And because of it—if he were ever brought to trial—he would hang.

Sloan restlessly paced the room while Rikky looked on. "I'm ready to sail," he told Rikky. He hesitated briefly. He had not gone near either of the Powells since the night Brianna had run from him.

"When is the execution to be?"

"August nineteenth."

"Go to Robert Powell for me, Rikky. Don't even talk to Brianna—see him. Tell him that the noose grows tighter, that we must leave before matters get worse. Perhaps the night of the hanging will be best. There will be many sickened by the sight, determined to keep quiet, even if we should be caught upon the streets."

"If I've been receiving my gossip right,

even our governor—who cares not to take a firm stand—is willing to assist 'departures,' shall we say? In certain cases."

"Those of his friends, Rikky. Powell is not among the elite of this society. He's a poor farmer, nothing more. This will be done on our own. Two men guard the rooms and Brianna has been free to come and go. She will leave; then I'll take on the guards and smuggle Powell out to the waiting ship."

"I'll pick up Brianna," Rikky offered.

"No, you will not. Because you intend to stay here. I will not be able to come anywhere near Massachusetts once this is accomplished—at least, not until this madness dies out."

"Oh, come! I'm a lord of the realm!" Rikky declared.

"Still, I'd not have you involved."

Rikky waved a hand in the air. "None would dare accuse me."

Sloan was about to protest, then decided the matter could be settled later. "We will see."

"I think, though, Treveryan, that you should see Powell yourself," Rikky said slowly. "He has great faith in you."

Sloan scowled darkly. "I've no wish to meet with his wife again, except when I must."

"I'll get her out tomorrow morning. Then you can speak with Powell without any confrontations."

Sloan agreed to the plan. Rikky picked up Brianna in his splendid coach to take her shopping along the wharf. He convinced her that she needed an outing. Sloan waited until he saw the coach disappear, then received permission from the guards to see Robert.

Robert was sleeping when Sloan entered the room, and for a chill moment Sloan started. His cheeks were so gaunt and narrowed that for several seconds Sloan believed he was staring at a corpse. But then Powell opened his eyes, and there was still fierce life in their dark depths.

"Treveryan," Robert muttered. A small smile touched his dry lips. "Is this why my wife has departed?"

"Aye," Sloan said bluntly.

Robert's smile deepened sardonically. "When I am gone, Treveryan, see that she finds happiness. She suffers with me and pines for you. When I am gone, I will thank God that she has you."

"What are you talking about?" Sloan demanded harshly. "I've come here to talk about saving your life. By God, man! You were not meant to be a martyr!"

Robert closed his eyes for a moment, still smiling, a little bitterly. "Whether they hang me, or the Lord takes me on his own, we both know that I am dying."

Sloan emitted a sound of impatience, and Robert opened his eyes to survey him. "Treveryan, my wife prefers to be blind. I grant her that illusion. I am dying. I saw your face before you knew I was awake; you looked like a man staring upon the ragged refuse of a soul departed. We both know that I am dying. My great fear is that I will not do so

371

soon enough to see Brianna swept from this turmoil."

"I promised you," Sloan said hoarsely, "nothing will happen to her. And I've come to tell you that the time has come. We will make good our escape."

Robert sighed, staring up at the ceiling. "When?"

"August nineteenth."

"The day of the hangings."

"Aye."

Robert seemed to digest that information. "She won't do it—she'll be convinced that a move would kill me. Don't tell her anything. When the time comes, just see that she obeys." He tried to pull himself up to a sitting position. "You'll do that for me, Treveryan? For by heaven, I've no strength to fight her."

"Aye," Sloan said softly, "I'll do it."

Powell surveyed him with his curious dark eyes.

"She'll hate you for it."

Sloan did not reply to that. "Stop concentrating on death, Powell. The sea air can do many a wonder for a man."

"As you say, Treveryan," Robert replied, smiling ruefully. "I'll not break faith with you, if you will not with me."

"I will not, Powell."

"One more thing, Treveryan."

"And that is?"

Powell winced, drawing a deep ragged breath. "When I am gone, take your son. Give him what is his. I gave him all that I could, and that was much love. But when I am gone you must take him, with or without his mother's consent."

A trembling had started inside Sloan's gut, and again he wondered fiercely why Robert Powell couldn't have been a cruel bastard, a man to fight or despise.

"You promised not to harp on death!" Sloan said harshly.

"I am not harping, but I am saying now what I will not be able to later. Now, I am done with it. I give you my most solemn vow that I will do my utmost to live."

Sloan left him then—pleased that at last they were coming near to action. The *Sea Hawk* lay in the harbor, waiting and ready. Sloan had no doubt that he would overpower the guards with no difficulty, leaving them trussed up, and departing with Powell. A nightmare was coming to an end.

All that was left was the wait for the day to arrive. As he always had, Sloan came to the sea to wait; he spent his twilights on the wharf, staring out at his ship, thinking on a dismal future. Because Powell was not lying; he was a dying man. Sloan knew the face of death—he had seen it in Alwyn.

And what then? Brianna would be heavily laden with guilt—he knew her so well. She would blame herself, and she would blame him. He stood with his feet planted far apart, his hands on his hips, and his fingers tightened convulsively as he muttered angrily to the breeze, "Damn her! This time, I do damn her." Well, she could rot in whatever hell she chose to make for herself. He was done with it.

But then, there was Michael. His son. Robert Powell had given Sloan his blessing to take the child and to give him his natural inheritance. And, by God, he would! Perhaps Brianna could deny and repel him, but the child was his, and he would take him, with or without his mother's consent, just as Robert Powell had charged him.

Sloan counted off the days, and on the eighteenth he awoke with a feeling of light-heartedness. He felt like a man in his thirties again, in his prime—rather than like a man worn beyond his years. One more day. Tomorrow night, he would be at sea again, facing the wind, feeling the wheel beneath his hands. And, by God, he would cure himself of this! He would live again. He would leave Powell and Brianna in New York—with the child, as long as Robert lived. He would not have to be a part of Robert's death, and when the time came, he would come for his son.

In the meantime, dammit, he would live! Without war, without continual pain—without insanity such as this!

Perhaps he would go to London—make a new peace with William and Mary, which would be necessary if he were accused of abetting the escape of a witch. Court life would be colorful and filled with women in whom to bury himself, and forget her.

Storm clouds were brewing to the east, but

the morning, remained bright. He wondered idly where his host had gotten to, since Lord Turnberry was not by nature an early riser. He was staring toward the water, sipping at scalding tea, when he started, hearing the sharp slam of the door at the rear of the house. Rikky came striding toward him; his handsome features were drawn and he was alive with tension.

Sloan was quickly on his feet, eyes narrowed as he watched his friend's approach. "What is it?" he demanded. He felt the invasion of a dread that tensed his muscles, tore at his gut, made a mist of the day around him.

"I've just come from the home of some of Stoughton's kin. There's to be an examination at Corwin's house, Salem, at ten this morning." He drew a deep, shaky breath. "They've pulled in Brianna."

Chapter 20

There was something very frightening about the way they came for her. It was not like Scotland, where she could hope to run and fight, nor was it like England, where she'd been condemned before she was caught.

It was all very quiet, and very polite. The constables were just at the door, and then they were handing her the warrant—and insisting that she come with them immediately for her examination.

She handed back the warrant. "This is absurd, and I can't possibly leave my husband. He is very ill."

Her show of cool outrage didn't make any difference. She was told that a woman would be sent to stay with Robert, and she might have a minute to take her leave of her husband, if she so chose.

Brianna closed her eyes tightly, then entered the bed-chamber with a heavy, heavy heart. She was not so frightened as she was worried. Forcing a smile, she tried to show him a face of complete bravado. "It seems, my husband, that it is my turn to stand before these fools!"

His eyes closed. "No!" he gasped. His pallor terrified her, and she sank to the bed at his side, holding his cheeks between her hands. "Robert! Have faith in me—I am not afraid of them. Believe me when I say that I've met the devil in the flesh already in Matthews; these men at least take time to question, misguided as they may be. Oh, trust me, Robert, it will be well!" She paused, gathering strength and will. She'd never spoken about Sloan to him; now she had to. "Robert, no matter what happens, whether they condemn me a thousand times over, I will be all right. Treveryan will spirit us away. And I am not on trial yet—I must go up for examination first."

He opened his eyes, and his fingers came, trembling, to her cheeks. He touched her softly, as if to memorize the contours of her face and the feel of her flesh. She cried out and leaned against his chest, holding him tenderly.

"Goodwife Powell!"

The constables were pounding on the door. Her time was up. Robert threaded his fingers through her hair. "No fear, my love, know no fear."

She tried very hard to smile at him. "I am not afraid, Robert, except that they are taking me away from you. But it will not be long; it cannot be long."

"No," he said. "It will not be long."

She hurried to the door, then smiled back at him. "I love you, Robert," she told him, and then she rushed out, before her courage could fail her.

When the constables reached for her arms, she wrenched herself away. "You needn't escort me. I see no girls yet whom I might afflict with my gaze or touch. And I am perfectly capable of walking on my own."

When she was taken to the home of one of the magistrates for her examination, she almost lost control. Some of the ministers were debating furiously against the use of "witch's teats" for evidence, but prisoners were still being searched for such things on the body. And though her clothing was not cruelly stripped from her as it had been in England, she was taken to a private room by several goodwives and told that she must disrobe or have the matter removed from her hands. Seeing that a protest would serve her only further humiliation, she shed her things and stood in silent lockjawed fury and misery while she was poked and prodded and felt with disgusting intimacy. Nothing so cruel as the prick was used here, nor did it seem necessary. She had a small mole on her shoulder, and the goodwives were solemn as they surveyed it.

"We will look again later," one of the matrons promised her, meaning to be kind. "Perhaps it will be gone."

"No! It will not be gone!" she assured them. "It has been there since I was a child, and therefore, if I am a witch, I've been one for years!"

She had good reason to regret her outburst later. From the private room she went before the magistrates. She was ordered not to look away, and so she could not see the group of girls and young women who screamed and cried as if they were poked by knives—but she heard them. Her arms were held now by the constables, and she was not allowed to shake them off. All she could do was stare straight ahead.

"Who afflicts you?" the magistrate demanded of the girls.

"Goody Powell! Oh, she strangles me! Where she touched me in the flesh, she strangles me now! Help me, dear Lord, I cannot breathe!"

"Oh, I see her! There she sits upon the structure beam; it is an incubus of Satan that she suckles, a creature like a wolf!"

A cacophony of voices rose, high and shrill

and so profuse that order was lost for several minutes.

"Why do you afflict these girls?" the magistrate demanded of her.

"I do not!"

"Then who does?"

"Their own sickness!"

"You merciless witch! Appease their pains!"

She was dragged to the girls and forced to touch them. They quieted, and the matrons were brought forward. The kindly women stated that she was perfect in flesh and form, except for a mark upon the shoulder. Before the testimony was done, one of the girls started shouting out an oracle again, stating that the devil, too, had found her perfect, and cherished her for his sabbaths.

"Oh, you will rot in hell for a liar!" Brianna could not help but scream out.

One of the constables wrenched her arm. She was not behaving very well for a Puritan goodwife standing before the duly chosen law.

A farmer stepped forward then; a man she was certain she had never seen before. But apparently she had seen him, somewhere, because he knew of her.

"She were a witch in the old country, sirs. My brother did hear that she was tried and condemned in England."

"Goody Powell—is this true?"

Chills eased their way through her, slowly, seeming to numb her against thought and speech. She could not lie. If she were caught in a lie, nothing else she said would have any bearing.

"I was condemned—but by a puppet court, and by a man later recognized as mad."

The screams started up, and the girls were hushed. Someone came up to say that she had looked at his cows—and that the animals had consequently drowned themselves. She realized then that the man was a villager who had frequently cut his cows through their vegetable garden—and whom she had ordered not do so again.

"She cursed my cows, she did!"

"What do you say, Goody Powell?"

"That if I were a witch, I would take myself from this room."

"Not even the devil has power so great," she was told solemnly.

This evidence she could fully scorn, but then an elderly woman came to the front and spoke with a soft fervor. "She did ruin her husband, she did. She forced him to wed her when they were at sea—I knew a woman on the same voyage, you see. Goody Ratcliff said that her child was born too early, and that the devil had charged her to find a human father, within God's chosen fold. Goody Ratcliff, too, had a dream in which she saw this woman come to Husbandman Powell at night, and force him to set his hand to the devil's book. How else would Robert Powell have come before us if he had not been tempted by the likes of her?"

Brianna felt ill—maybe she was the cause of all of Robert's troubles.

"Goody Powell!" The magistrate addressed

her sternly. "Did you bring the devil's book to your good husband and set him into a life of wizardry?"

"He is no wizard!" she snapped back.

And then, curiously, the room went silent. She was not allowed to turn, so she couldn't see.

But she knew that the firm strides approaching the magistrates' bench belonged to Sloan. She could feel his presence, and his air of power seemed to bring lightning to the room.

"On what evidence do you try this woman?" he demanded.

"We are not trying her here today, we are examining her."

"On what suspicion?"

The magistrate sighed patiently. Sloan was, after all, Lord Treveryan—famed for his adventures under King William's command.

"Witchcraft, my lord, the torture and torment of innocents. She was a known offender once—"

"Do you charge her for England, then?" Sloan's voice thundered out. "For I have in my possession papers clearing her, signed by our sovereigns William and Mary themselves!"

He should have been ordered out of the room; but no one thought to order him. One of the magistrates spoke up.

"My lord, we do not charge her for England. We charge her for the mischief she causes here."

"Then I would take her into my custody until her trial."

"My lord, I cannot allow that to be. She will be remanded to the Salem prison, until such date for trial is set."

"*Ohhhh!*" One of the girls screamed. Brianna took a chance to turn about. It was one of the youngest of the accusers, a girl of about twelve. She was clutching her side and twisting around vehemently. "He strikes out, too, I feel his sword. He is angry, and he moves about the room with his blade flashing!"

There was silence. No one had, thus far, gone to such extremes to accuse a lord, a known friend of the king.

In that silence Sloan's face hardened with the dark fury of a brewing storm. When he spoke, it was with a calm and grating elocution more frightening than the quick barbs of the magistrates.

"Should I hear my name mentioned—just once—I'll have a writ sworn out immediately charging two thousand pounds for the defamation of my good character!"

He looked magnificent standing there, rigid with his fury, green eyes like a rage of fire. He wore a blue velvet frockcoat, fawn breeches, and high black boots. No hat adorned his head and his hair was dark and neatly clubbed. Never had he appeared so much the nobleman, or the knight ready to do battle.

"Now, then." He turned back to the magistrates. "When will we see legal procedures here? When will concrete evidence be laid, and those who wish to testify in her behalf be given the chance to speak?"

The magistrate cleared his throat. "At the trial, my lord." Brianna believed that if they hadn't already come this far, the man might well have let her go, convincing the girls that they were "mistaken" about her identity. Powerful names had been mentioned before, without the accused ever being charged. It was one of the reasons that people were beginning to whisper on the street.

And Brianna was certain it was also a reason she could not be set free now; damning testimony had been given against her. If she did not appear for trial, the common folk would be wondering how it was possible that someone influential—or with an influential friend—could escape the net of the godly men determined to clear Massachusetts of the devil's clan.

"Then I will see you at the trial, gentleman," Sloan said simply. He turned about and strode out of the room.

Brianna realized bleakly that he had never looked her way.

Salem prison was not so bad, she tried to tell herself. The jailers tried to keep it clean; but even so, it was summer, and it was hot. She refrained from lying on her bunk until she was exhausted, because she was certain it crawled with bugs; she could occasionally hear the shuffle of rats about the walls.

She was in a small cell with two other women, sisters from Andover, still stunned that they had been charged. They were very godly women, calm and stalwart, and told her immediately that they would surely hang, for they would not confess to such "cow's manure!" as was being bandied about. Brianna had not known anything about Andover, but the sisters told her that Ann Putnam and Mary Warren had been sent there as seers, since the town had none of its own. But after signing over forty arrest warrants on the say-so of their touch, Justice Bradstreet had refused to sign any more, and was now in peril himself.

Brianna was glad to be in with these unshakable ladies, because from the cell next to them frantic cries and moans could be heard; a young girl thrashing out and crying that she was "bewitched" rather than a "bewitcher." Across the tiny hall an older man groaned with pain, but for what reason Brianna could not tell. The sisters told her in hushed whispers that constables sometimes came to take people away from their cells, and when the victims returned, they were half crazed and ready to say anything.

"That is illegal!" Brianna protested.

"It is not 'torture,' so say they," offered Mathilda, the older of the two.

"It is 'confinement' for the purpose of confession," Emily said scornfully.

"There is greater judgment," Mathilda said with a grim smile.

Brianna was sorry that the two elderly women were as severely shackled as herself, for movement was very difficult. They had their Bibles with them, and they spent their time finding psalms that brought comfort.

Late at night, when the sisters were sleeping and she lay in darkness, she heard a whisper, and her heart soared, for she was certain it was Sloan.

It was not. Philip Smith was down the hall a bit, and across, from her. He was calling out her name. She struggled out of her cot, wincing as the irons chafed her flesh, and hobbled to the grate.

"Philip?" She couldn't see him in the darkness. "I didn't know we were so close!"

He laughed a little hollowly. "We're all rather close here. I just wanted you to know that I'm near. Take heart; we will survive this."

"I know, Philip!" she whispered back, and somehow it did seem better. She was among people of sound mind and determination and she was proud to be with such unyielding company, though she could feel only pity for those who had come unhinged and confessed.

She trudged back to her cot, and, amazingly, she slept.

The next day was very black for all the prisoners of Salem. Five of their number went to the gallows that afternoon—John Proctor, George Burroughs, Martha Carrier, George Jacobs, Sr., and John Willard. The last, like Philip, had been a constable who had resigned after arresting too many friends.

One of the prisoners who had been to the

385

hanging came in the early evening, and all who could gathered close to hear him speak.

"They died well," he said. "Every last one of them. Proctor met his God with pride, for he made no confession. He protested his innocence to the end with honor and humility, and by our Lord, I was touched to see his demeanor! And George Burroughs, the old minister from Maine they claimed to be the king of the witches, recited the Lord's Prayer without a hitch or falter."

The prisoners fell into a heavy silence. Martha Carrier, hanged that day, had long enjoyed a reputation as a witch, but she had gone to God with denial on her lips. Here, in their cells, they could not help but believe her innocent. Yet her execution did not weigh so heavily on them, for her reputation alone could have damned her.

Proctor had been a respected man. Prone to anger, but respected. And Rebecca Nurse, a month in the hands of her maker now, had been the most pious, perfect Puritan mother and grandmother to be found. If those two could be hanged, anyone could.

The meal hour came, and still silence hung like doom about them. Brianna began to feel the vestiges of panic tightening her throat. She had been here a day now, and no one had come to see her. Perhaps Sloan would forget her; he had every right to do so. Except at the examination, she had not seen him since the night when the moon had touched her heart and senses and she had...

No! she told herself. Better to hang as a witch than to betray a husband who had given her the greatest loyalty.

But she couldn't help falling into a gloom of self-pity, and as the night waned, she called to Philip.

"Have you heard anything of Eleanor?"

He didn't answer right away, then said slowly, "She is safe, near the sea. I'm tired, Brianna, I do not wish to talk anymore."

Puzzled, she went to her cot. The sisters were asleep. Their soft snoring was strangely lulling. Brianna felt a new surge of hope in her heart as she mulled over Philip's words. He hadn't wanted to talk; he hadn't wanted others to hear him, she thought was the true message. Something was afoot. She had to be patient.

And pray.

Midnight brought a half-moon out from the clouds, and the night was filled with eerie darkness and shadows. It was a good night for the business at hand, Sloan thought. Shadows could conceal a goodly number of sins.

He had gone to Boston to hire a wagon that might easily be used for carrying goods and harnessed two of the finest, fastest horses he had been able to find. He did not expect to have to race through the streets, but he wanted to be prepared for the possibility.

Rikky insisted on accompanying him. "I'll not show myself, Treveryan. But I can be your eyes when you cannot look."

Sloan had at last agreed. If worse came to worst, Lord Cedric Turnberry would have to abandon his holdings in Lynn and find refuge in New York too. Sloan had ordered Paddy and George to be near the wharf in the *Sea Hawk*'s skiffs, but he did not want them on shore. There were no soldiers about, just constables who were as preoccupied by the day's executions as was everyone else. He was sickened by the deaths, and wanted no one killed, not his own men, not even the officials who were afraid not to do their jobs.

He and Rikky set out at midnight.

"The 'witching hour,' " Rikky said dryly. For once, he had abandoned his finery and was clothed in simple black like Sloan, to blend with the night. He flicked the reins, and the horses started moving slowly. The streets were silent; a drizzle had begun, and it seemed a fitting, dismal omen for the end of such a day.

Neither he nor Sloan spoke as they traveled along, both hunched against the drizzle. Rikky held the reins, and he knew where he was going. Sloan had decided that he would have to take Robert Powell first, even though the jolting of the wagon would disturb him. Robert was alone; he doubted if there would be an outcry until late in the morning. Once he had been to the prison, time would be dear. There would be many people involved—and an uproar was possible.

Rikky stopped the wagon some distance away from the small house with the two rooms where Robert was under guard. Sloan slipped

388

silently from it; Rikky would come forward when he saw him at the door with Robert.

Sloan's sword was at his side, nestled in its scabbard. A pistol was wedged into his waistband. He hoped that neither weapon would prove necessary—but neither did he intend to fail this night. He also carried a good length of heavy hemp, slung from his side beneath his frock coat.

He was immediately challenged, when he moved up the walk, by a young constable, a boy no older than twenty. "Evening," Sloan said. The boy looked at him curiously, as if trying to decipher his features in the darkness. "Your door's ajar there," he said.

The young man turned. Sloan brought his fist against the back of the constable's neck, and he fell silently, to the ground. Sloan stepped past him. He opened the door and stepped inside. An older man was dozing near the hearth. Easy, too easy, Sloan thought. He gripped a pewter candle holder and moved forward, hitting the man on the head.

He slid from the chair and Sloan hurried back outside for the youth and dragged him in. Working quickly, he bound and gagged both men and left them close enough to the fire for warmth.

Then he hurried into the bedroom, anxious to leave with Robert Powell. Again, Sloan thought that the man was sleeping. He quickly lit the candle at the bedstead, and moved to awaken him.

But Powell was not asleep. He was watching

Sloan with heavy-lidded eyes. He smiled, very weakly, and shook his head. "Get out of here, Treveryan. Too late for me."

"Damn you, Powell! It's not too late."

"Can't...walk."

"You don't need to. I'll carry you." Sloan reached down, lifting Robert Powell's wasted frame and the blankets. "Can you hold me?" he asked.

Robert tried to slip his arms around Sloan's neck. He could not. "It doesn't matter," Sloan said. "The wagon is outside."

"Wait!" Robert gasped.

Sloan saw that he was trying to indicate the bedstead.

"There's nothing we need," Sloan began, but Robert tried so desperately to say something that Sloan paused and lowered Robert back onto the bed. He went to the drawer and opened it.

"The paper...take it!" Robert wheezed. "Please! Guardianship...for Michael."

Sloan nodded and stuffed the paper into his coat pocket. "All right, hold on to me, we're going," he said as he lifted Robert once more.

Robert didn't reply. Sloan looked into the eyes that stared at him unseeingly. "Powell?"

There was no answer. Sloan realized suddenly that the steady wheeze of Powell's breathing had ceased. "No," he whispered, and he clutched him more tightly. "Damn it, man, you can't die now! You are free!"

But Robert Powell had found a freedom of his own. Sloan laid him back on the bed and frantically sought a pulse, a heartbeat, anything. "Robert Powell, damn you!" he repeated, but his words could not elicit a heartbeat or a breath.

Sloan stood back and pressed his temples miserably between his hands, caught in a turmoil of sorrow for the man who should have been his adversary. Then he reached forward and closed the dark eyes forever. He drew the covers over his face. He wished he could still take Robert with him, but knew that his body might hinder their escape.

"God grant you peace in heaven, friend," he said quietly. "And God grant me your forgiveness."

He took a long, shaky breath, and then another cleansing one, reminding himself that the night's work had just begun. Whatever the future, whatever his own desire, he had also made promises to this man that he intended to keep.

Rikky was in front, waiting for him. Sloan hurried to the wagon. Rikky was frowning. "Go," Sloan said.

The horses started down the street. "Where's Powell?" Rikky asked.

"Dead," Sloan said simply, and they continued.

Rikky left Sloan at the Salem jail and Sloan walked up to the door. Rikky had learned there would be four men on duty. Two would be the men that Sloan had already met and they would have to be trussed up.

"Can't come in here—Oh, it's you, Lord

Treveryan!" said the middle-aged guard. The man frowned. "Late, isn't it?"

"Aye, it is, Smithens, isn't it?" he queried cordially. Smithens nodded. Two of the other guards were seated together in a corner, drinking ale and conversing avidly. Sloan didn't know where the fourth might be, but it didn't matter just yet.

"Smithens, I apologize for bothering you at this hour, but I met kin of one of your prisoners this afternoon, and swore to deliver a message." Sloan raised a brow questioningly as he fingered his pocket and let Smithens hear the tinkle of coins. Smithens looked over his shoulder at the other two. They were still in conversation.

"Seeing how it's you, milord," Smithens said slowly. He raised himself, fumbled about a wall peg for his keys, and beckoned Sloan to follow. "Who are you looking for, milord?"

"Smith, Philip Smith."

"Come along, milord."

Sloan followed the man through the first door, noting gladly that Smithens did not lock it behind him. Why should he? For the most part his prisoners were women and old men—and people still so stunned to find themselves accused that they would not think to fight.

It was very quiet as they moved along, for most of the prisoners were sleeping. Sloan looked out surreptitiously for the missing guard, but did not see him. Smithens stopped before a cell. "Smith—Philip Smith. You've a visitor."

There was movement in the cell, Philip rising. He saw Sloan, and smiled broadly. "My Lord Treveryan. What a pleasant surprise."

Sloan caught the constable's hand, and stuffed it with coins, then indicated the door. "Would you mind? What I have to tell my young friend is of a very delicate nature."

The constable shrugged and fitted the key into the lock. Sloan pulled his pistol from his waistband and brought it quickly down. Sloan caught the guard as he dropped, and dragged him into the cell. Taking the coins from the limp man's hand, he said quickly to Philip, "Get the keys, and find Brianna."

"I know where she is," Philip said. He looked at the other two men in his cell, who were awake now and staring at them. Both were young men from Andover. "Lord Treveryan, my, uh, companions—"

"Can come, too, as long as they've a mind to move quick and work aboard a ship." The other two were up quickly.

"God forgive me," Sloan muttered, "that I cannot clear this place of its wretches!" He gritted his teeth, heaving as he dragged the constable beneath a cot. He looked up, and Philip and the others were watching him. "Get Brianna!" Sloan whispered. He beckoned one of the other men to follow him.

He returned to the main door. Casting an eye on his youthful companion, he opened it and stuck his head out. "Excuse me, good men, but could you come back? Constable Smithens is having a bit of a problem." He waited, smiling. The constables frowned at one another, shrugged, and came.

As soon as they entered, Sloan and the youth set upon them. One went down with a well-aimed blow to the jaw. The other fell with a little sigh, as if he had gone to sleep, when the youth brought his shackles slamming against his neck. Sloan and the youth hefted them up and brought them back to the cell. Sloan set to work tying and gagging the guards.

By then, Philip was out in the hallway with Brianna. She looked white as snow in the dim light, worn and too thin. Her eyes came to his like huge blue saucers. She was trembling, but silent and calm. Sloan didn't spare her much of a glance then.

Philip was down on his knees, working at the irons on his feet. "Have you seen the last guard?" Sloan asked him anxiously.

"No, my lord. But I found the key to the irons!" Philip whispered back with husky joy.

There was a touch on Sloan's arm. It was Brianna. Her hands, still shackled, were lightly on his elbow. "Can we take Mathilda and Emily?"

"Who?"

"Mathilda and Emily. Sisters. My cell-mates," she whispered.

He almost groaned aloud. Two old women were staring at him anxiously from the cell. One had a trembling lower lip, the other stood very, very straight—neither looked to be the type to beg.

Or "confess," he thought, to witchcraft.

"Aye, aye!" he muttered. "We'll take Mathilda and Emily!"

Philip had freed himself from his irons. He set to work on one of the other men. "Hurry!" Sloan commanded. Holding his pistol close to his side, he eased back to the door and looked out of it. He still could not see the fourth guard, and that worried him. He came back down the hall, managing almost complete silence despite his heeled boots.

"Hurry!" he again commanded Philip. One of his companions was free and he had set to work on the other.

Again he felt a touch on his shoulder. He turned to find Brianna's eyes on him again. "Do you have Robert?"

He stared down at her and hesitated just a moment too long.

"Where's Robert?" she demanded, and her whisper rose to have the substance of sound. She backed away from him, her chains suddenly clanging on the floor. "I won't leave without him, Sloan. I mean it. I will not leave without him."

"Shush!" Philip warned them.

The color was completely drained from her face. She didn't know what was wrong, but she was backing towards her cell as if she meant to stay there until she could get an answer. There was something very desperate about her eyes, a look that, at this moment, was very frightening. He turned away from her and grabbed the keys from Philip.

"I'll do this," he said, then added coldly,

"Philip, find something, gag her, and throw her over your shoulder. She's already chained."

He heard her gasp—but that was all—as he set to unlocking the last shackle of the second youth, and those of the two silent matrons, who weren't about to protest his action—or even whisper out a word.

There was a little thump. Sloan turned around to see that Philip had carried out his orders—Brianna was slung over his shoulder and there was a strip of linen wrapped tightly about her mouth.

"Let's go," Sloan said uneasily. Damn, but he wanted to know where the last guard was. He led the way along the hall, and checked the outer room. Then he inclined his head, indicating that one of the youths should go first, then help the old women along.

Suddenly there was a strangled gasp, and a cry. Sloan turned back; the second young man had just been attacked from behind. The fourth guard.

There was a loud thud as a scuffle ensued. Sloan swore softly and dived into it, grabbing the guard's hair, pulling him off the youth, and sending his fist hard against his face. He fell with a loud groan, and Sloan was not only sure that the prisoners would start awakening, but that the whole neighborhood would be up in arms.

"Go!" he commanded.

He didn't even worry about the lot of them streaking out into the night. They ran to the wagon. Sloan helped one of the old women into the back, then he started for the front.

"My Lord Treveryan!" Philip called to him quickly.

"What?" Sloan rasped out.

"What about Brianna?"

"Leave her just as she is," Sloan said flatly. "We've still got to reach the ship."

He hopped up beside Rikky, who cast him a glance, then flipped the reins, and the horses started moving. "Slow?" Rikky asked.

"Nay—fast."

"As you command, Treveryan!" Rikky replied. "Giddup, there!"

The horses bolted down the street, the wheels turning like spinning stars. The dull drizzle continued all around them.

Sloan closed his eyes. *God help me,* he prayed silently.

When he opened his eyes, he could see the wharf. And lights flashing, out on the water, coming closer and closer.

The wagon ground to a halt. Sloan hopped from his seat and hurried around to the back. Emily—or was it Mathilda? —hopped into his arms. "Bless you, dear young lord!" she murmured.

He smiled. "See those boats? Get to them!" She nodded, turned to her sister, whom Philip had just assisted, grabbed her arm, and hurried to the dockside. Sloan saw one of his men—Paddy, he thought—rise to help them. "Go on!" he told the two youths. Philip was reaching into the wagon for Brianna.

"Lord Treveryan," Philip murmured awkwardly, "Shall I take her—or shall you?"

Sloan clenched his jaw and swallowed tightly. "You take her, Philip. Once we're on the ship, you can free her. Tell her, tell her that I'm sorry, her husband is dead. But keep her the hell away from me tonight, understand?"

Philip didn't look as if he understood at all. But he replied, "Aye, Lord Treveryan."

The others were all headed to the dinghies; only Rikky stood beside him. Sloan lifted a brow slowly, then stuck out his hand. "I thank you, Lord Turnberry. I'd be damned if I know why you did all this, but thank you."

"Oh, I like adventure," Rikky said negligently—but then they both frowned; they could hear the sound of horses racing toward them in hot pursuit.

"Looks like you're coming along too," Sloan muttered, grabbing Rikky's elbow. They both raced for the dinghies.

"Room's in this one, Captain!" Paddy called to Sloan.

"Coming, Paddy!" The skiff was halfway out. Paddy had had the sense to push off when he'd heard the hoofbeats.

"Oh, what the hell," Rikky muttered, "I had a craving to visit New York anyway."

He took a dive into the water.

Sloan actually felt a grin tug at his lip.

Then he plunged into the water after Rikky.

Chapter 21

Sloan took the wheel as they moved out into the ocean. The weather was choppy and rough and the sailing difficult, but that was not why he chose the bridge. He wanted to hold the wheel. He loved the sea, and tonight, the gray rain and brooding darkness well matched his mood.

Paddy had asked him what arrangements he wanted made for the travelers. A number of the officers were willing to give up their quarters and bunk together, so there was really no difficulty about privacy. George had offered his cabin to the sisters—it was a short voyage south to New York and he'd be on duty most of it anyway. Paddy had been happy to give up his cabin to Lord Turnberry. Philip and the lads would be fine, threaded among the other crew members, and Eleanor had been situated in a small cabin earlier in the day.

"Sounds fine, Paddy," Sloan told him. "All well done. Thank you, and extend my appreciation to the others involved."

Still Paddy hesitated. Sloan, from long experience, stared at him warily with a brow raised high.

"Where would you like Brianna?"

Sloan turned to the dark sea ahead of him. "Offer her the use of my cabin. Privately, of course."

"I already did that, Cap'n."

"You did?"

"Aye—with a mind to your preference. We've got them all down in the galley now. Hungry lot, they were. Seems a seaman's rations might be an improvement over prison fare."

Sloan grimaced. "So you offered her my cabin—minus me—and she refused?"

"Aye, that she did."

Paddy was surprised when Sloan shrugged. "Then tell her she must sleep wherever she likes."

"But, Cap'n—"

"Wherever she likes, Paddy."

"She's a mite upset, what with the news of her husband and all, Captain."

"That is her difficulty. You can relay my message, then see that someone spells me in another hour. I need some sleep."

"Aye, aye, Cap'n."

Shaking his head with disbelief and muttering beneath his breath, Paddy went on about his business. Sloan continued to watch the sea, keeping slowly and carefully to the open water—there were numerous shoals here if one got reckless.

He spent his time thinking—and yet not thinking at all, for when he would try to piece together his thoughts, they were nothing but fragments and images. They all kept coming back to one—Robert Powell, staring at him with sightless eyes.

He really wasn't feeling anymore. It was strange, because he had spent years fighting. The pirates who still prowled the seas for booty, and then the Irish at William's behest. Men like Matthews. He'd seen carnage and death far worse than the trauma now plaguing Salem. He'd lost Alwyn.

But nothing had ever made him quite so numb as this night, as the entangled emotional involvements he'd come to be a part of here.

He was glad when George came to the wheel, greeting him both cordially and respectfully, and warning him that he would find correspondence on his desk—along with a bottle of dark rum. Sloan thanked him and ducked down the stairs to his cabin.

George had lit the lantern on his desk. The bedding on the bunk was fresh, and as George had promised, there was a heavy shot glass along with the rum on his desk.

He should have lain down to go to sleep but he didn't. He was so tired that he couldn't sleep. He pulled off his boots and coat, then moved behind his desk, sank down in his chair, and lifted his stocking feet to the desktop. He poured himself out a long shot of the rum and drank the fiery liquid down in a gulp, shuddered, and poured himself another. This time he sipped it, his eyes falling without volition to the bunk.

He'd never been able to sit in his cabin without imagining her aboard the *Sea Hawk* again. Well, she was aboard and the way things were between them, he could imagine himself insane for the rest of his life.

Except that he had determined he wasn't going to go near her again. Maybe he was feeling too harsh this evening; it was natural that she would be very upset, no matter how obvious Robert Powell's condition had been. He was on the defensive because he knew what was coming. And he was just damned determined to have his walls up ahead of time.

He set his teeth and picked up the first envelope, grasping a pearl-handled letter opener to slit it open. It was from a merchant in Virginia seeking to arrange a shipment of tobacco. Another was a promise of payment, and still another a request to take on another sailor. It was while he was reading the last that his door suddenly burst open. He instantly knew that no member of his crew would have entered so, and he tensed, eyes narrowing as she stood there in the doorway for a minute, then charged for his desk.

"I want to know what happened!" she demanded, her voice shaking. Her fists were clenched at her sides, as if she could stop trembling by the action.

He leaned back in his chair, watching her with all the cool control he could muster. He set the letter opener slowly down on the table, then crossed his arms over his chest.

"It's customary to knock at doors, madam, especially when the door is the captain's and you're a guest on a merchant vessel."

She ignored him completely, slamming her fist down on his desk. She was wild, very barely in control at all. Her eyes glistened with tears, but she was not crying. Her hair was free of caps and pins and tumbled about her shoulders, and her breasts heaved with her agitation. He smiled slightly, bitterly, thinking that there had never been a time when he hadn't thought her uniquely beautiful.

"I want to know what happened! I told you I would not abandon Robert, yet you left him, and then—then I hear from someone else that he is...is dead. Damn you, Sloan! How could you leave him?"

She was precariously close to tears. He longed to reach out and comfort her, yet he knew the futility of such an action.

He picked up his rum and took a sip, surveying her over the glass. "I'm sorry," he said flatly. "I could not carry a corpse with me for your inspection."

She took a step back from the desk, as stunned as if he had slapped her. "Oh, you bastard! How can you be so cruel?"

He made no move, except to set his rum down and pick up and slit open a letter. "I went for your husband first, madam. Since you care not to trust what I might say, you are free to question Lord Turnberry. Robert died. I am sorry. I am not God, and life is one thing that I cannot always command."

She was still for a minute, then coldly accused him. "It was a convenient time for his death, don't you think?"

On that he looked up from his correspondence, allowing light of dry humor to touch his eyes. "Madam, if you think I bore him ill, you are quite wrong. And if you think I would do murder on your account, you sadly flatter yourself and malign me. Now, you were offered this cabin, quite properly and privately, and you did not wish to find accommodation here, so I will appreciate it if you leave me."

The tears hovered ever close in her storm-swept eyes; he held himself in rigid check.

"I do despise you, Sloan!" she whispered. "And, no, I do not want your cabin, or anything else for that matter! You should not have bothered with your superbly gallant rescue! Your strength does not make you any better a man!"

He looked down unseeingly at the letter again. "Your husband bade me vow to free you, Brianna. I keep my word."

"Well, then, all is fine, isn't it? I am free. I'll thank you now for the passage."

"For the passage?" he asked her politely. "It's quite possible that I saved your life."

"I'm not sure what my life is worth!" she spat out, and then gasped as she heard her own words. But she wasn't about to back down, not that evening.

"Well, then, thank you, Lord Treveryan. Thank you again, and again, and again, and I am so damned sick of thanking you! If they take me for a witch in New York, bless them and I shall buy the rope myself! But until that time I will take my son and quit your company and pray never to see you again."

He looked up, smiling. "My son, Goodwife Powell? Have you forgotten that?"

"By the law—"

"Ah, you've seen yourself, girl, I would think by now, that the law works in most wondrous ways."

"And what does that mean?"

"Nothing, really. If you've finished with your accusations and assertions, I'd appreciate being left alone."

She emitted a wild cry and flew around the desk, ready to pelt against him in uncontrollable fury and misery. But as negligent as he had appeared, he was on his feet with the speed of a winter's wind, catching her before a first blow could land, and twisting an arm behind her back, causing her to cry out.

His touch was like ice; and, as always with him, she had lost.

"Madam, I'm not in the mood to handle you this night. I'd given orders that you were to be kept away from me, yet I don't find it hard to understand that you could maneuver some other poor fool. Well, I am done with it now. I am sorry about Robert Powell, as sorry as I have ever been to see a man's life wasted. But it was not my fault, any more than it was yours. Now, you may call me cruel, or bastard, or any other epithet that comes to your lovely lips, but not in my presence. You turned down my cabin, yet you came here to accost me. The cabin will be yours this evening, and you will not leave it, because I will not be accosted again. You will have to learn to accept the paths life takes, girl—and I'll not be your martyred scapegoat while you do it!"

Suddenly he pushed her across the cabin, causing her to land on the bunk. Vaguely she heard his footsteps as she tried to right herself. He was leaving.

The cabin door closed—and locked.

She ran to the door, banging against it. The strangest sense of déjà-vu filled her then, causing her slowly to sink before the door until she was sitting, grasping her head furiously between her hands, as if she could crush away the pain there.

She started to cry at last, not loudly, not hysterically at all. Tears fell silently from her eyes for Robert Powell, and she could not help but hate herself for what had come to pass. She had married him—without loving him. And all the time he had been struggling along, she had betrayed him in her heart. Lying at his side she had dreamt of Sloan. While Robert had lain a prisoner, she had kissed Sloan and almost forgotten that she had ever taken marriage vows at all. Robert had died accused and alone, and very possibly imprisoned because of her. She sat there remembering the darkness of his eyes and the gentleness that never failed to dwell within them. She thought of him holding Michael and of his great determination that nothing should ever happen to her.

At last she rose and moved to the bunk, so listlessly that it seemed a great journey. She fell down on the mattress and closed her eyes.

Would she ever learn to bear such sorrow? She wished that she had died—but then she repented of such a thought, for there was Michael to consider. She would teach him Robert's fine values of love and honesty and goodness. She would live with him quietly, close to the land. And she would never let the illicit passions of her heart and soul injure Michael as she had injured Robert.

Yet even while these thoughts tore at her mind, she wondered at the fury and emptiness she felt toward Sloan. He'd risked a great deal for her; at her plea he had taken the sisters from the jail. It had not been his concern, he could have left at any time.

Now he said that he was done with her, and that was what she wanted, wasn't it? To live a life that would bring pardon from God for the terrible sins of her soul.

She thought of Robert again. Smiling, laughing, speaking gravely. It cut through her like a knife; he was gone. Dead, and she would never see him again. She would never be able to thank him, to tell him that he had been one of the finest men, surely, who had ever lived....

Somewhere in the jumble of it all she fell asleep. She didn't hear the door open, or ever know that Sloan had come in to stare down at her.

Or that he shuddered with the same sense of déjà-vu that had struck her. It was so familiar, watching her lying there, at last asleep. It had been almost four years since he had first done so. He had watched a girl then, and now she was much aged by the passage of years, yet not old at all. Matured—and still young enough to believe that heartache could be fought, rather than experienced and slowly quelled.

He thought to touch her, to shift her more comfortably on the bunk, but he did not. To touch her was dangerous. He left the cabin and did not lock the door. When she awoke, they would be docked.

Rikky came for her in the morning, and Rikky, gently solicitous, led her along the wharf for her first glimpse of New York.

There were people everywhere, an abundance of people all manner of dress, with all manner of accents. From the women who hawked bright ribbons and cakes, to the old seafaring men pushing their catches, the place seemed incredibly alive. The sky was beautifully clear, and beyond the weather there seemed no hovering of gray here—no pall of doom. People smiled and laughed, and they did not rush by their neighbors in their fear or speak in hushed whispers.

Rikky had to pull her out of her absorption with the people about her. "Come—aren't you anxious to see your son?" And of course that query sent her scurrying along behind him.

She was somewhat startled when Rikky directed her toward a very magnificent coach finely emblazoned with his family's motto and emblem, a snake's head facing a lion. The seats inside were of velvet and silk, and she realized that not only was she pathetically drab, but filthy.

"Is it your aunt's coach?" She asked Rikky uneasily.

"Aye."

"And why is it here?"

He chuckled slightly. "Lord Treveryan did pave the way for us earlier."

"Oh," she murmured, stiffening. Mention of Sloan's name somehow reminded her that Robert had not been dead a day; that somewhere he would be receiving a pauper's funeral, with little care for the mortal remains of an accused "witch."

But when the coach carried them along a tremendous sweeping drive to one of the finest houses she had ever seen this side of the Atlantic, her thoughts turned to Michael. She couldn't wait to hold him yet cringed at the filthy sight of herself in the face of such vast wealth. For a moment she realized that she had survived on the charity of others, and quickly became determined that she would not remain dependent on others long. She would start a new life for her and her son.

The great doors opened as Rikky led her up the curving stairs of the porch. There was a woman dressed in a gown of light yellow and white. Its cleavage was low, and bowed ribbons were caught throughout the voluminous skirt, showing the delicate lace of the petticoat beneath. There was a scent of roses about her; she was both beautiful and elegant, with tawny light curls caught at her nape and bright gray eyes that seemed as silvery as the moon. She smiled, and Brianna felt even more her own tawdry filth.

But it was a welcoming smile, and even as they reached the doorway, the woman was berating Rikky in musical tones. "Cedric—you do take your time!" A hand was extended to Brianna—a soft hand, untouched by calluses, as her own were now. But there was warmth to it, and Lady Alyssa's grip was a strong one.

"Brianna, I've a room all prepared for you, with a steaming bath," Alyssa said, pulling her into the house. "I'm so dreadfully sorry for your loss... We'll remember your dear husband in our prayers. But your son waits you now—"

At that moment, Alyssa was interrupted by a high shriek of delight. Brianna's eyes became riveted to the magnificent oaken stairway near the entry, and then she fell to her knees, arms outstretched, her heart thudding as she watched her child upon the stairs. But Michael had accustomed himself to them well; he sped down their length with his little feet never seeming to touch, and in seconds he was in her arms. "Mama, Mama, Mama!" He buried his face in her neck, and she was holding him tight and murmuring his name in return when she recalled at last that they were not alone. She looked up at Lady Alyssa and Rikky and with difficulty swallowed back the threat of a rush of tears.

"Thank you," she told them, "thank you both so very, very much."

Rikky laughed. "I didn't do a thing—except choose to take one of Treveryan's voyages of adventure!"

Brianna stiffened slightly, and hugged her child. His child, but not his. She should be so very grateful to him but she couldn't feel anything but numbness and the overwhelming shadow of guilt. If she had not sinned so greatly in her heart, mightn't Robert still be alive?

Now when she looked at Michael with his eyes so startlingly green, she felt a tremor touch her. What was the future? She would have to take hold of it quickly.

"Michael!" Her fingers moved over his small cheeks, and she tried to smile. "Are you well, Michael, have you been good? These people have been very kind to us, you must be very, very good."

"I've been very, very good!" he told her solemnly. "Tante Alyssa will tell you so! May we stay here?"

She clutched him against her. "Michael, it isn't our home," she murmured. His wriggling body stiffened, and she repeated herself sharply. "Michael—this isn't our home!"

She gazed up guiltily again; Lady Alyssa was distressed as she looked at Rikky over their heads. She knelt down and tapped Michael's shoulder. "Michael—you will be here for some time yet, so let's not worry about leaving, shall we?"

Michael pressed his face against his mother's shoulder again. "Where is Papa?" he asked her at last.

Brianna did not know what to say. She couldn't bear him to be in tears, nor did she quite know if he would understand, though he was a very mature child, molded so by the society in which they had lived. "He..."

"Your papa cannot come for a while," Rikky lied smoothly, and he stooped down to pluck Michael from his mother's arms. "Now, young man, your mama has had a hard journey and needs a long bath! You leave her be for a moment, and she will be back with us."

Michael nodded gravely. Then said, "And where has Sloan gone? He will come back soon, won't he?"

"He's gone to the governor's, child, and yes, he will be back soon. Now go along with Rikky, and I will take your mama up to her room," Alyssa answered, then placed a hand upon Brianna's arm and led her toward the stairs.

"You really mustn't be afraid anymore," Alyssa was saying. "Our governor here is a mean skeptic against such proceedings as have taken place! We harbor at least a dozen 'witches' here already—a number who are his friends, and a number who are not!"

They had reached the upper landing; halls jutted off in either direction. Alyssa led her to the left and pushed open the first door. Brianna stepped inside.

The room was immense, and comfortable. There was a huge claw-footed tub, a stand with snowy towels piled high, a canopied bed with wafting draperies, a finely carved secretary, and a wardrobe against the wall, holding dozens of gowns.

Brianna gasped and stepped back. "I cannot stay here! I cannot accept this!" she muttered. Her eyes lowered. "I intend to find work quickly, but I can never repay you for all that you have done!"

Alyssa was silent for a moment, then said shrewdly, "We shall worry about such things later. I'll leave you now. Should you need any assistance, there's a cord by the bed. Give it but a tug, and Dulce will come. Choose what you will from the wardrobe—and for heaven's sake, let me burn these things you're in!"

Alyssa departed with a little smile. Brianna could not resist the tub, and in seconds she had peeled away her prison-tainted clothing and fallen into the delightful steam. Yet she felt no real pleasure from it. The steam seemed to surround her heart and mind, and she felt no pain either—just a terrible dullness and lethargy. She discovered then that if she did not allow herself to think, she would not feel anything, and she would not hurt.

All the gowns in the wardrobe were exquisite, but Brianna didn't much care anymore. She chose a dress in a dark russet with a minimum of ornamentation and came back down the stairs. Alyssa and Rikky were arranged across from one another on wide armchairs, and a large black woman was serving tea in delicate china cups.

"Michael is taking a nap, Brianna," Alyssa informed her quickly, noting the anxious look about her eyes.

Brianna nodded. "Thank you."

"Ah, Brianna!" Rikky came to his feet, eyes sparkling. "There is the beauty I've come to know and cherish. Dulce" —the black woman turned to him with a broad grin—"Brianna. Brianna, should you ever need anything, just call upon Dulce, or her man, Jeeves."

"Yes, miz, you just call on Dulce!" the woman said.

Brianna tried to smile. Smoothing down her skirts, she murmured, "Thank you, Dulce, but I intend to give you little trouble—and to find a position of my own as soon as I might."

There was a strange silence in the room; then Alyssa stood, pouring tea for Brianna. "I think I've a solution for you. You may work here. Dulce is rather helpless with a needle. I shall hire you on as a seamstress."

"Oh, no—" Brianna began to murmur, but Rikky interrupted her.

"Your son is happy and healthy here. Would you risk his health and well-being on a foolish matter of misguided pride?"

There was a sharp rap on the door. Dulce went to answer it, and as the door opened, Brianna heard Sloan's voice, low and smooth, with his trace of accent. He chuckled over something Dulce said, then came to the drawing room. He was dressed rather magnificently in navy breeches and a red shirt and his sword; a gold-trimmed coat lay over his arm, for the sun had risen high and the day was warm.

His eyes fell on her, quite coldly, but he did not approach her. He came to Lady Alyssa instead, smiling rakishly as he kissed her hand. Then he greeted Rikky, and at last said, "Good day, Brianna."

"Good day," she replied simply, and lowered her lashes, aware that he was surveying her with a wary curiosity, as if she were some unique thing to be explored.

"So how is the dear governor?" Rikky inquired.

Sloan laughed. "Patting himself upon the back for being the shrewd realist that he is and berating the officials of Massachusetts for allowing such a thing to go on." He chuckled again. "I've a mind that if they were stringing up none but poor old hags, he'd not be so concerned about the matter. But he's had friends among the accused, and so he has made himself a certain kind of hero."

Brianna stood as Sloan spoke. With her eyes low she spoke to Alyssa. "If you will forgive me, I would like to—be alone today." Being around Sloan penetrated that fine wall she had created, and she did not want that.

She returned to the beautiful room Alyssa had given her and threw herself onto the bed. She stared up at the ceiling. *Think nothing, and you will feel nothing,* she reminded herself.

She did not know how long she had lain there when the door burst open. She rose, startled by the sound. Sloan stood there, as rigidly cold and angry as he had been the night before.

"I thought you should like to know," he told her harshly, "that I have arranged for Robert Powell's burial. He will be taken to South Church in Boston for interment."

Brianna lowered her eyes. "It is another thing for which I must be grateful," she said coolly. "I will do my best to repay you."

"Will you?" He inquired dryly. "I want nothing from you, Brianna—except that which is mine."

She stared at him again, very alarmed by the tone of his voice. But he was already giving her a mocking bow. "You needn't fear my presence here. I've work to do, and I'll not be back now—for some time."

The door closed. She lay back down, still feeling nothing. He was leaving, he had said. She could stay here and see that Michael had decent food and care and surroundings while she decided what to do. In time she heard Michael's voice, calling her name petulantly, as if he needed to assure himself that she was there. She rose and hurried to him.

Rikky left with Sloan aboard the *Sea Hawk*. They traveled south to Virginia for a tobacco shipment and to deliver mail from New York.

At a tavern there the two men began to drink together, and in time, they were well warmed and near drunk.

"Lord Cedric!" Sloan confided drunkenly to his friend. "If you were me, what would you do? Gentleness will have no bearing on the lady—nor does patience fare me very well. Where have I made a mistake? I should be able to comfort her—I cannot. Perhaps I should stay away longer—I cannot, for I don't trust her. The child is mine, and I intend to take him."

Rikky took another long draft of his ale, then clanged the tankard against the table. "Here! Here! You've made no mistake, my friend, except to love too deeply and too well. I think I understand our lass in question. For the suffering she has caused, she feels that she must suffer. Misguided fool as she is, I don't believe she'll ever come to you on her own."

Sloan inhaled sharply. "She loves me!" he said vehemently. "By God, I would swear it!"

"Oh, aye!" Rikky laughed. "She loves you. But she will not accept it. My advice to you, Lord Treveryan—captain of the sea but not of his own heart!—is to take the matter into your own hands. Produce this document given you by her husband, now at rest. She will cease assuming that she has legal recourse! Give an order—and it will be followed. And when you sail away from the coast of tragedy, she will come to terms."

Sloan scowled as he watched Rikky, then stood so abruptly that he almost knocked the table over. "Come on—we're leaving."

"The tavern?"

"Nay, Virginia."

"Tonight? You're scarce fit to sail the ship!"

"I'll not sail her—Paddy will."

When he sobered and they were in New

York, Sloan hesitated about returning to Lady Alyssa's house.

Rikky laughed, taunting him. "Are you afraid? Is the lord of countless battles afraid of one slim lass?"

"Rikky, you press me sorely."

"Wake up, then, Treveryan! You are as bad as she!"

"Umm," Sloan muttered. "Then let's get on to your aunt's house, shall we?"

It was nightfall when they came. Dulce informed them that the ladies had long been abed.

Sloan started determinedly for the stairs. "Lord Treveryan," Dulce said, "I done told you that they's asleep."

"And I heard you, Dulce. Thank you."

He came to her door, but it was locked. He banged on it. She came, anxiously and half asleep. When she saw him, and the tense thunder about his face, she paled immediately and drew into the room.

"What are you doing here?" she asked him raspily, and in her blue eyes he saw nothing but cool defiance. Yet his heart was touched too; she was in a simple white gown, laced at the throat, and the desire she could kindle too easily touched him like a rampaging fire.

"I must return to London and Wales," he told her curtly. "I leave tomorrow—with Michael."

She gasped. "You cannot! He is by law my son. You—"

He caught her shoulders and pushed her heedlessly into the room, back to the bed, where he forced her to sit.

"Sloan Treveryan," she warned fiercely, "you cannot do this! We are not alone in some desperate place! You cannot push me so and manhandle and—"

He laughed, and placing one booted foot crudely on the bed so as to lean his elbow upon his knee, he produced from his pocket the document that Robert Powell had given him.

"Read it, mistress. I am taking the child. Now, you may stay behind, if that is your choice. I shall go to London and claim him before the king and queen, and he shall be legitimized as my son. Then you will never see him again, for I am finished with traipsing around the world to drag you from one disaster after another. Or..."

He let the word trail.

"Or what?" she spat out furiously.

"I can take you with me. But if you do come, you will stay with me. And you will repay me. Every night that I so choose, you will repay me."

"I am a widow!" she cried out to him. "How can you be so callous and—such a bastard!"

"Brianna, say whatever you like, feel whatever you like. But I have decided that I can no longer play this game. You will curse me however you like, but under your breath you will still whisper to me that you want me. When I come to my cabin tomorrow night, you will be waiting, bathed and clean and fresh and smelling like roses—and with a meek pretense of eagerness!"

He spun on her then, quickly, and left the room before she could reply. He closed her door and leaned against it and smiled as he felt the reverberation of her pillow crashing against it.

He chuckled then, certain that Rikky was right. But to be on the safe side he hurried down the hall to the room where his son slept. He stretched out carefully by the little boy, amazed again that the child could be his own flesh—and so very much like him.

Minutes later, he heard a soft scampering of footsteps down the hall. The door creaked open and she entered, and started to tiptoe for the bed.

"Nay, Brianna," Sloan said softly, and she jumped. "I'll not take my eyes off him until we're far at sea."

"Bastard!" she hissed, and a slight sob escaped her as she ran from the room.

Sloan touched his son's hair. "I know that she loves me," he whispered. "She just does not know how to reach for happiness anymore."

Chapter 22

Brianna did not sleep much through the night. Fury kept her awake. But by the morning, she was resigned. Sloan held not only the physical power—but the legal power as well. Brianna would never allow him to leave with Michael and without her. She swore to herself that she would leave calmly, with her head high.

It was difficult when they came to the wharf that morning. She hugged Alyssa with all the warmth and fervor she could express. "Thank you, Alyssa. For Michael and myself."

There was moisture in Alyssa's eyes. "I will miss you and Michael. I had come to think of him as a little bit mine. But—here, we mustn't get like this. I know that you will come back. Sloan has an eye upon a lovely manor up the river. He's thinking of buying it. So we shall determine that we'll see one another soon!"

Brianna didn't bother to remind Alyssa that her position with Sloan was extremely precarious. He'd ordered her onto the ship— that was all. He'd made no promises for the future—he'd only made demands.

Rikky gave her a monstrous hug then. "Best of luck!" he told her. Then he kissed her again and whispered, "They've always been wrong. You're a sorceress, not a witch. A highland nymph, to catch the heart of man! My love goes with you—all three!"

"Ye must come aboard now, Brianna!"

Paddy was there, setting a hand upon her shoulder. Rikky and Alyssa were gazing past her. Sloan was near the great wheel of the ship. Michael was atop his shoulders, waving.

"Good-bye!" Brianna kissed Alyssa one last time, hugged Rikky, and turned to hurry along the plank.

Paddy shouted out an order; the walk was lifted, and thick hemp ropes were thrown from the dock.

The *Sea Hawk* was under way.

Brianna did not go to Sloan and Michael; she maneuvered past the sailors to the aft and waved to the shoreline as long as she could. She had loved it there; the people, and the peace.

"With or without him, I will come back!" she whispered fervently to herself. But then there was a touch on her shoulder and she turned to see George Percy's familiar face. She had to smile at the welcome she saw there.

"Welcome back, my lady!"

"I'm not a lady, George, but I thank you for your greeting." She held silent for a moment, then added softly, "After all the trouble that I have caused."

"Caused, Brianna?" George chuckled. "Nay—the wind causes tides and the sun causes heat—but of us? We move along, sometimes as we choose! Come, now, and I'll show you the little cabin arranged for your son. It's affixed to the captain's own, so you'll not feel he's far away."

"Thank you, I'd like to see it," she murmured.

He led her belowdecks and she saw that it was the small cabin where Eleanor had stayed the night they had run from Salem. The bunk was fine, the cabin was neat. And there was a set of toy soldiers upon a small desk. A few old and worn primers, a little ball—and a strange assortment of tins that all seemed to fit into one another.

"Where did you come by these?" Brianna murmured.

"At a shop along the wharf. The captain sent me yesterday," George replied cheerfully.

"He did, did he?" Brianna said sweetly, curling her fingers around one of the little primers. He'd known all along he could force her hand, she thought angrily. Tears stung her eyes. Damn Robert! she thought. How could he have given Sloan the legal right to steal Michael from her?

She set the soldier down. "George, would you be so good as to retrieve Michael for me?"

"Well, I'll try," George said uneasily. "But it seems he's happy enough with his fa—with the captain, ma'am."

Brianna lowered her eyes and wet her lips angrily. Did everyone know the truth of it, then? And did it matter? Sloan wanted the child legitimized; he wanted to make him his heir. All well and fine, he would grow to be the lord of a vast estate...

A rotting pile of stones, I'll daresay! she thought with annoyance. She had always been a little frightened of his holdings, and of his position. And yet once...

Once he had said that he would marry her if he could. But now he hadn't asked her aboard the ship as his wife. He hadn't asked her at all, but rather demanded that she pay her passage.

"George, I am Michael's mother. He is not yet three and a half years old, and I do not believe he should be on deck with all the rope and gear and sails. He could get hurt."

"Ah, nay, begging your pardon, ma'am!" George exclaimed. "Why, they've all been at the wheel since they were just little things, all the Treveryans, that is. Why Paddy said Sloan held a wheel beneath his father's hand when he was but two."

"I'd like my son, George."

"Aye, I'll—uh—go tell the captain."

George left her, and Brianna looked around the small cabin. There was a window here too. A very small one, but she could look out and see the deep changing colors of the ocean. "Damn you, Treveryan!" she muttered. "If you aren't always forcing me onto a ship!"

There was a tap at the door. She called out to enter, and George came back in, appearing very unhappy.

"I'm sorry, Brianna. The captain says that Michael is quite fine with him, and if you do not trust him, he is sorry. He says that he will send him back at suppertime so that you may dine together, and then put the lad to sleep."

"Tell Captain Treveryan—" Brianna began

explosively, but stopped to take a deep breath. She was not going to carry this fight on with George as a go-between.

"Bring him to me as soon as you can, George," she said. George nodded, then left her. Brianna sank down on the small bunk and stared out the tiny window to the sea. How long ago had it been since she had sat for the first time, staring out? It had been Scotland she was leaving behind and she was in turmoil then too. She had just sold her soul to a devil then—the devil Treveryan!

And she was doing so again. How long had it been since she had lain in a bunk beside him, felt him touch her, tenderly, and with the most searing intimacy?

She smiled then, remembering those first days when she had seen him in Salem again. She admitted that she loved him, and Sloan swore that he had loved her always...

She started pacing the room, muttering to herself. In her mind, she saw him in all his guises; the man who had faced Matthews with a swagger and sword; the supreme aristocrat who had charged so furiously into the courtroom; and the crystal-cold stranger who had thrown her from him, determined that he was no cause of Robert's death. She couldn't remember what she said to him that night, the hurt and the shock had been so great to her. "I cannot give myself to you!" she whispered to herself. "It would not be right, and I swear that I am a curse to love! How many 'witches' have been persecuted from shore to shore?"

Where will this lead us now? She told herself that she did hate him a thousand times over and yet she had already begun to tremble for the night that lay ahead of her.

The day passed in this manner, then Michael was returned to her. He was so excited about sailing the ship that she could barely make out his garbled sentences. But when Paddy appeared with dinner plates of fresh smoked fish and New York harbor's finest vegetables and summer apples, Michael began to calm down.

"I'm going to sail her alone one day, Mama. I will! Sloan has said that I will."

"I'm your mother, Michael! I shall say what you do!"

He stared at her, his huge green eyes watering with confusion, and she relented. "I'm sorry, Michael. Someday—but a long time from now—you shall sail the ship."

He was happy then, thrilled with his soldiers—if not impressed with his books. But after he had started to play with the soldiers, he turned one in his hand.

"They are not so nice as the ones Papa made," he murmured, and then he turned to look at her. "Papa has gone to live with the angels, and I will not see him again."

He started to cry, and Brianna picked him up to hold him to her. "Who told you that, Michael?" she asked him.

"Aunt Alyssa. She said I mustn't mind, because God loved him dearly and would care for him for us."

God loved him dearly... Surely, that was true.

"Come, Michael," she said, "I will tuck you into bed and lie with you awhile."

She put a nightshirt on him—a beautiful one, given to him lovingly by Alyssa. She stretched out beside him, and his whimpers became yawns, and he said at last, "Papa will watch over us from heaven. He loved us, Mama. And Sloan will watch out for us here."

She tensed, hating how already Sloan had managed to ingrain himself upon his tiny heart, and yet wondering in a far corner of her mind if Michael did not have a better grip on the truth than she did herself.

In time he was asleep. Brianna thought about curling in with him for the night, and totally defying Sloan's orders. If he came, he would find her asleep with the child and...

Possibly drag her out of the bed, she thought ruefully. By being here she had made her commitment—although he certainly wouldn't be pleased, she fumed. Oh, she would be there! But if he thought he could force her into anything other than fury and loathing, he was wrong!

She left the small cabin and moved down the hall to enter the larger captain's cabin. Near the bunk was a rough-hewn tub, filled with water, spouting a thin mist of heat. And on the bunk she found a note that sent her into a fury again.

It wasn't signed, nor was it addressed. It said merely, *Clean and fresh, smelling like roses—and eager!*

She threw the note down, stamped on it, and thought she should let him come in—and douse him in the hot water. It was a pity, she decided then, that she could not manage such a feat.

And as the seconds slipped by, so did her nerve. She did not know him anymore. Was it possible, if she pushed him too far, that he could really see to it that she lost Michael?

She wasn't very familiar with rum, but she decided she needed a good dose of it now. She uncorked the bottle and swallowed such a vast sip that she choked and coughed and wheezed—and burned from her head to her toes.

But it was an impetus that she needed. She decided that she could get her clothes off, and herself into the tub. And that she could pick up the rose-scented slab of soap left her.

Footsteps in the hallway warned her that someone was coming. She jumped from the tub and hurriedly swathed herself in one of the linen sheets from the bunk. The footsteps were coming too slowly, making every fiber of her body dance in curious alarm—and fascination. She raced to the rum bottle for another long swallow—and was caught in the act when the door opened and Sloan stood there. He eyed her coldly for a minute, then turned his face from her as he closed the door and bolted it.

When he faced her again, she was clutching the rum bottle close to her, and a sardonic grin touched his lips.

"Sustenance, Brianna?"

She shrugged defiantly, her fingers twining close about the bottle. He moved into the cabin, unbuckling the sword he seldom seemed to be without, and casting it down on his desk. He sat to remove his boots, and then, without taking his eyes from hers, began calmly to disrobe, pulling his shirt over his head and tossing that, too, carelessly onto the desk.

He grasped the rum bottle and shook it slightly to remove it from her grasp. "May I?" he inquired politely.

She released the bottle and backed away from him. He took a long sip of the rum, then ordered, "Come here!"

"Come here! Just like that!" she shrilled defiantly. "You've nothing to say, no apology, no shame—"

"Nay, I haven't a word to say. Come here."

She did not; but he didn't seem to notice. As she backed away he followed her until she could go no farther. And then his hands caught hers, pinning her to the wall, and her hold on the sheet was lost. It drifted to the floor. She saw his eyes, the richest jade, and then his mouth touched hers with neither fury nor fever, but gently, heated and moist and seductively, until she gave in. She tasted the rum again, and she tasted him, warm and male, and she began to tremble inside with an uncontrollable yearning. His chest pressed to hers and hard muscle crushed against the softness of her breasts, taunting and wonderful. She felt the hardness of his hip against hers, the strength of his thighs. And his tongue, playing deeply in the recesses of her mouth, seeking hers, filling her with a burst of sweet- ness that she could not fight.

He moved quickly, drawing his lips from hers, lifting her his arms and staring into her eyes as he carried her to the bed. She felt as if she could barely move, so entranced was she. He shed his breeches, watching her all the while. Nervously, she waited for him and for her life she could not have said if it was with dread—or with anticipation.

He covered her body with his own, his hard-muscled legs wedging hers apart. And he took her hands again, holding them as he looked at her. She moistened her lips, already wet from his kiss.

"I'll hate you for this," she told him, but her wavering voice betrayed her words. His lips found hers again with an explosive hunger that brought a moan from her. Pleasure raged to a soaring desire with the sure and eager touch of his hands on her, caressing her breasts, cradling and arousing them. His body moved against hers, teasing it, and his mouth left hers to trail erotic patterns over her flesh, kisses that burned and made her quake.

But still he did not take her.

She closed her eyes determined that she endure—not enjoy. But his assault upon her senses continued; his tongue teased along her feet and her ankles and she shuddered from the effort to quell the churning rise of passion that lit a hot fire within her.

His touch moved along her thigh, and he stroked her, watching her face. She felt his eyes and, so compelled, opened her own, wishing she might wrench herself from him and hide her ragged breathing, her writhing body.

He came to her, leaning beside her, holding her breast again, moving his hand to her hip. "Do you really hate me?"

"Aye!" she cried out. It was not, then, the skillful play of his hands on her but the demand in his eyes that made her cry again. "Nay—nay, I do not hate you!"

"Then love me," he commanded her fiercely. "As, so help me, I love you."

She threw her arms around him, meeting his lips with her own, starving for the beauty of his tenderness—and passion.

Her hands threaded through his dark hair, her fingers traced the fine lines of his cheeks, and she drew away from him, searching out his face and his eyes.

"I love you," she whispered fervently again. "I love you and I want you. Please, Sloan, now!"

"I thought that you would never ask," he told her hoarsely, and with a thrust of silk and steel, they were one.

How long did love last? For it seemed an eternity of sweet reaching. Yet that which she sought came too soon, though she could not have borne another minute. It seemed that the ship left the sea, sailing amidst the stars, and at the end they touched the depths of the endless sky.

But even as she lay beside him, tears suddenly filled her eyes. And he, stroking her cheek, quickly sat up, harsh, again as he spoke to her.

"By God, I never meant to hurt you again! I just wanted you to live! Have sense, Brianna. I did not take your Robert's life, nor did you. He was dying, Brianna, even before they took him! You never harmed him; he loved you and he loved the time he had with you. I know what you feel—whether you can believe me or not! I have loved, though it's not the same, and it hurts, by God, it hurts! But life goes on for us, and I will not let you strip us of a future!"

She shook her head, reaching up to touch his cheek. "I—I'm crying because I'm—I'm so sorry, Sloan! I don't know why I could never see it! I railed against you even when you had saved my life a third time! I know that you did all you could for Robert. I could not see it before because I did not wish to. I just felt so horrible... Sloan, I did love you all the time. That was what hurt so badly."

He caught her fingers, and kissed them gently. "You never hurt him, Brianna."

"I'm not so sure," she murmured.

"You did not. You gave him what joy he had in life. Brianna, he wanted us to go on. He begged me to promise I would make you happy."

The tears stung her eyes. "He did?"

"He did. Ah, Brianna, he was a fine human being, and though I cannot deny I love you now, it's truth, I would have done nothing to take you from him."

"Oh, Sloan!" she murmured to him, and she

curled to him easily, loving and needing his arms about her. "Do you think we can truly find happiness?"

"Aye, we can. It is only elusive to those who do not seek it!"

She nestled against him for a long time, glad of the heat of his chest, of the slight rasp of his chin against her forehead. And she held him fiercely, for she might well have lost him through her own foolishness. But he did love her, tremendously. What other man would do so much—even help her fight her own demons?

"Sloan," she said at last.

"My love?" His fingers moved idly among the rich tendrils of her hair.

"Am I always to be the one to ask?"

"To ask—" He broke off his own worried query with a chuckle and moved quickly on top of her, pinning her beneath him "Oh. Nay, I suppose I'll not make you go so far. Madam, what say you? Shall we have God bless this union at last?"

"Sloan!"

"Nay, my love, I shall do better." He slid to his knees at the side of the bunk. "Brianna, will you be my wife? The chatelaine of my castle, mother of my present and future children—and first mate of my heart around the seas, forever?"

"I've a naked lord at my feet!" she murmured. "How shall I take this?"

"As a naked lady; I see only one way. Answer me, aye! Swear that you will love me all my days, then take me back into your arms and let us begin anew."

She brought his hand to her lips and fervently kissed the palm, then stretched out welcomingly to encompass all of him.

"Oh, aye, my Lord Treveryan!" she whispered heatedly. "Aye!"

Three days later they passed one of Their Majesties' English ships at sea. Sloan sent out a beacon, and they grappled the ships together.

The Captain of the trader *Queen's Mercy* was a jovial, rounded merchant, thoroughly enchanted and entertained by the idea of marrying another ship's captain at sea.

On the twentieth of October 1692 Brianna became Lady Treveryan among the good-natured cheers of both crews. Michael was a little awed by the ceremony, but he learned that it meant he would never have to leave either Sloan Treveryan or his mother, and so he was quite content.

That night Sloan and Brianna, with their sleeping son between them, stared out at the stars that blanketed both the sea and sky.

"Are you truly happy, lass?" Sloan asked her.

"Aye, that I am." And then she twisted to look at him over their son.

"I was just thinking of the first time I came aboard this ship! Locked in a cabin—and told to stay put! And now—well I've no intention to spend my life with you sailing away, so I shall be aboard constantly, you know. And if you think I shall remain in a cabin..."

"There will be no locks and chains upon you, love."

"You do not need them, you know," she told him. "Long ago, you chained my heart."

"Well, your nature is such that every once in a while you must be taken a little into hand."

She sniffed indignantly. Michael moved against her and she turned to Sloan. "I think we'd best put him to bed now. Sloan, when do you think we should tell him the truth?"

Sloan thought long before he answered. "Brianna, he is young. I say this not to hurt you, but when he is grown, he will not remember Robert. Yet, when the time is right, we will tell him everything. We owe it to Robert—and we owe it to Michael. Robert was, in his way, a very great man, and Michael should always know that he was loved by such a man."

Brianna nodded, and stood on tiptoe to kiss his cheek. "Thank you, Sloan," she whispered.

He set his arm around her, and they moved across hemp and rigging to go belowdecks. They placed Michael in his small bunk and went into the captain's cabin, smiling as they both started to douse the lanterns at once.

"Tell me about Loghaire, Sloan," Brianna urged him later when they both lay awake beneath the moon.

And so he did. He told her about the

rock-hewn castle, and about the sea, and about the gray mists and the flowers on the slopes when springtime came. But when he was done, he turned to her and said, "I shall never give it up, but I like New York. It's young and fresh and exciting, and I'd have a home there."

"Can we really?" Brianna asked excitedly.

"Aye, we can. We will."

She was silent for a moment, and when he prodded her she said, "One day I wish to go back to Salem. To laugh in the magistrates' faces, perhaps. And yet it's more than that. Oh, there was terror there, but there are good people, too, and sometime I would like to see how they have fared."

"We will go back—when you wish, and when the time is right. Such madness does not last forever."

He pulled her into his arms.

"We've a world to sail, my little witch. My sorceress. I feel that we may fly as the clouds do, for the past is behind us, and perhaps through all we have suffered, we will have learned to cherish our lives, and to live richly." He rose above her, kissing her, touching her, setting her aflame as only he could do.

She laughed suddenly, catching his eyes in the moonlight. "My Lord Treveryan—I do believe that I did, in truth, become the devil's mistress. For you, my love, are a devil of the lustiest kind!"

EPILOGUE

In the fall of 1693 Sloan and Brianna returned to New York. Sloan purchased the house he had so wanted. It was an immense rambling mansion, surrounded by both fields and sea, and Brianna found the same enthusiasm for it as Sloan did. They had not given up the ancestral home in Wales; they had just both somehow become colonists, and felt a yearning for that western side of the ocean.

They had known, however, before they left Wales, that the Salem witchcraft trials had come to an end. The last hanging had been that of September 22, 1692. Public protest had finally started to rise in unison and been given some assistance from outside influence. Joseph Dudley—once deputy governor under Andros—had plied his mind to the legal question and written to a number of the French and Dutch clergy. Their response had been filled with no-nonsense good sense—how could the girls, they wondered, possessed by some demon of soul or mind, point out evil in others? They did not call the girls "mountebanks," as Brattle of Boston was doing, but they suggested a pathetic illness.

Governor Phips of Massachusetts, who had

never known where the truth lay, took swift and decisive action. By the time a special court of oyer and terminer met again, spectral evidence was no longer to be accepted. Three were condemned—three who insisted that they were witches—but Phips, refused to sign death warrants.

The man had determined to wash his hands of innocent blood. In May of ninety-three he issued a general pardon. The jails were to be cleared.

Brianna, in moving into her beloved home in New York, really had no great passion to return to Salem at that time. But Eleanor, who had married her Philip that long ago day when they reached New York, came to see Brianna, and informed her that many of the accused—though pardoned—were still in prison because they could not pay their jailer's fees. Fields had lain dormant in Salem during the year of havoc and the relatives of many had fled Salem, so they simply had no way to pay.

Brianna mulled over the information for a while, then implored Sloan to take her to see what they could do. They couldn't free everyone, but they did what they could.

And it was while they were there that Brianna also felt a gnawing penchant to return to the farm that had once been hers. For some reason the place had not been seized. Sloan found her later, seated on the deacon's bench, staring about her with a little smile.

She looked at him sheepishly and a bit ruefully, and he thought then that no matter how long he lived, he would never cease to think her eyes the most beautiful he had ever, seen, the most expressive—and bewitching.

She stood, greeting him with a kiss. When his arms came comfortably around her, she said, "Sloan, I know you'll think me mad, but I'd like to keep this place too. Since Powells came here and died here...well, I am family. I couldn't live here again, but it's beautiful property, Sloan! Eleanor and Philip have been talking about returning, and I thought we could let it to them until they bought a place of their own."

She spun about then, looking up at him eagerly. He smiled, kissed the tip of her nose, and then her lips.

He realized then that she had never asked him for anything worldly. Not plate, not gowns, nothing. "If you wish it, my love, then we shall keep it. But we shall have a rather large number of homes, don't you think?"

She laughed. "It's quite possible, too, that we shall have a rather large number of heirs. Michael shall have the title and Loghaire—but what of the child we're expecting in the spring?"

He was stunned by the news—awed and completely overjoyed. He hadn't been there to see Michael born; he'd never held a tiny babe and known the wonder of anxiously awaiting a child.

He came to his knees and kissed her hand, and swore roughly that they should have a dozen homes if she wished. She touched his dark hair and marveled aloud, "Sloan, that you should love me so is surely the greatest wonder of life. Once I thought that I was cursed, but no woman has ever been so blessed!"

It wasn't their second son, however, but their third, Robert, who loved the farm—enlarged and improved with the years—with all-encompassing passion. Like his father and his brothers—and even his two younger sisters—Robert loved the sea. The Treveryans owned a fleet of ships by then; ships that serviced the Colonies, and ships that sailed the ocean. But Robert Treveryan always returned to the farm, just as his eldest brother always returned to the castle in Wales, and his middle brother, Sloan, always returned to the grand house in New York.

And it was Robert who learned of his mother's wishes one day. They were walking along the Salem wharf; Sloan and Brianna had just returned from a voyage to Loghaire, and while Sloan supervised the unloading of the cargo, Brianna had greeted her third son with maternal glee and spirited him away.

Robert, at thirty, had his father's adventurous spirit and the rugged appeal of a very good-looking devil, but his looks were his mother's. His eyes were as blue as a summer's day and his hair was as dark as the night. While Brianna observed her son with the greatest pride, she had no idea that he was returning the assessment.

In her early fifties, she was still as slim as

a nymph. There was but one streak of white to her hair, and it added mystery and sophistication to her beauty. Perhaps to other eyes she had aged, but never to him, Robert thought—and certainly, never to his father.

She wasn't usually a "nagging" parent, but on this particular day she had been after him about settling down with a wife so that she might see an abundance of grandchildren. He was wondering how to hush her politely when she ceased the discourse of her own accord.

His eyes were leveled at the Burying Point, and she smiled suddenly, as if she had thought of some secret joke.

"Do you know, Robert, I'd like to be buried there. Oh, don't look at me so strangely! I'm not intending to die for a long, long time, not until you've given me some grandchildren! But I'd like to be there, right in front of that old magistrate Hathorne! For all those questions he put before me!" She fell silent for a minute. "I think I forgive him. And Corwin. And even Matthews..." She paused, grinning at him wryly, and he thought he must be seeing her just as she had been as a very young girl. Young and so lovely that an envious person might readily have called her "witch."

"I forgive him, but I'd still enjoy a chance to make him squirm for eternity!" She laughed and pulled him along. Sloan would be waiting at the wharf, and Robert knew that she had never been able to bear leaving his father for long.

Years later, when he did kiss her good-bye

for eternity, he remembered her words. And he laid her to rest where she had pointed that day, beneath the spidery limbs of a sapling tree.

As the years passed, the roots of the tree encroached upon her marker, enwrapping it. Just as the New England fog swirled in and out throughout the centuries, enwrapping her memory in legend.

Author's Note

There are no witches—are there? Of course not. We of the twentieth century are very much aware that hags do not fly across the moon on brooms, hurrying to obey the summons of their master, the devil.

In the seventeenth century even learned men believed in witchcraft, and people did "practice" witchcraft in varying degrees— fortune-telling, palm reading—and practiced some very criminal rites, such as La Voison did at the French court. To practice witchcraft was a crime punishable by death.

But innocents suffered under that pretext by the hundreds and thousands. In various towns in Europe thousands upon thousands were burned for the crime. In Scotland they burned, and in England they hanged—in great and pathetic numbers.

Salem happens to be the dark spot in our country's history. And no one can deny that women such as the pious and very coura-geous Rebecca Nurse and men like the gruff John Proctor were completely innocent of any such practice. But too often it seems that the Puritan fathers are unjustly condemned for being just that—Puritan fathers. Belief in witchcraft was just as common among the other Protestants and the Roman Catholics of their day.

Where did the reality lie at Salem? Centuries later, none of us can really know. Many theories have been expounded—some claiming that petty land quarrels instigated performances from the afflicted girls. Others believe in a true state, not of simple hysteria but hysteria in a very clinical and physical sense.

I tend to agree with this theory. The writings of the Puritans' contemporaries suggest that there were indeed terrible afflictions, and it must be remembered that clinical hysteria can cause physical manifestations.

There is also the suggestion now that a virus in the wheat might have caused some of the girls' hallucinations. But one would have to wonder why such a virus would only afflict so few. Perhaps the virus was guilty of producing some of the evidence offered in court—like that of a herd of cattle seeming to go insane and commit mass suicide owing to the evil eye and threat of a "witch."

There have been many books written on the "witchcraft" of Salem, Massachusetts. For readability and differing opinions, I suggest Marion Starkey's *The Devil in Massachusetts* and Chadwick Hansen's *Witchcraft at Salem*. Also, in the course of writing this book, I had the opportunity to obtain a three-volume set of books originally compiled in the thirties by the Public Works Administration containing verbatim transcripts of the Salem witchcraft outbreak.

They are titled *The Salem Witchcraft Papers,* Volumes I, II, and, III, and are published by Da Capo, Press, Inc.

Finally, there is no better place to study this history—pathetic and shameful, but noble, too, in the supreme faith and courage of so many—than the Essex Institute.

About the Author

Heather Graham lives in Florida with her husband and five children. Formerly a professional model, she has written thirteen best-selling historical romances, including the *New York Times* bestseller *And One Rode West.*